Requiem of Celestia

Quinton A. Foote

Explore the World of Litore on all social media platforms and wherever you get your podcasts!

www.vendevarsaga.ca

Table of Contents

Major Populations
Human
Elven
Dwarven
Dragon-Blood
500 Kilometres
Uncharted Territory
Serenstrom
Noga Sea
Spire Lakes
Port Ortu
Dwarves of Silver Rock
Boundless Ocean
Scale Isles
Rhogar
City of Rays
Nether Keep
Blue Waste
Glacier River
The Southern Great Road
Argos
The Great Road
Scorching Sands
North Sea
Magma Isles
Shallow Bay
Silva
Kaia's Sea
Morass Prairie
Gauntlet Ridge
Skydore Mountains
Iridaunia
Drum City
Squally Sea
Gis Vanzlor
Volcano Flats
Recarit
Flooded Forest
Hovering Humans
Elemenzin
Moon Mountains
Shadowscorn
Lower Lake
Sapphire Sea
Argot Keep
House Adda
The Eastern Great Road
House Elda
House Titari
N

Celestia: The Pantheon

Celestia, otherwise known as the Pantheon of Gods in Litore is where the 12 greatest beings reside. The plane of Celestia takes on many appearances, depending on which of the 12 holds claim over that particular domain or who may be visiting. We can considered this text as the collective knowledge of all those minds across Litore's two ages whom have studied or worship Celestia. Much of this guide is borrowed from the varied holy texts of the 12 but it should be recognized even those texts have been translated and rewritten countless times over the eons. It should be known that some of this information has been gathered via testimony of only the most pious followers.

Many have theorized the gods of Litore created all they see today, from the Boundless Ocean to the deepest depths of the Underworld. As far as the 12 are concerned, this is what they would have us believe; so for our intents and purposes moving forward that is what we will assume is true. Some folk have claimed that the gods do not exist, but we cannot waste our time on such delusions, for the gods have made themselves known many times to the faithful and faithless. They impact our every day in one shape or another which has led me to put this collection of my *studies together in an effort to understand the arcane weave better. There is neither Power nor God who claims dominion over the arcane and many wizards like myself has theorized it radiates from Litore's very core. If indeed the 12 did create Litore, then surely they must be responsible for what we call 'magic.' In the pursuit of knowledge and power as all wizards strive for, I have listed below the Pantheon and their dogma in the hopes that one day, someone will decode the mystery and heal our world with the fullest mastery of the arcane and divine knowledge.*

I have surpassed my 700th year in this world and now find myself in the 'between', I have seen all manner of dark and light forces spread their gloom and love upon the earth we tread. My time nears its end as it must for all, even the gods I think, and so I feel it in my bones but that above even the desire for endless knowledge that in the pursuit of a world without conflict there must be one thing, trust. As I trust that this guide will aid in the pursuit of a better morrow.

- Alden Alabaster Cornelius

- <u>*Aceia*</u> *(A-see-ah)*, God of Shadow and Assassins - Dogma: **Only in Darkness is One truly revealed.** Sigil: A hood and shoulders with no face.

- _Āina_ (Ah-i-n-ah), God of the Forests and Land - Dogma: **Be resilient as grass, sweet as fruit, strong as stone, and a sprawling heart like the roots which you walk upon.** _Sigil: A single tree with a wolf standing proud._

- _Brailin StoneSower_ (Bray-lyn), God of Justice, Allfather of Dwarves - Dogma: **What once Was, can Never be Again.** _Sigil: Three Mountains._

- _Kaia_ (Kai-ah), Goddess of the Sea and sailors - Dogma: **Let the Sea set you Free or fight the Waves and find watery Graves.** _Sigil: Ocean waves with a single searaven._

- _Lokor_ (Low-core), God of Battle - Dogma: **Perseverance is the measure of Power.** _Sigil: A round shield with a sword and spear crossed atop it._

- _Mahem_ (Maw-hem), God of Chaos - Dogma: **Burn to Build and Build to Burn. Chaos is the World Blood.** Sigil: A single drop of red blood.

- _Ordo_ (Or-dough), Goddess of Order - Dogma: **Order is the heart of Civilization.** Sigil: Two hands locked in a firm grip at the wrist.

- *<u>Pirelia</u>* *(Pie-rel-e-ah)*, Goddess of Fire, Birth, and Renewal - Dogma: **The hottest Fires brand Strength Incarnate.** *Sigil: A ball of flame with a heart inside.*

- *<u>Sesara</u>* (Seh-sar-ra), Goddess of Life, Peace, and Sustenance - Dogma: **Life begets Life.** Sigil: A buck and doe grazing in front of a river.

- *<u>Skalgr</u> <u>'The Diamond Dragon'</u>* (Skull-gur), God of Death - Dogma: **Death is the final King.** *Sigil: A skull with one half still alive, eye closed.*

- *<u>Zeries</u>* *(Z-air-ease)*, God of Lies and Trickery - Dogma: **Nothing is what it Seems.** Sigil: Two sinister looking eyes.

- *<u>Zemez</u>* *(Zem-ehz)*, Goddess of Literature and Knowledge - Dogma: **Knowledge is Power disguised.** *Sigil: An open Tome.*

CHAPTER ONE

Son of the Ocean

Ven stared at the two figures sitting where Faenla and the searaven had just been. They leaned against each other; their hands tightly interlocked as they bore heartwarming expressions.

"Son?" he surprised himself by asking aloud. Ven looked back at Queen Saphier to see she was utterly frozen in time. He told himself this must be some trick, or illusion. The tall and divine female Kyst stood up and slowly stepped toward Ven. He keenly noted her scent, reminiscent of a warm sunset sea breeze. She placed her smooth, turquoise-green hand on Ven's storm-coloured cheek.

"My heart soars unlike ever before to finally look upon you with my own eyes. So handsome and strong." Kaia's eyes glistened like the sun reflecting off still water. She held her captivating gaze on her son, never stopping looking into his opalescent and monochromatic green orbs.

"Mom," scraped between his lips, barely conscious of the words. Kaia pulled him in and embraced Ven tightly. He felt like a child as her height was so great, his head barely resting against the flat of her shoulder. The hunter did not reciprocate at first, and looked to the elf who was now standing. He too was tall, shorter than Kaia but still several heads above Ven. He was rugged like the mountains and lean like the great cedar trees of the north. Ven never embraced her back but eventually Kaia dropped the hug to let Āina approach. Ven found himself straightening up, subconsciously wishing to feel as regal as his counterpart.

"I have watched your progress through Faenla. A father only ever wishes to be proud of his son, and no father has been more so than I. You are, and will be, everything the world needs." Āina's sounded like the resonance of a thousand-year-old tree refusing to uproot in the wind. Yet, as surreal as this was, Ven felt a familiar distaste in his mouth and anger pulse through his gut. He took a step back and looked at them with scrutiny.

"Parents raise a child, guide them through youth with love, wisdom, and discipline. You call yourself my parents, yet I near my 34th year and only meet you now. That makes you strangers and little else." Ven nearly choked on the words, for he truly believed this was the god and goddess of the land and sea. While he had never found validation in religion—as most Kyst around him did— he was not about to embrace them with undying love, especially if he was their child.

Kaia's face turned dark and stormy with rage, much as the ocean did and with as little warning. This made Ven's heart skip a beat, but the ever firm and solid hand of Āina rested upon her shoulder.

"He is right, my love. Though he is our only born and we have watched him his entire life, Ven was all but unaware of our presence. His hesitation is to his credit." Āina gave his son a comforting smile. Kaia's face quickly turned back to one of peace and understanding.

"Of course, forgive me. For you to become mighty, all you have endured was absolutely necessary. 'Grown alone so to be never owned'," Kaia recited. Those words struck a memory in Ven, for they were a part of the prophecy he found in the old sunken temple of his ancestors: *From the sea, a saviour will arrive. A Kyst bred to fight, born to mend. Grown alone to be never owned.*

"How am I to mend anything? I can't even keep those closest to me safe. Everywhere I travel I breed chaos and loss." Ven's tone clearly betrayed his lack of self-respect.

"You cannot mend the world and all within alone," Āina explained. "'Grimìr'—you know its meaning?"

Ven looked cock-eyed at his father. He knew it to be an old-elvish word roughly meaning "demi-god". "Grimìr, the chosen or children of the gods," he answered skeptically.

"You and the others of your kind will usher Litore into the Third

Age. It falls to you, my son, to unite and lead them all." Āina seemed to be entirely ignorant to the greater meaning and difficulty of that statement.

"The gods will soon fade from this existence. You are the key to uniting their children—our children," Kaia offered with the belief and encouragement that only a mother could give to her child. The hunter gripped the stone wall with one hand, unsure of what to say or do next, when something sinister dawned on him. He looked at the two gods with equal parts fear and fury.

" *'Grown alone, so to be never owned.'* It was you two, wasn't it? Who killed anyone who got too close to me." And just like his mother, Ven turned a darker, stormier shade. "You've done nothing but take from me. Anyone I held dear. Do you have any idea what it's like growing up isolated, alone, an outsider to the people surrounding you? I've known nothing but self-doubt and longing for what I could not have. Now you reveal yourselves to me, TELLING me what I have to do. Even for gods, you are more entitled than I ever could have imagined." He forgot who he was talking to as he took a single step forward, putting hand to hilt. "What about Scáth, did you let Rexous take her so I would be without?"

Kaia scoffed, pausing briefly before speaking, "Although they did not die by our hand, they did by our will. Yet, we cannot touch the other Grimìr." Ven did not ease his grip or move his hand from his tailbone where his ancient sword was strapped.

"Although he was at times cruel and ill-tempered, Aceia was our dearest friend. It is no surprise that you have fallen in love so deeply and completely with his daughter," Āina said with a wry grin. Kaia looked to her own true love with sparkling eyes of serenity. Ven's mind raced far too fast for anything to make sense, except for one thing—that he needed Scáth now more than ever.

"I am done here. What you want from me means little now. My life was complicated before this, and seeing as how you two are responsible for that I think I'll clean up your mess how I see fit. The other Grimìr will be better off besides."

"You don't get to be done here. No one does. Everyone and everything has a part to play and they do so whether they like it or not," Kaia growled with a gale.

"Is that the trick of the gods then? Worship inspired through fear?"

Ven's criticism was a clear invitation for Kaia to do her worst. Goddess of the Sea and Storms narrowed her eyes and Ven felt a truly palpable energy crackle throughout the room.

He smirked at her. "People have been trying to scare me my whole life; they've either died or been left bitterly disappointed."

Āina cut the tension with a hearty belly laugh as he watched his dearest bicker. "You two are truly cut from the same cloth. You are free to do as you wish my son but let me leave you with a single request. That sword you carry is of my very own making. It has a sister that you need to wield before the Celestial Renewal is upon you." Ven looked at his father. "You will find it buried beneath this very forest, lost to time, and with it, the truth about our arrival and your destiny. A truth you must learn, for history is doomed to repeat unless the newest generation is equipped with the knowledge to break the cycle."

Ven was not having any of it. He now understood; his entire life of being an outsider, the inescapable feeling of loneliness, was by their very design. "Be gone from my sight. I am not your son and I will not do your bidding." Ven turned his back to them, looking through the natural window, over the motionless world. A few ragged breaths passed and the world did not return, nor any indication of their departure present.

He screamed, "Leave!"

Once the gods had left time resumed, Ven quickly feigned excuses for Queen Saphier to leave his chambers. Ven himself did not leave his room until the following night, nor did he receive any food or accept any visitors. As he saw the light being sucked down over the ocean's horizon, he made to exit the Shallowbay rebel hideout.

"Where you off to?" The massive half-orc, half-elf known as Agan Dusk caught the elf at the cave mouth, causing Ven to shudder in irritation.

"That's a stupid question."

"It's a stupid idea," Agan replied to the petulant Kyst.

"It's better than waiting." Ven continued to walk out of the hidden cave that had become the rebel Kyst's hideout.

"It's hard not to treat you like a child when you won't stop acting like one. If you go, you will die and Scáth will be forever lost to us."

Ven stopped at Agan's blatant insult. "Give us a few days to think and plan, Ven."

The famed hunter swiftly turned and walked up to Agan. "You don't know Vakar, you don't know what he is capable of. In the few months I left him, he committed genocide, poisoned the innocent, and turned an entire country against me. Scáth will be hurt every day, and every day Vakar will grow angrier, and so too will her punishments grow in horror. So take your precious time and think of a plan while I do what needs to be done." Ven's jaw barely unclenched while speaking.

"I will not walk this quest with you,"

Agan said, thinking Ven was acting this way in an effort to convince the others to act.

"You err in assuming I want you beside me," he retorted, and the words surprised Agan by how much they stung. The huge fighter watched his good friend enter into the harsh coastline.

"What's that about?" Onstera's voice rang out behind him. Agan turned to see the Quesitor in a linen undershirt, silver hair braided over her shoulder and her sword belt strapped neatly around her wide waist. Faenla's blue eyes pierced through the darkened halls of the cave as he lumbered to stand beside them.

"Ven insists on going at it alone," a defeated Dusk answered.

"Will he truly meet his end?"

"I know nothing of this land or it's people. I have an idea on how to secure Scáth but it's complicated."

"Youre instinct has gotten you thiss far, no sense in questioning it now," Onstera said as she brushed by Agan to follow after the Kyst. Faenla went to join her, but Agan lifted his arm to rest it on the huge wolf's back.

"I need you this time," he said softly. Faenla stared at Agan's fiery yellow eyes and saw it was true, so stayed put.

The hunter was nearly thirty minutes into the forest after leaving the hideout and was already feeling slightly better for simply moving through his natural terrain again. They had only arrived the night before and he was in no mood to sit around; Scáth was taken from them, and he knew where to find her. So that was plan enough. It was late now, the forest floor grew dark, yet Ven moved with confidence. After hearing a twig snap behind him, he instinctively drew his artifact short-sword, 'Hunter's Protection.'

"You cannot go after her."

Ven turned to see Onstera standing behind him, the silver in her eyes washed away by adrenaline, turning a blood red. He knew what that meant, and he noted too the silver sword resting easy in her hand.

"I defeated you at Gauntlet Ridge. You can't stop me," he blurted before turning and continuing on.

"You were in balance then, your anger makes you-" she let her silence hang in the air as she chose the next word, "-insignificant."

"You don't know anything about me," he said, never stopping his stride.

"I know you do not trust your closest allies." That did stop Ven.

"I trust them with my life, but not with hers."

"Your wolf came to me after you told him to stay behind. Agan has led armies into war, yet you ignore their advice. I've known you only a short time, so I suppose it is possible you are stupid enough to ignore their counsel."

In one swift motion, Ven drew and threw his trident at Onstera's head. With impeccable agility, she dodged the whizzing polearm as it sunk deep into a half-rotted tree stump.

"Weak," she mocked. His heart skipped a beat; the act of attacking a friend fueled his lack of faith in himself, catalyzing his inner turmoil. Acting on impulse, he sprinted for her.

She gave him a disappointed look as she pointed her matte-silver sword at him. She fired the small bolt that travelled from the hilt down a groove in the blade face. She did this to make Ven focus on something else so she could throw a small dart into his thigh. Ven grunted as the dart bit him like a wasp, and he watched as Onstera climbed nimbly up to stand atop a stump that was bigger than most training gyms. He tore the small dart out of his leg and threw a dagger at the Quesitor, which split in two as it soared for her. She needn't put effort into the dodge, she simply leaned to the side. Heart racing, he sprinted towards her. His anger increased as she stuck him twice more with darts while he climbed.

As he crested the edge of the jagged wood splinters, she kicked him square in the face. He fell off the stump and landed hard on his back.

The wind was pulled from his lungs and his vision narrowed as the rage turned everything red.

She looked over the edge down at him. "Not so 'Mighty' after all." She disappeared back into the centre of the stump that acted as an arena. Ven rolled over and punched the ground as he forced the air back into his lungs. Veins popped from his forehead as the all too familiar rage took control. He nimbly climbed up the stump once more and came over the edge into a roll.; unnecessarily, as Onstera was standing on the far side, waiting for him.

"Embarrassing. I've seen Quesitor younglings more intimidating than you."

The sheer look of rage would have scared any on Litore, but Onstera understood she had every advantage here. Ven ran and jumped at her with his short-sword in hand. She spun and kicked him in the chest, fully stopping the Kyst's flying momentum. She redrew her hand-and-a-half sword and slashed Ven across his leather chest plate as he was still mid-stumble from the kick. He looked at her as if she would regret that.

"Rage makes you weak," she scolded as she weaved and parried a number of strikes Ven delivered.

"Stop pissing me off then!" he shouted in her face as they locked swords. The sound of scraping metal bit at both their ears. Onstera, with her considerable strength over Ven, shoved him back a series of steps.

"It won't be long before your enemies find out they must simply irritate you to kill you. Maybe if you did a better job of protecting your dearly beloved, she would be here to teach you that instead of me, little boy."

Ven let out a hoarse battle cry as he went back at the blood-seeker. Anger had unbalanced him, but he was still one of the finest warriors in Litore, of that he was confident. He swept low at her heels, forcing her to jump over his sword. He immediately threw his weight into his shoulder and shoved Onstera over the edge of the stump.

She fell right into a muddy pond and Ven leaped down after her. He drove his sword into the water where she had landed, yet his blade found no purchase but mud. After the water had settled, she revealed herself from behind an upturned root system.

"Apparently it makes you blind as well," she laughed at him.

"How?" he asked through gritted teeth.

"I was out before you even leaped in. Listen to me Ven Devar," she said, walking closer to the Kyst. "Take a deep breath, centre your heart and soul." She stopped directly in front of him. Ven closed his eyes, for the mere sight of her made his blood boil. He struggled to calm himself, turning all his senses toward his hearing and the sweat dripping down his back.

"Anger can be a powerful ally. It has saved me many times, but it will be your downfall if you can't properly harness it," she calmly whispered to him. Ven knew she was standing face to face with him now. She smelled of earth and power. She placed a hand on his chest and could feel his heart slowing. She admitted to herself he was handsome and his prowess as a warrior attracted her. "I could teach you how." Ven could feel her lips barely brushing his, teasing him. The anger still coursing through his body and the adrenaline moving his muscles convinced him to lock his lips with hers. The instant they touched, Onstera hit him in the temple with her sword pommel.

Ven awoke on the edge of the muddy pond, cold and wet in the blackness of night. As he slowly lifted his body up, his movement caused the ripples across the water to glow. He rubbed his head where he had been struck, wishing the throbbing pain to abate. The crackling of embers could be heard behind him and he saw Onstera comfortably sitting next to it, gesturing to a leaf full of food for him.

Ven felt the chill even more intently as he pulled himself out of the water and walked with soggy clothes over to the heat of the fire.

"Why did I hit you?" she asked, as if the answer should be obvious. Ven looked at her beautiful olive skin glowing against the soft fire light and felt that same lack of attraction he always did for her.

"My emotions kissed you," he answered bleakly.

"Even now I do not doubt your loyalty to Lady Scáth. When we are enraged, our decisions become not our own. Which is why you will not go after her and why you'd fail if you did."

This time, he could not disagree. He saw then a wisdom in this human younger than himself. "You don't strike me as the religious type, Onstera," Ven said, and she thought it was a curious remark but nodded in recognition. "Then maybe you are the perfect person to speak to. I myself never held faith in the divine. Of course, to not believe in them is to say we don't breathe air, but many on Litore choose to live life without honouring them. Unfortunately, the masses devote their entire existence to beings they've never known. Why is that do you think?"

"Folk need something to believe in."

"Why not believe in their neighbour, their kin or even themselves?" Ven posited the question and Onstera had a surprisingly quick answer.

"A neighbour might bed your partner, kin might steal your wealth, friends will betray, and one never lives up to their dreams. But the gods of old are above that. They offer something greater than yourself. They offer undying love and belonging. Or so they lead us to believe."

"I've told you about my lack of belonging and growing up without love. Yet Kaia and Āina came to me and revealed themselves to be my parents." Ven let the words hang in the air like fog and watched closely for Onstera's reaction. Perhaps it was because she knew him to be in a delicate state of mind, or she did genuinely believe him, but she seemed impassive about that declaration.

"You are the child of gods?"

"No. Dragon-bloods are the children of the God of Death, dwarves are the children of the God of Stone and Justice. I am the son of gods. Which in truth is the root of my life's turmoil. They left me without family. They killed anyone who got too close to me my entire life so I would be without attachments." He watched again to garner her reaction to this and she listened on with eager ears. "Scáth is the daughter of Aceia, which is apparently why we are connected so."

"Is it not good to have the answers you've sought for so long?"

"Yes and no. I just want normality. My entire life I have ran from the titles and responsibilities. I desire adventure, family, and a place to be loved. And now they tell me that before the year is over, all the gods will be dead and I must unite the other Grimìr, for the end of the Second Age is upon us." Ven couldn't help but call her out for the smirk she was wearing with severity in his tone. "What?"

"I just kicked a demi-gods ass," Onstera laughed to herself and Ven squeaked a small chuckle at the absurdity of it all. "It all seems a tad dramatic doesn't it?" she said more than asked, hoping to garner some brevity.

Ven wasn't having it. "If we fail, the Third Age will be bathed in bloodshed."

Onstera was smiling once more, which irritated Ven slightly, until she said, "Looks like we have a purpose again." Much to his delight, that filled him with a sense of hope and optimism. It was short lived, however, as she asked, "Agan is getting a plan in motion to secure Lady Scáth and he made it clear we're not needed. So what should we do?"

Ven was displeased by that but did well to hide it. "Well, the way I see it, my people are in a civil war and I must somehow find the other Grimìr. I wouldn't pick one over the other," Ven chortled.

There were 12 gods in Litore, and many 'powers' like The Caretaker of the Evar Spring Glade. Onstera was sure Ven didn't mean each of the 'powers' had children.

"In theory, that leaves nine children to find. Besides the few gods who would select specific races, like Brailin StoneSower of the dwarves and Skalgr of the Dragon-bloods, the rest are as good as anyone in the entire world. At least your civil war is happening right here."

Ven nodded, as much as he would rather try finding the others of his kind, that would be worse than searching for a needle in a haystack.

"Back to the hideout then," he answered reluctantly.

After their short trek back to the seaside cave, Ven was immediately pounced on by Faenla. The wolf put all of his substantial weight on Ven as he lay atop the Kyst, pinning him down with his great paws and dragging his tongue across his elf's face. Ven gave into the kisses and eventually managed to roll the great wolf off him. Faenla rolled onto his back and received great scratches from Ven before Onstera joined in.

The blood-seeker had never even touched the wolf before now, for though everyone in their group assured her he was friendly, a lifetime of primal instincts told her to keep her distance. The more she saw of Faenla, the more she understood he was like a big puppy rather the most vicious wild killer she'd laid eyes on.

"I'm glad to see you've returned Devar." Ina Enallea stood a few paces away, watching with a wide smile. The Kyst elves learned so much from the coastal wolves that they treated them with a sort of reverence. Never was a wolf to be killed, unless in self-defense, as they were instrumental in the natural balance of the forest. So many of the rebel elves fighting Vakar's rule saw Faenla as an omen.

"I'm here to help however I can," Ven said getting to his feet just to dip into a respectful bow.

"Good, follow me," Ina replied, spinning on her heel and turning to walk deeper into the cave system. Ven felt the lingering precipitation clamp to his skin the further he went in, until he reached a large room filled with a magical fire that spewed no smoke. The room was mostly lit by a great iridescent map, shimmering against the far wall. Ven noted the map was translucent depending on where you looked at it, but it offered an impeccable three-dimensional view of the entire Great Northern Rainforest, right down to the notable landmarks scattered throughout. Onstera and Ven were both lost in its intricacy when Saphier entered.

"Fascinating, is it not?" she asked aloud to the pair.

"It's as if you could walk right into it and appear where you were looking," Onstera said, and Ven let out a small chuckle, for what a wondrous thing that would be.

"Don't get too close," Ina barked as she sidled up to Saphier behind a great, oaken table that was littered with tomes and candles. The hunter and Quaesitor both turned to regard the two elves behind the table.

"I was joking," Onstera replied.

"I'm not," Ina said without missing a beat.

"It took many great sages and a collection of ancient and experimental magic, but we think it's fully functioning now. If we're going to beat Vakar we'll need every advantage," Saphier explained, and Onstera thought she picked up on some personal level of hatred at the mention of Vakar.

"How would one return here if they set out through the map?" Ven queried.

"Not unlike how Rexous and Scáth vanished when we found you —" Ina answered, or began to.

"But we'd like to be more efficient," Saphier said, throwing a small, sky-blue pebble in Ven's direction. He caught it without effort and inspected it closely. Its surface was smooth and oval in shape, the only identifying mark on it being a single kystin rune that looked like one half of an arbutus tree.

"So what is your strategy then?" Onstera questioned the two apparent leaders of the rebels. Saphier looked to Ina and gave her the go-ahead. Ina's olive-coloured skin appeared much like Onstera's, save for the fairness all elves shared. The blood-seeker watched her move to the map and was more interested in the way the Kyst moved her hips than the hue of her skin or the allure of Ina's vibrant hazel eyes. Ven noticed Onstera looking Ina up and down and nudged his ally to pay attention as Ina was already speaking on their next move.

"River Luvium, in many regards, is the capital of Kyst society in the Great Northern Rainforest, so naturally Vakar has stationed his second greatest force there. As it stands, Silva has 2,000 soldiers and River Luvium has half that."
"How many do we have?" Ven interjected, clearly hoping he could attack Silva and be done with it.

"Roughly 300 hunters and 200 sages. Not enough to consider a frontal assault anywhere but Greenwave," Ina said with gusto but was clearly trying too hard.

"Yet, our sources tell us most of Greenwave's native soldiers would flock to us if given the chance," Saphier added.

"I'm not hearing a plan in any of this," Onstera noted skeptically. Ven gave her a sideways glare but Ina and Saphier both grinned.

"You're on the coffers, Onstera. What do you propose?" Ina asked. Ven looked even more perturbed to find out Onstera was still being paid after delivering him.

"You have no option but to infiltrate and turn the people against Vakar's forces. By the sounds of it, that won't take more than a spark" Onstera Dentoress answered plain and simple. "Which settlement is the least happy about their new king?"

"Red Oak," Saphier answered, positive about her intel.

"Then Vakar would have stationed his most loyal Kyst there," Ven declared confidently.

"Seems like a good place to start trouble," Onstera said with a smirk.

"Trouble is not what were after. We need a plan," Ina shot back.

"Chaos will start this rebellion, Commander? General? What am I to call you?" Onstera asked flirtatiously. Ina sent a raised brow at Saphier, not sure how to respond.

"Rank and power is what got us into this mess, none of us will hold station above the other," Saphier answered sternly. Onstera laughed aloud at that.

"Please, you may as well turn that pretty behind around and leave the forest now then. Chaos might win you this war but order among your numbers is paramount." Onstera looked to Ven as if he should divulge some information, but he kept rigid and did not speak. "Look, you don't pay me enough to lead your rebellion and you sent the only actual veteran of a war away this morning. You'll have to come up with something. In the meantime, I think Ven has news he'd like to share with you." Onstera wasn't above forcing Ven's hand on the matter. He glowered menacingly at her, just long enough to dream up an excuse.

"Onstera is going to train me to better deal with my rage," he said awkwardly. Onstera rolled her eyes but Ina and Saphier gave courteous but confused nods. "I do have one question—what about the Kintar? I know Vakar attacked them, but surely they have berserkers alive that want revenge."

Ina and Saphier looked at each other in surprise before Ven received the obvious response. "I understand that Silva had a small number of Kintar living in it, but we do not tolerate those blood-hungry monsters under any circumstance," Saphier said with a dower expression.

"Those 'monsters' have more reason to be upset than you do. They very well could be the difference between us losing or winning this war."

"You would be wasting our time Devar, you cannot simply erase an entire age of hatred between our races because all of a sudden it suits you." Onstera watched this interaction from an outsider's perspective and noted the rising aggression from Saphier and Ven. She noted too the obvious discomfort Ina Enallea was displaying.

"Why not?" Ven asked through gritted teeth.

"Because it's not how the world works," Saphier answered, as an older sibling condescends a younger.

"You wanna bet?" Ven said furiously, and within two heart beats he touched the part of magical map he knew to be Claw Canyon. It was as if the map had reached out and pulled him in headfirst. Onstera was utterly unsurprised by Ven's rash behaviour since she had only just recently convinced him not to go after Scáth. She heaved a great sigh before walking over to the map.

"Please tell me exactly where he touched so I don't end up on the wrong side of the forest," she requested as if it were some mundane chore she was about to start. Ina quickly darted beside her, grabbed her hand, and touched the same spot Ven had.

CHAPTER TWO

Old Habits

Agan watched as Onstera left the cave to follow Ven. He looked at Faenla; his coastal-blue eyes seemed at home to the half-orc, but he needed the wolf all the same. "Let's go see about heading west."

"Unfortunately, Master Dusk, Scáth is not vital to our cause." Queen Saphier gave Agan her decision in the cold and damp cavern that was their war room.

"I would disagree. Ven Devar is absolutely crucial to your cause, and he will not lift a finger unless he knows a rescue mission is to be mounted," the impossibly large half-orc responded with severity. Faenla was standing next to Agan, the wolf's legs so strong and nimble, his thick black fur adding so much size to a beast that was taller than most of the elves here. He rested his piercing eyes on Saphier, the white spots on his fur looking like stars, adding to his almost mythical appearance. All of this consumed the queen, and she was reluctant to say no with Faenla giving her such a judicious stare.

"We will send our finest hunters to accompany you in her rescue," the queen, as beautiful as the legends said, offered to the fighter.

"I know you have lived a long life, but that is life within the borders of your world. No matter how many elves you send, they will not succeed. Although my years are insignificant compared to yours, I have lived as a sellsword, guild-master, and renowned veteran of many battles. I have endured much, Your Grace, and every instinct I have begs tact and above all else, stealth."

"What do you suggest then?" Saphier asked impatiently.

"There is a woman in Rhogar, her skill as an assassin is incomparable to any on Litore. Let me bring her here, and not only will she secure Scáth without anyone in Vakar's army knowing it, but she will be invaluable to your cause moving forward."

"The power and wealth it would consume to send you to Rhogar would leave us with little, let alone to hire someone of that calibre," she answered skeptically.

"If you are not willing to sacrifice all that you possess, then you have already lost and I may as well secure my companions and go our separate ways," Agan laid his piercing yellow eyes on the queen.

Saphier was not used to men talking to her this way. Her beauty was said to be a gift from Āina to spite his jealous lover, Kaia. This meant most men and women were in awe around the queen and often fumbled over themselves when discussing anything. That is not to say Saphier wasn't a brilliant and sophisticated elf, for few could match her intellect; however, the last man to talk to her like this nearly killed her. Yet, she found it difficult to deny Agan's words, for they were wise and spoke of the harsh reality that lay ahead of them.

"If I do send you across the world, how will you get back? It would take a half-year by horse," she asked, knowing he'd have some unconvincing answer, but feeling stubborn enough to ask it anyway.

"I'm owed a great many favours in all corners of Rhogar," he said, suppressing a grin. Saphier gave a great sigh of resignation. She looked him up and down; Agan was of a rare breed of elven and orcish heritage. She wondered if perhaps he was half-Kintar, for his skin was mostly green until it faded to red across his face and scalp like a sunset. He was a hulking figure and had small tusks on his lower jaw that barely crested his lips.

"Prepare yourself, I will have the circle ready for your departure first thing." Saphier said and left no room for Agan to reply. He found the wolf and gathered what supplies he could before getting some much needed rest.

Before the crack of dawn, the half-orc and wolf had the queen and she simply raised a hand and beckoned the them to follow. Agan followed the queen out of the hideout and further up the stone plateau. Nearing the end of the stone beach he saw a boulder and Saphier nimbly dart around it. She went around on the ocean side, for it was clearly a rockslide from the cliff to their right. He had to press his back against it to shimmy along the narrow path. He looked over the edge of the plateau to see jagged rocks breaking the waves a few metres below.

Making it around the boulder, he saw another kilometre of stoney shore and half-a-dozen sages. They were already preparing a complex pentagram with gold paint on the sea-spattered ground. Around the border of the circle were strategically placed braziers, burning a sweet red. After a moment of watching the sages complete their tedious work, one of the Kyst gave his queen a confident nod.

"Have you travelled this way before, Master Dusk?" Saphier asked.

"I have, Your Grace," Agan replied. Faenla went about sniffing the golden image before looking back at the half-orc.

"Then step within and visualize your destination clearly."

Agan took a deep breath, chose his destination wisely, and vividly pictured the mining city of Argon. He walked into the centre of the pentagram, inviting the wolf to join him, to which Faenla hesitantly accepted. As they came to a halt in the centre, the braziers exploded violently in a jet of red flame. As the flames grew they came together, and Agan was forced to shield his eyes from the heat and blinding light coming from the wall of fire. He felt an immediate pressure change in his ears and then frozen air nip his skin.

Dropping his arm, he looked around to see a timber-built city surrounded by high, snow-covered peaks. He dropped to one knee for a moment to regain control of his senses which were barraged by the new surroundings and having gained thousands of metres in elevation instantly.

Looking up, he saw the unmistakable kilometre-wide hole in the centre of Argon. Huge cranes and mighty log homes were built around the mine entrance. It was a multi-day walk down the spiral road to the base of the mine and with new mine shafts to enter at regular intervals. It was here, some eleven years ago, that Agan was sent in to investigate if the Dwarves of SilverRock were in the Ruptured Range. As a matter of fact, they had mined a hole into Litore's mantle, then dropped a cylindrical stone the size of a small mountain down the shaft, setting off the first Quake of Harazune.

Agan felt his heart racing and a nausea overcome him, as this is where the Adazji Guild met its end. He breathed deeply, closing his eyes, trying to force the image of his fallen friends from his mind. He was forced to bury so much of his past deep, deep within himself, lest it consume him body and mind. Faenla gave him a nuzzle on the shoulder, beckoning Agan to lead. He put a large hand on the wolf's neck and the pair made their way to Argon.

Down in Copper Street, four Dragon-bloods carried an ornate palanquin with long Water Dragons carved on either side for handles. Four more Dragon-blood guards walked with the palanquin, each boasting heavy armour and long sabretooth ram fur-lined cloaks. Every seam in their clothing had thick grey and white fur peeking through. This did great things to keep them warm but also made their already large appearance even more imposing. Only one guard, with dark orange scales, had a helm on his head with golden dragon wings sprouting from the sides.

A fine layer of snow dust swirled along the cobblestone when a long, thin knife found its way into the skull of a servant carrying the palanquin, his blood showering the ground. The other three carriers were not strong enough to make-up for the sudden excess weight and the whole structure smashed into the ground. A large and fat Dragon-blood rolled out of the palanquin as it fell. With impeccable synchronization, the surrounding guards took up defensive positions around their lord. As one of the servants went to help him up, he was also met with a knife through the neck.

"Shields!" commanded the helmed Dragon-blood. The four guards surrounded the lord as they all looked for where their attackers could be. Everything went still and quiet as all by-standers quickly fled the scene, leaving only the moaning winds to fill their ears. The tension broke as the two remaining servants fled into the nearest alley with commendable speed.

"You must fly back to the manor!" the helmed guard shouted at the mayor, who was cowering behind their shields.

"I can't, damn you! Do your jobs and get me to safety," he responded, with no lack of disrespect, for the comforts of wealth and an easy life had made him too plump for his draconic wings to carry him.

"We're moving, stay in formation," he ordered his three soldiers, and so they moved in perfect harmony to keep the lord protected on all sides. As they came to an intersection, one guard caught a knife in the shin, causing him to break formation, subsequently catching another knife between his serpentine eyes.

"They're everywhere!" the lord screeched in terror.

"No," the leader said to himself, understanding now what he was up against. Just as this occurred to him, a spear soared down from a roof top, splintering straight through one guard's pine shield and skewering him to the cobblestone. The leader looked up to see a shadowy figure - hood, hair, and cloak billowing in the wind.

"On my command, stay between us and run," he spoke sternly to the lord, never taking his eyes off the figure above them. They vanished into the thin air and the helmed guard gave his mark. The three of them sprinted for the lord's manor. They were making great ground and the leader knocked several civilian Dragon-bloods out of their way as they ran through the streets.

The rear guard thought they stood a chance when he spotted the manor and noticed the bulbous lord was keeping to the golden winged leader. That was the last thought he ever had, as they passed a dark alley and another spear fired forthwith, directly under his arm pit and through his heart. The lord and lead guard never slowed, not until the ladder kicked open the gate and the lord ran onto the manor grounds. The guard turned just in the nick of time as a spear came flying at him. He caught it with his shield and the pole arm came to a halt halfway through it. He dropped the broken shield just as he heard the lord burst into his home.

"Jarith, Drek, to arms now!" he shouted for his household guards who had remained behind on what started out as monthly inspection of the mines. When he received no response, a cold chill ran down his spine. He slowly turned to see Jarith, a yellow Dragon-blood of some renown, slumped over the second-floor handrail, blood dripping from his neck to splash the floor tiles below. The lord quickly threw the door open to leave and saw the helmed leader facing the manor on his knees, with his head gripped firmly by his hands, resting between his legs.

He quickly shut the door again and locked it before quietly sobbing to himself. He slowly, and without care, walked towards his office. He noticed a spear-head protruding from the office door. It swung inwards with ease and as he entered he found Drek, a purple Dragon-blood, skewered to it. He lamented the death before entering further into his study, fully accepting his fate now. The room was dark, and he felt chill on his bones. He wondered if it was already the chill of death creeping inside of him. Determined to feel one last moment of warmth, he lit a match and tossed it into the hearth.

As the oil-soaked wood burst into life and the room filled with light, a ShadowScorn woman was revealed from the darkness to be seated in his chair. She wore dark-black leather armour and a silk red cowl under her chin. Her hair was braided tight at the sides with bangs that helped enshroud her face as her hair forever misted into ethereal shadow. Her skin shifted with the light from an onyx black to a soft grey. Her eyes poured shadow out the corners and congregated across the bridge of her nose. The lord jolted back in sheer fright.

The human Scorn lifted a glass of liquor to her lips, downing the whole drink before letting it shatter to the floor. "I could have poisoned you, slit your throat while you slept, or killed you in the street. So why didn't I?" The Dragon-blood tried to speak but could only swallow his words, vibrating with angst and trying not to imagine those possibilities. "Because you deserve to know what true fear is. They paid me to kill you not because of the corruption, or squandering of the less fortunate, or outright stealing the city's coin. So why am I here?" Her tone became ever more threatening as she demanded his confession.

The lord simply shook his head, understanding that denying her this was the only thing left in his power.

"Say it," she demanded, but the lord remained steadfast in his cowardice.

"Say it!" she screamed.

"Slaves! I sold slaves," he erupted in confession, followed by sobbing. "I'm sorry, I'm so sorry. I should have never, I know that." He dropped to his hands and feet, begging for his life.

"The Dragon-bloods of our day allow too much to go unpunished, but your King Dusanith's zero tolerance for slavery is to be commended." Kithlyn stood from the high-backed leather chair and sauntered to the bent over lord. She slowly flicked her wrist and from her bracer emerged a long, slim knife that slid perfectly into her hand. "You can stop begging for your life, it's non-negotiable. If you have something useful, say it now and I'll make it quick."

After a few sniffles of defeat, he spoke, "Check under the seat, there is a log of everyone I've ever sold too." Kithlyn could tell by his tone that he truly did understand the wrong he had done.

"May the Diamond Dragon have mercy," she whispered, before plunging her knife into the base of his skull. Kithlyn was nearing the end of her first century in life, and by ShadowScorn approximation she had several more centuries to go. By all accounts, she was the most prolific assassin in Litore, largely due to her unique heritage, which had been seen by all as a massive misfortune. But all those doubters were blinded by ignorance, for the ShadowScorn species were placed on Litore as benevolent creatures, yet they possessed the capabilities to defeat any adversary.

Kithlyn quickly discovered that the seat cushion of the leather chair lifted and found a cloth-bound journal inside a small compartment, filled with names and locations of slavers and those they sold to.

"Effective as usual, if not a little more theatrical than I remember," a gruff voice sounded from the doorway.

"One must find ways to keep the passion alive for one's occupation," Kithlyn responded, never taking her eyes away from the contents of the journal.

Agan chuckled at the old adage the Adazji guild used to speak.

"I am not helping you."

"What makes you think I want anything other than to see an old friend?"

The Scorn assassin moved, never looking at Agan, to an oil painting of the now deceased lord. She tore it off the wall to reveal a safe.

"The first time I met Agan Dusk was to aid in his revenge. The second was in aid of his redemption. The third led me to a war that nearly split our continent in two. Each time we meet, I am pulled nearer to death." By the time she finished her line of thought, she had expertly picked the locked and thrown the safe open. She took a step back in shock. This put Agan on edge and he was quickly behind her. Inside the safe was a small chest, a faint thumping sound within. Kithlyn turned on her heel and faced the hulking half-elf.

"Speaking of death, you should be dusty bones by now."

Agan was now the one not making eye contact, as he walked to the safe to peer inside.

"First I'm hearing of it. You're the one who fell down Harazune's infinite hole." Agan was almost transfixed by the sound. He put both hands on the lid and slowly opened it. Within was a beating heart. When Agan turned around to see what Kithlyn was thinking, he found empty space, followed by an audible sigh escaping his lips.

In truth, he knew convincing Kithlyn would be a monumental task, which he came expecting, but what he wasn't prepared for was to find the Heart of Pharyn. He closed the lid and shoved the small coffer in his bag. After stepping in a pool of blood, he remembered where he was, and made a prompt exit.

Kithlyn wasted little time in heading back to one of her many safe houses. Argon was a large city, so she keenly bought up entire apartments and manors for herself to lay low in. After disappearing into the darkness around her and shadow-walking into her apartment on the top floor of an otherwise empty building, she spoke a command word and a magical darkness lifted from the floor to cling to the ceiling like swirling cloud cover.

She checked the thin wire across the inside of her door to ensure it was not broken and no one had been inside since her last visit. Since the War of a Thousand Dragons she had barely left Rhogar, for it was the largest country on Litore and offered more lucrative contracts than anywhere else. She was possibly the most prolific assassin across the continent and had a rocky past before settling amongst the Dragon-bloods. This ShadowScorn felt more akin to the children of death, and it felt more like home than the countless other places she had travelled.

Her infamy did, however, work against her from time to time. She was known by King Dusanith, so as long as she was careful, trouble never arose from the crown. But Rhogar was far from a unified country. There were more dukes, jarls, and lords than she could point her impressive collection of knives at. She had a stack of enemies that would give anything to have her head set upon a spike and proudly displayed within their vast lands. That fact did nothing but bolster her ego. She was a ShadowScorn and every contract completed was revenge for her kind. Proof that the Scorn were a species not to be trifled with.

Yet for all that, she had little in-common with her with true kin anymore. For Kithlyn Whisp had met a fate like so many of her kind and hadn't seen the City of Shadow since her 16th name day. Although the renowned woman could have returned many times, she could never bare it. Life behind those walls was no better than life in a rat trap. She likened it to how the lord she just killed must have felt in his mansion, to be in your safest place and understand there was no escape, no hope of a morrow.

She lit a small hearth and sat with crossed legs in front of the flames, stoking it every so often. She sipped a tea and tried to find some semblance of peace; for even though she was a veteran assassin, taking a life, no matter how evil, stung her soul.

Her introspection was halted as a small metallic orb shattered her window and rolled towards her. With impeccable reflexes, she lifted herself up with the flat of her palms and rotated her pelvis to spin and kick the ball under her bed. It hit the back wall and exploded with a light as violent as the sun. She faintly whimpered in pain and shielded her eyes, then keenly heard the sound of footfalls throughout the building.

She opened her eyes and saw nothing but searing blurs across her vision. The door to her apartment burst open and the sound of a glyph sizzled, followed by an ear-ringing explosion. She felt the heat of the fire wash over her just as a charred corpse hit the wall from the force of the explosion.

Still blinded, she darted out the room and into the hallway where she heard three sets of footsteps charging her. Running in the opposite direction and counting her steps, she leaped over a trip wire that would electrocute on contact. After several more heart pounding seconds, Kithlyn heard the trap work and a loud thud behind her as one of her pursuers convulsed on the floor. She turned ninety degrees and forced the darkness in the hallway into her eyes until she could see again. Just in time, as a club swung out of an apartment door aimed for her head. She ducked and slid across the floorboards, grabbing the ankle of the assailant as she went. Reversing momentum, she leapt on them and drove a knife into their heart just as another ball exploded with light.

Aside from the sheer blindness she suffered, the pain of it was almost enough to consume her. She understood another pair of footsteps were coming from behind her and she was cornered with no way out. She rolled into the open apartment and slammed the door shut, driving a knife through latch to buy her a few extra seconds to recover.

Closing her eyes once more, she focused on drawing the lingering shadow into her very being. The door shook violently as the intruders attempted to break it down, but even so, this seasoned assassin breathed deep and calm, centring herself. Her room began to glow a soft yellow, which grew with intensity as it would with the rising sun. Suddenly, the banging on her door stopped and she could tell with closed eyes that her room was bathed in sun light. She turned slowly to face the window, for the darkness of midnight should have been upon them.

A great winged humanoid hovered there, 12 metres off the ground, staring frightfully at her. They were covered in feathers that were entirely engulfed in flame. Kithlyn lifted her hand above her brow, attempting to get a better look at the creature. Its fiery visage grew in brightness until she could bear it no more. The humanoid flew straight through the window and grasped her by the neck. The flame from the creature was intense, but its touch did not burn. Within a few heartbeats she was overcome by the heat and slipped peacefully into unconsciousness.

The hulking fighter and colossal coastal wolf stood on a small mountain, looking down on a cart carrying a metallic box. The unrelenting wind and snow assailed them as they watched atop their vantage point. They were heading north and out of Rhogar through the Ruptured Range, a belt of mountains that appeared as though they had erupted over night, for they were sharper and steeper than any other in the world.

From Agan's view, he could not make out who or what the bright creature siting on the drivers' bench was. Not until a short while later, when it sprouted massive wings and took to the sky, trailing a bright line of orange fire behind it.

CHAPTER THREE

Daughter of Shadow

Scáth suddenly found herself in a pitch-black room, circular in shape and wooden in nature. She was breathing heavily as the adrenaline of battle was fresh in her veins. She whipped her head around trying to discern where she had just landed and where her companions were. No matter where her gaze fell, she saw nothing but rich wood, save for a single metal door with no handle.

She quickly stepped up to it and gave a great push but found no purchase. She started to bang on it and soft thuds echoed back. An unfamiliar anger filled her heart, and before she knew it she was the kicking the door with every ounce of strength she could muster. Eventually, she gave in and rested her forehead against it in defeat.

What had happened? Why was she here and where was *here* anyway? A hundred questions and concerns fluttered around in her mind until she heard a large clunk as a lock lifted from the other side of the door. She quickly threw her back against the wall and waited with scimitar in hand. As a tall and slender Kyst male walked inside, she slid behind them, kicked the door closed, placed her scimitar against his throat and twisted one of his arms behind his back.

"Where am I?" she whispered angrily in his ear.

"Silva," a calm and confident voice answered.

"Silva burned."

"We rebuilt it."

"Get me out of here."

"Can't. Well, I should say I won't."

"What is stopping me from cutting your throat then?" she threatened.

"Nothing you're aware of. So you should do it." He invited her to do so as he pressed his neck harder against her blade. Scáth felt for a moment she would spill his blood in a heartbeat, yet she found herself unable to kill in cold blood. She shoved the Kyst forward a number of strides and held her weapon out at the ready.

Vakar turned to face her and straightened his robes out as he did.

"Hello, Scáth."

"Vakar," she nearly gasped. "What's going on here?"

Vakar looked around as if it was obvious. "You are a prisoner, a piece on the board, one plan in a greater weave of strategy."

"Ven misses you. He wants things back to the way they were." The Scorn immediately went to seeing reason.

"It's your fault things changed in the first place, Princess," Vakar said derisively. "Life will never be what it was before that fire."

She scoffed at that. "If a rabbit is sick and you eat its meat, is it the rabbit's fault you fell ill? I was a victim from the moment I was abducted to the moment Ven, Athvar, and Agan saw more in me than what I was raised for. I am sorry that the Kintar burned Silva trying to get me, from the deepest, most sincere part of my heart Vakar, I am sorry, but it was not my fault."

"I made sure they were sorry, but you haven't even begun to repent." He had a macabre smile that unnerved Scáth, yet she had grown in courage and confidence since the last time she was in the Great Northern Rainforest.

"You're threats will not intimidate me. I have suffered more than you know and lived a life of fear twice as long as you've been alive. I no longer cower to wicked folk like you, for fear is the source of your power."

Vakar began to circle Scáth, leaving them in silence as he inspected her with veiled intent.

"Ven has taught you the way of the warrior I see," he said as if that fact meant little. "Has it occurred to you that I gained this level of power not through fear, but knowledge, Scorn Queen? You gave up your familial line, now King Sindrum Silver, first of his name, sits upon the throne you were destined for, isn't that right? In the briefest of moments, you skimmed true power when you lead your people in the grand foyer of Shadow Palace. Yet it churned your gut, crumbled your courage and soured your heart. For weakness is at the root of your soul and no amount of training or kind words from a traitorous Kyst can change that."

Scáth was surprised Vakar knew so much from the Siege of Shadow. That information could only be sourced one of two ways, she thought. One being Vakar was in league with Serenstrom. The other being, use of forbidden magic to source the knowledge.

"In case you misheard me, your insulting words are like wind against stone. They mean nothing and bounce off with no effect. I hear they call you 'cunning' but so far I've only known you to be a snivelling elf who can't handle losing."

Vakar knew she was attempting to elicit anger, and he hated that it was working. This was not the Scorn he so briefly met all those months ago.

"Since reason seems to elude you, shall we try physical force?" Vakar asked by putting his hand on her shoulder and a zap of arcane electricity sprawled across her body. Scáth involuntarily tensed, her muscles seizing before abruptly loosening and dropping her to the hard ground in revolting agony.

She heard a loud whistle and the door swung inwards. Rexous and three other Kyst Hunters walked in. Rex held a small orb that gave off a bright light, filling the room in a blinding yellow hue. The three other hunters roughly grabbed Scáth and dragged her out of the room and into one more suited for captivity.

The Scorn was barely conscious as she felt herself being strapped into a wooden device suspended off the ground by a single chain. Rexous watched his hunters do this, ensuring no shadow was in the room for her to call upon. When the hunters finished binding Scáth's ankles and wrists, they promptly left the cell. Vakar watched eagerly from the door as Rexous inspected her restraints.

"Ven mourned for you. You were like a brother to him," she muttered at the hunter.

"We hated each other," he answered impassively before turning to leave the room. He stopped in front of Vakar as Scáth said one more thing.

"No, you didn't."

Rexous didn't look but he knew Vakar was watching his reaction closely. However, the once Prince wasn't given a chance to react before Eevie Hara met them at the door. Eevie was the closest thing Vakar had left to family, being the sister of his dearly beloved Qiri. She also happened to be the Prime Commander of the Kyst Hunters in this new army. Her bright, amber-coloured skin and luminous hazelnut eyes immediately caught Scáth's attention. The Scorn strained her hearing the best she could to decipher Eevie's whisper.

"A Kintar Berserker from Claw Canyon just killed an entire platoon of our hunters." The three Kyst noticed Scáth looking their way, and Rex and Eevie made their exit.

"Please Princess, you really are desperate if you think playing on his emotional side will help you here. He was cold before I stitched his rigid soul back into his body." Vakar shot her a disappointed glare. The King of Kyst went to leave and slam the door behind him, but Scáth's tender and caring voice stopped him.

"The only difference between a hero and a villain is how they deal with their trauma. The thing is, it's never too late to become one or the other." Vakar couldn't understand if she was warning him or offering redemption. He considered maybe both, and surprised himself by gently shutting the door.

Scáth let her head limply hang as her body was uncomfortably suspended against the vertical table. She considered how she might get herself out of this situation. The last thing she wanted was Ven or Agan risking their own safety to rescue her. She was resolute in the fact that she would not be a hindrance to her companions. She had grown into the person she had always dreamed of being after the Siege of Shadow. She had lost more than she could have ever thought, led her nation against all odds, made the most important decision of her life by giving up the throne, and was the only one capable of thwarting the final General of Serenstrom. Reminding herself of all this gave her the confidence to know she would escape.

On the return journey from ShadowScorn, she had practised relentlessly in the art of shadow-phasing. Yet for all her hard work and dedication, Scáth understood her abilities were completely unlike the rest of her kind; she could not fade into the lingering darkness and appear somewhere else in shadow; she could not generate spheres of writhing darkness or change the shade of her skin from white, to grey, to onyx black; however, she had mastered one skill—the ability to be a solid or as incorporeal as shadow itself. So, after long meditation, she focused on her ankles and wrists until suddenly she felt herself slide off the table and her feet land softly on the wood.

She looked back at the contraption that was holding her, brushed her hands together as if cleaning them and wore a look of satisfaction on her lips. She looked up at the hovering ball of light in the centre of the room with squinted eyes, then to the heavily-locked wooden door, when an idea struck her. She stared at the glowing orb of light and focused through the pain stinging her eyes. She found the harder she concentrated on removing the light source from her vision, the darker it was becoming. Eventually the entire orb had been literally drawn into her pupils and the room was left pitch black. She blinked tightly, and as her eyes opened, the light within faded like a dying star. She couldn't suppress another smile as she accomplished a feat unheard of to the rest of her species.

She walked over to the door, inherently without making a sound, as even her leather armour and hefty pumasheep cloak didn't make a ruffle. She pressed her ear to the door, listening for a long while, and was confident there was only one hunter or sage guarding her door and few people ever passed by.

She trusted in her skill to subdue a hunter, for she was trained by possibly the greatest Kyst hunter of them all. However, she feared what she would do if a sage was guarding her door. Ven spoke highly of the Kyst Sages and their immense power, and she knew too of the power the priests of Aceia held in ShadowScorn.

Yet none of that mattered if the next phase of her plan failed. She would have to try something she had never found the courage to risk. Scáth would attempt to make her whole body insubstantial and pass through the door. A combination of the traditional shadow-phasing and her own unique ability. But she was mortified at what might happen if she lost concentration midway and found half or all her body stuck inside the object she was attempting to phase through. What manner of horror would that feel like; her imagination didn't need any help in conjuring images of only half her torso reforming while the other half stayed behind in the door.

Nevertheless, she would not let her companions risk or sacrifice themselves without doing the same. She steeled her nerves and reminded herself of what it felt like to be truly one with the darkness around her. The feeling of utter weightlessness, the pressure of gravity released in one euphoric moment. The Daughter of Shadow placed her hands upon the door, feeling the ancient wood against her palms and fingers. She eased her weight against the door and focused on the feeling of freedom from the physical world. In a heartbeat, she fumbled through the door, catching herself mid-stumble forward and reforming as the light from many candles bounced off her ghostly white skin.

A Kyst female dressed in ornate robes that Scáth recognized as a traditional sage uniform, was left wide-eyed and stunned for two seconds too long. Scáth swept the sage's legs out from under her, and before the Kyst hit the ground, the Scorn gripped her collar and punched her squarely in the face. A spurt of blood issued from the sage's mouth and Scáth quietly rested her body against the floor.

She surveyed her surroundings quickly, noting a thin, spiralling hallway that was clearly built against a tree, for there were doors located only on the inside wall. Small windows on the opposite wall let in the red hued moonlight. She knew they must be up high if the moonlight was this strong, as little (if any) light shone through the canopy. The Scorn heard footsteps coming from down the hall and knew if this sage was found unconscious the whole place would be on alert. Scáth quickly slid the locks open on the door and dragged the unconscious Kyst inside.

She listened closely for the footsteps to pass, then slipped back out. Before heading down the hall, she gingerly locked the door, ensuring the sage wouldn't be a problem later. Scurrying down the helical walkway, she heard a familiar voice from one of the doors to her right. Faint candlelight spilled out from the room onto the floor from the crack in the doorway.

"Are you questioning me?" Scáth heard Rexous snarl. She wouldn't have considered pausing if the conversation included anyone else, so, she sidled up close to the wall and peered inside.

"I thought that was obvious," Eevie retorted. Rexous' growl, albeit low, resonated towards Scáth.

"If you didn't want me back, why did you allow him to resurrect me?"

"Your arrogance always made me sick, you know that? I did everything in my power to stop him from souring our world with your presence upon it again. He doesn't listen to me anymore, or anyone for that matter."

Scáth had never heard anyone speak that way to Rexous before and she recognized the voice to be Eevie Hara. "Kill Ven Devar, or by Kaia's vengeful fury I will make every borrowed breath you breathe a tormented one."

Eevie stormed out of the room but Scáth had already quickly continued on her way. Soon, she was peering through a large, carved archway that opened out onto one of the magnificent bridges connecting the kilometre-high cedar trees.

She was momentarily filled with a wave of conflicting feelings. Everything looked just as it was before Silva burned to the ground. Great ferns and fungi glowed with brilliant bioluminescence while the tree canopy seemingly hugged you, offering a front row seat to the heavens. Then, the recognition that this all went up in flames because of her, less than a year ago. Thousands dead and those that lived, scarred forever more.

"I'm impressed you got out." Eevie's words had Scáth spinning in fright. The hunter's face was not smug or vile, but sympathetically disappointed.

"You cannot keep me here," Scáth replied defiantly.

"You don't understand; if you cause trouble, his wrath will grow, giving you less time."

Scáth's mind raced through ten thoughts in a tenth of a second before it occurred to her that Eevie was trying to help. "You know I have to try."

The Kyst did not have the time to respond. Scáth did not make it two steps through the archway before Rexous leapt down from above to block her exit. Scáth, utterly surprised by the appearance, rocked several steps back. Eevie had used that split second to close the distance, and stood stern as Scáth bumped into her.

"I know you do. As would I," Eevie spoke solemnly before cracking Scáth in the temple with the hilt of her sai. The Scorn hit the ground with a thud, eyes shut.

"Get up, little sister. Darkness is calling."

Scáth felt the soft silk pillow against her cheek and the warmth of wool blankets across her body. She also felt the caring but firm hand of her brother nudge her awake. She sleepily opened her eyes and saw Scarnin standing at her bedside, the pupils of his eyes giving a soft glow in an otherwise pitch-black room.

"It's time to train, get up or else they'll start calling you the 'sleeping princess'." Scarnin's voice always had such a unique effect on Scáth, for it calmed her with a sense of familiarity but enraged her as only an irritating brother could. As she sat up in her bed, a wave of concern and discomfort hit the princess; something was off here but she couldn't place it, like a missing word on the tip of your tongue. That thought was abruptly ended as Scarnin threw a thick winter cloak in her face.

"Be in the courtyard in ten or I send a Ghost of Aceia to get you," the Prince of Shadow ordered before vanishing into the lingering darkness. The last thing Scáth wanted was to be escorted by a ghost through the annals of ShadowScorn Palace, so she promptly draped the cloak around her shoulders, pulled up the hood, and sprinted for the courtyard.

The thick cloud cover above obscured the three bright moons of Litore, the largest of all being Caelestis. Scáth walked out onto the courtyard that overlooked most of the city. In the very centre of the smooth laid stone was a large blossom tree, its bark a stark black and its leaves a matte white. It was planted by their grandfather King Armin; over the centuries the bark and leaves had soaked up the lingering shadow and become an extension of its surroundings. Scáth had spent innumerable hours sitting by that tree, thinking about how it adapted and transformed to become one-of-a-kind.

"Come, sit." Scarnin waved his palm to a spot in front of him, already sitting cross-legged in the soft soil around the tree. Scáth walked softly through the dirt and sat down, resting her hands on her knees.

"Close your eyes little sister," Scarnin instructed, and Scáth complied. "Calm yourself—I can sense your unease from here."

As she attempted to relax her body, a pounding headache ran through the back of her skull.

"It hurts."

"What hurts?" he asked.

"The back of my head." Although her voice was strong, a tear rolled down her cheek.

"Pain is a reminder you're alive; the more you ignore it, the worse it becomes. Focus on the exact point of pain, fall into it, and let your muscles relax around it." Scarnin was surprisingly soothing in his tone and Scáth did as he said. Within a few moments of focus, her pain began to subside.

"Good. Now command your mind to let go of your worldly attachments. Become one with the city, then the land, the sky, and finally, the universe around you."

Scáth envisioned herself outside of her own body. Seeing herself as a single blade of grass to the whole of reality. Just one more organism breathing life in this single instance. Her whole body visibly drooped just a bit as her physical strings were severed.

"Excellent. Now, focus on your soul and its innate connection to Aceia."

"How?" she wondered aloud, for they had never reached this part of the meditation before.

"Your body is the vessel; it carries you through this world. Your mind perceives your surroundings and makes sense of it. Your soul is who you are. You are the Princess of Shadow, Scáth ShadowScorn. Fearless, courageous and wise, but locked in a prison of physical and spiritual torment. Very few in our kind fail at harnessing shadow. Those with the greatest inner turmoil left unchecked will never achieve the possible. So, what is your inner blockage?"

"Perhaps my inner turmoil is our high-walled prison."

Scarnin simply shook his head. Scáth sighed before straightening her posture and spending a great deal of time looking within. She had a list as long as her nightgown of things that drove her crazy, but she knew none of those were the real cause of her inability to become one with shadow.

"I don't know. There is too much to sift through," Scáth answered finally, defeated by her lack of understanding.

"Is it because you are female?" Scarnin asked nonchalantly.

Her eyes fluttered open in rage. "Pardon me?" she spat vehemently.

"Close your eyes, sister." he replied, never opening his own. She rolled her eyes with grandeur before closing them again and re-centering herself.

"No, it is not because of my gender, Scarnin."

"Because our mother hates you?"

That had her face screw up in confusion and hurt, yet she did not open her eyes.

"Why would you say that?" she asked with predictable sorrow. "She does not hate me. Perhaps there is an underlying layer of aversion, but we still love one another."

"Quit lying to yourself. She knows you'll never amount to what you should have been. Night after night we come out here and you still can't grasp the most basic shadow technique." As Scarnin spoke these words, a great wind swirled around them and the cloud cover dispersed, showering the world in the red moon-light of Caelestis.

"I never lie to myself."

"You are scared and will amount to nothing. If you are lucky, you will serve the one purpose a female has." The prince's tone was so calm and confident, the words struck Scáth profoundly. For a split second, deep in her meditation, Scáth saw a flash of Scarnin's funeral.

She angrily opened her eyes and saw that Scarnin was replaced by Oren the Administrator. His dark and hateful eyes were silhouetted by the red moonlight to create a terrifying visage. His usual smirk of superiority was present but it unnerved Scáth more than usual.

"Please, little Princess. This is your inner turmoil; you lie to yourself with every breath. First royal Scorn born a female. Every opinion you've ever voiced has been seen as nothing more than noise, if perceived by anyone at all. You tell yourself daily that you matter, that soon those around you will heed your words. Soon, someone might care." Oren's smirk filled the princess with rage and his words hissed like a snake, but were the absolute truth.

"You know nothing of me. You're a poison dripper," she said, looking for any kind of response to hide the fact she was fighting back tears and the urge to attack him.

"I've known you from the minute you were born, I've known your father and grandfather. You, little princess, are a show piece and nothing more. A pretty face to calm the masses, weak in bone and soft in thought."

Scáth fought the urge to jump at the petty Scorn man. Instead, another image of Oren laying in the palace dungeon, shackled to the wall, flashed briefly in her mind.

"No, you are the weak one," she replied, resolute. Another great gust of wind kicked up around her, causing a great heap of white blossom leaves to fall upon them. Before the wind settled, Scáth was faced with Ven Devar. And whatever she thought she was beginning to understand about her situation vanished from her mind at the sight of her beloved.

"Are you okay?" Ven's tender and caring voice calmed Scáth.

"I'm not sure." Her distress faded quickly into a smile for her Kyst.

"You will be, so long as you're not alone," Ven said sweetly, returning the smile. Yet, the kind words didn't sit well with the Scorn.

"You think I'm incapable of caring for myself?"

"Well, yeah," he answered hesitantly. "How many times have I saved you from death? Or Faenla and Agan? The one chance you had to repay us, Athvar died." Ven looked longingly, not wishing to hurt her with his words but unable to lie. Scáth let her eyes fall to the ground, somewhat ashamed and embarrassed she thought he had believed in her.

"I didn't know you felt that way."

"Don't be sad, it's why I love you. I need someone to protect, who relies on me for their very survival."

Scáth shot her gaze up at the hunter, holding a wicked stare on him. She fought against the sweet look he always had for her, and his honest innocence she had fallen in love with. She looked from him to the great black blossom tree. She shook her head in frustration and peered through the stone balustrade to look down on the grand entrance of the palace. She saw a great battle and many legendary heroes laying asunder, one Solsta elf standing above them all in gleaming gold and white armour. One last image flashed in her mind —the moment she drove the scimitar Ven gave her through that elf's heart. She looked back to Ven and spoke confidently.

"It's not true and it's not why you love me."

Ven's image dispersed with a swirl of violent shadow. After a contorting mass of writhing tendrils were tamed, a tall, lone humanoid stood in front of Scáth. Its body was without definition, short hair misted upwards to look like fire while shadow poured from it's eyes as if it were perpetually weeping.

Scáth instinctively jumped to her feet, kicking up soft soil as she did. She instinctually reached for her hip where a weapon would be, but of course found nothing.

"What are you? What is this?" she shouted, desperate to understand. The tall figure stood there motionless, shadow pouring off its whole body like plunging water. "I demand you tell me!"

"Don't ask the wrong questions, child."

"Where am I?" Scáth blurted angrily.

"In the deepest recess of your mind. For the mind is the most powerful place in existence." Its voice sounded like a coarse but fading whisper. She looked around once more, a picture-perfect representation of ShadowScorn. The crisp night air felt so real upon her skin but there was a weightlessness to her spirit she could only associate with dreaming.

"You are Aceia." Every instinct of hers was confident in that. In return, the figure gave a slight nod.

"And who are you?" they asked knowingly.

"Scáth ShadowScorn, First Princess of Shadow, First Scorn Queen," she stated proudly, fully remembering everything up to the point where she was hit in the head on Silva's great bridges.

But the ghostly onyx figure shook his head. "You are Scáth the Lady of Shadow, Daughter of Aceia. My only heir."

She stood there unmoving, unblinking, utterly stunned by the remark. Yet, she couldn't help but feel like this was another lie. Perhaps this was Zeries, God of Trickery, fooling her.

"No, Arwr and Katia are my parents. If this is in my mind, then you are nothing but a figment of my imagination," Scáth tried to reason aloud, as much for herself as to deny this entity.

"Your mother hated you because you were not hers, your father loved you because he, like you, has known me. I sacrificed myself when Ivan the Revered won his siege. The only true piece of me that remains now, is you."

"I don't believe you." She resisted, although some part of her could not deny it.

"You are different in all the right ways. A bridge between your species and the rest of the world for the new Age of Litore. You must unite the world in an era of peace."

Scáth was torn from her stare on the figure as a bright light was beginning to form in the sky above them. She understood now this was either the strangest dream of her life or there was some truth to what she was hearing.

"When is the Second Age over?" she asked. Once again, the figure shook his head, letting her know not to ask the wrong questions.

"Are there others? Like me?" She spoke hurriedly as the light in the sky grew brighter.

"One for each of the gods. I was close with Kaia, there is little doubt as to why you have fallen in love with her son." Aceia spoke with a sense of worry now and Scáth held her hand out to block the light from stinging her eyes as it nearly encompassed the entire sky. "Be wary my daughter, for not all the Grimìr will share this goal in mind."

Scáth barely heard the final words, as the light in the sky was now all-consuming, until eventually she could not perceive anything.

Scáth, The Daughter of Shadow, awoke sprawled out on a familiar cobblestone floor. Her eyes were instantly assaulted by a blinding shimmering light surrounding her. As her eyes slowly and painfully adjusted, she first noted the light was actually a semi-translucent wall that encircled her in a barely two-metre radius. She slid her elbow back to support herself as she half leaned up.

"It pains me to say I'm impressed." She heard, then spotted, Vakar on the other side of the shimmering wall, with Rexous and Eevie on either side of him. "But I do appreciate a challenge. I don't suggest touching the wall unless you want to scar that delicate porcelain skin of yours." Vakar's smug pride was written all over him. Rexous wore his famously impassive stare, but Scáth noted Eevie wore a look of shame on her face. The three Kyst left the chamber before Scáth slid her arm back onto the floor and shielded her eyes in defeat.

CHAPTER FOUR

Chaos Incarnate

Vakar methodically stepped between the colossal trees that were nourished by a slow running creek. It was the same trail he walked with Ven the night before Silva burned. He replayed that 30-minute journey to the beach, as if reliving the event now.

"Thanks for coming out here with me, I needed to get away from that place." He heard Ven's voice in his head.

"You always want to get out of there," Vakar said aloud flatly, not teasingly like he had on that walk the prior year.

"Don't you? Ever want to get away?" Ven's question rattled around in his mind like a pestering insect.

"From time to time, but then I remember why that place needs me. My friends, my studies, continuing our culture."

"Sounds nice," Ven said, upset by the comment.

"You have me, Ven." Re-saying the words now felt sour on his tongue, and had Vakar stop in his tracks for a moment. How utterly inseparable the two Kyst used to be. How quickly that had all changed. "You have your life as a famed hunter, and you know as well as I, Eevie never shuts up about you."

Ven snickered at that. "I simply lack the courage to speak to her and I fear Qiri would quit hunting with me if I was to court his sister."

Vakar started his walk again. "You, who single handedly defeated Hoarfrost, a greater demon from the Underworld, fear speaking to that dorky hunter? Maybe I will tell Qiri to stop hunting with you so you must journey with her. He would you know; he does whatever I tell him to do." Vakar's face changed to the same loving smirk it did back then when talking about his soul mate in life.

"I am, from the bottom of my heart, happy my two closest friends found true love in each other." Ven clasped Vakar's shoulder, and Vakar could feel the pressure now, gripping him like a ghostly hand.

"It will happen for you too my friend, and when it does, I will know that happiness you speak of." The words slapped him in the face now; he wished he could have stayed true to that, yet he now held Ven's one true love prisoner. It donned on Vakar then that perhaps Ven always was the wise and compassionate one. For some reason, this fueled the hatred he currently felt; however, that almost insignificant piece of him that knew Ven was not to blame for anything had one more argument.

"Maybe it will, maybe it won't. Truthfully, I don't believe I am suited for love. I've always done better on my own."

"Ugh, save the melancholy for your journal." Vakar remembered Ven sneering at that comment, but in truth the famed hunter had let out a small laugh.

"Is being a sage and settling down truly your greatest ambition?" Ven asked *accusatorily.*

Vakar had simply answered 'yes,' but now he said with a growl, "Revenge."

"Boring, you could do so much more." Ven spoke with a deeper understanding of Vakar then the sage realized.

"Like making sure the Kintar never hurt another Kyst." Vakar's every word was laced with malice unchecked and veered from the past.

"Think of the adventures, the lives you could touch and change for the better. We could do it, you know? Change the world, just the two of us." Vakar remembered Ven being so optimistic and hopeful.

"I could even kill you." The words brought Vakar a surprising sense of relief now.

"Instead of guilting me about appreciation and the lack thereof I seem at fault for, why not bestow some actual wisdom?" Ven had said after the usual lecture he received about not appreciating all that the folk of Silva had done for him.

"Here is some wisdom for you. Life is unfair. And those who have more than most shouldn't complain about what very little they can't seem to possess," Vakar said bitterly now, just as he had then.

"Perhaps those possessed of more would give it all to possess the little they do not. Forgive me brother," Ven said, holding emphasis on the use of 'brother', as these two were unrelated but spoke about the other as if they were family. "I shall quit bothering you with my greater concerns and hopes in life."

Vakar remembered feeling truly sorry at the time for not being more patient with his closest ally in life, but now he took satisfaction in those words.

By this point they had reached the beach, and Ven had gone fishing. Vakar now sat down in the very same spot and, without effort, created a fire from nothing to warm his damp bones. He nestled into the soft upturned sand and fell deeply into his book, titled *Fables of the Thousand Dragon War.*

The war had broken out over a decade ago between the Dwarves of Silver Rock and Dragon-bloods of Rhogar. Its many conflicts had ramifications across the entire continent, most notably the Quake of Harazune. It was also prudent information for Vakar to reinforce his knowledge as the half-elf, half-orc Ven now travelled beside was a key player throughout that piece of history. And although he couldn't be sure, the vessel he spotted in the distance sailing towards him carried a particular Solsta Elf that he suspected had several parts to play in the famed war. He had come to this beach not to just reminisce and find rare solitude, but to meet with a mysterious figure known as Aolendìr Tardinian. Vakar looked up from his book to watch the sleek schooner gliding across the waves ever closer.

The Kyst put his book down and calmed his mind for the encounter about to be endured. Perhaps twenty minutes had slipped by when he heard a small rowboat scraping against the beach. He opened his eyes to see a devilishly handsome elf approaching. Aolendìr was tall with bronze, sun-kissed skin, his thick and long tied-back hair was bright gold, matching his glistening eyes. His neatly maintained beard came to a spectacular point as it peaked through his popped collar that met the lobes of his pointed ears. A cunning and conceited smile gave the impression of an elf that knew much and had extraordinary experience. Vakar immediately sensed a least a dozen powerful magical relics hidden throughout his many layered robes and cloaks. Vakar did not stand to meet his guest but instead held his hand out for

Aolendìr to sit across from him.

"You must be the King of Kyst I've heard so much about. Let me say it is a genuine honour to meet someone-" he paused most dramatically, "-of such young repute."

Vakar raised a brow at that. "And should I be honoured to be in your presence?"

"Ask the bards of Iridawnia or send a riverraven to any the royal courts of Litore. You'll find my reputation varies in every region of every country." It was very clear to Vakar that Aolendìr was assesing him as he had when the Solsta approached. "Good read?" Aolendìr sent his chin in the direction of Vakar's book resting beside him.

"I suspect you could fill in many of the gaps." He sounded flat.

"What under Āina's green earth gave you that impression?" Aolendìr said smirking.

"And here I was warned you were a master liar."

"And who might I ask warned you?"

"Our mutual friend in the west. How does his expansion into the Magma Isles fair?" Vakar answered then asked.

"He's a wealthy patron who thinks himself smarter than he is, not friend material." Vakar was actually taken aback by the unamused tone Aolendìr used. "And to answer your question...poorly. What religious crusade hasn't gone terribly and proved detrimental to the indigenous peoples. Yet, he has the coin and enough zealots to accomplish just about anything, I'm afraid," the Solsta elf ended with a look of suave amusement. "So, although I do admire the Great Northern Rainforest," Aolendìr paused to look around; the sun was setting, showering the kilometre-high cedars, firs, and arbutus in golden sunlight, "we are both busy elves. What do you wish to gain from me?"

"You talk a lot. So please keep it brief when addressing me."

"I am a master of many trades, the art of speech among them." Aolendìr laid a look unto Vakar that told him he wasn't going to hold any of his wit back.

"I have achieved much in my three decades of life. But you are a someone whose lived five human lifetimes and lived each more grandiose than that last-"

"-You flatter me," Aolendìr winked.

"Don't interrupt. I seek betrayal and is betrayal not the lifeblood of chaos?" At those words, Aolendìr's demeanor was visibly intrigued.

"It's a true honour to be allowed within the confines of Silva," Aolendìr said genuinely, as he was taken aback by the sheer beauty of the city in the trees. "Is it some magic that preserves it all? For everything feels fresh and new," he questioned the King of Kyst while dragging his hand across the strips of bark on one particular tree. Vakar did not slow in his stride towards the royal tree and Aolendìr looked at the Kyst's back with curiosity as he followed. So he uncharacteristically kept quiet the rest of the way and although he was on the receiving end of many strange stares, he offered wide smiles and friendly nods to the elves going about their daily lives.

Before he knew it, Aolendìr was within the royal hall and a great, high-backed throne with vines and seasonal-coloured leaves slowly weaving their way throughout the chair. He peered upwards to see a cathedral-like ceiling that was pitch black except for glowing fungi appearing like stars in the night sky. He noted many hunters standing guard on either side of the hall, each and every one of them holding their gaze on the outsider. Aolendìr, however, walked through the room with unparalleled comfort in the strange setting. As if he himself were their divine ruler.

Vakar payed no attention to his subordinates and continued to the spiral walkway at the far end, leading them upwards. The walkway was on the outside of the tree and was covered by thick branches and leaves. To their left were rooms and doors every few metres that blended seamlessly with the tree trunk. As they neared the top, Aolendìr stopped dead in his tracks and faced one of the doors. It took Vakar a second to notice this before he too stopped and turned to face the Solsta.

"What is she doing here?" Aolendìr eyed Vakar suspiciously. Vakar was stunned to realize this mysterious elf somehow knew Scáth ShadowScorn was in that particular room.

"Why do you care?" he asked almost threateningly.

"I can't understate the importance of that Scorn."

Vakar walked back a few steps to come face to face with the golden elf. "I seriously suggest you understand that I never underestimate anyone or anything."

After a tense moment, Aolendìr grabbed his fine, silken shoulder cape in one hand and bowed low. "I consider myself warned."

"Then if you'll follow me." Vakar led them the last distance to the very top of the tree where his large, circular study was. In the centre was a great green pentagram, intricately carved into the wood. One half of the ten-metre tall wall was devoted to books, many of which Aolendìr knew to be magical. The other half of the room was a raised arcade with a great oaken desk strewn with papers and quills, a mediation area, and an alchemy lab.

"Cozy."

Vakar was watching Aolendìr closely for one particular reason—to see if he would perceive the small stone pillar holding a crystal ball. And to Vakar's surprise, the visitor not only spotted it, but said something most strange.

"Well, I guess that makes us brothers of a sort."

Vakar's face screwed up. "Come again?"

Aolendìr's wide grin revealed his perfect teeth. "Don't they call you 'cunning?" When he only received a deadpan stare, he continued. "It's one of twelve artifacts the gods placed on Litore. It's also one of the only things that'll get you a quick visit from a Negator if you're not careful." However, once again, he received little in the way of a response. "Did I lose you at 'artifact' or 'Negator'?" he queried caustically.

"Anyone arcane or divine knows of the Keepers and their pet Negator's. They don't scare me."

Aolendìr looked unimpressed and decided to leave it at that. "Well, good Kyst, do you know which god that belongs too?"

Vakar shook his head slightly in frustration. The Solsta grinned slyly. "Zeries, God of Lies and Trickery."

"How does that make us brothers?" Vakar asked incredulously.

Aolendìr fake curtsied, "Mahem," referring to the god of Chaos.

Vakar finally failed to hide his true expression. "I would have not been chosen by such a deceitful god."

"Oh?" The enigmatic elf feigned surprise. "Did you not lie to Ven about your intent? I seriously doubt you came to lead the Kyst of Sanctuary Island by asking the previous monarch to step down. And how did you convince the other elves of the Great Northern Rainforest that Ven Devar was slaughtering his own kin to unite them under your banner?" Aolendìr spoke as if he had all the answers, and of course he knew how to respond to any question.

"I had nothing to do with the spat between Rexous and Ven that led to all those dead Kyst," Vakar said defensively.

"But you used that lie to your advantage, through means of great trickery. And you ask me why Zeries has chosen you," Aolendìr chortled.

"And what makes you so special? Everything I've seen so far is fairly underwhelming. Vakar spat as he began feeling irritated by Aolendìr's attitude and this unsavoury news.

"You think yourself powerful, and most would agree, but you've surely heard of my extensive reputation. Else you would not have sought me out. So here is a free piece of advice—do not think for a moment I have to do or say anything because you flapped your lips." For the first time since they met that morning, Vakar saw this Solsta could be as threatening as he was charming.

"Noted," the King of Kyst replied reluctantly.

"So, it's time you told me more about my being here. For I surely feel like turning around and returning to my ship," he said while patting a large sack of coin in his breast pocket that Vakar had recently given him as payment for arriving.

"You're right—if you ask the right people, your reputation is vast. I rose to power after my people suffered a great tragedy and the one in charge of leading us ran away on a hero's quest. I've gotten this far on intellect alone. However, some of the Kyst did not take well to my self-appointed title. My army now faces a rebellion, and I find myself at a loss. I am no military tactitian."

"You want me to dismantle the rebellion?" Aolendìr raised his dark eyebrow while approaching the crystal orb.

"I want you to infiltrate it and do what your reputation speaks so highly of." Judging by the smile Aolendìr wore, Vakar knew he would oblige. "Ven Devar has recently returned home. He was travelling with the ShadowScorn Princess, that's how we abducted her. Since then, he has flown into an unbalanced rage and fights alongside the rebel Kyst."

"It would appear not just the Kyst," Aolendìr said, carefully peering into the orb. This came to Vakar as yet another surprise, for he knew that only a powerful arcane user could activate the crystal. Yet, an even greater shock hit him when he saw Ven walking beside a Kintar that had been causing immense strife for his army since their cull of Claw Canyon.

Aolendìr moved his gaze from the four figures within the orb to Vakar, fixing him with a slightly amused glare. "In all your tomes, have you never come across the words 'the enemy of my enemy, is my friend?' Did it never strike you that this decimation of the Kintar might push them to join the rebel Kyst?"

It was then Vakar's turn to fix the Solsta with an agitated stare. "It did. I was confident that over 60,000 years of hatred would keep them apart."

Aolendìr shrugged carelessly. "Even the best of us miscalculate our enemies. I will infiltrate the rebels and learn all that I can. If I cannot guarantee my safety or deception, however, intel may be all I can offer."

"That's it? Everyone I spoke too said you'd be much harder to convince," Vakar pointed out skeptically.

"It's not every day I get work with a fellow Grimìr." He winked coyly before beginning to exit.

"We have not agreed upon a price," Vakar called out after him.

"Nothing you can't afford," Aolendìr said with his back still turned to Vakar as he strode out of the room, offering the Kyst no more time to interrupt. His attention quickly left the now empty doorway to the crystal orb, showing Ven walking down into Claw Canyon with a particular Kintar.

Aolendìr lackadaisically strode through the great tree, offering respectful nods to any Kyst he passed. Soon, he came across the doorway that would bring him face-to-face with the Daughter of Shadow. Much to his surprise, the door was now guarded by a sage, luckily quite young in appearance. Aolendìr stopped and squared up to the elf.

"Evening, good Kyst." Aolendìr grabbed his silken shoulder cape and dipped into a flourishing bow. The young Sage wasn't sure how to respond, so gave a faint nod. "I find myself wandering your great halls after meeting with your majestic king. He assured me you'd be standing here and could grant me access," he spoke with unparalleled confidence, delivering his lie with the same assuredness as telling someone he was in fact a Solsta Elf.

"My apologies, but I cannot grant that which you seek. I answer to Head Hunter Eevie Hara and Grand Sage Pine Evergreen, they commanded me to grant no one short of themselves or the king entry."

"Ah yes, there is nothing more heartwarming than someone who can follow orders without fault. I see there is no convincing you otherwise." Aolendìr bowed once more before taking a second to look the sage up and down. His robes were a dark burgundy that clung neatly to his body, tight sleeves accented by lavender threads. "Those robes are most exquisite, I myself fancy a good set. May I feel?"

The Sage who was most proud of his newly crafted robes gave a big smile before holding out his arm for Aolendìr to feel the soft, woolen material. The instant he gripped the forearm of the Kyst, a pulse of warm energy swept up the Sage, glazing his eyes over.

"It's me you dullard, move aside for your Grand Sage or I'll have you scrubbing King Vakar's chamber pots," Aolendìr barked haughtily before the Kyst stood straight and stepped aside. The Solsta stepped past him and opened the door before leaning back in beside the sage. "Oh, and forget I was ever here." Then he quickly and quietly closed the door.

Aolendìr at first shielded his eyes from the blinding light that filled this entirely empty room. An almost furry bark layered the circular walls, which he immediately sensed a great deal of magic was laid upon. A shimmering cylinder stretched from floor to ceiling that was no bigger than a metre and a half in radius. In the centre, with their legs crossed, sat Scáth ShadowScorn. She gave a most curious look to Aolendìr.

"It's a genuine privilege to meet you, Princess." Aolendìr dipped low once again.

"I am a princess no more." She noted the elf pause most quizzically before regaining his poise.

"My apologies, I thought this was the classic princess locked in a high tower scenario." Aolendìr paused a moment looking around. "Well, tree."

"Have you come to rescue a princess?" Scáth mocked.

He smirked. "Not this time I'm afraid." He noted the Scorn looked weak, sickly in a way. He could not be sure but considered it must be due to the lack of darkness in the room.

"Then what?" She suddenly appeared irritable. "You work for the genocidal maniac I presume. Who abducted me to wound his oldest friend. Yet, I assure you, nothing you can do will hurt me more than sixty years of being a Scorn."

"I don't doubt it, milady. I don't hurt the innocent anyhow," he answered honestly, but Scáth scoffed. "In truth, I've been hired to find your counterpart. I thought you may be able to shed some light on his true nature. Since you two were destined for one another."

Scáth was taken aback by how sincere Aolendìr was acting but couldn't help feel that he was trying to garner something else. She knew then that he was a master of wit, but very few could match Scáth's wisdom.

"Good, then Vakar feels helpless and inadequate to deal with Ven alone. I can't possibly imagine why he thought resurrecting Rexous was the answer; perhaps those around him hold him to a higher level of cunning then what's deserved."

Aolendìr smiled faintly. "Do you not think Ven himself will come to rescue you?"

"What makes you say we are destined for each other?" Scáth deflected the obvious answer to his question. Aolendìr smiled before squaring up closely to her shimmering prison. The Scorn felt a sudden headache overcome her before it quickly faded.

"Your dream, the one with your brother, meditating in ShadowScorn Palace. How often have you had it?"

Scáth looked at him differently now, knowing he had just read her mind. "You peer into my mind then ask me a question. What kind of a game is that?"

"I needed to know if you knew who you really are, but I do not wish to invade your thoughts." The Solsta peered over his shoulder, studying something beyond the wall. He then turned back to face Scáth. "I fear I have overstayed. One final free piece of advice, Daughter of Shadow. Vakar is one of us. If you did not before, I suggest you tread lightly around him."

Aolendìr bowed most graciously before spinning on his heel and exiting briskly.

CHAPTER FIVE

The Warrior

Ven's stomach hit his chest as he was suddenly falling suddenly from the sky, muscles locked as if stunned in place as the forest canopy rushed towards him. He wanted to throw his arms up in front of his face to brace as he connected with the tree's, yet he was unaffected by the lashing of branches. Ven looked down and prepared himself for when his feet met the ground. The weight of his body returned and the pressure built in his legs, until he gave way into a forward roll through the massive sword ferns and dirt.

The Kyst stood quickly and surveyed his surroundings, astounded the map had worked so effectively. He quickly noticed the huge rift in the ground, as if a great talon had clawed the earth. Ven had never laid eyes on it, but was confident this was Claw Canyon. He walked a few paces until he could peer into the vast canyon. Looking down, he had expected to see great structures clinging to the rock face as the stories he heard growing up detailed. Instead, he saw the basin littered with those impressive homes and buildings, the rock face showing barren remnants of the settlement that once proudly clung here. Often single walls of a houses were left clinging to the cliffs, displaying stark reminders of the lives that were abruptly ended.

The mighty hunter stood there, sick to his stomach, the pang of injustice fuelling the rage that had been boiling over since Scáth's abduction. From what the hunter could tell, there was minimal movement in the canyon basin, but there were Kintar. In the instant of a heartbeat, he felt the weight of a weapon rest on his right shoulder, and the bone white blade tip came into view.

"One reason why I shouldn't kill you is all you get."

"I want to avenge those who lived here," Ven answered without taking his eyes off the people recollecting their lives below.

"Remove your hood and turn around."

Ven did so slowly, staring into the eyes of Njor Swordsplinter. The Kyst saw a Kintar larger than most with dark red skin and the look of one who had lost everyone and everything.

"I am Ven Devar, and this is my fault."

Njor looked him up and down and decided quite simply this was not the Kyst he followed in the raids ordered by Uthul 'The Betrayer'.

"You're not making a great case for yourself," he huffed.

"I was in the far east when everything after Silva's destruction happened, but those events occurred due to my absence. I've come to offer myself over to your people, and leave my fate in your hands," Ven said, lowering his head. Njor kept his greatsword rested on Ven's shoulder and stared hatefully at the Kyst. He would have loved nothing more than to separate this elf's head from his body. Yet, for some unexplained reason, Njor felt an inner turmoil against that action.

Ven and Njor both heard footfalls quickly approaching their direction. The hunter looked up and Njor deftly spun as Onstera was flew through the air with her foot out to kick him over the cliff. Instead, her foot made contact and buckled until her whole body fell limply at Njor's feet. Ven was astounded; the Kintar hadn't budged a centimetre from the hefty blow. Onstera quickly rolled backwards and got up into a defensive stance and before Ven could tell her to cease, the Quaesitor came back at Njor with a heavy strike of her hand-and-a-half sword. Njor swung his free hand against Onstera's side, and she was lifted off her feet and soared quicker than a cannon ball until she vanished into the forest.

It was Ven's turn to react, and he nimbly darted in front of Njor with *'Hunter's Protector'* out stretched at the berserker's throat.

"Who are you?" Ven growled. Njor looked down on Ven with a sense of serenity inappropriate to the situation.

"I lived my life as Njor Swordsplinter, until I met my end in the cull of Claw Canyon. Lokor, God of Battle, breathed his last life into my corpse and I was born again."

"You just sent one of the most skilled warrior's on Litore flying through the air like an arrow from a bow with the swipe of your hand —how?"

"Lokor's strength flows through my veins."

"If you've killed her, your life is forfeit." Ven sheathed his short-sword on his tailbone with lightning effect before sprinting off in the direction of Onstera.

Ina was already at Onstera's side when Ven finally found them, rested against a tree.

"Is she okay?" Fear was evident in his voice.

"Nothing broken from what I can tell, but she's out cold. Did a Tree Giant hit her?" Ina asked, clearly stunned by the force Onstera was sent back into the treeline with. Ven just shook his head doubtfully.

"Help me get her up." The two hunters each grabbed an arm and carried the unconscious human back to Njor.

"Well, is she dead?" Njor asked out of courtesy more than concern.

"Luckily for you both, no," Ven replied dryly which had Njor smirk in amusement. "First, you're gonna help us heal her, then we're gonna discuss the future between our people."

"You're a confident little elf aren't you." Njor said without a hint of charm. The hunter eyed the massive Kintar angrily;, even though this berserker was a head taller than him, size couldn't frighten Ven. "Follow me,." Njor added, as he was already turning to lead the way down into the canyon.

As they reached the basin of the canyon and more Kintar came into view, it did not take long for deathly stares to fall upon Ven and Ina. It was very apparent the only reason they were not being torn to literal shreds was because Njor was giving them an escort. The two Kyst saw the reverence in which the Kintar looked at Njor and guessed he was their newly appointed leader.

The trio, plus an unconscious Onstera, reached an animal- skin tent that had several berserker's sitting outside, next to a barely hot fire. The group of Kintar warriors looked at the encroaching outsiders and stood on guard with palpable enmity. Njor waved them to stand down and all but one did; a Kintar shockingly similar in size to Njor, who was already tall for his race. He threw his hand into Njor's chest. Ven keenly caught the berseker's hand bend unusually and Njor felt no resistance, however he gave his kinsmen the respect and stopped.

"What are you doing with them?" The Kintar asked Njor in their harsh, and guttural language of kintish.

"Offering them aid," Njor answered, as though that should be enough.

"We should be peeling their skin from their feet like boots and suffocating them with bags of their skin," the berserker threatened, never taking his eyes of Ven. The hunter wasn't fluent in their native tongue but understood enough. Just as Ven was about to speak something that he knew would have made the situation worse, Njor interrupted.

"I'm tired of running that circle." This appointed leader made his intent as ruler clear, and with it carried an underlying challenge to anyone who thought they knew better. Njor took a step closer to the tent and furled the flap with one arm before the underling spoke again.

"What if the rest of us aren't?"

Njor looked at the handful of warriors around him. "You know where to find me," he answered solemnly. The berserker dropped his eyes to the ground and sat back down. As Ven and Ina passed him, Ven conjured his inner turmoil into a menacing glare. He understood well, as just displayed by Njor, that Kintar only respected strength.

Upon entering the make-shift infirmary, the two hunters instantly spotted a hunched over crone within, pouring vials and crushed up herbal compounds into a small, simmering cauldron. The smell of burning incense filled Devar with a surprising sense of ease, although it barely masked the stench that naturally filled the air here. Without further instruction, he and Ina placed Onstera on a small cot while Njor approached the shaman.

"This woman needs your healing touch."

The old shaman turned to face the group, showing her entirely clouded over eyes and saying nothing in reply to Njor. She walked straight up to Ven, standing several heads shorter than him. She looked up at the hunter and placed her withered fingers upon his cheek.

"Why is the Mighty Ven Devar in Claw Canyon?"

Ven's eye's immediately darted to Njor, hoping to garner his reaction; if Njor had one, he wasn't showing it.

"How do you know me?"

"I know all who enter my tent." Her voice rang out with the wisdom of a long life. "And few in all the Great Rainforest have gone without hearing your name." She placed a disarming smile upon him, which quickly had his hesitation taking a back seat.

"I wish to heal old wounds and build a bridge between our two worlds."

She turned her head to face Njor Swordsplinter and gave him a knowing nod. Without a word, the reincarnated god left the tent. Ven watched him go, expecting a word or answer as to why, but they received none.

"Come now, young Kyst, I'll need an extra set of hands to heal your friend." The old crone began handing bandages and splints to Ven and Ina before emptying her cauldron into a skull bowl.

The two young hunters gave each other a concerned look; why did Njor leave without warning? Stuck in a tent with their backs against a soaking wet cliff didn't scream favourable odds if they were ambushed. Ina's predicament had worsened from the minute Ven saw their new map in the cave hideout. She, unlike Ven, was deeply rooted in their traditions as hunters. She planned her every move, calculated the outcome, then planned again and again. Yet, Ven was at his apex when he could think freely and creatively. In his mind, plans just got in the way of seizing the moment. Ina was left concerned, for very few Kyst ever entered Claw Canyon and fewer still left unharmed. However, one lesson she could fall back on, is to trust your fellow hunter with your own life, and right now, Ven was all she had.

"You two don't hide your unease well and I'm blind!" The old crone laughed, as she was wiping away a trickle of blood from Onstera's forehead before stitching the wound up. Ven and Ina shared a curious stare.

"It's just, Ven and I had nothing to do with the recent attack here. The Kyst and Kintar have been warring since the birth of the Second Age, many attempts at peace have been struck before and every one ending in betrayal." Ina explained her concern with faint hope and honest doubt.

"So, it's peace you seek, but you do not speak for all Kyst?"

"Yes," Ven answered.

"Neither does Njor, but as we sit here he gathers the remaining Kintar of the canyon so you may plead your case."

Ven's eyes widened. "What if they don't like what we have to say?"

The old crone gave a wicked smile. "You better make it a good speech."

An hour of tense glances between Ven and Ina later, Njor walked back into the tent. He looked at them with his piercing amber eyes and simply motioned with his arm to follow as he made his exit once more. Ina stood, relieved that the wait was finally over and was quickly behind the Kintar. Ven, however, stared unceasingly at Onstera, who was now fully stitched and bandaged up, enjoying a deep rest. His opalescent green eyes then floated up to the shaman. The old crone met Ven's intensity before giving a stern and reassuring nod. He sprang up from his chair, for he feared he muscles might glue him to it from anxiety. He was several-dozen paces behind Swordsplinter and Enallea as they entered a huge makeshift building of fallen timber. Ven quickly surmised it had been crudely thrown together using remnants of the once impressive city that clung to the cliffs.

As he brushed aside a leather skin barely covering the entry, he was starkly reminded of the brutality of Kintar, as the skin was clearly humanoid and most likely kystin. It filled him with rage but that was quickly extinguished as he saw what remained of Claw Canyon's people. Water dripped through the layered ceilings, and the sound of coughing and muffled crying came from every corner of the room. The healthy, badly broken, and elderly were all in a similar state of despair. Ven guessed there was less than a hundred Kintar in here and nearly every one of those heads turned to face the two Kyst Hunter's. For the first time since he lost Scáth, his face wasn't rigid with rage. His brow wilted and a look of true empathy was evident. Ina, lead hunter of the rebels, was no less revealing about her heart. Her vision went blurry as the tears welled.

Njor turned back to them, and made eye contact with Ven, before giving way and motioning him to address the room. In truth, giving a speech was the last thing he thought he'd be doing here, much less on the topic of peace when all his heart desired was revenge. He walked in what he considered was the centre of the room. He looked around and received entirely hateful stares, except for one— a single Kintar looking at him with hope. Ven instinctively dropped his gaze to the mud floor.

"I suspect most of you know who I am, probably for more slights and crimes against your people than not. No doubt first because I slayed the ice demon, Hoarfrost, but what they do not say about my legend, is I did not defeat it alone. I remember Bonesaw, the berkserker Claw Canyon sent to fight the demon, even though we arrogant Kyst did not ask. It was she who had shown the most bravery and landed the most blows to Hoarfrost, and it was her sacrifice that showed me how best to defeat it."

Ven narrowly ducked as a loose hunk of wood was thrown at him.

"How dare you speak her name!" A Kintar shouted from somewhere in the building. He looked to Ina for support, but she remained quiet.

"My point is, only together can we survive, face Vakar alone, and this is the fate of anyone who opposes him." Ven motioned around the room.

"Why would any of us choose to trust you?! You're the one who used us to attack those Kyst settlements, which led us to this catastrophe." A different Kintar, one seated close to Ven, shouted before a large group of them hollered in agreement.

"No. You first gave them that reason when you burned Silva to the ground. You don't think burning one of the largest settlements in the north wouldn't call a raise to arms?" The famed hunter pointed concisely, which had the room only to grow in bluster. "Fine, if any of you even survive the next month, we can all go back to fighting each other. Just know that my kind will outnumber you a thousand to one and have the power of an empire," Ven said angrily, while making eye contact with Ina to leave. But a voice quickly rang out, coming from the young Kintar that had shown Ven kindness when looked in the face.

"So it's true, the Kyst have really united?" They asked, sheepishly. He merely nodded in reply. "Then there is no hope." They added forlornly. Ina took a step closer to Ven.

"So long as you don't give in, there is hope. Myself and the Kyst of Shallowbay have been leading a resistance, that's why we're here."

"With you at our side-" Ven chimed in, "-we could call the other Kintar of the north to our aid. If the Kyst of Shallowbay and the Kintar of Claw Canyon join forces, the Great Northern Rainforest will know anything is possible."

The Kyst were left in a hum of quiet chatter as those in the room began to discuss their thoughts. Now it was Njor's turn to step in.

"I've fought off many attacks since that night of destruction, and each one has claimed more of us despite my god- given gifts. It may not be next time, or the time after, but it will eventually prove too much for us."

"Heretic," a metallic voice spoke from the entrance. The hunter's immediately saw the look of disdain appear on Njor's face. They turned to the entrance and spotted a large Kintar dressed in black and white armour, sporting a metal face mask. They knew this to be a Templar of Lokor, a band of devout followers that saw their collective demise in recent years; however, some managed to cling to their rather radical ways and continued to practice their rites. Many species and races had pledged their life to the Templar's, but none more so than the Kintar, as they were some of the most prolific warriors in Litore.

"Kaldoon," Njor acknowledged his presence.

The looming figure walked up to Ven, generally, the Kyst were taller than Kintar— having evolved to climb trees- while the Kintar remained below; but this fully plated and masked figure manage to look down on Ven. "Why does this prancing elf still breathe?" The masked Kintar asked anyone but the Kyst. The famed hunter's eye's narrowed hatefully, but once again Njor interrupted before Ven could respond.

"We're discussing our collective future."

"If Lokor really chose you, why do you act against his tenets? Battle is what he craved. Not peace." The Templar moved his gaze from Ven to Njor.

"He's dead. It does not matter what he once wanted because Celestia is crumbling."

"The Father of Battle may never die," the Templar said reverently.

"Then get on your knees and bow before me, squib."

Ven and Ina shot each other wide eyed looks as the Templar, who could show no emotion through his mask, clinched his fists.

"What? Are you scared your god's avatar will finally put an end to your pitiful cult?" Njor prodded and the Templar's body grew angrier. "Don't you think if the Templar's of Lokor were worthy he would have prevented their downfall?"

Ven was in slight awe as Njor continued to insult this Kintar, without care of what the end result brought.

"Let's find out," the Templar challenged before exiting. Ven and Ina remained still as the majority of the occupants left to witness the fight. They looked to Njor, who was clearly angered by the turn of events.

"Damn," was all he muttered to the Kyst before he too went outside. Ina was first to leave and Ven shortly thereafter, deciding he should witness this considering the outcome would dictate how they'd be leaving the canyon.

As they stepped outside, a low fog had settled in the canyon and the sun, though still in the sky, hung too low to cast any light in the basin. Several fire pits had been lit, offering spots of heat and yellow mist. The observing Kintar all moved to one side, ensuring they would not be in the way. Njor's mahogany red skin glistened in the swirling dew, his furs offering minimal warmth or protection. His vivid amber eyes scanned the Templar for any sign of weakness, the slightest limp or hesitation. Of course, the Templar in his full plate-mail and gaunt metal mask hid everything about the humanoid within.

Njor pulled his sword off his back—a rather famous weapon from which he earned his last name. It was carved from the horn of a Timber Dragon, giving it an unparalleled sharpness and durability, that often shattered lesser weapons. The Templar gripped two mallets on his hips and as he did, the Old Elvish runes on the metal heads began to glow sunset-orange. Ven was watched the two Kintar so intently, and his heart already pumping so much so that he didn't notice the old shaman approaching. She stopped in between the two warriors, her cloudy grey eyes somehow appearing more intense in the this fog.

"You both agree to uphold the laws of your ancestors?" Her question was answered with two stern nods. "Then you have selected your chosen weapons; you will receive no others, you will no receive no help, nor aid during the battle. The battle does not end until one of you is on their way to the Evar Spring Glade."

Ven thought she sounded rehearsed in this speech and no doubt she had given it a hundred times in her life. He wondered if she always sounded so averse to be giving this speech or if this type of fight was usually met with more cheers than the still silence about them. The old crone walked over and stood beside Ven and Ina, and the whole canyon went still. In the time it took Ven to blink, Njor had closed the 10 paces to Kaldoon and swung his great sword. The Templar had side-stepped and Njor dug his feet into the earth, skidding another metre before turning back to face his opponent. The two Kyst's had their jaws dropped as neither had ever seen someone move with the literal speed of lightning as Njor just had. Ven saw first hand he had the strength of true giant-kind, but this was uncanny.

"What magic is about him?" Ina quietly said to Ven, he gave no response though, and in truth she expected none. The chosen of Lokor rushed once more, with his sword arm out, he spun 360 degree's and delivered a whirlwind slice. Kaldoon dropped low and drove one of his mallets into Njor's kneecap, the force of which flipped had Njor flip round over end to land on his back. Kaldoon was quick to give a small leap, driving both his weapons down. Njor rolled out of the way just in time as the mallets exploded against the slick stone, sending shrapnel into the air.

Njor got to his feet and tossed his sword away. This seasoned berserker had spent over a century battling and he understood now his sword would not do him good against someone this quick to react, even with his new found speed. Kaldoon, thinking Njor was a fool, quickly closed the distance. He swung hard but Njor grabbed his wrist and twisted is backwards. The mallet fell right into Njor's awaiting hand, but that left Kaldoon's other weapon- hand free to strike. And strike he did—the small hammer struck Njor in the cheek, which sent him flying to the side. His flight was finally halted as his back struck a great rotted tree that had been used to destroy a section of Claw Canyon's settlement.

Kaldoon wasted little time in getting back into melee range of his sworn enemy. Njor was feigning greater injury than he was suffering. When the gap was no more than five paces, Njor threw the mallet aimed for the Templar's head. It connected squarely against his forehead, Kaldoon hit the ground before anyone could breathe. The mallet continued to soar until it collided with the canyon wall, yet it did not stop there as the mallet bore several metres into the rock face before losing momentum. But everyone's eyes were on the motionless

Templar and Njor sliding his foot back from his throwing stance.

Everyone gasped as Kaldoon rolled over, supporting himself on his forearms., when his gaunt metal mask fell to the ground, splitting in two pieces. Even Njor's eyes widened as his foe managed to shake off the hit and get back to his feet. The two Kintar squared up once more, then Kaldoon revealed his face. A battled- hardened elf with sickly white skin, although that was barely visible under the intricately designed black tattoo's that covered much of his face. Red eyes that truly appeared to burn with the underworld's flame starred back at Njor Swordsplinter. To make Kaldoon appear already more terrifying than what was natural about him, there was small random pieces of metal weaved across his face, no doubt from wounds that were too deep to heal or entire chunks of bone that were torn from his skull, which made Kaldoon appear already more terrifying than what was natural to him.

"Now you see me," he snarled at Njor, but the berserker hardened his resolve. The last thing he wanted to do after the declared 'cull' of his people was kill to one. However, Kaldoon was not a name, rather a title. Needless to say, even Njor considered their tactics before their recent decline to be extreme and at many times, ill-judged, often throwing compassion and conscience to the wind in the name of battle. Now it was a known fact throughout the Kintar community in the north that Njor had been reborn through Lokor's final act of divinity, Kaldoon would sooner die than live in a world where anyone other than him was granted that gift.

So Njor dipped back into a fighting stance. Kaldoon choked up on the grip of his small- handled mallet and dashed for his foe. Njor watched every move Kaldoon took, every flinch of his muscles. The Templar came in fast and swung for Njor's ribs, yet the berserker invited the strike, quickly dropping his elbow and pinning Kaldoon's wrist between Njor's arm and ribs. He looked down on the Templar and saw Kaldoon had recognized his mistake. Njor quickly followed with a head butt that sounded like a pick-axe breaking stone. Kaldoon dropped to the ground hard, followed by several devastating punches to the face, splattering the pair in blood. Njor heaved with blinding rage as each punch followed.

Ven watched on in abject horror; is that what he looked like when he lost control—a primal animal? The last punch was delivered with such strength that a small wave of dust, dirt, and blood was sent in all directions. His knees still wrapped around Kaldoon's arms, Njor breathed menacingly through his nose and looked at the crowd of Kintar, showering everyone in his terror. To everyone's shock, Kaldoon was not dead, as he spat a mouthful of blood in Njor's face hovering over him. Njor reached around against the cold damp stone to find the magical mallet. He gripped it and slowly raised the hammer above his enemy for a death blow. It seemed to Ven he was holding the mallet with a level of hesitation, surely the kill was a single swing away.

Njor looked down upon Kaldoon, the Kintar's red eyes looked back up at him, pools of blood running down his face like red tears. Njor went to drop the hammer, but heard an all too familiar voice call out.

"Beast," echoed through his mind as the foggy image of his wife standing before him plagued Njor's muscles. Ven instinctively lurched forward as Njor was about to kill his enemy, but instead his arm fell to his side. The famed Kyst looked in the same direction as the Kintar and thought he spotted a ghostly figure.

"What is he doing?" Ina whispered to Ven.

"You didn't have to leave me," Njor spoke out to nothing but a memory. He watched as the wavy figure of his wife turned to leave before vanishing as quickly as it had arrived. The mallet slipped from his bloody knuckles as he slowly climbed off Kaldoon. Njor then made direct eye contact with Ven and they shared an exchange of strange understanding. It was interrupted when the old crone shambled over to Kaldoon and checked his pulse.

"You did not kill your enemy Njor Swordsplinter."

"I will not kill out of tradition or any circumstance that does not absolutely require it. I am no longer that elf, we are no longer those people."

"Then from this point forth, you are banished," She answered in absolute. Njor looked around at his people and saw they would not follow him, so he gave a small nod before walking up to the two Kyst.

"There is nothing left for us here. Let us grab your friend and depart."

CHAPTER SIX

The Phoenix and The Assassin

Kithlyn was stuck with her arms to her side, standing upright while her shoulders smashed the small metal walls with every bump the wooden cart hit on the road. A bright orb of light hung above her head, preventing the child of darkness from calling upon any shadow, innate or external.

"Who's driving this shit cart?" Her voice was bitter and sounded even more so as it reverberated inside. After she received no response, she forcefully elbowed one wall. "I know it's not steering itself!" Within a few heartbeats, the wall she elbowed glowed red hot. Kithlyn reflexively flinched with a yelp.

"A familiar foe."

"You gotta be kidding me. It's been a decade Scarlet, get over yourself."

"I'm taking you back to Redwillow," Scarlet's voice crackled like a roaring flame.

"The Underworld you are. That dump is a long way from here, you really think your flaming feathers can keep me contained that long?"

"Flaming feathers?" Scarlet scoffed heartily. "Let's hope you make a better prisoner than bard."

"Ouch. Hey, how's the church treating you? I hear no one has heard from Pirelia since the war." After several silent heartbeats, Kithlyn continued to poke. "That good eh? Do you think there's been any more Phoenix Folk since you, reborn in the ashes of injustice? Or has Pirelia given up on Litore all together?"

"Should we test that theory?" Scarlet asked threateningly. Kithlyn laughed.

"Please, when I die it will be to the Underworld for my soul. Your temperate goddess want's nothing to do with me." Kithlyn was left in the silence of her own thoughts as her attempt to elicit some response failed. "Since the distance is actually quite great, how many of your followers are transporting me?"

"Why would I give a master assassin information on her captors?" Scarlet voiced sarcastically.

"I just want to make sure that when we are eventually attacked, you all stand a chance. You must understand, I do not intend on dying in a cage." Again, no answer came. "You might be enough to deter marauders or the Fires of Fel, but the monsters that plague this land will think of nothing but the taste of your flesh." After another moment of silence, Kithlyn roared. "I will not die in this cage!"

"We heard you the first time."

Kithlyn sighed heavily. Her life had been long and full, far more so than any other of her kind. She had considered more than once that perhaps she was the ShadowScorn who had seen more of the world than any before her. She had been kidnapped and sold to a wealthy family in Elemenzin, trained as an assassin to do their bidding. It didn't take long to become stronger than her captors, so she murdered the entire House of Durakai and started her own life. She brought whole crime syndicates to their knees, ended multi-generational vendettas against her, brought kingdoms to ruin with a single flick of her blade, and played a key role in the War of a Thousand Dragons. Kithlyn knew if her life was to end now, she would die knowing she had lived an extensive life. Since earning her freedom by blood, she had spent her whole life killing those who would freely bind the innocent.

Her mind kept returning to the surprise visit from Agan Dusk. Every time his rugged face and fierce yellow eyes popped into her mind, she ignored them. They had spent so many years side by side, rescuing one another, keeping each other safe in events so perilous that not even fantasy could match the truth. She had never known love and never given it, yet it was during their—at times—physical intimacy that she knew trust and comfort. Perhaps, she considered, that was love. Although she could never admit it, she reminisced fondly over a dream where the two had grown old together, far from civilization and its eternal struggle for dominance. Yet, the Quake of Harazune shifted the entire world, and the two had not seen each other since.

Then the half-orc, half-elf she spent a decade trying to forget reappeared out of the blue and in need of her help once again. She was resolute about not getting pulled back into this life—it only ever brought hardship.

Kithlyn was torn from her reluctant contemplation by the sound of several locks on her prison door sliding open. Her door was thrown open and she tumbled out, landing firmly on her feet. Her eyes were assailed by glistening snow in broad daylight and high mountains all around them.

Scarlet Albright, a towering avian humanoid who resembled a hawk, gripped Kithlyn with her red hot hand still ablaze. The Scorn recoiled, expecting to get burnt, yet felt nothing but the firm grip around her bicep.

"We camp."

"It's morning," Kithlyn retorted, as if Scarlet were blind.

Scarlet tactfully ignored her and forced the assassin down on a log. The Phoenix then walked a few strides to a bundle of wood, knelt, held her hand down upon a log, and within a single breath a hot fire was crackling.

"Convenient." The shadow around Kithlyn's eyes was waning but still offered a darkness that bolstered her personality. One of the priests, a human woman that Kithlyn suspected was in her early twenties, set up a tri-pod with a pot attached over the fire. She spotted only two others in their troop, a human and a Solsta elf, both female priests. They were unfurling everyone's bedrolls and gathering more wood while the other woman filled the pot with water and food.

"You only brought three people?" Kithlyn looked insulted as she addressed Scarlet.

"No, only three people survived your retrieval."

She smiled and laughed a little, not in true jest but simply to irritate her captors. The Priest of Pirelia poured a ladle of stew into a bowl, spitting in it before giving it to the Scorn.

"Oh darling, that only makes it sweeter." Kithlyn smiled coyly and plunged the spoon into her mouth. She managed to hold her tongue while everyone ate their food, but that was only because she was studying each of the priests. Gathering every minute detail of their person and relationships amongst each other. She noticed the elf was continuously coughing with a particularly wet wheeze; the priest who handed out the food gave a painful flinch of her right shoulder every time she raised spoon to mouth; and the other woman looked at Scarlet with a curious level of disdain.

Despite the nourishment she just had, Kithlyn couldn't help but feel weak. She knew this to be a direct result of being starved of darkness. When she made her move, she would have to be precise and well planned. However, the fear of growing ever weaker weighed heavily and she knew with each passing hour her form would continue to wither.

"So, who has the honour of escorting me while I relieve myself?" Kithlyn of course waited till all of her captors were settling down to rest before asking this. She looked to Scarlet with a smirk that rubbed the Phoenix wrong.

"Hold it."

"I've been in that cage all night," Kithlyn said, getting to her feet. "When a lady's got to go, she's gotta go." As the Scorn went to walk behind the cart, she heard a resounding snap and found herself immobile. After straining for several seconds without a single muscle responding she found herself able to speak.

"Did you just cast a spell on me?" she questioned indignantly.

"I said hold it," Scarlet answered with an air of superiority. For six long hours, Kithlyn was stuck under the beating sun, frozen in space. Her muscles would be aching if she could feel them; it was an unnerving sensation, like being conscious while your body was lost in a deep sleep. Every passing minute left her with a greater sense of rage, solidifying her resolve that her captors would have to die. The thought that she had erred in refusing Agan crossed her mind several times during her paralysis; it buzzed around her mind like a fly she was unable to swat. In truth, Kithlyn doubted she could defeat Scarlet on her own, yet her old companion would be more than enough to tip the scales in her favour. As dusk approached, and the Scorn had conceived of a dozen ways to kill everyone here, Scarlet walked up to face her.

"Everyone answers eventually."

"Naive as ever, I see. I've brought more people to justice than you ever could."

"Perhaps, but Pirelia demands you pay for your sins."

Kithlyn chortled. "No she doesn't. You haven't heard from your fire god in years. This is Scarlet Albright, Phoenix of Pirelia, feeling petty and powerless, looking for a cause as all pious idiots do."

"Well this petty and powerless Phoenix has you in chains." Scarlet gripped Kithlyn's arms, putting them down by her sides and wrapping another set of heavy chain link restraints around her body.

Scarlet's diadem, with a single red ruby encrusted in the front, gave a slight pulse and Kithlyn felt her muscles come back to her. She hit the ground and her body felt like fire, utter agony as every muscle had seized from hours of immobility. She stifled a small whimper from the unbearable pain before forcing her body to calm and work through it.

"If it's not too late, you may relieve yourself now," Scarlet said smirking.

Agan Dusk and Faenla were sitting atop a ridge several hundred metres above Kithlyn and her captors. He had placed the thumping chest in the snow while they rested, finding being near it was taking a toll on his mental state. He hadn't taken his eyes off Kithlyn for hours; he was a patient warrior, a master tactician. However, for one of the few times in his life, he was itching to get down there and free his dear companion.

So distracted was Agan that he did not notice that Faenla had left some time ago. He looked around for his massive ally, but only spotted Faen's large paw prints going over a steep ridge. The sun started to dip, and he noticed Scarlet was now speaking to Kithlyn while the other priests of Pirelia woke up and broke camp. He looked around worried as Faenla was nowhere to be seen.

He put the box back in the bag and, much to his relief, the colossal wolf came sauntering back. Agan stood up slowly as Faen's mouth and long, black snout were soaked in blood. The half-orc approached, Faen's head hung low, his piercing blue eyes staring back at Agan with a massive, white, and furry arm in his mouth. The wolf spat it on the ground and Agan knelt to pick it up. After inspecting the arm that was nearly a metre long, Agan gave a slight chuckle of disbelief.

"Remind me never to tousle with you." Agan rubbed Faen between the ears, astounded the wolf had slain a Vildfir alone—a species on Litore known for their range of savage demeanour to their friendly and affable personalities. Standing on average three-metres tall, covered in thick hair, the Vildfir were just smart enough to be considered intelligent but unmatched in strength. It was a stark reminder for Agan that he had let his guard down, and without Faenla here he very well could be in a mountain side cave becoming a Vildfir's next meal.

Agan stood and began to walk away until he realized Faenla wasn't moving. He scrunched up his face in confusion, then Faen swung his head back towards the steep ridge. Agan scaled the ridge the best he could and peered over. Far off in the distance, he spotted at least ten bright-white Vildfir walking parallel with the road. He assumed Faenla must have killed a scout, which did not bode well for Kithlyn and her abductors come night fall. He slid through compact snow back down to Faen and the duo quickly made their descent to the Southern Great Road.

Agan found his first stroke of luck as thick cloud cover offered extraordinary conditions for maintaining appropriate stealth. Faenla's blue eyes were like floating orbs as his black and white speckled fur never failed to blend flawlessly with the night. The duo kept their distance, but never let Kithlyn's cage out of their sight.

It was deep into the rein of darkness when Faen's head shot upwards, straining and flicking his ears until he pinpointed the origin of the sounds. Agan quickly followed Faen's line of sight and saw a half-dozen figures on either side of a ridge, their great hairy silhouettes waiting in anticipation, ready to ambush with every advantage. Faenla and Agan made brief but meaningful eye contact, and they sprinted for Kithlyn.

"I can't see anything ahead of us," the priestess driving the cart muttered in frustration to Scarlet sitting beside her. In response, the Phoenix Folk jumped off the cart and lead the way, while increasing the flame and light around her ten-fold. Scarlet was keeping an even pace as the path narrowed and the mountain walls beside them nearly obscured the night sky. She looked up and thought she could see stones laying precariously across the thin gap. She dimmed her flame again to adjust her avian eyes to the darkness—too late as a spear soared silently over her, cutting a straight path to the cart. The driver was skewered to her bench; in shock she looked dumbfounded at the pole protruding from her gut before breathing her last. Scarlet let out an echoing screech followed by a beam of thick fire. It blasted harmlessly between her attackers as snow-white Vildfirs began jumping from an impossible height, landing powerfully on the ground.

Inside the cage, Kithlyn heard the sounds of battle outside and rolled her eyes before shouting, "I told you!" with as much indignance as possible. Barbaric and rough war cries were sounded and she instantly recognized them as Vildfir.

Outside, one of the two remaining priests fired a spell of viscous energy out of her amulet. It struck a Vildfir, leaving them looking more like melted cheese than anything. She was, however, immediately gripped and hoisted up from behind. It was not a quick death, as the Vildfir squeezed his head-sized palms together, caving in her rib cage.

Quick as the wind, Scarlet flew and drove her pike into the Vildfir that just killed the priestess. She flapped her wings and was vertical in the blink of an eye to open her next foes throat. Scarlet flicked her head as her only remaining companion let out a shriek as four of the half-giants surrounded her. At the same time, two Vildfir ripped Kithlyn's cage down and began running off with it, thinking it was some great treasure. Scarlet stood there for longer than she would admit, deciding between who to go for, before flying to her final priestess' side.

The Vildfir carrying Kithlyn were heading straight towards Agan, who pulled out his iradinium axe. Before the rear half-giant could register what had happened, Faenla shot out from nowhere with immense strength and pulled him to the ground by his throat. The colossal wolf made quick work of the thing. Kithlyn's cage hit the ground with a thud and she gave a faint yelp.

Agan halted his feet while rearing his arms up; skidding across the ice, he hurled his double-bearded axe over his head, straight at the last Vildfir. The great behemoth raised his arm up in a feeble attempt to stop the axe. It cut clean through his arm, only coming to rest after burying itsself into its chest. The other end of Kithlyn's box hit the ground, followed by a frustrated curse. Faenla looked back to Scarlet and her companion desperately trying to stay alive in a lost battle.

"Wait!" Agan shouted, sensing the wolf's urge to help. He gripped the axe's haft and pulled it out with a squelch. His iradinium blade effortlessly cut the lock on the cage. Agan didn't get the chance to open the door as it was kicked open, Kithlyn shadow-stepping several metres away ready to fight her captors.

"Ugh, don't expect a thank you." She rolled the small whites of her entirely black eyes.

"We gotta go, now." Agan was already rushing away when he noted that the wolf and Scorn were not budging. "She threw you in chains, Kith," Agan pleaded.

"I know, it should be easy to walk away." Kithlyn had a hint of turmoil in her voice.

Faenla looked from the two Priestess' of Pirelia to Kithlyn, cocking his head ever so slightly in some attempt to better understand the Scorn. He turned to Agan and stomped one of his fore paws hard in the snow. Agan let out a frustrated grunt before stomping between and past his companions towards the distressed.

Scarlet worked a mesmerizing routine with her elegantly designed pike. Although her strikes were mere grazes, it allowed her only remaining ally to cast powerful spells against the snowy species. More than once, Scarlet's flaming feathers were gripped by the Vildfir, who then immediately let go with a great yelp of pain.

"I can't hold this, My Lady," the priestess expressed with overt exhaustion. Scarlet went to touch her ally and restore her with divine energy but caught a great club to the shoulder. The force of it had Scarlet in a barrel roll midair before colliding roughly against the stone wall. Her body rag-dolled into the snow and remained still and dim.

With the priestess surrounded and her back against the icy stone, she closed her eyes and prayed to Pirelia for deliverance. The death blow did not come, as Kithlyn shadow-stepped atop one Vildfir's shoulder, plunging a dagger in each of its eyes. Faenla bit at the ankle of another before yanking so hard he tore off the half-giant's leg at the knee. Agan followed suit by slicing at the last Vildfir's hamstrings, dropping them to their knees, where he grabbed a handful of hair atop their crown and sliced across their neck.

The priestess opened her eyes, her body shaking wildly. "You, you came back?" she asked in disbelief.

"Wake her up," the assassin demanded, nodding her chin towards Scarlet. Faenla followed the priestess' every move, standing over the unconscious Phoenix. The priestess placed her middle three fingertips on Scarlet's head; her amulet glowed, and Scarlet lazily opened her eyes. Faenla's enormous head was near Scarlet's face. He studied her intently as the two made eye contact. A sense of dread washed over Scarlet as Agan drove his axe into the legless monster, silencing its painful moans.

"I can't say I prefer this situation to the last," Scarlet announced, trying to stand, but Faenla barred his bone snapping teeth at her, still unsure if he could trust her or not.

"I've seen that wolf bite a feral in two, what do you think he would do to your hollow bones?" Agan asked, advising her to remain where she was.

"Are you hurt, Serene?" She asked her ally, and the priestess shook her head.

"What awaited me in Redwillow?" Kithlyn asked of the two.

"Redwillow? Really?" Agan spat at Scarlet in mock disappointment.

"Nice little reunion we have here, the Scaleless Dragon and the Shadow Mistress back at it again. But aren't you supposed to be dead?" Scarlet questioned Agan.

"Not so lucky I'm afraid." His bright and cutting eyes had never been more sincere.

"Who's the wolf?"

"A friend of a friend," Agan replied with a hint of pride, clearly the cause of Faenla's suddenly perked up ears. Scarlet's beak showed what it could of a smile.

"Answer me." Kithlyn's tone dragged them back to their current predicament.

"Ironboot," Scarlet replied coolly.

Only Agan noticed Serene, the priestess, muttering a prayer of spell casting. With incredible reflexes he threw his axe at her—the haft, not the blade—striking her in the head. She hit the ground with a trickle of blood from her forehead.

"Next time, it's the blade," the half-orc warned.

"You're not a part of the Willow Guild, and Nordhum Ironboot does not send others to do his or the guild's work." Kithlyn continued to push her line of questioning.

"We have a mutual interest in your collection. The Willow Guild had a trade dispute to settle south of Three Gates so here I am."

By now Faenla had grown tired of Scarlet not speaking plainly and gave a throat crackling growl at her.

"There is a reckoning upon us," Scarlet quickly added. "The gods are dying, Nordhum has confirmed the absence of Brailin StoneSower. As you so astutely observed, I lost Pirelia's presence entirely."

Agan looked to his former partner and saw she was lost deep in thought. "What does that have to do with her?" he asked, almost accusatorily.

"We believe each of the gods have chosen a Grimìr, and who better than the Mistress of Shadow to be Aceia's champion?"

At that, Faenla gave a huff of approval. Agan rolled his eyes at the confidence and understanding that the wolf possessed; it often irritated him more than Ven's.

"I will let Agan decide; he freed me and so I am indebted to him."

Agan sighed at Kithlyn's words. He walked over to her and gently gripped her hand, meeting her backlit eyes that reminded him of the yearly eclipse.

"I need you to come with me, not out of debt or guilt, but because you believe it is the right thing. Until then, I follow your lead." He spoke with a much softer tone, perhaps only akin to how he spoke with his current flame, Aelis Andula, Commander of ShadowScorn.

"It's a four-day's ride, I want to be there in three," Kith declared without room for debate.

Scarlet nodded, and the four of them climbed onto the now cage-less cart with Faenla taking up scout.

Three days later, Agan couldn't suppress the smile that creeped across his lips at the sight of the idealic and prosperous town of Redwillow.

CHAPTER SEVEN

Daughter of Peace

"Heave-to, ladies!" Captain Tsuni Tal of the Horizon's Edge barked viciously as her ship was caught in the storm of the century. Captain Tsuni's fiery red hair had turned the shade of blood as the relentless waves and heavy rain soaked the crew and ship, threatening to flounder her prized possession.

On the main deck were dozens of hardened and experienced women unfurling masts, heaving on ropes and tying off others, while another handful began climbing the mast nets. Normally these women would have had wide smiles as they battled the ocean, thanking Kaia for the rush of adventure, but this time was different. The crew of the Horizon's Edge was in a sheer state of determination; remaining on deck had never been harder and to fall overboard meant certain death as the ship would be helpless to retrieve you. Further still, if they did not perform to their height of skill and follow every one of their trusted captain's orders, it meant everyone's demise.

"Bring out the storm sail!" Tsuni shouted once more. She wrestled with all of her significant strength with the wheel at the helm as it was spinning to port and they needed to turn starboard. She had her whole body wrapped around the helm, attempting to spin it the right way so the stern was running with the waves.

Ivan, standing on the main deck and attempting to help the sailors 'heave-to', realized it was a lost cause and looked up to Tsuni. At that moment, one of the handles connected to a spoke on the wheel snapped in her hand and the subsequent handle struck her in the head. She was thrown to the deck and the whole ship lurched to the left, knocking several people asunder and one unfortunate sailor overboard. Ivan sprinted to Tsuni's side with heightened agility. Much to his surprise, she shot back up to her feet, slipping and sliding back to the helm. He noticed a heavy stream of blood running down her face, but she just screamed at him to help her get them back on course. The two of them managed to spin the wheel so they were running with the waves.

"Someone pissed Kaia off!" she shouted at Ivan over the raging storm as they both held firm. Ivan, however, had his eye's locked to their now starboard.

"How can one wave move against the rest?" His tone was one Tsuni had never heard from him—it was utterly dumbfounded.

"Aye, it's rare."

"I guess we're just that lucky." Ivan nodded in the direction of the wave moving with immense speed, and at this distance it appeared tall enough to crash over Moon Mountain. Several shouts sounded across the main deck, quarter deck, and crosstree.

"ROGUE WAVE!"

Now it was Ivan's turn to see a new side of Tsuni as she let out a very small gasp.

"Abandon ship?" he dared to ask, and although he was completely out of his element, he saw no other choice. That brought Tsuni's unyielding heart back to the surface.

"I owe my life to this ship; I'll be damned if I abandon it now." Her voice was shaky—no doubt from exhaustion, the cold, and the blow to the head—but her brown, almond-shaped eyes told Ivan she meant every word.

"Then how can I help, Captain?"

"You've spoken of possessing divine power—can you harness the wind to fill the sails when I say?" she asked quickly, surveying her crew. Several of them had been badly hurt when the ship went array. Three of the cannons had come lose and were now 2000 kilos on wheels, ready to crush anyone or anything in its path. The ship's master-at-arms, a grisly woman known as Alaana, had already begun getting the mighty weapons under control.

"I'll try my best," Ivan replied. Tsuni thought she detected a hint of doubt but had no choice but to ignore it.

"It's all any of us can do now." She looked from Ivan back over to her crew and gave a whistle that sounded over the raging waves of pouring rain. At once, all the women on deck, as well as the terrified Aquon boy that Ivan had freed back in Port Ozos, turned to face their inspiring captain. "Each an er'one of ye has served with honour and distinction. Right now, our Mother is throwing everything she has at us. But we are women, the world has already thrown all its got at us, yet here we stand! Prove to Kaia, this be our sea, show her our story hasn't yet been sung!"

Everyone on the ship shouted in unison, proving their resolve against these insurmountable odds.

Finally, Tsuni shouted, "Drop every sheet, gals! Full speed is our only hope!"

Ivan watched in true awe of Tsuni; her natural leadership was extraordinary and the love of her crew inspiring. A love that was born not just from kindness, but a heavy hand and steadfast courage. However, Ivan the Revered, someone more people trusted in their religion than their Macer, was having a crisis of faith. It had only been a few cycles ago that he met a Keeper who told him Sesara was dead. He of course had told Tsuni of the rumour but kept his wavering devotion a secret, as what he truly needed was time to reflect and further investigate these claims.

Unfortunately, Ivan had not cast a single spell since he awoke in the Spire Lakes beside his horse. He immediately gripped his hands and begun uttering a series of old prayers, all in the name of Sesara. He knew he had cast spells in Serenstrom, and to great effect, but somehow he doubted he could anymore. Ivan was not about to confess that fear to Tsuni, now of all times. The famed paladin knew he would have to cast that spell, and it would have to be great, or it meant their death.

Ivan could feel the ship turning as it began to dip and rise, now horizontal to the waves, creating a nauseating churn in his guts. He had served through several decades of war and crusades and saw things that would turn your average folk to jelly. Right now though, he was happy to keep his eyes closed in prayer rather than staring down that mountainous wave.

"It's now or never ladies, tie yourself down or hold firm!" Tsuni gave one last command before they began their daunting ascent.

It was then that the young Dragon-blood and ShadowScorn teenager came up from below deck. The Dragon-blood quickly went to lashing the Scorn to the mainmast and the poor girl was whiter than usual, even for her species. The ivory-coloured Dragon-blood was clearly going to use his natural ability to spread his great wings and fly if the boat was to capsize.

Ivan felt the ship begin to race up the wave. Before long, the bow was so steep everything began sliding towards the stern. His feet slid across the slippery deck, forcing him to maintain balance while never missing a word in his rhythmic chant of the incantation. The ship was well over 45 degree's and still climbing when Captain Tsuni shouted for Ivan to release his spell.

The revered paladin finished his spell with a thunderous clap. The sails filled with wind and the whole ship lurched forward, forcing the hull deeper into the water as it picked up speed. Ivan watched in equal parts horror and awe at the might of the wave and knew that they were doomed. He had put every ounce of wisdom and divine power he could muster into that spell and they were barely half-way up the wave. His back hit the captain's cabin door; the bow was at such an angle that when he stood back up, one foot was on the deck and the other on the wall he had just struck.

Tsuni looked behind her as the stern and quarter deck of the Horizon's Edge were kissing the waves that promised doom.

"We're caught in the pull!" she alarmed everyone, as they now surfed with the wave instead of sailing over it. Tsuni clung to her ship's wheel and, for one of the few times in her life, prayed to Kaia for deliverance from this ultimate obstacle. She stopped praying when her feet lifted from under her and she was left hanging from the wheel. Craning her neck, she saw the bow of Horizon's Edge straight as an arrow pointing towards the storm clouds above. The sound of splitting wood, shifting cannons and cargo, were all drowned out by the screams of her faithful and beloved crew.

Aunna Morningthorne sat in front of a canvas and easel. Before her were the tropical, crystal-clear waters and sandy white beaches of the Magma Isles. Off in the distance, a volcano sprung from the ocean like a resilient seed, determined to defeat winter's bite. It was covered in the most vibrant moss and flowered trees she had ever seen. From the moment she set foot on Coral Island, she had been captivated by that volcano. Life clung to it richer than anywhere else, yet could not be nearer to annihilation.

Her moment of serenity washed away at the sound of an alarm bell. Her posture drooped, for it could only mean one thing, the same thing that had happened a dozen or more times in the few cycles since she arrived—battle. She had half a mind to ignore it, stay where she was in peace and never return. A nagging sense of duty, the same one that had nipped at her very being since she could remember, forced her up. She put her paint and brush down, smoothed out her long silk dress of turquoise hue, adjusted the diadem that rested around her forehead, and walked back towards their keep.

She walked through curving and wide-reaching palm trees, tall blades of thick grass, and waxy papaya plants. Her mission here, alongside Runa Ringnir, was to bring Sesara and her edicts to the Magma Isle's, along with gifts of immense wealth and desire to entice the local natives. In truth, it was to be a staging ground for their ultimate goal—settling a presence in the central-northern half of Litore. Aunna had sat on the council just shy of five years, the youngest ever to be granted a seat. In that time, she had learned that all the Macers previous—man or woman—felt the need to leave their mark in history, a deed that would see them not forgotten to the annals of time. The only Macer she had served, Charles O'Donnell, had reinforced that theory as sure as the snow was white. After yet another failure at capturing the City of Shadow, she wondered if this plan to bring faith to everything north and east of the Skydore Mountains was being done for the right reasons.

She paused amongst the foliage and plucked the most beautiful, sunset-coloured mango. She held it close to her mouth, teasing her lips and breathing deeply to take in its fresh scent. She opened her eyes to see Fort Ringnir preparing the soldiers of Sesara to meet the rebelling locals. Not an hour had gone by in the previous months when she hadn't remembered that fateful day that she had met Sesara herself. She often had to remind herself that it was real, not a dream or trick, that the Goddess of Peace, Life, and Sustenance truly appeared before her and called her daughter.

Of course, it was not without a dire warning—find the others of your kind and ensure Charles O'Donnell does not see the first sunrise of the Third Age. She understood they were not wanted here on Coral Island or anywhere in the Magma Isles; however, if she accepted her charge and came here, perhaps by her words she could share the true faith of Sesara, and not the modern twisted version it had become.

It had occurred to her that perhaps her former mentor and closest thing to a father she ever knew, Ivan the Revered, had vanished from their faith because he too knew someone must stop Macer O'Donnell. She was not dumb and could think of a hundred reasons as to why he did not say goodbye first or attempt to contact her since, yet that didn't make it sting any less. She felt like shedding tears at the weight of it all—the injustices, the unwelcomed settling here, and the grievances thrust upon her.

Her brow only furrowed for a second before her resolve hardened and her face grew stern. She held her chin high and made the final descent into the pretentious fort. Walking into the main bailey, soldiers hastened about her, orders were shouted, servants ducked for cover, and the ashen-coloured Dragon-blood Runa Ringir, Arch Paladin of Sesara, was orchestrating it all like a mad puppeteer. Aunna strode amongst the tumult as if it were beneath her, and of course that's how she felt. She did not stop until she was face-to-face with her counterpart, staring her in her angular, draconic eyes.

"Going to help this time are you?" Runa chortled. Aunna looked up at her. The Dragon-blood was several heads taller than her. The pair stood in front of the large, swinging wooden-gates that led into the fort.

"Look at your warriors, they cannot sustain much more of this," Aunna pointed out the obvious.

"They'll endure what I command them to endure. I am well read in the art of war—you , are not," the paladin said, trying to usher Aunna away with words before turning her massive maw towards her soldiers.

But Aunna was not done with this conversation. "Do not fail to remember who raised me. I know a great deal about the tactics of war. I also happen to know much more about the frailty of the mortal condition. It's your pride and heritage getting in the way of respecting your followers and causing their lack of respect for you."

Runa became so furious so fast, she exhaled and small roots of electricity crackled inside her flared nostrils. Aunna, however, had an impassive stare that resembled someone trying to pick something off a stale platter.

"All your negotiations have failed," Runa reminded.

"Yes, well this time you won't be with me," the cleric answered smugly which made the paladin grow.

"Wait here." Aunna began to step for the exit before adding, "Be a dear and open the gate, would you?" She continued her stride and Runa threw her hand up to signal the gate be opened. The instant Aunna's gown fluttered out of sight the gates shut behind her.

Aunna waded through soft, coral-white sand towards the raiding party of nearly twenty-five humans, twenty Aquon, and possibly a dozen Kyst or Solsta elves. She was surprised to say she could not tell which elves they were and considered that they could be a mixed-breed. They all shared sun-kissed skin, similar seashell and pearl jewelery with minimal to no armour. Several of them carried fine bows, but most sported small kris knives with coral or obsidian hilts and pommels.

Many of the locals looked at Aunna's raven-coloured hair and violet eyes with awe, but it solidified the fact she did not belong here. She stopped a few metres from the war party and a single human closed the distance. He was not exceptionally tall, his thick, wavy hair swept back just past his ears, his eyes a soft turquoise like her own dress. He wore a beautiful necklace of coral, pearls, and a carved obsidian wave proudly around his neck, and a similar one around his left bicep. She acutely noticed his eyes scanning her body as the silk dress billowed tightly around her curves.

"My name is Aunna-"

"-Morningthorne," he cut her off. "My father met you and that abomination you travel with many moons ago. He's dead now, as you well know."

Aunna felt a lump in her throat forming. "She does not represent the best of us. I try to. My condolences for your fallen mean little, I am sure. In an effort for peace, it helps when both parties know the other's name?"

"Caelen Rommach. Newly appointed leader of the Coral Island."

Aunna curtsied before offering a disarming smile. Caelen's lips quivered as he fought the urge to return it.

"What can I offer so that we may exist in peace and perhaps even benefit from one another?"

Caelen crossed his thick arms. "First, I wish you to come see our village and prove you mean no ill-intent. Second, we want weapons to protect ourselves from the Salt Slayers."

"The first would be an honour. However, we did not come to arm the free folk of the Magma Isles."

"We care not for you gifts and trinkets. We want steel that does not rust with each new moon tide like ours do. This is our wish, Lady Morningthorne."

"I understand. Allow me to return for one hour to gather supplies and a small escort to join you back to your village? If you would permit, Caelen the Fair."

Caelen was surprised to see Aunna understood his native tongue, for the translation of his last name was without flaw. From his belt, he pulled a small sack of weaved twine, and from that he grabbed black lava salt, putting a grain in both Aunna's hand and his own.

"A rare delicacy. Sharing it between two people is a sign of trust," Caelen spoke, and popped the glossy black grain of salt in his mouth. Aunna reciprocated, curtsied, and delicately made her way back into the fort.

"Well?" Runa barked impatiently.

"I am taking a small party of volunteers back to their village."

"Why?"

"As a sign of friendship, they've invited me to witness their culture and walk within their home. And I'll be requiring a crate of weapons. Not a large crate, but the steel must be good."

"What?" Runa snorted in disbelief. Aunna looked puzzled at her.

"Have you forgotten how to form full sentences Runa?" The Dragon-blood looked like she was about to strike her. "You've achieved nothing but bloodshed. The Macer wants relations with the varied species of this truly breathtaking archipelago."

"You would arm them so they may continue that bloodshed? They are savages and nothing more."

"In their eyes, so are we. Foreigners with a foreign goddess come to conquer and convert. And the only difference I see is we're the ones who moved onto their lands without invitation. A single crate of knives or whatever you deem fit will not give them the power to defeat us, but it will turn the tide of war into peace."

Runa stared the cleric down and the two powerful females did not budge for a long moment, as all in the fort halted their work to watch. Runa eventually shouted several names without flicking her eyes away. Understanding these were the people Aunna was supposed to take to their village, she interrupted the paladin.

"I said volunteers, Runa. You may send one soldier with me."

"I will be joining you."

"You slayed their former leader. You will remain behind to guard our walls. Perhaps this is just a ruse and they will send a different raiding party to hit the fort."

"Or perhaps they will slaughter you the second you step foot inside their village." Runa gave a genuine smile at that thought as the words escaped her.

"Then a great day for you it will be."

After a several kilometre walk along the sea-swept beach, Aunna and her retinue of six mostly healers, one artist and one botanist—followed Caelen and his people through the jungle. Over an hour later, Caelen stood by the entrance of a cave mouth, shrouded by long vines and roots of trees clinging to the rock face. After everyone had gone through, the Sarnese leader held out his hand for Aunna to take. Everything about her wanted to swat his calloused hand aside; instead, she gave him a smirk and brushed her fingers across his arm as she walked on into the darkness. She understood now why he offered a hand, for it was pitch black inside the cave tunnel. She was not phased, however, as she cast a minor spell of dark sight upon herself.

After a few moments, light poured from a small crevasse in the wall. Aunna squeezed herself through and was stunned by the jaw-dropping society before her. A great, sprawling settlement bathed in the sunlight from the massive hole in the stone ceiling. From it poured a river that made everything glisten and grow abundantly. Flowers and vines clung to the lip of the hole all the way down into the basin and continued throughout the homes and buildings. Birds flew down, around, and out again. Children ran through the mossy bed that made the floor of the whole basin, while folk tended crops and gardens.

Aunna felt a tear run down her cheek as Caelen slowly stepped beside her. "Everything we need is right here in Nedea."

CHAPTER EIGHT

Old Wounds

Ven and Ina led the way back to the Shallowbay hideout. The famed hunter couldn't help but look back every few seconds to make sure Njor Swordsplinter, who was carrying a miserable Onstera, was still behind them. It was a lifetime of being taught, drilled into his head, to never trust a Kintar. Even though there were a handful of Kintar living in Silva as he was growing up, they seemed different somehow —more Kyst in spirit than Kintar. He had grown to value Onstera's company, but to say he trusted her would be a stretch; she had lied to them from the moment they met at Gauntlet Ridge until the Shallowbay Kyst told them she was working for them.

He still had a rage boiling inside him and it scared him to admit it, for the rage had never been so consistent before. He had barely slept since their arrival, and then Scáth's abduction ensured any rest would be fraught. It was not his stay of rest that all Kyst meditated to achieve, sleep simply eluded him. Growing up, the anger came and went like the tide, but now it bubbled like a lake of lava slowly expanding, creeping to the surface until all was consumed by its heat.

He could not forgive himself for murdering those Kyst in Vakar's new army. He did not want to speak of it and the only two souls he might speak to were gone. It unnerved him that no one had brought it up since it happened. Were they afraid of him? Did they think he would turn his ire on them at the slightest mention? What frightened him most was he could not say he wouldn't. Surely Agan was not afraid of him, but he had left the Rainforest. Scáth always understood Ven's feelings better than he did, yet her insightful nature was not at his disposal. Even the wolf that was more a part of him than friend or family could ever be was not here to listen. Every time he put his mind to sort out his feelings, an overwhelming jumble of emotion blocked any progress. It quickly became a vicious cycle he could not put into words nor into a coherent thought, which meant he could not begin to help himself, leaving him feeling weak and boiled in his rage.

"Shouldn't we stop for the night?" Njor spoke up in his broken Kystin.

"Why? So your raiders and berserkers can ambush us in the night?" Ina shot back without missing a beat. The sun had all but set and the forest was left in a deep twilight as the plants, waters, and odd flying critters began to glow magnificent colours.

"You well know night is not the time of the Kintar. That belongs to you and the Gloom elves," Njor said matter-of-factly. He looked around suspiciously. "And I'd rather not meet those twilight elves this night."

"He might be right. If Onstera could sleep laying down she may be able to walk tomorrow," Ven added. Onstera's silver eyes cut through the air to pierce Ven's opalescent green ones. It shamed her to do so, but she nodded ever so slightly. Njor went and laid Onstera in a soft bed of moss against a small log before constructing a fire pit.

Ina went and stood close to Ven. The two hunters in their pumasheep cloaks blended flawlessly with the foliage around them.

"I will take to the trees, keep an eye on things from above," Ina whispered to him, side-eyeing the Kintar. Ven gave a firm nod of agreement and within a few seconds Ina was already several metres up a cedar tree. Ven went and knelt beside Onstera and checked over her wraps. With the fire crackling Njor turned to speak up.

"I apologize. I should not have struck you such as I did." He stumbled for the right words. "This strength is still new to me."

"I attacked you, and lost. I'm grown enough to accept that." Onstera's words sounded pained, but she ended them with a nod. Ven pulled his hand away and went to setting up a lean-to as a familiar rain began trickling through the canopy.

"How new?" Ven asked, while keeping busy.

"New." Njor's voice rang out deep, as if the exact time frame didn't matter.

"Where did you acquire it?" Ven persisted.

"After death took one look at me and left, Lokor's final act was to give me what was left of his power."

Onstera and Ven looked at each other knowingly.

"And he's dead?" Ven asked, already suspecting the answer but wanting to hear it from someone else.

"In my heart, I know it." The berserker sounded solemn.

"Was there any contact shared? Instruction's?" Onstera questioned. Njor looked at her with a crooked brow.

"What do you two know?"

Onstera looked at Ven and remained quiet. The famed hunter felt a stranger sense of trust toward Njor since seeing what was left of Claw Canyon, but that innate feeling was muddled by a lifetime of conditioned hate.

"The Third age is upon us. The gods are dead and dying."

Before Njor could respond, all three of them heard a whistle from above and turned their heads to a dark spot in the trees. Ven stood, trident at the ready to throw, but Njor stood tall and held out his hand to stay any attack.

"Witblade," he bellowed.

From the darkened collage of flora stepped out a large berserker. They were muscular and tall, tattoos elegantly weaving around their eyes, nose, and ears. Their dirty hair was braided back, a few stubborn strands hanging in front of their eyes. Witblade walked straight up till they were standing face to face with Njor.

"You leave our kind to walk beside these-" Rinya looked at Ven and Onstera distastefully, "-vermin?"

"It is better to walk beside those who do not kill out of absolutes than those who spill blood like wine."

"Spilling blood is our way. Why would Lokor disgrace us all by choosing the pathetic sob story that is Swordsplinter?"

By now, Ina had made her way to stand next to Ven and Njor was choosing his next words carefully.

"Perhaps he saw what I would become, what he wanted to become of our people. We killed in his name, now he is gone and I remain. And I say, 'enough'."

Rinya's disgust was apparent. Not so easily convinced. "You do this for her, not us. Being a pacifist won't bring your wife and daughter running back to you."

Njor did the only thing he could think of next. He gripped Rinya's throat and squeezed, hoisting them up in the air with a single arm as easy as hoisting a tankard in cheer. "That Njor is dead. I care not for them. Only the future of all Kintar."

Rinya looked down on Njor with hate-filled eyes, veins bulging across their temples, neck muscles straining against the pressure, but to no avail. Long after they all thought Rinya would have passed out, they gave Njor a small nod in acceptance. He dropped them and Rinya fell to their knees, rubbing their neck.

"I've followed you for most of my life. If you betray me now, I will spend the rest of my days making sure your second chance is for nothing." They stood tall again, then added with quiet malice, "Pick a different name, it disgraces the Njor Swordsplinter I fought beside all those years."

Ina considered this to be more tenuous than watching the ritualistic melee earlier that day. When Njor reached for the dragonbone bastard sword on his back and unsheathed it, Onstera wondered if this Rinya character had spoken too candidly. Ven and Ina both tensed their weapon arms, but Njor cut the tension swifter than this sword could cut flesh. He held the pommel in one hand and the blade face in the other, offering it to Rinya.

"I believe you speak true. You've earned this, more than anyone I know." Holding out the blade, Rinya appeared stunned at the gesture. They gripped the pommel and deftly swung the blend vertically to better view the magnificent weapon.

"Call me Njor SecondSpirit," Njor said with a somewhat awkward half-smile. Before Rinya had the chance to offer a kind gesture in return, Onstera piped up.

"Are you two ever going to shut up? A girl's gotta rest around here and your mulish grunts are keeping me up."

Ven and Ina were completely pulled back into the situation as their eyes sprung open in shock.

Rinya and Njor laid their dark, piercing red eyes on Onstera. Now Ina really thought this situation would explode; however, Rinya Witblade smirked and said, "Perhaps my eyes deceived me, I've never known vermin to be so sharp."

"Just like that?" Ven brought the briefest moment of levity crashing down like a giant struck low. Rinya turned their brooding ire upon him.

"It was said you led the attack with Uthul against your people. I was there you know, slaughtering those feeble elves with the widest smile. One look at you now and I can safely say it was not you."

"Do they call you Witblade for stating the obvious?" Ven's tone was lathered in spite. Rinya walked over to him. They were just shorter than the Kyst but that made them no less imposing.

"There are many things I love in this life—the comfort of a warm bed with some lass or lad to fill it, the sweet sight of watching my enemies life fade from their eyes. Yet, what simply pleases me the most is cutting out the tongues of blabbering welps and feasting on it before their very eyes."

Ven had a hundred things to say to this monster standing before him, a hundred things to deflate the arrogance from their inflated ego. It was staying his blade that caused him the most trouble. Had he even considered what it meant to truly broker peace between the Kyst and Kintar? Was it something he considered he could do? Or was he destined to put his ancient sword through this berserker's heart right here and now and halt this new era before it even began?

"We're not taking just anyone back with us," Ina piped up and went to stand over Rinya, looking down on them, for female Kyst were the tallest in all the forest.

"They go where I do," Njor said, walking up to them. Onstera for the first time felt uneasy; two Kyst and two Kintar having a standoff seldom led to anything good.

"One misstep, one offence given to Queen Saphier, and I'll kill without another word uttered," Ven promised to Rinya.

"Good," Onstera shouted. "Now all four of you shut up until I say you can speak so I may rest. I seem to recall that's why we stopped in the first place."

They all keenly noticed Onstera's eyes turn from the alluring silver to blood red as her heart now raced. Njor and Rinya went and sat by the fire and began roasting fresh game. Ven eyed the blood-seeker, then turned to Ina. She gestured for him to follow her.

They stopped next to a particularly divine pool of glowing cyan water with small, pale-green lily pads floating on the surface. Ina knelt down to fill her canteen; the ripples looked like someone had reached into the sky and touched a star.

"I won't bring that berserker back to our hideout before we're certain they are trustworthy. I doubted bringing Njor, but that other one is a risk I cannot take."

Ven nodded, understanding her worry. "What can you tell me of Sanctuary Island? I need to get back there before long." Ina knew Ven was referring to finally laying Athvar to rest with his people.

"Vakar has left a small military presence there. Shortly after you left, he poisoned Queen Ilthanis to gain control of a stronghold and add more Kyst to aid his plans. However, we have a scout living there and she has confirmed Vakar has not returned since rebuilding Silva. I believe it's guilt keeping him away from the spot he first committed murder."

"I am no military tactician, but would it not make sense to gain control of the Island? Surely it's natural advantages would be a great asset to the rebellion?" Ven spoke of the Island's vast and sheer cliffs that made all but two points of entry impossible. Game was also plentiful and the predators non-existent.

"Of course we have considered it, but once Vakar found out we had taken it, he would strike at us with the full force of his army." Ina, being the lead hunter for Shallowbay, was familiar with greater military tactics and had found no way around that problem. So Ven surprised her, and slightly concerned her, when a smirk consumed him.

"Full might? If there is one thing I learned from the Siege of Shadow, it is that the besiegers have no choice but to leave their rear weakened. While Vakar lays siege to an impregnable island, what settlement or stronghold would you like to liberate?"

It didn't take long before Ina Enallea wore the same smirk. "I would leave this night to get our forces ready. Will you be okay with Onstera and the others?"

Ven looked at the two Kintar sharing food around a warm fire and Onstera finally at rest. He felt confident he could dispatch the Kintar if need be, although a part of him felt foolish in that confidence.

"Do you have that potion of stimulation?" he asked. Ina pulled a small wooden vile from the folds of her cloak.

"Give it to her when she wakes. That and the Sanguis modifications will have her right as rain." She placed it in his hand and promptly began heading back to the cave hideout.

"Enallea," Ven shouted. She paused to look at him. "Thank you." He placed a warm and unsteady smile upon her.

"See you in a few days, Devar."

Ven watched the much wiser and calmer hunter walk away, looked back to the two Kintar, and instantly regretted letting her go. It was a mistake and he knew it. He knew too there was much to be done and in a short time. They could spend a few days tops searching for the other clans of Kintar or the ever elusive and melancholic Gloom elves.

Personally, he did not know which he would prefer to encounter, for he had had enough of the Kintar for one cycle and the Gloom elves were named justly. They were a spiritual people and seemed to guard an ancient secret that only they knew about, for they worshipped not the gods of Litore but the very stars above them. Their hair as pale as starlight, their skin a midnight blue, and their eyes seemed to reflect that which they spent long hours of the night starring at. Each set of eyes, completely void of pupil or iris, appeared to be just vast voids of star fields captured in time. They spent very little time on daylight activities and were mostly seen as nocturnal creatures. Ven thought that if there was ever a species of Litore to give the ShadowScorn a run for their money in the darkness, it would be these proud and solemn folk. He would first have to find them. He knew of where they liked to roam, near the borders of the forest or in the tree tops like the Kyst, but they were not proficient climbers like the coastal elves. It was likely they would be near the southern or eastern border of the forest where Vakar had the least interest. It would be a huge gamble, as the Gloom elves rarely ever took part in the affairs of others, and like the other folk of the world, despised the Kintar.

As he sat in the dimly lit forest floor with a keen eye on Onstera and their newfound companions, he lazily lifted his head and fell victim to a bushel of gnome-sized leaves falling from the canopy. They quietly and swiftly glided to the forest floor, glowing bright gold as the great oaks here did. As the clump of leaves softly landed in the dirt, their light slowly faded as the bioluminescence found no more agitation. One leaf did glow again as a chipmunk climbed off their ride with unsteady little feet. Ven watched in amusement as the critter wobbled for a few seconds before falling to its butt. It reminded him of the Chips, the chipmunk that used to follow Athvar everywhere. He had always envied the way his dear friend could communicate with animals, and they never tried again outright after the incident on Sanctuary Island. Yet for some reason, Athvar always believed Ven could attain that level of insight, and perhaps it was understanding gestures and subtle hints more than actually speaking and receiving a reply.

Ven pulled out a handful of dried fruit, laying most of it in front of him, balancing a single raisin at the end of his pinky finger. The chipmunk's little nose and whiskers slowly, then crazily, sniffed the air before slowly opening his eyes, only now noticing Ven. His eyes widened and jumped back up on all four little feet before scurrying back behind the soft golden leaf. Ven thought he had run off, but a moment later the little critter stuck his head back out. Sniffing the air once more, he scurried with as much caution as he could muster towards the tiny pile of dried fruit. After greedily gobbling that down, his little whiskers went back to work.

"It's okay, little one," Ven voiced with as much calm as he could muster. The chipmunk shot his head up and looked quizzically at Ven. As if he was stunned that he somehow understood or believed this elf. The tiny critter bounded over to Ven's finger, grabbed the raisin, leapt up into Ven's open palm, and ate his snack. Shortly thereafter, the critter looked up to Ven and squeaked. Ven placed another raisin onto his shoulder this time. The chipmunk promptly scurried up his arm and remained atop his shoulder for the rest of the night.

The longer I spend in my home, where the blood in my veins had evolved from my ancestors to become the coastal elf I am, the more guilt and shame weighs me down. When you are growing up, all you wish for is what you do not have. I have had more than a taste of what I desired for most of my life. Family and adventure. Connection and battle. Love and loss. How quickly what we desire turns to sour milk in our mouths. I once thought myself the 'hero' for abandoning my life and escorting Scáth home, and few would deny it was the right thing to do. I protected her, she protected me. I killed in her defence and the defence of her people. It weighed on me greater than anything had, but I never killed unless threatened. Or so I could convince myself. If I had met Onstera Dentoress in Gauntlet Ridge six months prior, I would have slid my sword through her throat.

Staying my blade, as I promised myself I would whenever possible, has drastically altered my life for the better. Yet, it all led me to fighting Rexous once again, then doing the unthinkable. A 'hero' does not kill unless absolutely necessary, and even then, perhaps not. Yet, I murdered. I slaughtered my very own kin like worms to a hook, helpless and without fault. I killed Kyst of the Great Northern Rainforest who had surrendered or were in full retreat. I can never take that back, I can never seek redemption from the dead, and so I can never be the hero.

-Ven Devar

CHAPTER NINE

Gloom

"I'll need an escort," Aolendìr informed Vakar as they sat around a large table with Pine, the Arch Sage, and Eevie, the Lead Hunter, in the King of Kyst's great army. Vakar nodded.

"Eevie, select a hunter to escort our guest to the Gloom elves."

Eevie stood with a nod and left the chamber. "Will you be needing a sage? Magic in our woodland realm does not act with such reliability as it does in the rest of Litore," Vakar advised.

"Nothing I can't handle," Aolendìr answered with a wink to Pine. The experienced sage scoffed and stood abruptly. He held his gaze on Vakar, sending a telepathic message. *"This one is not to be trusted."* Vakar heard the words ring clearly in his mind.

"Do my feelings mean so little to you?" Aolendìr asked aloud with a coy smile, laying his golden eyes upon Pine. The sage's face flushed and he quickly left the room.

"Must you embarrass him so?" Vakar scolded.

Aolendìr shrugged. "My advice is find yourself a better wizard."

"We are not wizards here."

"Clearly."

"We are as every bit as proficient," Vakar informed. The Solsta elf merely nodded with a small bow in respect.

"Before I go, a keen mind for curiosity begs I know what your intentions with the ShadowScorn are?"

"Use her to weaken Ven."

"You said it yourself; the boy elf has flown into a rage and now kills without question. He has done the unthinkable and aligned with the Kintar. How does stealing the one he loves weaken him? There is only one thing more powerful than revenge in this world."

"And what is that?" Vakar thought it was hatred.

"You're the one that every names 'cunning', figure it out and let me know."

"What would you do with her then?" Vakar asked impatiently.

"Send him her head." Aolendìr said without a hint of care.

That night, the suave, golden elf left the safety of Silva with a single Kyst Hunter for a guide. The hunter had introduced himself as Ehan. Aolendìr thought the elf was more akin to the Kintar given the sheer size and lack of grace about him. They stood at similar heights and even with the multiple jerkins, breast coats, cloaks, and high collared tabard the Solsta wore, Ehan appeared much wider and bulkier with his simple leather armour and pumasheep cloak. Aolendìr walked briskly a few short paces behind the hunter. He gazed at the sheer beauty of the rainforest at night. He had heard how the trees grew to such immense size here, but it wasn't until they had walked several minutes around a single tree that lay in their path did he truly understand.

"So, tell me about yourself, Ehan? Regale me with one of your adventures. If lady Eevie selected you for this journey you must be a mighty and skilled warrior." After no reply, Aolendìr rolled his eyes. "Then I suppose you are of no actual talent and this is merely punishment for some prior misgiving." He waited to see if that would elicit some response from the brooding and stoic hunter. It did not. "Is it because your new king put a female above you?" Aolendìr said it with a scrunchy face and tone that danced around something awkward. "So you're not a misogynist. That's a relief because I can't get enough of females personally. Ah! How could I not have seen this before—it's love. You love your commander but she does not love you back?"

At that, Ehan finally stopped dead in his tracks and turned to face his charge. Aolendìr expected a punch to be thrown or a quip to be exchanged. Neither arrived and Ehan turned back around to keep walking. The Solsta continued as well, remaining quiet until they settled down and made camp.

Ehan curled up next to a tree, pulling his hood down low and saying nothing. Aolendìr sat down on a log after wiping some debris off of it and stared intently at the hunter. After several minutes of this, Ehan broke his silence.

"Stop it."

"Stop what?" Aolendìr quickly retorted.

"Staring. Talking. Just stop."

"I haven't been this quiet for this long in years."

"Don't you sleep?" Ehan asked angrily.

"When I'm tired. I've been told I sleep-talk quite a lot I'm afraid."

Ehan sighed heavily and pulled his hood back. "What do you want from me?"

"You hate Ven Devar. Why?"

"Most Kyst hate him."

"Not how I've heard it told. He was the best among you. I'm sure it stung the proud and competitive egos you hunters possess. But to the commoners he was a hero, a legend, Guardian of the North. So?"

"He betrayed his kin, slaughtered hundreds of Kyst alongside the Kintar. He is the most hated elf in all the forest."

"If you really believe that then you are of no use to me. Travelling beside a dullard is the surest way to get yourself killed."

"I've 150 years of experience, no one is better suited to navigate this land," Ehan protested.

"Age is merely a number, not an indicator of one's worth. I needed information on Ven Devar, not whatever you offer." Aolendir motioned his hand dismissively.

"Good luck." Ehan said with fire in his voice as he got up to leave. He made it a dozen steps before he found his feet sinking into the earth. The soil surrounding him bubbled and burped as the large hunter struggled to wrench himself free. Aolendìr stood up, flattening his cloaks as he did and walked up to the Kyst. Ehan found himself chest deep now, the cold dirt settling back into a solid around him. In his feeble efforts to break free he only managed a single hand to remain unstuck.

"Oh dear, whatever will you do." Aolendìr moved and knelt in front of Ehan. The hunter swiped his free hand at the Solsta, who expertly grabbed his wrist and twisted with ease. A resounding crack echoed out and a splintered bone protruded from his wrist. Ehan wheezed in pain as he grimaced through the agony.

"Now, about Ven Devar." The suave and charismatic elf smiled over his prisoner.

"It's wonderful isn't it?"

"They look so big up here." A young and innocent voice replied.

"It is said that the largest moon, Caelestis, struck Litore with a shower of meteors. Sending a thousand, thousand chunks of the world into the sky, and from those pieces of land, Caelestis created the moon Soror, so it would know loneliness no more."

"What about Tarvus?" the little half-dwarf, half-elf asked his mother.

"Well, now that Caelestis and Soror were locked in the eternal dance of love; pushing and pulling each other, dragging the ocean tides in their wake. A great Cloud Dragon called Tarvus, who carried the sun to Litore each day, saw this new moon in the sky and worshipped it with each sunset. Until the first Mountain Giant awoke from her eternal slumber in the Skydore Mountains. She blamed the spirit of Caelestis for stealing her rock to create Soror. You have to understand little one, the first Mountain Giant, named Monsaxum, was as tall as Moon Mountain; her hair was clouds, her feet as big as countries. She grabbed a chunk of earth so large, many believe it to be the crater that formed Litore Lake. So, what do you think Monsaxum did next?" The Gloom elf mother's eyes shone with exuberance as she asked her child. The kid, stout like a dwarf yet almost lean like an elf, had brown hair and eyes of stars like all Gloom elves. He pondered his mother's question deeply.

"She ate it! I would be hungry after eternal slumber."

The mother laughed before pointing up into the sky. "Me too, my little rock. She threw it so far and so fast that it struck Caelestis straight in the heart. Having her revenge, Monsaxum rested once more into the Skydore Range. Then the whole world fell out of balance; the rain never stopped, the oceans sat still, and the sun could spring no life. So, the Cloud Dragon Tarvus, flapped his wings until a hurricane sent the sun spinning round and round, never to stop. Then he flew up into the heavens. He gathered all the pieces of Caelestis and healed its spirit. In an ultimate act of heroism, he perished in the stars. So the Moon Spirits pulled him close and covered him with their own stone, thus creating the third moon of Litore, restoring all things back to harmony." She rubbed her fingers through her boy's hair as he rested in her lap. In awe of everything, he snuggled his mother there in peace, feeling her loving caress, listening to the legends of his people, and imagined anything was possible.

The mother had short, pixie cut hair, accentuating her pointed ears. Her pale blue skin was covered in intricate tattoos of the stars, constellations, moon flowers, and many cultural and personally significant things. The silvery white of the tattoos matched and completed her hair. Her eyes were a hundred shades of blue, white, and red for they appeared like swirling fields of stars. Her ears twitched and a familiar concern washed over her.

"Go to your father." The mother immediately became sour as she leapt up and focused her attention below them, through the forest canopy.

"But I am to train with Diwyn Florienne tomorrow," he whined back at her in defiance.

"Now, my little rock. Flee." She planted a kiss on his forehead and touched the Redwillow pendant hanging from his neck. A great cloud of celestial bodies wrapped around the child, engulfing him before vanishing as the cloud collapsed in on itself like a dying star. The Gloom elf picked up her rapier and slung her bow back over her shoulder. Then she dove into the trees like a swan into water. She made herself thin using the sharp wide curves to her basket hilt to catch branches, slowing her momentum or redirecting it altogether. She descended until a single traveller came into view.

After trailing the Solsta Elf for several minutes, she leaped down behind him as he knelt beside a pool of water, refilling his canteen in a miniature water fall that trickled down from a mossy pool above. Standing behind him, she held her white wickedwood bow and knocked a star-steel arrow.

"Evening," Aolendìr said, dropping his canteen and raising his arms to clasp behind his neck.

"Only an outsider is stupid enough to wander the forest at night alone."

"I believe it, but I like to think of myself as more of a visitor to your wonderful forest," he answered with a wide smile. She, however, raised a white brow in slight disgust.

"What are you doing here?" Her tone salivated harshness.

"Looking for the Gloom elves, and since I've found one, allow me to introduce myself." Aolendìr turned, dipping into a low and fanciful bow. "Aolendìr Tardinian, at your service, milady."

He placed his golden stare upon her and put on his most smoldering expression. After she continued to look mortified at the bravado of the elf, he added. "And your name? If I might be so bold."

"Wynn Walker, and don't ever call me 'milady' again or I'll cut your tongue like fruit from a tree."

"We'll I'm sure you hold true to your word, Wynn, might I-"

"- Tell me what you're doing here." She snapped, getting back to her original question.

"I'm hoping to offer aid against King Vakar," his reply was kind but firm.

"What could you have to offer us? We leave him alone and he returns the gesture."

"Yes, but how long do you think that will last, my starry-eyed doe? Peace will always be tenuous. Soon he will want command of the whole forest."

Wynn hesitated for a moment. The Gloom elves were as reclusive as they came, seldom to be bothered with the other species of Litore. Their problems always seemed too middling compared to the vastness above. However, Wynn was not like most Gloom elves. Her history denied her such isolation.

"I've dealt with males like you my whole life. I've been abused, tortured, killed, and resurrected by males like you just so they could do it all over again. By all the gods, I should loose this arrow through your eye and rid another one from this world. I know that whatever you want lays beneath that fake smile and appalling personality. Fortunately for you, I agree that the others of my kind need to take action in this war." Wynn stopped speaking when she noted a smile form on his lips, as if he was getting what he wanted. She lowered her weapon and strode close to him, face-to-face. His pointed golden beard was flecked with a streak of grey, the few wrinkles forming around his eyes spoke of centuries of experience. His layers of cloaks and high collars added a metaphysical shield around him, bolstering his defense somehow. Wynn had never looked more serious, but Aolendìr kept his edge. "Make no mistake, once I determine your true intention, and find out it's not to my liking, you'll beg for the Underworld before I'm through with you."

The smile on his lips grew tenfold, and he nodded respectfully.

"You can't be serious." Rinya growled.

"I can, and I am," Ven replied as if taunting a sibling, but in truth he was holding back harsh words. It had unfortunately slipped that Ven was following the chipmunk he had made friends with after coming to a poor understanding that he needed to find the Gloom elves.

"Why are you following him? I've seen humans with more sense than this elf," Rinya complained to Njor. It was Onstera who shot a dirty glare at Rinya with her silver eyes, being the only human present.

The reborn Kintar answered his companion's doubts. "You remember Skurge. He talked with animals and they talked right back."

"He was a dullard, Njor! The clearest memory I have of Skurge is him blowing snot bubbles and popping them with his tongue."

SecondSpirit laughed at that and agreed. "Well, we haven't seen Ven do that. Yet."

The Kyst wasn't paying them any heed as his full attention was on following the chipmunk. Which he quickly came to learn was easier said than done. Ven was a fine tracker, not extraordinary but decent. Yet, following the tiny critter for nearly a day now had its troubles. For one, the route the chipmunk took was rarely one they could. Another was Ven found himself following an entirely different chipmunk before the original one came back and squeaked at him rather rudely.

Onstera closed the gap to walk behind a concentrating Ven. "Are you sure about this? They are literally laughing at you."

"Let them, it does not bother me," Ven said maintaining his line of sight on the guide. Onstera made a disgruntled noise. "It bothers you?" He glanced her way.

"I don't know why, but yes." She looked at him with a strange intensity. "They can't be trusted. We should abandon this partnership."

"I want to but if Njor is telling the truth, he's one of the chosen I have to find. If the way he struck you and fought Kaldoon in the Canyon is any proof, then he is Grimìr."

"Fine," she huffed. "Just please tell me we can stop following the chipmunk soon."

"If you know a better way to find an ever-elusive race of elves, I'm all pointed ears over here."

Onstera couldn't help a smirk that quickly faded when she heard the snickering behind her. It irritated her that she was irritated by their mocking of Ven. He didn't care, so why did she.

By now the natural light on the forest floor offered a soft glow to the world around her. She looked up periodically and saw the looming Caelestis shining red upon the tree canopy. It was the time of the Gloom elves, and for better or worse, she was prepared to meet them.

Ven halted suddenly and crouched low, throwing his hand up to stay his companions. Onstera noticed the Chipmunk crawl up his arm and hide in the folds of Ven's cloak. She thought she could hear soft voices in the distance—no, not voices, a single voice. Loud and proud, insistently speaking to another but receiving no reply. Then as quickly as she heard it, it stopped.

Ven slowly stood up, looking all around him as he did, raising his arms non-threateningly. Onstera Dentoress looked back and saw the Kintar make the opposite gesture, putting hands to hilts. She gave them a scowl and a harsh shake of her head, sending her platinum hair out wildly.

"We mean no harm. I am Ven Devar and we seek the Gloom elves of Glowen'ashen. We offer an alliance in these unstable times." Ven's voice sounded more assured than it ever had as it rang out among the trees. A gust of wind made the great timbers of the forest creak and moan in reply. He had the unnerving sense that someone was aiming a bolt at him to end his life. Yet, he stood tall and firm through the unease.

From within a large plant that glowed a soft green, a Gloom elf stepped out. Her hair starkly white and her skin a pale midnight blue, dozens upon dozens of intricate and now softly illuminated tattoos aided in her nighttime camouflage.

"I am Wynn Walker, an honorary of the Glowen'ashen people."

"It is a privilege to meet you, Wynn." Ven bowed low as he gave his kindness.

"There is another, in hiding. Why do they not show themselves?" Njor bellowed, glaring at Wynn. The Gloom elf seemed caught off guard by this.

"The one who spoke loud and with equal blunder to giant-kin," Onstera added poignantly.

"He is an outsider, and therefore not important to-"

"-Aolendìr Tardinian, at your service." The ever self- important Solsta Elf bowed with his shoulder cape in hand. He had revealed himself from thin air and immediately struck eye contact with Ven. However, the moment was stolen by Rinya as they burst out laughing.

"Ahh, I thought the Kyst were flamboyant," Rinya said, wiping away a tear of joy. Of course, Aolendìr seemed bothered not at all by this.

"It is true, I do enjoy showmanship," the golden figure said, fixing his waistcoat. "As it just so happens, I too am here to offer the Gloom elves aid in this civil dispute."

"You mean the upcoming war?" Onstera said incredulously when Aolendìr had barely finished speaking.

"Speaking of outsiders, it would I appear I am not alone in that description."

"She is a trusted ally to the Kyst. Her presence here is not on trial." Ven ended that line of questioning before it could gain traction. "If you have not shown yourself to the Kyst rebels, then you have heard of our civil war from the self-proclaimed king and you are not to be trusted."

"I understand your train of thought, however inaccurate," Aolendìr quipped. "Your rainforest is vast; if it were a country and had an elected monarch, it would be the second largest in Litore. I have been hired at no small price to aid the folk who would see Vakar gone, and life as it was, restored." He nodded his head low and softly closed his eyes, lathering his remark in sincerity.

"What are they doing here?" Wynn gestured towards the Kintar. SecondSpirit took a proud step forward.

"We are exiles from Claw Canyon. I tried to change the way the Kintar lived, and was rebuffed. Now we walk beside Ven Devar so we may still have a chance at bettering our home and those within." The impossibly large Kintar was stern in his speech, but acted non-threateningly.

"You walk beside someone who slaughtered his people and hope to do good?" she scoffed.

"Slander," Onstera shot back with surprising malice. "Created by the 'cunning' to better feed his own goals."

Wynn cocked a brow at the unlikely story. Ven keenly caught that and was quick to explain.

"Give it a moment of thought, it is no secret that we used to be like brothers. He used that in his story to underline the betrayal he felt. Or made up, really. I stand the best chance at defeating him, so he turned every coastal elf against me."

"He wasn't even in the forest when it happened. Look." Onstera held her hand out to Wynn, offering her a crinkled piece of parchment. She walked cautiously and snatched it from her silver, pointed nails. "It's all there, the contract my guild received in Iradawnia to collect Ven on their return from ShadowScorn."

"You're a Sanguis Quaesitor?" she asked flatly. Onstera nodded with pride and withdrew a pendant from under her breastplate. A circular ring surrounded by thorns with a hollowed-out centre supported a single drop of blood with an arrow piercing it. The sigil of her guild.

"Then you have my hospitality. Your guild fought beside my ex in the War of a Thousand Dragons."

"I was barely a woman grown then but I remember it well, as all survivors do." Onstera placed her hand over her heart in respect.

"The elders will hand me over to the Moonworms for this, but it would do me ill to turn you away." She looked hard at the two Kintar. "Any mishap or disrespect to my kin, you will not leave our enclave."

Rinya looked at Njor with humour. "Considering we're considered the 'bad guys' we sure have been threatened with death a lot since joining these cavalier elves."

"I assure you, they mean nothing by it," he said, staring at the collected group before turning to Rinya. "Just like you don't."

The chipmunk on Ven crawled onto his shoulder and squeaked joyfully. The hunter chuckled to himself and followed Wynn. Aolendìr stepped out of Ven's path, holding his arm up as if to grant him the right of way. He held his gaze long on Ven as the hunter walked away, wondering just what would he do with this young elf.

CHAPTER TEN

Ocean Bones

Ivan found himself sinking, heavy armour dragging him down to the ocean's bone crushing depths, Horizon's Edge and her crew being pulled down to the blackness below, silhouetted by the light of the surface world. He was falling, falling, falling, until his face hit the hardwood floor of the cabin aboard Tsuni Tal's ship. He groaned slightly and heard the squeaking of a rat under his bed. He righted himself and gripped his jaw in discomfort. He looked around before giving a deep sigh. He could have sworn the ship had sunk during a hurricane. It was so real—the fear, the screams, the feeling of all hope lost. It unnerved him, made him almost sick to his stomach, that he should be in the cabin and not lost on the Noga Sea. On the edge of his bed now, he sighed heavily before cracking his neck and back. He walked over to the door and put his hand on it, for some reason not sure what to expect on the other side. After steeling his nerves, he shoved it open. Fresh salty air and the clear blue sky greeted him.

On the main deck was most of the crew, including the children he had freed so they might be returned home. They were at full mast and the wind tickled his beard; he had found it difficult to maintain it the way he liked out at sea, so he embraced the length. Taking a deep breath, he walked up the stairs to the quarter deck where he found Captain Tsuni. Her red hair was down today, blowing madly in the wind but kept out of her eyes by a wide brimmed hat. She looked at Ivan with a warmer smile than he had ever seen.

"You need a cat," he said casually, leaning against the rail to face her.

"I've always fancied parrots myself." Her smile betrayed her tone.

"You've got rats, cats eat rats. Parrots defecate everywhere. Not ideal in," he didn't finish he sentence, instead motioning around to their limited space.

She looked at him with her almond shaped eyes, gazing deeper than what was apparent on the surface. Captain Tsuni's crew had grown fond of Ivan's company and counsel. He genuinely cared for their wellbeing and that was not lost on them. It had taken her longer to come around, and although she would never admit it, she too enjoyed having him on board. It certainly did not hurt that he threw a seemingly endless wealth at them for their services.

"What's wrong? Surely a veteran such as yourself isn't bothered by a few miscreants."

"Bad dream."

"Do ever you have good ones?" she asked rhetorically, knowing of his troubled past as Arch Paladin to the most powerful and corrupt church in Litore. His facial expression indicated that she had made a good point.

"Sometimes I dream of my daughter." He turned to look over the endless horizon of blue water and bluer sky, imagining the whole world and everything that was going on in the sliver of space where the sky and sea met. In truth, Aunna Moringthorne was not his blood daughter. Those in the Grand Church of Sesara never failed to remind him of that. Yet it was him and his brother who raised Aunna from the time she was a babe till she was a woman grown.

"I didn't know you had one. Where is she now?"

"Doing the Macer's bidding I expect. I didn't say goodbye the way I would have liked. Life often rushes you onward, leaving regrets in the space you recently occupied." He hung his head, weary and aching all over. He was not a young man anymore and life at sea was hard on the bones. "Doesn't matter." He decided he didn't like talking about it, so he quickly changed the topic. "Do you foresee a storm coming?"

She thought about it for a moment. "No, but the weather changes quick this time a year. And the closer we get to Rhogar, the closer we get to the Squally Sea. I expect we'll have little reprieve from the storms then."

"Maybe we should dock in Torn Harbour. I could arrange escort from there to return the kid." Ivan sounded optimistic but he was hiding something, and Tsuni sensed it.

"I'll sail us to the City of Ragos, as you've paid for. I've done it before. I know the waters," she answered with finality.

"We don't need to risk it."

"You paid to go there, we're taking you and the Dragon-blood lad."

"I don't care about the money." It came out harsher than he intended. "I want you and the crew safe. That is what I care about."

"Ivan, I've sailed around the known world three times. I have not seen my third decade in this life. I promise we will be safe." She was not used to being so kind but for some reason, she wanted Ivan to know that she cared. He did not respond to that, however. "Listen, I know since Port Ozos, you've been suffering a crisis of faith-"

"How can there be a crisis of faith when there is no faith. She is dead, the church isn't even reminiscent of what it once was."

Now Tsuni did not care about being kind. "Don't be a fool, the gods cannot die."

"She is dead. You said it yourself, the world has no good left in it."

"You returning these kids to their home is good, Ivan. It might surprise you to find out that as a drunken sailor, I've been wrong before."

Despite himself, Ivan chuckled at that. "You've got the spirit our world needs, Tsuni."

"Has it ever occurred to the pious that it's not religion we need, but each other?" She laid an almost curt look upon him.

"SHIP ON THE HORIZON, HARD STARBOARD CAPTAIN!" A sailor standing with the ShadowScorn in the crow's nest was leaning against the basket shouting down at them. Tsuni left the helm and her first mate, Sereene, grabbed the wheel.

Ivan was beside the captain in an instant, who already had her spyglass out, scanning for a ship. It didn't take long to spot, coming from the coastline.

"Damn." She handed the scope to Ivan then gripped the rail hard, locking her shoulders and hanging her head in contemplation. Ivan could see clearly it was a man-o-war and it flew a blood red flag with a skull wearing a crown, a rapier and flintlock pistol crossed beneath.

"You know this ship," he guessed, judging by her reaction.

"Captain Zerenies Zintos, undisputed Pirate Prince of the seven seas."

"It's twice the size of Horizon's Edge, surely we can out-sail it." Ivan lowered the spyglass and looked at her. Her head still hung low, her face obscured by her dancing hair.

"She's a faster vessel than she looks. And Zintos always keeps at least two pairs of wizards on board, they'll fill his sails with unnatural wind. No one escapes the Pirate Prince."

"How much time do we have?"

"If we dump supplies and cargo, we might stay ahead of them for a day." Tsuni looked across her decks at the crew, all anxiously awaiting orders.

Ivan moved closer. "Go to the Scale Islands, I can fill your sails as well." He could tell that she seemed to doubt him. Even with favourable winds, the Scale Isles were two days out. He planted a firm hand on her shoulder. "I won't fail you." She shot him a grimace his direction before whipping around and shouting orders.

"It's our lives or nothing gals! If we don't need it, overboard with it! To the Scale Isles!" Tsuni punctuated her final statement by throwing the wheel hard to port side. The whole ship lurched, the ropes swayed, and the boat creaked in what sounded like an exhalation of anticipation.

Ivan didn't waste any time in walking down below deck to help gather non-essentials. Only enough food and water to feed the crew for three days was kept; that left belongings, furniture, spare lanterns, oil, grey powder, and anything not nailed down to go over the rails. In a brief moment on the main deck, Ivan paused to watch one of the older crew mates hold a cask of rum a little longer, planting a kiss on the side before throwing it over. She stormed away as if she just lost a loved one. The paladin smiled at that, the wind tousling his hair with their increased speed. Nearly an hour had passed when Ivan climbed the near vertical steps up the quarter deck and to the stern.

"Impossible," he said, mouth agape.

"Might be time for some of that wind you promised," Alaana, the master-at-arms, suggested. Neither of them took their eyes off their doom that had closed nearly half the distance. A single cannon was fired from the pirate; the ball whizzed towards them, then made a grand splash a few dozen metres shy.

"Yeah." The great and revered paladin turned to face the helm, gripping the gold link pendant of Sesara around his neck. He closed his eyes and began to pray. He had never been so full of doubt in his life. The nightmare of last night still rang loud forming notes of doubt—he knew his goddess to be dead. He had cast spells in the recent past but not a one since his fateful meeting with that Keeper of the Balance. Nevertheless, he prayed, and after several moments of white knuckles around his doe and stag-carved pendant, he threw his elbows back and pushed his palms forward.

Captain Tsuni, first mate Sereene, and master-at-arms Alaana all watched with puzzled faces as nothing happened.

"Hmm," Sereene grunted. Ivan did not waiver. With his eyes closed, he once again repeated the prayer. A bead of sweat streaked across his aged forehead as he threw his palms forward once more. He could feel the supernatural rush of wind encompassing his body, yet it did not come forthwith. He could sense the disappointment and excusable stares behind him, but he would not quit so easily. With a booming voice he called upon Sesara, yet nothing followed. He gripped the rail that overlooked the rest of the ship, his rigid arms supporting his otherwise defeated person.

"Ivan?" Tsuni spoke. All he could do was shrug and shake his head, unable to look at them. "Tis alright. They'd be catching us eventually."

"Orders, Captain?" Alaana inquired.

"Nothing left to do but make a deal with the devil." Tsuni gave Sereene a firm nod, so the first mate went to shouting orders for the sails to be lowered.

Ivan turned to face the two hardened women. "I'm sorry, I don't know what's wrong with me."

"Don't go soft now, your help is still required. If we can't buy him off—which is likely seein' as he could kill us all and take whatever he wanted—we may be able to offer our services instead."

"I follow your lead," Ivan answered reverently.

"Shall I hand out the arms?" Alaana asked, referring to the handful of flintlock pistols and the several-dozen cudgels, axes, and cutlasses.

Tsuni nodded before adding, "For self defense only. We do not stand a chance if it's to come to blows between ships. Yet, if Ivan is everything he promised, we may stand a chance hand-to-hand."

Alaana nodded and strode off with the fervor of purpose. Ivan looked at Tsuni with frustrated eyes. "I just proved I am not. What are you thinking?"

"We'll die for sure if it comes to combat, Ivan. But the girls don't need knowin' that. Those kids you saved, I suggest you stand in front of 'em when they board us."

He considered the captain's line of thought and knew it to be a wise one. In particular, the Scorn girl would be of high value to the pirates and Ivan still cut an impressive figure when fully armed and armoured. He nodded and made way to his quarters where he would suit up.

Having dropped sail and left the ship to float, the Pirate Prince quickly came to port side and threw hooked lines at the Horizon's Edge. Ivan stood firm and looked up as the hull was nearly half again the height of their own. After watching a score of curious heads pop over the gunwale to look down upon them, Ivan quickly found the Scorn and instructed her to stay behind him. A gangway was lowered, and for a long moment nothing happened, except the waves slapping between the hulls.

Captain Tsuni waited at the bottom of said gangway for Zerenies, yet it was a strange, almost scholarly type that walked down first. Tsuni bent her brow curiously as the river gnome waddled down the studded stairs. Her feet were planted firmly, for her small stature seemed well built for the bobbing terrain. She wore strange pieces of glass around each eye, held together by a golden frame with Old Elvish filigree. Her long, sand-coloured robes trailed behind her and her soft blue hair was held together in a neat braid. Most curiously, Ivan noted the tome she clutched with both arms, holding tighter and dearer than if it were her own babe.

She stopped in front of Tsuni and asked, "Are you the Captain of the Horizon's Edge?" She pushed the spectacles up her little round nose as she did so.

"I am," Tsuni replied confidently. "Where is Zerenies?"

"Captain of the Ocean Bones, Pirate Prince of the Seven Seas, and Master of his Domain, Zerenies Zintos wishes you to join him in his cabin for supper." The gnome barely made eye contact with Tsuni and wasn't even bothering to look around.

"Who in the Underworld are you?" the fiery redheaded captain asked in sheer frustration.

"I am Tilly Tickletoe, servant to his Prince." Tilly delivered it as someone beleaguered by her station, not proud.

"If you bring me the first mate of Zerenies, I will join him. That way we can ensure a good exchange of hostages. And if you lie to me and bring me not his first mate, but a lowly sailor," Tsuni motioned to Ivan, "he will know."

Tilly bowed and deftly made her way back up the gangway. Ivan moved uncomfortably as he counted nearly forty pirates all casually leaning overboard, staring at Tsuni's crew like their next meal. Ivan found a resolve in that moment that he had not known for many, many years. The crew he had come to care for was comprised entirely of women. He did not care if it meant his own death, he would not let this band of cutthroats and thieves have their way with them.

He was torn from his contemplation by a large, dark-skinned man wearing nothing but billowing linen pants and an open-breasted leather jerkin. To tie it all in, a flintlock pistol on a bandoleer crossed his bare chest. His footsteps were marked by resounding thuds as the planks bent under his weight. He looked down on Captain Tsuni with a knowing smile before allowing himself to be cuffed by Sereene.

"Cut his throat at the first sign of trouble. You have the ship if I fail to return, but trust Ivan's advice—he's more experienced than any of us." Tsuni clasped Sereene's arm before walking aboard the Ocean Bones. She did not show it, but her heart pounded, and worry grew heavy as she knew there to be nearly two hundred in this crew. They cat called her and made lewd gestures as she followed Tilly, and those who didn't looked upon her with stark souls and hollow eyes. She could not be bothered by any of this, keeping her attention on what lay before her. Tilly swept to the side as they met an ornate door with the Prince's flag carved upon it. Tsuni did not wait for any more ceremony and wanted to show the crew she was not an easy target. She threw the ornate door open and slammed it behind her.

She found a surprisingly restrained interior, but a lavish meal spread across the entire wooden table. On one side sat the Pirate Prince, his leather cuffed boots elevated comfortably. He wore a bright-white, wide-sleeved button-down shirt with a turquoise silk scarf. His curls were vivacious brown and his beard thick and red. It irritated Tsuni to admit that he was brilliantly handsome; a dashing scar across his left eye completed it all. She was, however, aghast to see he was barely twenty-five years of age, which meant she was nearly five his senior. He held out his hand for her to sit across from him, a golden plate and silver goblet awaiting her.

She sat down but showed no interest in what sat before her. "Prince."

"Captain Tsuni Tal, it does me hart warm to see yer in command of a fine vessel such as ye are."

Her face screwed up at that. "What's yer meanin?" Her harsh and poor accent came through as it always did when back among pirates.

"Ye wound me, nearin' fifteen years ago now we sailed a short while together. Under Captain René aboard The Seafoam. True to say I was just a lad at the time but I had big eyes for the 'red maiden'." He smiled, taking a gulp of from his goblet and she winced at the reminder of the nickname.

"What can I do for ye? Surely ye coulda swamped me ship and plundered without effort."

"To be true it was me intent upon sighting ye. She's a fine vessel ye have, could be a sleek addition to me armada."

"And yet here we be breakin' bread." Tsuni hated dancing around an answer, it was her direct personality that made her a great leader.

"Ye be headin' to Rhogar, aye," Zerenies said as if he knew it for fact.

Tsuni looked at him suspiciously. "Aye."

"Good. King Dusanith has his whole fleet looking for me flag. I've cargo needin' delivering."

"The cargo?"

"A few folk the lads captured outside Serenstrom. Lined up a buyer with especially deep pockets."

"They be?" she demanded.

"Why the interest?" He planted his feet firmly on the floor now and eyed her curiously. Tsuni smelled the spicy rum in her goblet and finally tasted it. It was rich and warm and despite her best effort not too, she downed the rest in one gulp.

"Me reputation does not precede past the rails of the Horizon as yer's does. Me gals deserve an honest life, we may smuggle when the coin begs, but I draw that line at trafficking humans."

Zerenies laughed as he filled their drinks anew. "Fear not then for yar fellow human, it's dwarves we be sellin."

She adjusted her floppy and wide brimmed hat. "There must be something else."

Lifting the silver rimmed cup to his lips, he looked at her with lustful eyes.

"Show 'em to me," she snarled.

Ivan never took his eyes off the first mate of the pirate prince until he felt a tapping on his pauldron. Turning, he saw the Scorn girl, right where he instructed her to be. "Captain's been gone a long while."

"She'll be okay, patience and solid nerves are our greatest ally in these situations." He placed a warm smile on the girl, whose eyes were pure black with bright white pupils.

"Don't worry little girl, you'll have everyone aboard that ship to keep yar company real soon." The first mate laughed heartily at his own crudeness. Ivan saw the visible horror on the Scorn's face before he turned to square up with the pirate. The burly human stood a head higher than Ivan, but that mattered nothing to this veteran.

"Try and scare her again, and it'll be the last thing you do," Ivan said with a coldness he had lost touch with since his active-duty days. It surprised him to react this way but for too long did he stand by to those who might oppress or rule through fear.

"Ivan," Sereene said to put him back in line.

"Best listen to yer bitch." Not a heartbeat later, Sereene punched the pirate so hard in the mouth he spat out a tooth. The first mate slowly turned back and gave them all a bloody grin in return. The tension was cut as they turned to face the gangway to see Captain Tsuni returning. Shortly after appeared Tilly Tickletoe and the four dwarves, each clad in irons.

"What is this?" Alaana asked, alluding to the prisoners boarding.

"Our way out, " Tsuni replied without enthusiasm. The first mate held his bulging forearms out, the chains clinking. Tsuni nodded to Alaana to set him free. She did so, glaring him down as she unlocked his cuffs.

"Be see'n ye real soon ol' man," he said with a great smile, shooting the Scorn a wink before walking back up to his ship. Ivan wasted no time in questioning Tsuni.

"What are we doing with them?"

She eyed Tilly, still clutching her tome and standing nearby. "Delivering them to the City of Ragos." Ivan didn't take his eyes off her as a dozen pirates came aboard, reluctantly dropping crates of supplies haphazardly on the deck. Tsuni didn't look away from Ivan and her stare said it all, so Ivan let it go.

"Let us set sail, Captain," Tilly stated, adjusting her spectacles once again. Tsuni looked down at the gnome. "The prince has sent me to ensure you fulfill your end of the bargain."

The fiery captain rolled her eyes in frustration before impatiently barking orders to get them on the way again.

CHAPTER ELEVEN

Trickery and Lies

Vakar was sitting in his large circular study, as he did so often of late. After the reconstruction of Silva and the abduction of Scáth, this King of Kyst had barely ventured outside his comforts. He had grown obsessed with the crystal orb that allowed him to spy on anyone, anywhere in the world. It had revealed much to him, not least of which was Ven trotting through the forest, gathering allies to fight him and his new kingdom.

He did not trust in his new servant, the Solsta elf Aolendìr, but he did trust in the coin and magical artifacts that bought his service. From everything Vakar had heard of his reputation, once he was bought, he would complete the task without err.

So Vakar turned his mind to another problem—he was drowning in those of late. This one was due to the overwhelming difficulty they were having in keeping Scáth locked up; she was growing exponentially powerful. This brought back the conversation he had shared with Aolendìr about being demi-gods, and that his orb was one of twelve artifacts put on Litore. If Scáth really was Grimìr, then was she even containable? If Aolendìr was to be believed, then Vakar himself was chosen of Zeries—but why? He had always been faithful to his gods of Land and Sea, more so the latter he knew. He rarely gave Zeries a thought, and when he did it was out of insult or disgust for his domain. Yet, what little research had turned up about the god of lies and trickery referenced several moments in time where a stone pillar, translucent orb, and rose appeared. If this Solsta elf was a chosen himself, it would surely explain his prowess and reputation. Which meant he had goals outside of collecting coin. So what were those goals exactly? He had exhausted the libraries of the north regarding demi-gods, he himself at a loss. With little else to go on and needing to learn more about what it meant to be Grimìr, he decided to pay Scáth a visit.

He now had two sages and two hunters stationed outside the Scorn's cell at all times. She had lured one sage in and convinced him to set her free; how she accomplished this was still anyone's guess. On a separate occasion, she managed to conjure enough shadow from within herself to blot out the shield of light surrounding her and pass through it. As he approached and opened the door, he did not pay his guards heed. It took him a moment to adjust to the blinding light within her cell, at first holding his hand above his eyes to better see his prisoner. She sat in the middle of the hollow beam of light, legs crossed and in deep meditation. Her mouth was gagged and her arms tied behind her back, so Vakar waved his hand and the gag dematerialized. She opened her eyes which under normal circumstances looked like miniature hurricanes of swirling shadow, but now appeared aged and cloudy with cataracts.

"You've actually punished yourself more than I have. Is this some tactic to have control over when and how you'll be dealt with?" Vakar inquired as he conjured a chair to sit on. She looked at him, weak and frail. The near cycle of blinding light starved her of any darkness that allowed the shadow within her to recharge. "Doesn't matter," he said without giving her the chance to speak. "I actually commend your efforts. Did you know, many wild animals would gnaw their own foot off if it were caught in a trap. Unlike those in Serenstrom, I can't pretend like I am ignorant enough to believe you ShadowScorn are little more than animals, but I am curious to see how far you will go to be free. Given the natural sore spot it is for you and your kind, I expect you will go further than most."

"What would you like from me?" Her voice was flat, though she meant it to be harsher.

Vakar feigned a smile. "What do you know of the gods?"

"Plenty."

"Of just Aceia or the others as well?"

Her heart skipped a beat hearing Aceia's name spoken aloud. "All twelve and the known Powers. I am twice your age and spent most of that time locked in a castle. Don't pretend to be the only learned person here."

"Understood," he confessed. "In all your studies, what have you read about the Grimìr?"

Now it was making sense to Scáth, for Aolendìr had warned her that Vakar was like 'them', and at the time she didn't exactly know what it meant. However, she had nothing but time to reflect and contemplate while imprisoned. Although her dream by the black tree in the City of Shadow with her brother was fresh in her mind, she didn't believe—nor want to—that she was the daughter of Aceia. Aolendìr had almost insisted it was the truth and now with Vakar prying for related information, it really did appear the gods had each placed a chosen or child upon Litore.

"It is nearly impossible to decipher what was truth and what was legend. It has been theorized that the gods have had hundreds, if not thousands, of chosen or children throughout history. There are tales of many great heroes and villains that *do* the impossible, feats and atrocities that would be unimaginable to average folk."

"Surely with enough digging, one could separate truth from fairytale. And surely, is legend not derived from reality?" He almost leaned forward he was so intrigued by the possibility.

"You can't possibly believe that you might be one?" She laid the most skeptical and dismissive stare she could upon him. She did not want him finding out the truth that at least Aolendìr believed for as long as possible.

"I said nothing of myself. But, if I held the Daughter of Shadow in my grasp, well the possibilities are endless. You know, the Church of Sesara has some most impressive knowledge on mental conditioning."

Scáth knew this very well, as Agan had spent a decade as a brainwashed attack dog for the corrupt rulers in Serenstrom.

"You've got bigger things to worry about than me," she trilled.

"Like what?" he sneered at her light-hearted mockery.

"Your closest allies already lose faith in your leadership. A civil war is apparent. And you're so incapable of dealing with Ven yourself, you commit the most atrocious magic known to this world and resurrect Rexous. You've even turned to hiring outsiders to do your work for you. As daughter to a truly benevolent ruler, I can say you make a poorly king." She seemed all but interested in his plights; this surprised Vakar, as he would have guessed his troubles would have pleased her. "Why you took me just to add to your struggles is beyond my understanding. For we both know, my companions and the rebel Kyst would never let him come."

"You presume to know him better than I?"

"I do." Scáth was resolute in this, which left Vakar sitting with his thoughts for a long while. His initial reaction was anger fuelled by jealousy, but he didn't like that.

"Perhaps you do, I fear neither of us knew each other as well as we might have thought. However, you serve a higher purpose in my kingdom than mere bait." Vakar couldn't hide his sinister feelings. For the first time in this conversation, Scáth felt the upper hand slip away. "What you said earlier was true, those in my newly formed kingdom are already feeling a certain discomfort. I imagine those new to being ruled all act the same. So what could be better for morale and earning trust from the common folk than offering them the catalyst that set all this in motion."

Scáth's heart sank. "I don't believe you," she lied.

"I had hoped against hope Ven may come, but you're right. He's off having adventures once again, with a new lass, not thinking of you at all."

"You just spoke of the endless possibilities of having me at your disposal. You can't do that if you feed me to an angry mob." She was trying to remain calm by sounding out why he needed her.

Vakar nodded slowly. "But, if you've taught me anything since your captivity, you may be the strongest willed person I've ever met. I do not believe even Nuada, Power of the Underworld, could control you, but I say let's give her a chance." Vakar stood from his chair, which dissipated as he did. "I understand now what Ven saw in you. I am sorry, not for his sake but for yours, that it must end this way, after all you endured."

It was the sincerest apology she had ever received, and that left her speechless.

Vakar strode through the great royal tree, making his way up the wide, smooth spiral walkway. He kept his hands locked behind his back, stalled in a contemplation that left him oblivious to his surroundings until his keen hearing heard tempered voices. He paused a moment as he recognized the angered voice of Eevie coming from a door slightly ajar. A soft orange hue spilled through the door-jam. He touched the artifact pendant of Silva around his neck and became completely invisible. Slipping through the doorway, he found Eevie, Rexous, and Pine arguing around a live-edge arbutus table. The orange light was the product of an illusionary fire that covered the tabletop.

Rexous eyed the slight movement from the door. Vakar sensed this and thought he had already erred, but when Rexous got up, he slipped by the formidable hunter and stood in the corner of the room. Rexous gave the door a firm slam.

"Rex, you're living proof he has gone mad," Eevie said angrily.

"Many wizards, sages, and scholars have performed the Resurrection Spell, and many of them were not mad," Pine quickly interjected.

"Of course you think it is okay, the pursuit of knowledge has rarely kept your kind from indirectly inflicting harm." Her malice somehow undercut the validity of the comment.

"Vakar has always been sweet and possessed of an unequivocal intellect. It used to drive me insane, however, now his heart has grown cold and ever more cunning. I'm glad he killed his softness—he'll rule more effectively," Rexous stated, staring at the magical, heatless flame dancing between them.

"Has everyone lost their sanity? He committed genocide and tore you from the afterlife! Your mother will be remembered as one of the greats in our history, how can you see him as an 'effective' ruler!" Eevie felt like screaming.

Rexous laid his heavy red eyes upon his female counterpart. "I hate him more than I've hated anyone. I do admire him; he's done the unthinkable in just one season."

Eevie scoffed before going to grab another flagon of wine. Vakar quickly moved out of the way as he spotted the wine beside him. Eevie paused and looked suspiciously at the empty space as the air moved around her. She lost her concentration when Rexous continued to speak. "I begged my mother to kill the Kintar of Claw Canyon. She refused, and paid the ultimate price."

"Along with nearly 5,000 Kyst," Pine added.

"He has brought peace to the greatest forest in Litore. At terrific cost, I do admit Eevie." He eyed her again as she sat back down, filling her cup. "Greatness demands great sacrifice," he said with heavy words before dropping his stare back into the centre of the table.

"Unbelievable. You already had the chance to kill Ven Devar twice in recent memory, and you failed. Vakar wasted time and effort in bringing you back. Things that could have been spent on bettering the kingdom he created through nothing but bloodshed and harassment," she answered brusquely.

"Rex is the greatest hunter in the north," Pine said to Eevie, both to get under her skin but also because many still believed that to be true.

"I would have thought that title went to the hunter who killed him outright?"

"It would be most unfortunate if our king was to hear you now," Pine added with an air of preeminence.

"Anything I've said here I would gladly say to his face. Unlike you cowards," Eevie retorted. Vakar grinned at that, knowing she spoke true.

"The five of us grew up together. We weren't all on even terms, but we do know each other." For once, Eevie was interested to hear what Pine was saying. "If I had to guess, Vakar doesn't think himself capable of killing Ven. Rexous either isn't skilled enough, which I doubt, or he won't do it. Which in turn, leaves you and I." Pine never lifted his gaze from her. "Despite all that has been said, your infatuation with the traitor has not gone unnoticed."

Eevie scowled at that, knowing Pine referred to the fondness she held for Ven growing up.

"That is hardly relevant. Any feelings I harboured for him died out when he betrayed the Kyst and slaughtered them up and down the coast."

Rexous moved slightly and Vakar's heart rate spiked some. In truth, it was still only he who knew Rexous was the one portraying Ven Devar, yet he knew the knowledge would breathe in the minds of others eventually. Pine laughed heartily and went to pour more wine to distract himself from the humour he found in her words.

"You're the general to Vakar's armies, so you're not stupid. Perhaps the love you once held for Ven has soured into blind hatred and that is why you do not see the obvious." Pine sounded like a petulant sibling. Eevie's delicate elven features furrowed in confusion. So the Supreme Sage looked to Rex. "Should I tell her, or you?"

The former prince was redder than usual, his eyes had yet to flash more since his revival.

"Before you consider thrusting your dirk through my heart, I'm wearing more protection charms than even you could penetrate," Pine said smugly. Rexous was weighing his options when Eevie looked hatefully at him.

"Say it," she demanded. Rexous gave a quick expression akin to doing a chore.

"I killed those Kyst. When Silva fell, I lost control, I wanted revenge. It was Uthul who found me and laid the seeds of death in my heart. So I poisoned Ven's name while getting close to my father." He noted the predictable look of shock on both their faces when he admitted Uthul had been his father. "So when he trusted me, I killed him. With nothing left to lose I found Ven and died peacefully knowing he died alongside me." Rexous shrugged during the stunned silence. "You can imagine my dismay to find out he lived when I did not."

Eevie sat there, tears threatening to stream freely. She closed her hazel eyes and shook her head in denial. "And Vakar knows this?"

"He does." Pine answered when Rex remained still and silent.

"Who are you two." There was quiet in the room, until her chair legs scrapped across the wooden floor and she stood. Rexous thought she would kill him, and by all means he meant to let her. He nearly begged it of her, but she walked away before he found the courage. Vakar watched her leave; he hated himself seeing Eevie this way, so hurt and lost, and he still felt less than he should. He turned his attention back on the two still remaining.

"I admire you." Pine broke the silence like a window shattering in the dead of night. "Much like how you admire Vakar, I think. You sold your soul for something you believed in."

Rexous looked at him for a heavy moment. If Pine's life depended on it, he would not have been able to guess what Rex was thinking.

"To the Underworld with your admiration." He got up to loom over the small sage. "For future reference, no amount of magical protection will keep my blade from your heart, if that is my wish." With no emotion but the venomous threat, he departed the room. Pine sat there for a long while mulling over the conversation, drinking his wine periodically as the jumble of possibilities and concerns washed over him.

Vakar left the room through the door Rexous left wide open and stood in the long, slightly curving hall, pondering his next step. The smallest seed of fear took root in his mind as he thought of what this revelation might mean for Eevie's allegiance. He counted on her to lead his army of hunters. They did not at first take to such a young hunter being appointed general, but she quickly won the respect of any doubters. However, that all undoubtedly hung in the balance of the next few hours. So he decided he needed to dig deep and find whatever compassion he had left in him, and convince his once sister-in-law to stay by his side.

Having dropped his invisibility, Vakar strode through the throne room and out into the midnight air. Silva was built so high into the kilometre-tall trees that it was front row to the celestial heavens. Bathed in red moonlight from Caelestis, he promptly made his way to Eevie's tree house. There were several kinds of structures in Silva and her house was built in a circular shape, tucked tightly between the trunk and one of its many colossal branches. Walking a small bridge that connected her own tree to the rest of Silva, Vakar knocked on the oval shaped door. It was embossed with a detailed image of two Kyst peering through the foliage mid-hunt to watch their prey.

After another knock went unheard or ignored. He walked along a wrap-around deck that offered an unobstructed view of the lush green forest surrounding the house. He stopped to peer through a wicker window where he saw her, laying on the ground, knees tucked up to her chest, shoulders bobbing followed by gasps of crying. She was leaning against her bed, holding an oil painting of her and her brother, Qiri. Vakar was familiar with the painting; she had managed to save it in the tumult the night Silva burned. On more than one occasion, he had come over just to look at the remarkable life-like painting of his true love. After a while, it had become too painful to stare at anymore, the more alone he became the less he could handle looking at how happy Qiri had been. All he could imagine now was his handsome face beneath the ground, being eaten by grave worms and swelling up before collapsing under the weight of its own decay.

Vakar suddenly felt like he shouldn't be intruding and made to leave. His shift of weight creaked the wood and Eevie shot her gaze towards the sound.

"What are you doing?" she sniffled, although Vakar thought she still somehow sounded threatening. He paused, feeling stupid, before turning back to the window.

"I don't really know," he admitted. She huffed in frustration before standing up.

"Come on, I picked some fresh tea leaves this morning." She left her bedroom and Vakar stood outside, feeling like the adolescent elf that he was for the first time since that fiery nightmare incarnate. He took a step to the right as if to go through the double-wide back doors, then quickly thought better of it and went left, to use the front door again.

He found it open this time and Eevie was putting a kettle on the wood burning stove. "Get the lamps, would ya?" She spoke softer this time and Vakar simply snapped his fingers and every oil-burning lamp in the spacious living room burst into life. It was so cozy he thought, even more so than he remembered it being. Beautiful hand carved furniture filled the room, and a large carpet woven from reeds patterned an elaborate arbutus tree across most of the floor. Many pumasheep wool blankets, dyed bright colours, were draped over various surfaces, offering a softness to the otherwise hardwood interior. Vakar sat down on a tall chair at a small circular table. It sat four comfortably, and he remembered the Hara family all scooting in closer to one another when he was graciously invited for dinner. Qiri and Eevie's parents were always so welcoming to Vakar. Always making sure he had plenty of dessert to take back to his empty home after departing for the night. They had done a remarkable job in reconstructing the burnt home to its former glory, but it lacked a certain familiarity. Especially seeing how weird it was for Eevie to be living here all by herself; no parents, no big brother, just memories to keep her company.

His roaming eyes saw the oil-painting back on the wall and he quickly averted his line of sight just as Eevie came and slid a steaming cup of tea in front of him. They didn't say much at first, but it became apparent that she was glaring those big hazel eyes at him.

"You can say it," he said flatly.

"How could you? You knew it was Rex, not Ven, and you used that to your own advantage."

"I used it to everyone's advantage. Our people are safe, unified for the first time since the First Age. What does it matter who was blamed for it? Rex and Ven are both equally guilty of heinous crimes," he spoke calmly, hoping it would rub off on her.

"Ven did nothing wrong. You know I've been in love with him since I knew what love was. And you let him take the fall anyway." The tears collected around her lashes again, but she fought them off.

"He brought that Scorn into our home and we all suffered the consequence."

"He did the right thing." Eevie would not let him say otherwise. Vakar said nothing, understanding they would not settle the debate here and now — or likely ever.

"Do you still love him?" he asked, a little more macabre than he wanted. Her face screwed up in anger and she looked away.

"You brought a serial killer back to our home, a traitor, and had us working alongside him. How could you ever think that was okay?" She turned the questioning back on him.

"It's not okay, Eevie," he looked hard at her. "It's necessary."

"For what?" she snapped.

"He's capable of more than any hunter. The only one who ever stood a chance at matching Ven's skill."

"He can't defeat Ven and even if he could, he won't. You've turned him against you the moment you brought him back to life."

"You're right. Rexous hates me but I know for a damned fact there is one elf he hates more," Vakar replied in a tone of finality. Eevie leaned back in her chair and sipped her tea. Vakar pushed his cup away and moved to get up but stopped himself to say, "Since you're going to find out sooner than later, Scáth is to be publicly executed."

Eevie looked at him without an ounce of surprise. "Nothing like a public execution to bring people together."

Vakar couldn't remember anyone looking so disappointed in him before. Deciding he had had enough of being lectured, he made his final statement.

"Good. Then you can be the one who swings the blade." He could tell the hatred in her eyes was at a boiling point. "Thank you for the tea," he said before quickly making his exit.

* * *

Vakar made his way back into his chambers at the top of the royal tree, wondering when exactly he lost the ability to feel anything more than the grumble of his stomach. He considered that perhaps he and Rexous shared more in common than what met the eye. That bothered him for some reason, which as always of late, pushed him towards his work. He had unified the northern Kyst, then successfully culled the Kintar. Now he had to bring stability to his kingdom and crush these rebels. With Scáth's execution being planned, he decided to check in on his new spy and see if he had found Ven yet.

He walked over to his crystal ball and focused his mind's eye on Aolendìr Tardinian. The image inside the orb began soaring through the forest, whipping through the trees like a racing riverraven. Soon the image burst through the foliage and continued to cross the open ocean. Vakar darted his vision as quickly as he could to try and spot any landmarks as to where it was taking him. An island quickly came into view and he recognized the city as Green Wave. The world's largest waterfall poured from the tropical rainforest above, straight into Kaia's Sea. The city of Green Wave itself was built neatly behind the massive falls in a large, open rock shelf. The image did not stop however; it kept going with greater haste straight into the waterfall, the moisture literally condensing on the outside of the crystal orb. The image then shot down, directly down, into the turbulent mixture of fresh and salt water. Down and down it went, the whitewash finally giving way to calm green waters in a tight tunnel system. Vakar knew now —this orb was not showing him Aolendìr or Ven. Soon the image burst through the surface of the water and there was darkness. Only darkness. He waved his hand trying to control the image past whatever was blocking the view, but only blackness was found.

Then a sinister voice rang inside his head, "Find me to find your destiny."

CHAPTER TWELVE

Redwillow

Their cart rolled through several billowing, red weeping willows that had tunnel-like paths cut through the vines, offering shade from the sun and a sense of being at one with nature.

"Like old times, huh?" Agan quietly said to Kithlyn as their cart bumped along the dirt and stone road into Redwillow. Kithlyn didn't say anything but her whole body breathed in the fresh air, and her ears took in the sound of running water as River Routh slowly flowed along to her left; it even branched off to a form a couple of small creeks that ran through the town itself. Redwillow wasn't home to more than a few thousand folk, mostly miners that worked in the iron mine and farmers that cultivated the rich land around them, although it did have a boom during and after the War of a Thousand Dragons. The citizens here seemed relaxed and jovial, far more than most places in Litore and it was the world-famous Willow Guild they had to thank for that.

Scarlet drove the cart through the town square where Agan and Kithlyn received emphatic waves from two halfings sitting on a wide wrap-around porch under a sign that read 'The Saddle Inn.' Kithlyn averted her gaze from the kind gesture, but the burly half-orc nodded with a slight smile. He recognized the male halfling with his shaggy brown hair as the purveyor and owner, Oin Bumblebottom. He wasn't sure if Oin recognized them from their brief stay in his inn over a decade ago, but he thought the halfling looked older and wiser, however no less enthusiastic about life.

They passed a statue in the square that once showcased the founder and explorer of Redwillow, Routh FineEye. Its plinth now held five statues of the Willow Guild, with his dear friend and Guild Master, Nordhum Ironboot, front and centre. He felt a sense of pride overcome him, knowing all that the guild went through to help bring an end to the War of a Thousand Dragons. It was quickly replaced with guilt, as he was coming here not as an old friend looking to visit, but because he needed something.

Right before crossing a bridge that spanned a small creek, Scarlet took a right turn down a smaller road. It quickly spat them out at the entrance to the Church of Pirelia, Goddess of Fire, Birth, and Renewal. Agan looked to his right across a small meadow and saw the Guild Hall. "I have no interest in your domain," Agan said leaping down. "Meet us at the hall." He offered his hand to Kithlyn, more out of reflex, being so used to travelling with Scáth. She promptly swatted his hand away and jumped down.

"You're getting soft," she mumbled, not caring for his kindness.

"I'll attend shortly," Scarlet answered while assisting her priestess Serene inside.

The veteran and assassin began the short trek to the hall. Agan was lost in a flood of memories; since his decade of brainwashing and the subsequent amnesia being lifted during the Siege of Shadow, things from his prior life had been slowly returning to him. It took smells, sounds, and familiar sights to trigger them, and being back here opened the floodgate.

"I promised myself I'd never return, you know," Kithlyn spoke up, a little less closed off than she had been since their recent reunion.

"Yeah." He didn't know that, but he completely understood. As they neared, the great three-story hall loomed over them, with the guard tower in the back right corner being the tallest structure in sight. They heard the creaking of chain links in the wind as a metal sign slowly swayed in the spring breeze. The top half was molded to look like a weeping willow tree while the bottom formed the trunk and read '*Willow Guild.*'

As they approached the wide sheltered porch, relief flooded Agan as he spotted a middle-aged dwarf wearing a chest plate of pure iradinium, sitting with his feet raised on the handrail and a foamy tankard resting on his round belly. The two of them stopped at the first step of the porch and realized Nordhum was fast asleep, his snores bellowing out like a bisonbear. His thick brown and braided beard fluttered with his breath, the two-horned crown sat crooked on his brow in his slumber.

Agan and Kithlyn shared a rare look and smile at each other. Agan walked the few stairs and dragged a chair beside the dwarf. Sitting down and chuckling at the fact Nordhum was still sleeping, he relaxed for the first time in recent memory.

"I'm gonna get a drink, hopefully Snark is still running the bar." Kithlyn passed them both and went inside. Agan threw his feet up on the handrail beside Nordhum's and watched the town go about its business. He saw Faenla walking around, sniffing the thick grass before flopping onto his wide back and rolling around without a care. A curious thought struck him then; he wondered if perhaps, sooner than later, he might want to settle down. It never appeared like an option to him before, but maybe after he helped rescue Scáth, laid Athvar to rest, and helped Ven settle his business, it could be. He wasn't particularly old, but after the life he lived, he certainly felt it.

"Good to see ya, ol'friend."

Agan turned his head to see Nordhum hadn't moved a muscle or opened his eyes.

"Your eyes are closed," Agan said with a chuckle.

"Aye," Nordhum responded with a smile and threw his arm out, offering the tankard.

The half-orc drank it in earnest and wiped the foam away from his lips. "Life seems good here, Nordhum."

"Oh, it is. Little else than Ferals and Siphons given us trouble these days." Ironboot turned his brown and experienced eyes on Agan now. "You look good, if not a wee bit grumpier."

Agan just grumbled which, after a quiet moment, brought them both to laughter.

"I'm glad to see ya Dusk, truly. But I've only known ya to carry trouble on your shoulders."

Agan nodded. "I know. I think my troubles this time might be everyone's I'm afraid. If it's any consolation, it wasn't my idea to come here and burden you."

"Aye, but we needed the Shadow Mistress. Shouldn't have been surprised to see you with her." Nordhum pulled his gaze back over the town as a great shadow flew with blinding speed. Agan quickly recognized the shadow and its huge wings.

"She's still here?" Agan asked, as Faenla leapt up with lightening grace and ran under the safety of the porch, skidding next to the pair.

"Oh yes, she grew her own small forest at first, but it didn't take long before it covered a couple square hundred kilometres or so."

"She doesn't cause any problems?" Agan asked, peeking his head out over the handrail trying to get a glimpse but she had already soared far away.

"On the contrary. The folk of Redwillow love her and she them. Willow patrols for hundreds of kilometres in every direction, the land is far safer with her around."

"You really turned the region into something special, Ironboot. I congratulate you." Agan looked around for a few moments and asked, "Is Aodhan still mayor?" Before Nordhum could answer, Agan turned his head at the sound of running footsteps from inside.

"The family is bigger than ever," Nordhum said as a small dwarf burst through the doors, chased by a tall Gloom elf, with stark white hair and covered from head to toe in nature themed tattoos. Agan's heart skipped a beat.

"You can't get me Aunty, Da will get you first!" The dwarf lad had brown hair and a stout frame like his dad but starry eyes like his mother and aunty. He jumped into Nordhum's lap before abashedly realizing there was a stranger here.

"Thron, that's not how we introduce ourselves, is it? This is an ol'friend of Da's." When Thron refused to pull his head from Nordhum's bushy beard, he whispered, "He looks scary, but he's softer than Aunty Faye and funnier than Uncle Krans."

Agan shot Faye Walker a curious look. She was leaning against the chair that supported Nordhum and her nephew; her eyes still appeared like galaxies and her smile was as warm as ever. Agan looked back to Thron who was now staring him down. Thron's eyes were still star filled but brown in colour, and his skin was a far paler blue than traditional for Gloom elves.

"Hiya, mister."

Agan fumbled for the right words as children were really, really not his forte. "Hi."

"Do you like magic?" Thron's voice got notably more excited.

"I do." That wasn't true at all, Agan hated the unpredictability of magic but saying 'no' felt wrong. The kid gave a wide smile and vanished from Nordhum's lap, only to reappear on Faye's shoulders.

"Watch it, kid!" Faye mocked frustration as she tickled his legs wrapped firmly around her shoulders. Agan looked at Nordhum in surprise.

"That's made parenting difficult," the guild master admitted light heartily.

"Can I pet your doggy?" Thron asked exuberantly.

Agan was surprised by this for some reason; perhaps because Faenla was as tall as anyone here, or because Thron wasn't scared. He quickly looked to Faenla who was sitting politely. He nodded and Nordhum's son jumped down from Faye and ran up to the enormous wolf. Faenla was twice the height of him, so he slid down on his elbows to rest on his belly. Thron laughed and hugged the wolf tightly. It was a rather heartwarming sight for everyone, that was abruptly interrupted.

"I see you've all caught up." Scarlet's voice snapped and popped like burning wood.

"Still plenty of that left to do," Faye answered. "Go and find Krans, help him with the animals." Thron rolled his eyes and stomped his foot. "Hey now, keep that sass for you Da." Faye thought for a second before adding, "Or Snark." She tousled his thick mop of hair and shoved him off.

"Only if I can take Luna." The tiny half-dwarf demanded he take Faye's spiritual companion, an Ammin of the Care Taker. A small, ankle-height creature appeared as if from a heat wave. From what Agan could tell, it was mimicking Faye as it looked like a little moving celestial body. He and Luna ran off the porch and went around the corner to the stables.

"He can see Ammins?"

"We're not sure why. He hasn't suffered any personal lost or bared witnessed to unnatural death," Faye answered.

"He's special," Scarlet chimed in.

Agan was starting to have second thoughts about coming here.

Perhaps he should have been more demanding in returning to the north—Scáth's predicament was time sensitive after all—and seeing the simple and happy life the Willow Guild had carved out for themselves, the last thing he wanted was to encourage any behaviour that would risk that.

"Let's go inside." Nordhum slapped Agan's shoulder and moved indoors. Agan watched as Scarlet followed but Faye remained behind, holding her gaze on him. He wasn't sure at first if she felt hostile towards him, until she moved up to him, squaring herself up. Her whole frame fit within his massive shoulders and torso. She ever so gently wrapped her arms around his body and hugged him tightly. Her condition left her skin cold against his, and her strength far surpassed his own.

"It's good to see you," her voice reverberated across his body, and after several breathes of hesitation, he hugged her back.

"You're the least gloomy Gloom elf I've met you know." He held her shoulders so he could look at her.

"We're all originals, might as well act like it." She punched him hard in the shoulder. "I haven't lost my edge though." Spinning on her heel she waved him to follow. As he walked indoors, it was just as he remembered, although things felt newer.

Two large suits of animated armour stood as sentry's, flanking either side of the entrance in the foyer. There were six ornate thrones positioned around an impeccably carved map in the floor. It detailed Litore's biggest cities, structures, and landmarks on a massive and accurate scale.

He looked around and to his left was Nordhum's smithy shop, to his right was the office of one Valoris Rhoshal, an Elemenzian monk, though Agan hadn't seen him here yet. In front of him was a beautiful courtyard filled with wildflowers, benches, and a great red weeping willow tree. On either side of the courtyard was a hallway that led to the back of the guild hall proper. In the right hallway was Faye Walker's infirmary, where she healed sick citizens and brewed potions and salves, among other things.

The left hallway had an entrance to the barn where Snark's twin brother Krans kept their horses and livestock.

In the back was a small tavern and kitchen, run by none other than Snark himself, a goblin with more piercings than Agan had ever seen on any living creature, adorned in a fine black frock coat. On one side of the tavern was a shop that used to be run by a particular Templar of Lokor, Corpsepaint, who Agan had respected more than most in his travels, and the other side acted as a shared space for the various friends and members of the guild.

Agan, once again, couldn't suppress a smile as Kithlyn was having her ear filled by the squeaking voice of Krans who, unlike his twin, had been kicked in the head a few too many times by his animal companions. He wore bulbous goggles and a worn-out vest with puffy pants.

"Ehhh, Mista Dusk, what a pleasure to have you back in the ol'hall." Agan looked down to see Snark holding up a tankard.

"Thank you, Snark. Glad to see you're keeping things in line around here." He grabbed the tankard and suddenly his heart stopped altogether as the image of Athvar flashed before him, replacing Snark. It was true that gnomes and goblins came from the same species and had diverged over the millennia, much like the Kyst and Kintar. Agan blinked and Athvar was still standing in front of him, but his neck was broken and his spine protruded through the skin. Agan's chest tightened, breath refusing to fill his lungs as he sank into his past trauma.

"Agan." Ironboot was now standing beside the half-orc when he finally came to from his panic attack. He sent his yellow eyes around the room, and everyone was looking at him most curiously.

"Let's get a move on. I can't stay here long." He was gruff and short tempered now, like he usually was. The peace and calm that had washed over him on the porch dissolved completely. Nordhum and Faye looked at each other with worry for their old friend, but they all sat down at one of the tables. Snark brought more refreshments and food before disappearing with Krans, scolding him for losing track of Thron.

"Well, here I am. What do you want?" Kithlyn started the conversation on an accusatory tone.

"Let me start by thankin' ya for joining us." Nordhum wanted to maintain positivity here. "Now, the severity of this meeting cannot be understated. There is no real easy way of puttin' this, so I'll just say it. The gods are dyin." Nordhum's brogue often put a lighter spin on things, but his physical discomfort was evident. He paused to garner the reactions of Agan and Kithlyn but their expressions were never telling.

"Everything comes to an end. Even the endless." Kithlyn appeared by all means to be relieved by the news.

"This isn't something to be happy about." Scarlet snapped her avian beak, her fire swelling. Kithlyn laid an unimpressed stare upon them all.

"Look, we don't need some speech on how this is possible or why it's happening. I get how this might be frightening for you two devotees especially, but Kith and I have never cared for the gods. This news does not concern us," Agan explained. He knew he was thinking not of the greater ramifications, but rather his objective, and would not be distracted.

"Hear us out," Nordhum pressed diplomatically. "Scarlet hasn't felt Pirelia's presence for many years, but Brailin StoneSower spoke to me of great portent—a celestial renewal."

Kithlyn made a point of rolling her shadow-eclipsed eyes.

"He has said for decades now, the gods have been planting Grimìr across Litore or picking chosen ones," the dwarf added.

"Congrats." The Scorn smiled sardonically.

Nordhum pressed on. "No species on Litore is more descendant of the gods than the ShadowScorn. And no greater assassin walks this world than you."

Kithlyn's face screwed up as their meaning began to take shape in her mind. Agan turned to regard Kithlyn as it began to come together for him too. He admitted the theory made sense; he had just spent over a month is the City of Shadow and still no one matched Kithlyn's skill. Surely, his beloved Aelis Andula was the greatest tactician he'd ever met, but he doubted she could beat Kithlyn in single combat. Yet, it was Scáth who kept appearing in his mind, the whole reason he was here in the first place. It made sense that the former and first Scorn Queen would be the Grimìr of Aceia, not to mention she was different than others of her species.

"We believe it's you," Scarlet announced what everyone was thinking. "The death of the last god will mark the end of the Second Age and the Third shall reign. Which means you and the other eleven descendants of the gods are responsible for ensuring our new era begins peacefully."

"What of the Powers? Faye, has she spoken to you of any of this?" Agan asked, for he knew the possibility for disaster was clear; however, all outcomes needed to be predicted. Why couldn't the Third Age start peacefully on its own? He knew better than most that action for the sake of action often led to misfortune.

"The CareTaker is as powerful as ever. Sadly, much like she did before the Quake of Harazune, she warned that a great energy of death is swirling around the Evar Spring Glade." Faye appeared genuinely disturbed by this, for the Quake of Harazune wrought unfathomable death and destruction across Litore.

"How do we know this isn't some ploy by Zeries, Mahem or Skalgr? Or damn maybe all three of them are in on it to trick us into something worse." Kithlyn was evidently more invested in the conversation now but was hesitant to so readily believe it.

"We know," Scarlet answered.

"How?" Kithlyn echoed mockingly.

"Belief in our gods, Shadow Mistress," Nordhum said with conviction.

Kithlyn snorted with laughter. "Belief in gods is for adults who have done wrong and are too weak to accept their faults. Escapism is for the craven. Serenstrom rapes my country and steals our people under the words of Sesara." Kithlyn was hateful now. "You," she stared angrily at Nordhum. "Commander Ironboot sacked towns, stole that which made people unique, slaughtered the innocent in the name of Justice." She met Scarlet's bright fiery eyes. "Don't even get me started on this bird shit, you self-righteous, hollow-boned hypocrite." Kithlyn stood up abruptly. "I look forward to watching you all lose what was most sacred to you, fall off your pedestals and join us in the real world." The Scorn looked at Faye—the two had always understood each other—and the Gloom elf stared back with compassion. Kithlyn fluttered her eyes to the floor and stormed out of the Willow Hall.

After a moment of uncomfortable silence, Faye stood up and followed after her.

"She's not wrong," Agan voiced heavily.

"Aye, but I've made up for my past transgressions and to be true, none of that matters if we don't act soon," Nordhum said, not defensively but to accentuate the severity of their warning.

"Listen, I don't think she's your chosen or Grimìr or whatever you're callin' them. But I know where they might be."

Kithlyn walked across the road and through the town square where she received more friendly waves. If her blood wasn't boiling she might have appreciated how welcoming everyone was. No one looked at her differently here for being a Scorn because the town was built on diversity, and frankly, hosting the world famous Redwillow Guild meant weird things often occurred. She continued on until her boots sunk into the soft sand of the Routh Riverbank. Under the shade of one truly beautiful red weeping willow, she threw her rump into the sand and stared out over the twinkling river. She felt the sting of tears swell in her eyes and the unfamiliar sensation of one trickling down her bright porcelain skin. She wiped it away with a finger, and upon inspecting it she saw writhing tendrils of shadow within. She balled her fist and her skin changed from white, to grey, to obsidian-black with rage. The shadow that perpetually escaped around her brow and bridge of her nose was exploding.

She could do things no other Scorn in existence could do; she was not about to have that hard earned fact taken away because she was some chosen of Aceia. No—everything she was, she made. It wasn't long before she heard the light footsteps of Faye Walker behind her. She sniffed hard one time and cleared her throat. Soon Faye was beside her in a large, heavy black cloak that completely obscured any bare skin. They were shoulder to shoulder and Faye swayed once into Kithlyn.

"Hey, girl," Faye whispered sweetly.

Kithlyn scoffed. "Hey, yourself."

These two had met near the start of the War of a Thousand Dragons and felt an immediate connection, not least of which was Faye's connected past to Shadow Scorn.

"Where ya been all this time?" Faye inquired politely. Kithlyn shrugged a little.

"After falling down the chute, I did a spell in the Underworld. Since then, I've been killing bad guys every chance I get."

"Sounds about right. Seems like a bit of a waste though."

Kithlyn groaned. "You're seriously here to try and convince me to do more with my life? Bad folk need killing and there is no one better for the job. If Aceia chose me, he chose wrong."

"I couldn't agree more." Faye smiled, which confused Kithlyn. "I loved Ruvean, and I won't ever find that kind of love again. He was the finest Scorn I had ever met. Your people welcomed me into their society when I had nothing, and it was beautiful. And then he was murdered by lesser who thought they were better. It took me a long time, but I had my revenge. I saw it to it that his soul could rest. And you know what?" Faye paused and Kith was hanging on her every word. "I felt no better because I did no real change. I feel the way you do, and though you may not see eye-to-eye with those inside the guild hall, you all want the same thing—a better world."

Kithlyn stared into Faye's large, celestial eyes before heaving a great sigh.

"Dammit you're good."

"So I've been told." She bared a coy smile for her old friend. "Come back when you're ready." She laid a gloved hand on the Scorn's spaulder and stood up. Faye was surprised when the assassin sprung to her feet.

"Agan came all this way for me, and I haven't even asked him why. He deserves my help first." Kithlyn wanted to make this clear, and hoped slightly that Faye would back her up on it if the others disagreed. The Gloom elf smiled warmly once more, and they walked back together.

When Nordhum, Scarlet, and Agan heard Kithlyn and Faye laughing as they walked back in, the Phoenix couldn't help herself. "Wonder who she's mocking this time."

"That's her genuine laugh," Agan quickly corrected, "and it used to mean the world to me," the final words just barely escaping his lips. The two returned to their seats, still grinning about something Faye had said.

"Feel better?" Scarlet asked. Kithlyn simply scowled.

"We don't have to get along, but I won't tolerate antagonizing." Nordhum used his guild master voice, which surprisingly carried a lot of weight behind it. Scarlet sat back, and in a show of faith, Kithlyn nodded.

"First, I owe it, once again, to help Agan. You and your troubles will have to wait," the Scorn said plainly.

"As it stands, Agan's plans are now our first priority," Nordhum answered happily. "And since you two were last here, we have had a wizard make a few improvements," he added with a fist banging the table, downing the last of his tankard. He grabbed an axe that was the size of himself and led them to the second floor of the turret. Upon walking up the spiral stairs and entering through the stone door, they saw a large circular room, empty save a massive pentagram carved in the floor. Nordhum stood in the middle and looked back at the group with a wry grin.

CHAPTER THIRTEEN

Glowen'ashen

Ven followed Wynn closely every step of the way. He surveyed his surroundings with obsessive interest. He wondered how the Gloom elves could keep their enclave of Glowen'ashen so secret. Everyone who cared to know knew the general area, yet the precise location of the settlement was one of the best guarded secrets in the vast forest.

For that reason, Wynn brought them to a large, jade-green pool of water with a roaring waterfall at the opposite end of the basin.

"Wait here," she instructed.

"Why?" Onstera asked. She knew why, but she was desperate to see the enclave up-close. It was a large part of her creed as a Quaesitor to know the unknown, like Gauntlet Ridge. She received no reply, and Wynn was quickly lost in the late-night foliage. Onstera sighed heavily and sat on rock, pulling out a waterskin. The two Kintar were talking quietly to themselves in Kintish. Ven noticed Aolendìr kneeling beside the pool, skimming the surface with his sun-kissed fingers. Ven went beside him, sitting down on the edge of the basin, kicked off his boots and put his feet in the water.

"It's a healing pool. Try it," he beckoned Aolendìr. This enigmatic elf was never one to shy away from a new experience, so he pulled off his cuffed boots and waded in. As he stepped in, the water around him glowed brightly, reflecting off his clothes and skin. Even greater was the soft tingling he felt as the water almost massaged his skin and muscles back from weariness.

"Wonderful," he said with great honour to be invited into the forest this way.

"Why do you want to help those fight against Vakar?" Ven was direct and abrupt in his question. It came naturally to him, not that he necessarily liked that aspect of himself, but this new version, where he left his rage unchecked, found it relieving.

"It's my life's ambition to do good. And when I heard the greatest forest on Litore was heading towards civil war, well..." Aolendìr turned away from the waterfall to face Ven. The Kyst cocked one brow.

"Seriously?" His voice full of distaste for the mock answer.

"You think I lie?"

"You're a stranger. Not a stranger like the two Kintar behind me—I know their culture, their practises, what makes them, them. My human companion belongs to a fabled guild known for protecting the world from its darkest evils. Even Wynn, who I met hours ago, lives only to protect this forest and her people. So yes, I think when a complete foreigner to these lands enters alone and pretends to be none the wiser while offering aid to an event that has barely left the confines of this forest, he is in fact lying." Ven's heart was racing. He was angered merely by having to explain.

Aolendìr scoffed in jest. "Then let us agree to never lie to one another." He paused to wait for Ven's answer, and the Kyst nodded firmly. "I am a war profiteer. A purveyor of the unacquirable. Not a sell-sword per se, but of that line. Although my true skill resides in the mind, I offer services that deliver chaos to the enemies and bolster the allies—for the right price of course." He grabbed his shoulder cape from the water and bowed.

"Vakar is the smart elf's bet to win this. A king's bounty would be your reward. Surely, we have only the difference between right and wrong on our side."

"Treasure can always be found along the way, my friend." The Solsta smiled coyly.

"If you're willing to steal." Ven pointed out.

"I prefer the term 'procure'." He smirked again and Ven rolled his eyes, swinging his feet out of the pool. Aolendìr noted the white marking that ran down each of his legs to end at his middle toe.

"Why do you think the Kyst have markings?"

Ven slid his last boot on as Aolendìr asked his seemingly random question. "What?"

"The elves of Litore all started from the same species, but the magic that radiates from the ground beneath us has expedited the evolutionary effect on every creature in the world. There are at least five major sub-species of elf, and you're the only ones with natural markings."

Ven screwed up his face like he couldn't be bothered to listen anymore. "Camouflage would be my guess."

Aolendìr nodded curiously before turning back to face the waterfall. Ven gave the back of his head a curious stare before going to sit on the rock with Onstera.

"You okay? I could hear your heart racing," she asked without taking her platinum eyes off the golden elf.

"I've grown angrier with every breath since they took Scáth, filled with sadness ever since my supposed parents made themselves known. All I want is to kill and hurt those who deserve it. The veil of lies he enshrouds himself with…" Ven stared at the thick bed of green moss beneath his feet, unable to find the best word, but Onstera understood all the same.

"Rage can be your greatest ally in combat, or your ultimate undoing. It will without a doubt cloud your judgment in the art of verbal warfare until you are left defenseless and stupid. I was six years old when the Fires of Fel murdered my father and everyone in our Sanguis Guild Hall. I spent the next twenty-three years chiseling that anger into something controllable." She fluttered her gaze upon Ven's stormy cheeks, and he felt her eyes on him.

"Teach me," he returned the stare.

"It begins with ignoring what your rage tells you. You are one of the most skillful warriors I've encountered, and that is saying something, Ven. I'm betting the Kyst Hunters taught you control and peace of mind?" He nodded. "It's the safest way to be effective in combat. Because the minute you tap into your anger, you lose all sense of right or wrong. You cannot effectively judge your next step. Your instincts shift and contradict one another. You will blunder and your enemy will kill you. Nine out of ten times you will lose that fight. But what if you could maintain that clear mind you have while tapping into the bursts of strength, speed and endurance to push just a little bit further?" she ended with a knowing grin. Ven didn't have to guess. He had seen on several occasions the way Onstera Dentoress had vanquished her foes unlike any other.

"How did you learn to harness the power of anger while keeping a clear mind?"

She looked over at the two Kintar sitting against a tree, eating their rations and talking in hushed voices.

"Njor, come spar with Ven," Onstera shouted. This made Aolendìr turn to regard those on land and Rinya smile devilishly.

"I wish not to hurt the little elf," he replied while popping a handful of meat chunks in his mouth.

"You're missing the point—I want you to hurt him," she said flatly. Ven looked shocked while Aolendìr and Rinya's smiles both grew wide.

"If you would, I'd like to put fifty gold talons on Ven," Aolendìr said with an irritating amount of suave.

Rinya leapt up. "You're on, Goldie." They dragged Njor up with them before walking to Aolendìr to show their coin. The Kintar Grimìr rolled his dark-red eyes before walking up to Onstera and Ven.

"What's the meaning of this, then?" he demanded impatiently.

"You Berserkers function off blind rage, correct?" Onstera inquired.

"It's more than that, but we use our rage to push past the wounds we have suffered in battle or the fatigue our muscles feel. We learn the art of war from the age we can listen and understand words, we do not let our anger cloud our judgment."

Onstera waved her hand back and forth to signal him to shut up. "I just want you to fight Ven, piss him off as much as you can. Got that, muscles?" She patted the hulking Kintar's bicep like a good little boy and Ven began to feel anxious about this. He was quick, but it appeared from the fight in Claw Canyon that SecondSpirit had the literal strength and speed of Lokor.

Ven and Njor both sighed loudly before squaring up to one another. Ven dropped his cloak, pulled out his straight-bladed, doubled-edged short-sword and crouched into his defensive posture. Njor pulled one of his newly acquired mallets off his belt and breathed in deeply. Ven watched his opponent keenly, watching for muscles to flex so he could roll to safety. Njor lunged his left foot forward and Ven rolled to the right, but it was a fake and the Kintar hurled his magical mallet straight into Ven's ribs. The sheer force of it not only knocked the wind from his lungs but sent him skipping across the ground several metres.

Njor slid his foot back and stood relaxed as Ven got back to his feet.

"I believe that pissed him off, alright," Aolendìr whispered to Rinya. They simply elbowed the Solsta in reply.

Ven's opalescent green eyes narrowed furiously. He unsheathed two throwing knives from his greaves, twirling one in his hand before gripping it reversed. He walked quickly towards Njor, and the Kintar reciprocated.

"Remember to think, Ven," Onstera reminded. Ven ignored her; the only thought he had was gutting this monstrosity before him. Now in range, Ven sent his hands into a whirlwind of strikes. Njor was quick, divinely so, and he managed to dodge and weave around most of them. Yet the hunter found purchase several times and his enemy had streams of blood running across his body.

Ven thought he saw his opportunity to put him down for good and he lunged his arm forward. A foolish mistake, and he knew it; Njor grabbed his overextended arm and side stepped, dragging Ven out so they were face-to-face. The Kintar delivered a punch that sent a shock wave off of Ven's iradinium-infused leather chest piece. He hit the ground so hard his body left an imprint in the earth. Njor grabbed the Kyst with both hands by the collar and hoisted him up high, without even a breath of effort. The hunter was brought out of his daze by sheer rage and spat a mouthful of thick saliva and green blood in Njor's eyes. He instinctively dropped the elf, but Ven already wrapped his legs around his neck. Letting his weight do the work, he swung down and around, throwing the Kintar into the ground. He ended up on top, left knee digging into SecondSpirit's stomach. Ven dodged a slow blow and repaid it by skewering his bicep clean through with his knife. Njor gave a bellowing Kintar roar, but Ven drove his fist into face. He punched him harder than he had ever punched before, again, again, and again.

The onlookers each wore a different face of shock at the sheer display of hatred. Aolendìr was seriously considering how he was going to dispose of Ven and wondered if that would even be possible.

He spat out a tooth and Ven went to drive his knife through his head. But the berserker reached around and gripped the hunter by the back of the hair. He pulled hard so Ven rolled with the momentum and the two were separated again. They got to their feet and Ven screamed at his enemy, sprinting forward again. Njor waited until the last second and spun to nail Ven in the head with his mallet. Ven blacked out instantly and his body flew over the basin of water, skipping like a rock until he eventually sank like a rock.

Onstera glowered at Njor, but he weakly fell to one knee. She ran to the water's edge to retrieve Ven, but Aolendìr had already stripped off his cloaks and jackets and was wading into the deep. Suddenly, he vanished in a golden puff of smoke and reappeared where Ven had sunk. He took a deep breath and dove under. Diving deep, he pulled out a long and intricately carved wand and the tip let out a series of pulsing lights. They fell to the bed of the pool, and he quickly spotted the Kyst laying unconscious in the pebbles. Aolendìr swam closer and pointed his wand at Ven. He could do it right now, simply cast the incantation and obliterate the Kyst.

Rinya and Onstera were standing in the water, the Quaesitor failing to hide her worry.

"What's taking so long?" she blurted.

"Maybe goldie is killing Ven," Rinya said casually.

"What?" Onstera sneered.

"Seems odd he just appeared in the forest, doesn't it? Everyone knows Ven is the only one who can touch Vakar."

Just as Onstera stepped forward to dive in the water, Aolendìr burst out with Ven around his shoulders. He was flying and soon he landed gently, placing Ven in the moss. The human ran to their side, but the Solsta held out his arm.

"Wait," he pulled a vile from his belt and gently rubbed the viscous goo on the wound across Ven's skull. Within moments, the wound sealed and Ven lazily opened his eyes.

Ven cracked his neck and wheezed. "Ow."

Njor was bent over as blood poured from his mouth, nose and stab wounds. "Good fight, little elf."

Soon, everyone was helping Ven and Njor deal with their wounds and take a much-needed rest in the healing pool. Nearly an hour later, Wynn and a centuries-old Gloom elf made themselves known.

"Is this what you all enjoy in your free time?" Wynn said aloud with no lack of judgment. Like a group of children, everyone fumbled for the right words.

"Training, believe it or not. Training of an extremely high calibre," Aolendìr chirped up in his playful manner, water still dripping down his pulled back hair. He then threw a bag of gold at Rinya and gave a wink for free.

The old Gloom elf slowly walked over to the Solsta; after inspecting him she placed a wrinkled, pale-blue hand on his cheek. He looked deep into her eyes of blackness, and knew she was scouring his soul. The stars in her eyes were unique, for they were red, as if with age.

"Am I to believe you all sought us out, seeking the same?" Her voice so frail.

"Ours is to unite the forest, restoring it from that which Vakar has made it," Aolendìr answered serenely, almost immediately mimicking her tone and way of speech. The Elder looked to the group, looked back to Wynn and gave a slight nod. Wynn walked past the Solsta and threw a blindfold at him, then offered one to each of the others.

Ven accepted and wrapped it around his eyes while Rinya groaned irritably. Once every outsider was blindfolded, a dozen Gloom elves made themselves known and walked the troop towards Glowen'ashen. Some minutes later, Aolendìr felt a shiver run through his body. Having been trained in the arcane hundreds of years prior, he knew they had just passed through some illusory magic. He didn't speak, but he understood how these elves were remaining hidden, and if the need ever arose, how to reveal them. They walked many, many more hours, stopping twice for refreshments and brief respite. Suddenly, Ven felt a stiff breeze billow his cloak and the light against his blindfold brighten exponentially. A moment later, Wynn pulled it off and he was breathtaken.

Gloom elves walked freely in loose hanging, breathable clothing of silvers, purples, blues, and black. A huge field was before him and a great pool hundreds of metres wide sat glistening in the center of everything. A single stone bridge ran through the middle of the pool that was otherwise completely untouched. People sat around the water as if in prayer, and Ven noted everything was showered in gold as dusk was approaching. The buildings were humble but elegant in their design. The grass and dirt around the homes were all bright colours, as if each one was a burning star. He saw too the ground was marked with geometric lines, forming a great constellation.

"You see why we want to keep it a secret?" Wynn asked him.

"Better than most but you know Vakar will find you eventually," Ven replied.

"Don't convince me, convince the elders."

His nod was clearly weighed by the pressure of that task. With a goal before him, and the right allies at his back, he knew they stood a chance. Wynn and the Gloom escorts brought the visitors to a hut, and beckoned them wait. The hut consisted of one wide, circular room, with the majority of the roof open to the elements. The floor was a mosaic of glass to reflect the night sky, and the wall opposite the entry was lined with six chairs. Those chairs sat upon a significantly raised dais and were protected by a crescent shaped table.

The five outsiders stood aimlessly at first, as the seconds turned to minutes. Ven noted a perfect circle of light on the floor, cast down by the sun and it was perhaps three quarters across the floor signalling that it was early evening.

"We may be waiting awhile," he said aloud to no one in particular. Rinya rolled their eyes and went to try the door they entered through.

"Locked," they moaned.

"I'm sure we're in for a long night." Onstera stalked to the wall and sat cross legged, back flush and upright.

"Agreed," Njor added before walking to the opposite side of the room and resting his head on his bag before closing his eyes. Ven and Aolendìr looked at Rinya expectantly.

"I'm not interested," they answered with a deadpan stare and found one of the raised chairs to sit in. Ven went and sat cross-legged and fell into a meditation. He sensed the Solsta sitting uncomfortably close but fought the urge to be snarky. An hour must have passed when he could no longer abide by Aolendìr's noisy aura and he opened his eyes. Like an irritating pet, the golden-bronze elf was staring at the Kyst, waiting for him to open his eyes.

"Those four aren't the liveliest I have ever met," the Solsta confessed to Ven.

"You might not be so lively if your home was on the brink of ruin. Where is your home, even?"

He shrugged earnestly before moving past the question. "What's the Quaesitor eaten up about then? Surely her kind never settles down in one spot until it's in the cold earth."

Ven stared in slight agitation. "It's not just my home in peril, all of Litore stares into the eyes of catastrophe." Aolendìr looked surprised at the young Kyst's wisdom. "I've been lied to and shown false hearts my whole life." Ven held his knowing gaze for a long pause. "War profiteering sounds like pumasheep manure. For there is a war of pure profit in the Magma Isles as we speak."

"Really? Perhaps I'll head there next," Aolendìr quipped.

"We're about to be interrogated by what might be some of the oldest elves in the world. Do you really think your charade will phase them?"

"Are you always this hostile?" Aolendìr countered.

"When I have to be. Which is frequently of late."

"That's good, Kaiason." He spoke the words with no hesitation and Ven's heart met his gut. His mind raced for answers, but the only solution he could conjure was to throw his hand his to hilt. Aolendìr only smirked as Ven reached for his weapon, for the doors had just swung open. Six Gloom elves entered, each more ancient than the last, followed by Wynn, who closed the door and pressed her back against it. The first Gloom elf, a rather small creature garbed in a very long and flowing white dress, stood over Rinya, who was still seated.

"Is this your chair?" the Kintar asked nonchalantly.

"Indeed."

Rinya puckered their lips to blow a kiss then jumped out of the chair, slid over the table, and joined their companions. Ven and Aolendìr hadn't broken eye contact since the entrance and their friends began to stand at attention. The Solsta finally broke the secretive tension with a flick of a brow and joined the others. Ven tried his hardest to clear his mind before standing next to Onstera.

The circle of light in the floor had faded to a dark red brought on by the moonlight of Caelestis. As the red light grew in strength, the glass began to glow and reflect against the walls. Involuntarily, Njor, Aolendìr, and Ven pinched their thumb and forefinger between their eyes to fend off an excruciating pressure.

"Forgive us," the youngest of the Elders spoke in an eerily calm tone. "The twilight magic of Glowen'ashen can be... punishing to those arcanely blessed."

Rinya and Onstera gave threatening scowls to those seated, but it took only a dozen or so heartbeats for the pain to pass. It was then that Aolendìr began patting a few specific spots on his raiment.

"You've muted our magic," he accused.

"We have," a weary and dry voice responded.

"How could we determine if you speak true, while magic could conceal your barest intent," the youngest elder happily shed light on the situation. Ven shot the Solsta a superior grin at the difficulty he was about to have. "What is your, intent?" the youngest Elder asked.

Ven took a step forward. "To unite those who wish to fight the plague that is Vakar. Everyone in the forest was free and do not wish to live under one ruler."

"Most of Litore lives under the rule of kings and queens, even Elemenzin rules by an Emperor now. Vakar has already set up peacekeepers across land to protect those who cannot defend themselves." This elder was quiet, a reserved elf in body and mind.

"What of the genocide against my people?" SecondSpirit's powerful voice skipped around the room. He glared at each of the presiding counsellors.

"You burned their home to the ground, they burned yours. I am hearing nothing new," perhaps the second youngest elder, an ego-driven male with more celestial tattoo's than bare skin, spoke.

"Our generational war is our own. The Kyst and Kintar have battled since *one* became *two*," Ven said defiantly. Njor sent Ven a nod that signalled his agreement. Another step in understanding each other.

"In all the battles we shared, tens of thousands have died over thousands of years. Vakar killed tens of thousands in a single day. Do you not think he will come for you next if you do not bend to his every will," Rinya added to Ven's point.

"Perhaps it is just we believe the Gloom elves are hardier than the Kyst or Kintar. Or maybe we care not for those who bring their personal squabbles to our home."

Rinya and Njor scoffed in unison. Onstera cocked one brow in embarrassment on the Gloom elf's behalf. "Is that how you all feel?" she questioned the elders.

"We do not all see eye-to-eye," the youngest elder said while eyeing up the arrogant Gloom. "However, we dream only of the stars. We offer worship to the great cosmic heavens above. Sometimes we are quick to forget the world around us."

"Take it from a seeker of blood and secrets, nothing can remain hidden forever."

"Pray, what is a Sanquis Quaesitor doing with the famed Ven Devar?" the diminutive elf asked.

"Although he could not know at the time, I was hired by the rebel Kyst to make sure he made it to them in one piece. Now I am training him."

"What could the Mighty Ven learn from the likes of a bounty hunter?" the arrogant elf belittled.

"A bounty hunter? Nothing I'd suspect." She ended her words with an equally belittling smile.

"I believe you six above most would agree we never stop learning. Knowledge of the rarest kind can be found in the least expected places." Aolendìr paused to offer Onstera a look of respect. "And we only stop learning when the Ammins have come for us." He noted that the elder on the far left and definitely the oldest, nodded slightly. "Peace for all times is a simple impossibility, for balance rules this world and the cosmos above. So balance dictates there be strife. Truthfully, I am someone who profits off times of strife, for peace brings little else than forgettable days and too many babes. Alas, I am a creature of balance, so I work towards peace all the same. This great mass of forest upon which we stand is unlike any other in all the worlds, and it has known war for too long. I have pledged myself to bringing your home back into balance. All that remains to be seen is, will you?"

Ven nearly rocked back at the words from the Solsta, they appeared so genuine and seemed to make perfect sense.

"Are the five of you going to fight this war alone?" the arrogant elder remarked.

"Many of the Kyst are in open rebellion, but you already knew that." Ven's tone bit harshly. "What Kintar are left could be persuaded to fight," Njor added, "if they knew those they fought beside believed in true reconciliation. My people have been falling from their ancient tenets for many years now. I know from personal experience there is only oblivion down our current path, so we must adapt or die." Njor keenly caught the scoff of Rinya after his speech. So too did the all the elders.

"You do not agree, child?" The ancient elder spoke once more, eyeing Rinya curiously.

"I'm a killer. Born to swing a blade, bred to end lives, and taught to do it better than any on Litore through the lessons and texts from millennia of like-minded ancestors." Rinya looked at their old friend, who seemed a bit betrayed. They sighed heavily as their inner stubbornness caved, if not for themselves then for the sake of their friend. "But the elf I chose to follow says we must adapt or die. And Rinya Witblade has not had their fill of this world," Rinya ended with a slight bow and stepped back.

After a moment of the elders speaking amongst each other, and no sound reaching the companions, the female elf whom had been proceeding this meeting spoke, "What would you have us do then? Simply marching against Vakar and his kingdom would spell doom. We have only a few thousand warriors against his?" she ended, clearly inquiring if they knew the strength of his forces.

"6,000 Kyst Hunters, half that many sages," Onstera answered solemnly before adding, "Queen Saphier would have your chosen leaders meet with her and the commander of her forces, Ina Enallea, to discuss further actions."

"She lets a sell-sword speak for her people?" the youngest elder retorted.

"If you and your elders are half as wise as you think you are, you'd know the Sanguis Quaesitor's are far more than just sell-swords." Onstera laid a heavy silver stare upon them.

Ven took several steps forward so that he was arms-length away from the crescent shaped table. "You can sit here exchanging sharp words and pretend as though you care. But lives that call the Great Northern Rainforest home are lost everyday while you sit here contemplating the stars and decide if you give a damn about the world around you. I for one am sick of waiting on others to do the right thing." Ven's opalescent eyes grew watery and his heart pounded as a look of sheer indignation crossed his face. He spun on one heel, wild green hair whirling around, and stormed to the door. He paused to stare down Wynn who did not move out of his way, as she was looking to the elders for her next step. She received a nod and moved aside. Ven threw the doors open and walked out into the night

CHAPTER FOURTEEN

Shadow in the Light

Scáth was laying on the hardwood floor, curled up in the fetal position. The tube of light she was stuck in was not big enough for her to stretch out properly, although it mattered little, for her muscles were in a state of atrophy. Utterly starved of darkness, her skin had turned a sickly grey, her eyes glazed over and cloudy. Her hair lay lifeless on the floor, no longer misting into ethereal shadow. She had fallen asleep like this the night before, or perhaps it was the day before; she had lost all sense of time inside this tree after they had sealed every crevasse.

She had fallen asleep thinking of Ven, wishing beyond all else that she would pass away quietly with her true love in her thoughts. She had lived more freely in the past year alongside Ven than she had in the past sixty stuck inside ShadowScorn. They had both seen the wide world and they had seen it together. All she could hope for now was a natural death that robbed Vakar of any glory. Scáth had accepted the fact no one could come for her, not inside the heart of Silva, the new capital of Vakar's kingdom. Once she had accepted that fact, it brought her a sense of peace. She would never forgive herself if someone died attempting to retrieve her. She had lived longer than most in Litore, more comfortably than most, and had true friends and family to share it with. As the reality of death encroached, a fleeting sense of excitement tickled her—excitement to see her brother Scarnin and father Arwr again in the Fields of Eternal Night.

Her eyes lazily fluttered to the door when she heard mumbled arguing. A great thud sounded and a second later, Eevie Hara walked in. She slammed the door behind her as if to accentuate some point. Eevie took a deep breath, regaining some measure of calm before walking up to the cylinder of light. The Kyst knelt down and it took the Scorn a rough moment to sit upright, but after some strenuous effort, she did so.

"Yes?" Scáth's soft caring voice had turned coarse and dry.

"Tonight, you will be executed."

"Okay," her reply sounded like a solution to a stubborn problem. Wrinkles formed across Eevie's light green-coloured face.

"That's it?" the hunter chortled. "The Daughter of Shadow rolls over so easily?"

"I suppose so." Scáth wasn't feigning interest, she simply had no interest left.

"No," Eevie grunted defiantly. The Scorn seemed perplexed. "You've been running circles around those pretentious males and you were locked up the whole time."

Scáth digested the meaning of that for a moment. "They defeated me, I am but a shadow of my former self. Weak and frail."

Eevie shook her head. "Your story cannot end here. This fight needs you."

"You do not sound like someone who fights for Vakar."

"Vakar was set to marry my brother, you know? They had a tree ready for them to start their new life together. Vakar, Ven, and I were all born in the same spring. We learned together, trained together, made mistakes together. When Ven and I started training as hunters, we became close, if you could call it that. He always seemed out of place, for whatever reason that resonated with me. Then when his father Renic died, the only person Ven would talk to was Vakar. Of course, being the stubborn little elf I was, my heart only grew stronger for him. I guess I like the mysterious ones," Eevie scoffed in jest of herself as she wiped tears away from her face. Scáth felt as though she was beginning to understand why Eevie was telling her this. "Ven was paired up with my older brother Qiri. He was only five years our senior but old enough to continue Ven's training. Flash forward a decade or so and Ven slayed a demon no one else in the north could. Vakar and Qiri's love is in bloom, and I'm still the dorky hunter with a crush on a famous elf who barely knows she exists."

"But of course he knew you, and probably loved you in his own way," Scáth managed to offer empathetically.

Eevie smiled, "Just not in the way a young elf hopes." Scáth smiled back and nodded knowingly.

"Then you showed up," Eevie's tone changed quicker than the winds of winter. "I watched as he paraded you through our home, showing enthusiasm and talking more than he ever had in his entire life. In one night, I lost Ven, my brother, my family, and my home. All because you appeared where you did not belong." Scáth went to say something, but Eevie held her hand up. "I do not blame you, Scáth. If a tree falls and destroys a home it was clinging too, you do not blame that which supported it. Rather the soil that that rotted and gave way and the wind that knocked it over."

"You truly mean that?"

"I know your story. You were not here of your own will. Ven did the right thing in giving you safety, he could not have known the thick weave of events that would follow."

"Do you still love him?" she forced the question out. Eevie quickly looked away from the withered Scorn.

"You said I do not sound like someone who fights for Vakar. That King of Kyst is not Vakar." Eevie ignored the question, not because she didn't want to answer it, but because the answer changed nothing.

"If you help me, they will kill you."

Eevie stood up and bowed respectfully before exiting the room. Scáth wanted to say something, but the right words would not come.

She laid back down as the exertion of that exchange depleted her mentally and physically. She felt a glimmer of hope, the first one in a long time. But how could she make any kind of escape in this condition? Even with the aid of Eevie, she knew the prowess of these hunters and sages would make it impossible. She considered Eevie was playing her, toying with her in some sort of sick game as the distant lover of Ven.

Jealousy had played a large role in her life back in the City of Shadow; as princess, countless others only dreamed of the comfort and luxury Scáth enjoyed. Somehow though, this did not feel like jealousy, and she knew trusting Eevie was her last hope. For some reason, that story she heard about the life here before her arrival, seemed like Eevie was explaining that she had accepted, Ven had chosen Scáth so completely. That brought a faint smile to dry and cracked lips. And knowing too that Eevie did not blame her for the destruction of Silva was freeing, as Scáth still believed it was her fault, even if it was indirect. At least knowing that someone who was impacted so harshly—as Eevie was—didn't want her dead, brought the Scorn some comfort.

Not ten minutes later did a similar set of events occur outsider her cell door. Thinking it was Eevie coming to break her out now instead of tonight, she was utterly dismayed to see it was Rexous.

"You," Rexous seethed. Scáth didn't say anything, instead struggling to her feet, determined to stand tall. "Even locked up in a cage of light you manage to bring misery."

"You don't need an external presence to make you miserable."

"I was not miserable before you arrived that fateful night," he retorted.

"That's not how I've heard it. Some folk are just born angry. It does not make you any less," she said kindly, considering that perhaps, much like her upbringing as royalty, Rexous had never been shown a soft hand. Constantly being held to the highest standard possible, taught never to let your subjects see weakness. Never taught to appreciate the simplest thing in this life—who you are.

"What?" His voice bit keenly, truly unnerving her.

"In all of your brooding and sulking around, it never dawned on you that perhaps you and I have quite a bit in common?" Her tone made it clear she was explaining the obvious.

"We have both slaughtered the innocent." He meant to take her off this pedestal upon which she spoke. She felt a wave of consternation at that truth, for she had not considered that overlap.

"I have killed directly, and I suppose indirectly, yes."

"Do not dare to compare our childhoods, Scorn," he spat.

"What childhood?" she quipped. "I told you, Ven spoke of you like a brother, one he didn't particularly like, but nevertheless. I know much of your past. What I know most assuredly is princes and princesses do not have what most children are afforded."

"And what is that exactly?" Rexous asked, already intent on laughing at her answer.

"To be a kid."

Her words sent a chill crawling across his skin like a thousand tiny spiders. He fumbled for the next words: he wanted to laugh, but not obscenely; he wanted to cry, but the tears wouldn't come; he wanted to scream, but instead stood still. Silent.

"So what," he whispered dismissively.

"So everything. You were not shown compassion as a child and now walk through life tasting a bitterness in everything."

"You seem compassionate enough for the both of us," he said, lifting his eyes from the floor to meet her own.

"I learned that from my father, a good ruler has compassion for all. It was trust and a voice I was denied. To know my real self, locked within a castle, it became impossible." She lost herself for a moment in reflection. "What do you think you made up for? Often when denied one thing we compensate with another."

"My skill," he answered quickly.

"No." She pointed through the shimmering wall of light to his heart. "Something deeper."

Rexous looked down to his chest, then back to the ShadowScorn. "Charity," he answered, sounding bashful. "All I ever wanted was for my people to have everything they ever needed or wanted."

Scáth looked back to him with a wide and genuine smile; it quickly faded, and his face turned to stone, then a hateful grimace.

"Before I died that is. Before my soul was torn from the world beyond and crudely stitched back into this mortal vessel."

Scáth shook her head, nearly in tears. "No, that is still within you."

"Shut up!" he roared, spittle hitting the barrier between them. "Damn Vakar and damn those elves outside waiting to see your head roll. It should be me thrusting that blade through your black heart before Ven's very eyes. I'd do anything to break his spirit, to see him crumble piece by piece."

"Do it," she threatened as tears streaked her skin. "I'm tired of being threatened by weaker creatures. Drop this shield and kill me. Or accept that you were given a second chance to mend the wrong you did."

He scowled outwardly and winced inwardly. "You truly are a pain in the ass." He turned on one heel to make his exit, stopping at the door as Scáth prompted him.

"Why didn't you kill me atop Glass Mountain? You had me helpless, Ven couldn't have stopped you, but you let me go anyway."

He looked over his shoulder to regard her one last time. "A mistake I wouldn't make twice." The door slammed behind him.

"Liar," softly escaped her lips with a breath. After too many minutes of standing idly, she laid back down wishing that was the last of her visitors. She closed her eyes, wanting to find sleep so desperately but it alluded her as the reality of certain death loomed larger and heavier than this cage of light around her.

Hours passed and she had not moved a muscle; she was within her own body, lost in the infinite space of her mind and memory. Understanding that your time was coming to a close offered an out-of-body experience she had never known possible. Scáth figured that all in all she had lived a good life, with people she loved and admired. It was not without its hardships and complications but again she knew that is what made life sweet—the bad brightens the good. The past year was, without a doubt, the best in sixty plus, with adventure and friends, survival and beauty, death and love. She wouldn't trade those memories for anything in the world, not even a ticket out of this predicament.

Regrets had never really made sense to her; she figured that regrets were just the seeds of growth. Without the catalyst required to learn and improve as a person, how could we become creatures of admiration? No, any regrets she could have had were necessary events to becoming the Scorn she was. Perhaps, she mused, there was one regret, although she thought it was more of shame, a shame that she did not get to live the life her and Ven wanted. She did not get to feel his most tender touch, have a family, or grow old together. To find a love so true as him and be robbed of that, she was sure now it was a shame.

Eventually, she heard the inevitable, as shuffling and several voices murmuring outside her cell came to a head when the door was opened. Vakar strode in with Pine, Eevie, and Rexous in tow. The King of Kyst made his way right up to her while the three lingered by the door.

"Well, let us be done with it," Vakar said with a surprising lack of enthusiasm. Scáth had assumed he would revel in her death as he insinuated.

"Not excited, my King?" Scáth lathered her words in sarcasm.

"Little excites me these days. Will you behave when I drop this cage of light, or do I need the assistance of my companions?" He motioned behind him. She reflexively looked at Eevie, wondering if the hunter showed any sign at all towards their previous conversation; however, she appeared as if it were another day on the job.

"I have nothing left to give," Scáth admitted, physically and mentally overcome. Vakar nodded, waved his hand, and the artifact necklace glowed green, the magical light dissipating with a wisp. Scáth instantly felt a sense of relief, as if a persistent stinging pain had just been lifted. The king lifted his hand towards the hunters and sage and they ushered the Scorn out. Rex and Pine led her out the door while Vakar and Eevie walked shoulder to shoulder just behind.

Her legs could barely support her for she was so lethargic. The supple boiled leather she wore now chaffed hotly against her skin and a sense of irritation filled her. The feeling quickly fled, being replaced wholly by sadness. She put one foot in front of the other, determined to appear strong as she walked towards death.

By the time they exited the royal tree, Vakar was leading them, Rex and Pine on either shoulder and Eevie still rear-guard. As she stepped into the night, she inhaled deeply, relishing the fresh air and soaking up the darkness around her like a sponge to water. It only then occurred to her something was off—why would Vakar do this now? Of course, he knew she thrived off the blackness of night. Perhaps he meant to show the people of the Great Northern Rainforest that even in darkness a Scorn could be killed, thus eliminating any superstition about them.

She saw the sky was clear and the moons of Litore bathed everything in a soft red hue. So too were there more plants and fungi glowing brightly with every colour under the rainbow along the bridges and common spaces of Silva. Walking across the great cedar bridge away from the royal tree, Scáth spotted an executioner's platform in the main town square. It seemed so out of place in such a scene of raw natural beauty, this structure of pure macabre.

She held her chin high and scanned the citizens who had come to watch. Hundreds of Kyst, maybe a thousand, had crammed into the square to see her die. They left no space between them, they filled every bridge connecting to the square, they clung to trees and sat on buildings. She noted many different expressions; some waited with sick glee, others with glistening eyes of sorrow. She began to feel exposed the closer they go to the scaffold, as if naked in a dream, and a dream is what it felt like. Countless eyes undressed her and there was an eerie silence, for not a soul made a sound; not even the hoots of hummingowls or the chittering of chipmunks could be heard. As she walked by, she saw a child with bright green eyes and hair, much like Ven's. Scáth gave her a warm smile. The child responded by dragging a finger across her little throat. The gesture made Scáth sick as it was done with a conviction that no child that age should possess. It made sense to her now, just how much these northern Kyst hated her.

They reached the small flight of stairs to summit the platform. Rex and Pine stopped as Vakar took the first steps. Scáth paused before Eevie put a hand on her shoulder, offering her a warm nod. She reciprocated and continued up the stairs, the hunter's hand still helping her forward.

Upon reaching the top, Eevie rested a considerable amount of weight on her shoulder so the Scorn stopped, allowing Vakar the majority of the space. He paced across the wooden planks several times before pausing most dramatically. He slowly raised his hand in the direction of Scáth and said, "Our damnation, come to justice." Like the first thunderclap of a storm, the cheers and raucous applause broke the tension. Scáth dropped her head in shame, whispering soft prayers to Aceia for a quick death and to be reunited with her brother and father in the Fields of Eternal Night. Any hope she may have held for Eevie breaking her free had quickly fled at the sight of the sheer numbers in attendance.

"Nearly a year ago, this ShadowScorn," Vakar pointed accusingly at Scáth, "was brought into our home by the traitor, Ven Devar." The crowd booed and shouted words of hate at Ven's name. "It was her presence here that lured the Kintar to our home, that caused the death of so many loved ones, friends and family. Tens of thousands of years of our history reduced to ash." Vakar finished by waving his hand at Eevie. The general of his army pushed Scáth forward to the center of the platform and shoved the Scorn to her knees. Eevie held her hand above her head, palm open. Vakar focused and spoke a small incantation. In the palm of her hand formed an emerald hilt. As she closed her grip, a heavy shimmering blade coalesced from a whirling smoke that shot out of the hilt.

"Thanks to the resilience, dedication, and strength of each and every one of you, we have rebuilt the greatest structure in the Great Northern Rainforest. This night marks a very special occasion for the Kyst, new and old to Silva. With the execution of Scáth ShadowScorn, we leave the past behind and enter a new era of peace and security." The assembled Kyst roared in applause once again, the sound of their collective voice combining to create a near static white noise. Scáth could bare to look at the crowd no more, hanging her head in horror. Eevie rested the wide blade at the base of Scáth's neck and everyone went silent.

"Are there any last words you wish to speak?" Vakar asked of her.

Scáth looked him dead in the eyes, the vivid darkness returning to her glare after been starved of shadow for so long. "Your mistakes are your own. Such as this ended, so it will begin again." She held her gaze until Vakar, shaken at the threat, looked away to Eevie and gave her the nod to execute.

"Forgive me," Eevie whispered and although Scáth heard it, the remark did not feel directed at her. The hunter raised her conjured sword high, and the silence was broken as a long, drawn-out howl of a wolf echoed from the forest floor. It ricocheted throughout the treetops as if it originated from the heavens. Eevie looked around, trying to determine where it could have come from. She noted Rex already had his dirks out at the ready and was moving towards a bridge edge.

A look of sheer rage came across Vakar and he shouted at Eevie to do the job. Scáth knew that howl like the voice of a loved one; she knew now there was a chance at fighting. Perhaps she could phase through the blade when Eevie delivered the killing strike, but she feared she was too weak to call upon her inner shadow for that.

"Do it!" Vakar shouted again. She lifted her sword high, hands trembling, and just as she was about to fell the blade, another howl was heard.

"Enough of this," Vakar roared and threw his hand out towards Scáth; the instant a bolt of incineration leapt from his fingers, a black dagger skewered his hand, sending the eviscerating magic into the crowd of civilians. Eevie quickly turned to see where the blade had appeared from. Scáth sensed this and rolled sidelong, wrapping her legs around Eevie's ankles and twisting with all her weight. The general hit the ground hard and Scáth rolled atop her, slicing her wrist bindings in the process. In the time it took her to accomplish that small feat, she noted every magical light had been extinguished, leaving only the bioluminescent plants.

Between the pile of ash that was so recently a handful of Kyst and the mystical darkness, pure panic broke out among the spectators. A dozen hunters and sages were now standing around Vakar, but a stream of black daggers pelted them like hail, killing many of them instantly while a few lucky hunters dodged or parried. The sages faired better, enacting shields of force, but many still fell as the daggers came from every direction.

"Come with me," Scáth offered hastily to Eevie.

"This is my home."

"Not anymore." Scáth ripped the magical weapon away and held her free hand out for Eevie.

"Kill her!" Vakar yelled above the tumult. Eevie looked longingly at the offered hand but remained still. Scáth could wait no longer and jumped off the platform, running for the royal tree as a score of Kyst were on her tail. She ducked into a roll as a line of arrows soared around her, but she deftly got back to her feet and was met with an orb of darkness. She almost recognized the magic as that of her homeland. Having no other choice, she dove through the darkness that filled the entrance. Coming out of it, she found the throne room empty. She began to run to the far end when a hand wrapped itself around her waist, and another over her mouth. The figure quickly pulled her back behind a statue in an alcove set against the wall.

"Agan sent me, remain still if you would," Scáth heard a voice whisper in her ear. She took a leap of faith in trusting the person who had not revealed themselves, but the mention of Agan was enough to momentarily calm her. She wondered who it could have been the infamous half-orc would have sent instead of himself. Then it dawned on her. It was the master assassin he spoke of, a fellow Shadow Scorn.

"Kithlyn?" she whispered through a gasp.

"Shh."

A series of footsteps rushed past the alcove and the room became silent again. Kithlyn let go of Scáth, who turned to face her. Scáth was aghast by the appearance of this Scorn, shadow literally wept from her eyes and across the bridge of her nose. Her eyes appeared more like the eclipse of moons, giving off flickering light behind an iris of impenetrable blackness. A hood clung tightly to her head while her braids misted away as all Scorn hair did.

"Be ready to shadow-step out of here to the forest floor," Kithlyn said, peeking around the statue to survey the throne room.

"I can't," Scáth admitted sheepishly. Kithlyn turned back rather slowly to dead-pan stare at her.

"Pardon?" the assassin asked rhetorically. Scáth shrugged, not appreciating the tone. Kithlyn sighed heavily. "Thanks for the heads up, Dusk," she said under her breath, turning back to regard the throne room just as another score of hunters rushed passed. "Do you know how to get down then?"

"Agan said there was no one better suited for these kind of tasks in the entire world. And you're asking me how to escape?" Scáth crossed her arms unimpressed, deciding it was important to make a strong first impression here, especially because she had wished many, many times to meet this particular ShadowScorn who had defied all odds and expectations in creating a life for herself outside the City of Shadow.

"We don't have time for this. Do you know a way down or not?" Kithlyn pressed. Scáth smirked and stepped in front of the assassin, making sure the coast was clear before sprinting across the room and behind the throne. Kithlyn wasn't a metre behind her, keeping close but more importantly an eye out. As one hunter come out of a side door just before the throne, she didn't make it two steps before Kithlyn sent a dagger into her mouth.

Not a sound issued out from their hurried footfalls, nor a ruffle from their clothes, for no species on Litore was more naturally gifted in stealth than the Scorn. Scáth placed her hand on the back wall, dragging her ghostly white hands across the oiled wood. Her fingers felt an insignificant lip, but she knew this must the secret tunnel Ven had used all that time ago, or at least the rebuilt one. Scáth muttered an incantation in Old Elvish, expecting the secret door to release and grant passage. When nothing happened, Kithlyn less than softly pushed her aside and waved a stone across the spot. The stone glowed with red rune then faded again, just as the door slide in and over.

"A magical lock-pick if you will, get inside quickly," she told Scáth, indicating her to continue leading the way. She did not hesitate and entered the small tunnel, Kithlyn quickly behind her. After several moments of navigating winding tunnels, Kithlyn had to ask.

"How did you know about the secret door?"

"It's not my first time escaping this wretched place." Scáth looked back to see Kithlyn had almost entirely melded with the darkness, just as she herself had. "Thank you."

Kithlyn was not accustomed to the kind words so simply nodded in reply. It was a tender spot for her, a travesty against her people, and although she had her moments of questionable morality, Kithlyn lived to see people have freedom, most of all her fellow Scorn.

"Where is Agan? And Ven?" Scáth could not wait to ask. She hoped she was minutes away from being reunited with her closest companions.

"I know nothing of a Ven. Agan and some of the Willow Guild are with the rebels. No one could get the wolf to remain behind, so he awaits us."

Scáth pressed forward, now with a smile for little else could have made her feel as safe as knowing Faenla was waiting for her. She decided it was good the others had not come, especially Ven, for that is exactly what Vakar wanted.

"Move ahead of me, there should be another secret door against that wall." Scáth pointed to the wall in front of her and Kithlyn waved her stone once more and the wall slid open. It revealed a thin spiral staircase leading up and down.

"Not half bad, princess," she remarked coyly, motioning for Scáth to lead once more. Scáth entered into the stairwell and began cautiously heading down. Upon reaching the base with no one finding them, Scáth began to ask Kithlyn to open the last door when it suddenly opened up itself. Kithlyn quickly dove to the side of the door, obscuring herself as Scáth stood firm, hand still on the conjured sword.

Rexous stood on the other side, dual dirks already out and hatred emanating from his scowling face. "Ven told you about this hidden exit after he found me."

"He did. He saved you this way if I remember."

"Always the hero, never the villain," he shot back.

"Ven is full of darkness, as are we all, Rexous. You are good too, you can prove that to yourself by joining me, start anew with this second life." Scáth meant every word, yet out of the corner of her eye she saw Kithlyn shaking her head. Rex took a step forward, spinning and inverting one of his dirks. Scáth reflexively took a step back. "Give me one good reason you'd rather live in hate than redemption."

"Not everyone deserves a second chance." With his last word, he threw the dirk for Scáth. She did not flinch as her chest became incorporeal, forming into pure shadow, allowing the weapon to pass through without harm. Rexous and Kithlyn both wore faces of shock.

"I won't offer this again Rexous, you will lose otherwise."

"I've already lost." He lunged for her and as he passed the doorway, Kithlyn snapped her arm out, driving the iradinium knuckles she wore into his temple. Rexous was unconscious before he hit the ground and slid to Scáth's feet.

"Let's go." Kithlyn grabbed Scáth's shoulder, pulling her onward. A few dozen-metres away from the royal tree, Scáth looked back to see if Rexous was getting up; instead, she saw Eevie standing in the doorway, motionless.

Only a few minutes of fumbling through the dense woods later, Faenla bounded out from behind a tree, bearing Scáth to the ground and soaking her with licks.

"Faenla," she said joyfully, getting to her feet and wrapping her arms around Faen's huge neck, burying her face in his thick soft mane. "I missed you."

CHAPTER FIFTEEN

Limits of Conviction

Aunna stood there in the cool cavern air, tears clinging to her cheeks as the sheer beauty of this settlement, named Nedea, filled her heart. Fitting, she thought, for its origins in Old Elvish meant 'paradise.'

"It's perfect," she mouthed. Caelen smiled and rested his hand on her shoulder.

"Come see what the Sarnese of Coral Island have built for themselves." He gently lifted his hand away and began walking down the stone-cut steps into Nedea. Aunna wasted no time, causing her to nearly slip more than once on the slick stone as her eyes darted across the cavern. She had seen so much of the world and knew in her heart nothing was as beautiful as what laid before her now, yet she couldn't exactly say why.

"Watch your step now," Caelen mentioned as he stepped on three circular stones placed in one of the many streams that ran throughout the settlement. She nodded kindly in recognition, pausing on the second step as she noted a school of tiny fluorescent fish swimming quickly around the water. Gracefully she leapt onto the spongy moss and lichen and was immediately flanked on all sides by children, gawking and giggling. They rubbed her silk dress between their fingers and reached for her long hair all the while speaking in their native tongue.

"Hello," Aunna said with an ear-to-ear smile, not sure if they understood her.

"They say your eyes and hair are like the berries that grow on morningthorne bushels," Caelen explained.

"Indeed, those berries are my namesake," she said bending down to let the smaller children get up close to see her vibrant purple eyes and raven-coloured hair. The fact these children were made up of humans, Solsta, Kyst, and perhaps many cross-species of the three was not lost on the cleric of peace. She stood again and Caelen spoke in his language. She thought it sounded so much like waves lapping against sand, and the soothing rush of water slowly smoothing those rocks into grains over the centuries.

Many of the girls dispersed but a few stubborn ones clung to Aunna's hands; Caelen rolled his eyes and led them further into town. Most of the structures and homes were built from palm tree logs, thus taking on unique shapes as they were rarely straight. Many were painted vibrant colours and had beautiful coral carvings built in as supports while others were purely decorative. Aunna saw one of her healers already offering aid to the elderly and unwell, while another offered out minor potions and tinctures of healing to the Sarnese healers. Near the centre of town she saw her botanist and artist looking up at the gigantic hole in the ceiling, showering light and life down into what would otherwise be a barren place.

"Come here, I want you to have something." Caelen caught her attention as he led her to a small hut with a palm frond roof and walls that only reached waist-height so it was otherwise wide open. An elderly woman was inside hard at work crafting jewellery. Aunna looked down as the girls clinging to her and they all giggled before playfully bounding off. When she looked back, the jeweller was repeatedly cupping her fingertips to the base of her palm. Aunna moved forward, slightly panicked at the insistence of the woman, but Caelen simply laughed. The elderly woman wore her loupe always in her eye, somewhat like a monocle.

Upon reaching the hut, the jeweller grabbed Aunna's chin and pulled her close; she inspected the cleric deeply with one eye comically enlarged by the magnify glass. Muttering something in her language, the old woman moved away and flipped open an ornate chest, pulling out a long necklace of woven coral. At the bottom dangled an obsidian turtle pendant. The jeweller had Aunna lean over the counter so she could put the necklace on. The elderly woman made a sound of satisfaction before decidedly moving back to a workbench. Aunna fumbled through a small sack and pulled out several gold coins, but Caelen quickly put his hand out to stop her.

"We do not trade currency here, there is no need. These shoun's," he said pointing at her necklace, then to a similar one of a wave around his own neck, "are of cultural significance to the Sarnese."

"They are most beautiful, I am truly honoured by the gesture," she said with a small curtsy.

"The sun-turtle is a most rare and sought after omen. Sarla here has been bestowing these pendants for hundreds of years."

Aunna thought this strange as the jeweller appeared to be human, but she considered whether 'Sarla' could be a title. "What does the sun-turtle represent?"

"Sun-Turtles are ancient, some of have been known to live longer than Kyst or even Dragons. They are warm to the touch, bright, wise and above all, value peace and union. For my people and the others that call the Magma Isles home, the sun-turtles have long since been regarded as guardians to us." Caelen stopped speaking when he noticed his guest fall into herself, fondling the pendant around her neck and staring intently upon it, almost studying it.

" 'Thank you' is insufficient, but it is all I can offer." She smiled and made eye contact with her host; his penetrating turquoise eyes caught her off guard so she quickly pointed to his wave pendant. "And that?"

Caelen grabbed his own pendant and held it out as much as the coral chain would allow. "The wave, eternal, relentless, and each one unique. A symbol of strength, resilience and constant change. No turtle, but a good second," he winked. Aunna shocked herself with a snorting laugh. She looked around and breathed the humid floral air in deeply.

"I see why you want things to remain the way they are, especially without an outside presence." Her whole energy shifted, like light of the sun stolen by a cloud. "The leader of my faith has settled on Coral Island to launch a greater campaign from. I'm afraid we are not going anywhere."

"I know." He reflected sorrowfully for a moment. "Which is why I want you to join us."

This made Aunna rock back on her heels. It was so sudden, so personal and presumptuous. To betray everything she stood for and worked towards her entire life. "Pardon me?" she remarked rather malignantly.

"I am not ignorant of your religion. It stands for peace and life, yet for thousands of years it reaps the land and burdens your followers. *You* do not. Sarla sees the deepest part of one's soul. You are far more aligned with the Sarnese than the zealots of Sesara." It seemed to her that Caelen was almost lecturing her and that did not sit well.

"I will not turn my back on my life's work." Her tone was painfully sharp.

"I'm not asking you too, I'm asking you to enact real change. The people of these islands will never bow to an outsider. It is a hopeless endeavour your Macer has tasked you with. You will never know this sea, its islands, and its many secrets well enough to beat us. The minute any pirate disagrees with the rules your church lays down they will do what they do best. You lost the minute you chose the Magma Isles."

Aunna remained quiet in the face of that declaration. It bothered her how sound of mind it was, and even worse was the fact that they were only here as a launch pad to the Great Northern Rainforest, which many Macer's had contemplated over the centuries; it was obviously abandoned for many reasons, the most important being that it could never be tamed. With Macer O'Donnell sulking from his mere defeat after being so close to capturing the City of Shadow, he decided this was how he would go down in history—the first Macer to settle and convert a section of that most wild and dangerous land.

"That may be well and good, but I hold a position of extreme influence. If I am to inflict real change on my church, there is no better spot for me to do it from," she spoke empathetically and wondered if maybe under different circumstances she could do as Caelen beckoned —live a life without immense responsibility.

Caelen surprised her by dipping low into a bow and coming up with a warm smile. "I can only respect one so devoted to her cause. Please, stay a while longer, we are having a celebration of life tonight. Stay, sup, and soak up our culture." Aunna furrowed her brow with a sweet smile and nodded slightly.

Caelen left her then to experience Nedea as she wished. Truthfully, she didn't know where to start. She was slightly deterred by their conversation about loyalties, but she was never one to waste an opportunity sulking. She started by checking in on the retinue she brought along; the healers were speaking Sarnese thanks to a few magical charms of language transference. They were sharing knowledge and gifts, large smiles and sounds of laughter from both parties. Her botanist, a man named Gren Greenteeth—she was not sure what his true last name was, but the amount of leaves, twigs and grass he chewed on often stained his teeth green—was busy sketching and taking notes on many of the cave flora. After listening to Gren ramble on about why this particular succulent glowed a dull hue of black instead of the normal orange, she patted him on the shoulder and spotted her artist. She was perched most precariously on a thin ridge half-way up the cavern, easel and canvas in front. Aunna found the way to her after a young Sarnese Solsta showed her the way. She went to stand behind the artist, an old friend known only as Arta.

"You capture the colours unlike anyone else, sister." Aunna sat beside Arta on the small foldable bench.

"Thank you, Madam Morningthorne." Arta stopped and gave her friend a sarcastic side eye.

"What will you do with this one?" Aunna asked, referring to the completed piece of art.

"I think I will leave it with the Sarnese."

"Can you believe we're here to convert these people? They don't need anything we have to offer."

"That Solsta who led you up, he asked me to stay in Nedea." Arta now looked at Aunna full on.

"Caelen asked the same of me."

"It is tempting, isn't it? There is something so serene here."

It was easy for Arta to make a case from up here; this vantage point perfectly highlighted the unique beauty of Nedea.

"There is. As if Sesara brushed her fingers along these very stones," Aunna answered.

"Maybe it's just you," Arta countered reverently. That had the Arch Cleric looking puzzled and somewhat bewildered by her old friend's remark. Arta simply shrugged and resumed her painting.

"What would possess you to say such a thing?" She came off more hostile than intended but knew it to be a good thing.

Arta sighed and put her brush back down. "Your presence of late, has been..." she looked around the cavern as if searching for inspiration, "... harmonious."

"Harmonious?" Aunna mirrored in surprise.

"Nobody was thrilled about this Magma Isles assignment, well no one you selected. Runa's followers are as loony as ever. We were honoured of course to come along, but the malcontent on the journey over and the subsequent fighting against the natives has been brutal," Arta finished a little short.

"And?" Aunna prodded.

"You've managed to bring a level of serenity and motivation to us that some are saying they've never felt before. Not even from our Macer."

"Shh," Aunna whispered and shook her head. "Don't say things like that. Despite what we wish to believe, it is not safe for us to share such thoughts."

"Aunna, it's true, for many of us you've filled the void left by Ivan's disappearance. A true leader believing what Sesara intended all along —peace."

"I will always be there for those who need me or for a reminder of the tenets of our faith. Hear my warning, sister—talk of being the new Macer will only end in tragedy." Aunna placed a gentle hand on Arta's. "I am sorry." She stood up and without another word, descended back into Nedea.

Night had just stolen the sky and Nedea cooled off significantly, prompting many to put on thin shawls or wrap themselves in blankets. Aunna was now seated with her handful of followers in the center of town. Before them was a large wooden pyre, with an elven corpse laid peacefully atop it. The body was dressed in fine clothes of woven reeds and a crown of flowers atop their head. The Sesaran visitors saw each and every citizen holding a paper lantern, inlaid with wicker designs, often of waves or palm trees. A group of children approached and handed each of them a lantern of their own. Aunna noted the kids were not nearly as playful or filled with glee as they had been previously. A real sense of reverence and grief had settled over the town as more and more citizens showed up. Soon, everyone was seated on the spongy moss in a circle and a Sarnese man next to Aunna reached to grab her hand. As Aunna accepted, she noticed everyone was holding hands, completing an unbroken circle.

First, Caelen stood and placed his lantern atop the pyre without a word. He sat back down, and the person to his right followed suit, and so on and so on until every person in attendance had placed their lantern atop the pyre. Aunna and her group had never felt so honoured before, to be invited into such a personal aspect of life for these islanders. So they placed their lanterns in accordance and soon Sarla, the Soul Reader, had both her hands placed on the pyre of driftwood. Aunna's sense of awe quickly dissipated as she noted Sarla mouthing a chant, perhaps not wordless, but too quiet for anyone to hear. To Aunna's eyes it appeared as though the elderly woman who had given her the turtle necklace was getting younger.

An internal light manifested in her chest, growing with each heartbeat before splitting and moving down her arms. The light leeched from her fingertips into the pyre and the whole thing burst into flame. Aunna couldn't suppress a necrotic feeling from witnessing Sarla gain youth from this dead body, yet somehow the whole process oozed love, not evil. Sarla didn't lift her fingers from the fire for far too long, it seemed to the Sesaran visitors. Arta looked worried, not sure if she was about to witness the old woman burn herself alive or not. Instead, the Soul Reader breathed a great breath across the flames and all the lanterns illuminated and began to soar. Sarla fumbled back a few steps, clearly weakened, but Caelen was quick to support her.

The lanterns floated up, up and out of the cave and through the hole in the forest floor until they became synonymous with the stars. As the attendee's watched on in awe, Aunna felt a familiar presence about her. In the dancing flames was the image of Sesara, for a moment Aunna thought to smile until the visage became clearer. Through the dancing flames reaching ever higher, she understood that the deceased goddess was solemnly shaking her head.

Aunna looked back up to the floating lanterns and saw nothing, but she heard a single Sarnese man gurgle and fall over with a single arrow through his throat. She looked back up not see stars but instead a curtain of arrows. Hundreds were in attendance some ran for cover while others sat there screaming in horror or frozen in shock and confusion. Aunna and her retinue jumped up, her healers immediately going to aid those injured. As the Sarnese began running in every direction for the safety of their homes, Aunna caught a deathly glare from Caelen. Of course he thought it was a set up, why would he not.

An arrow whizzed by her head, cutting a clean line through her ear, she winced in pain but was distracted as a magical ball of fire collided with a hut and burst into flames. Aunna touched the gem encrusted diadem and brought her hands together, with a word of power she slowly raised her hands skyward. An iridescent yellow shield of light began to glow and expand exponentially. It looked like rain drops on water every time her massive shield of energy caught and arrow or bolt of energy.

"Get them out!" Aunna screamed at Caelen. He returned a gaze of acknowledgement but it was far from friendly. He sprang into action, delegating orders to those he knew would help with the evacuation.

Arta ran up to Aunna and began casting a similar spell to aid her friend. The resistance was increasing tenfold as the barrage of missiles grew.

"How did they follow us?" Arta asked with hands held above her head and thick strain in her voice.

Aunna shook her head, unable to break her weakening concentration for even a second to answer. The shield had grown to cover half the cavern by now and Aunna's diadem was throbbing, like a migraine sending waves of pain throughout her neck, shoulders, and extremities. Although neither of the clerics could see it, a great winged Dragon-blood was soaring down into the cavern, head first with their iradinium sword tip leading the way. Runa drove her sword into the shield, sending waves of destructive magic into it. Aunna looked up to see her counterpart pushing with all her physical and magical might to break her defence. Beating her huge draconic wings, Runa gripped her sword with both hands.

Aunna felt her spell about to shatter and felt too the gem on her forehead fracture like a bolt of lightening. Her spell broke and so did Aunna, falling to her knees from sheer exhaustion. Runa shot through the barrier with unprecedented speed, sword aimed right for the Arch Cleric. Arta saw this and sprang for Aunna, shoved her aside and was immediately impaled through the chest. Runa drove the priest straight into the rocks and roared menacingly at her. Aunna matched Runa's scream at the sight of seeing her dear friend and ally so brutally murdered. She lifted her purple finger nails like claws and static light began skipping between them, Runa knew this devastating spell well and cocooned herself in her huge leathery wings. Aunna still screaming let the spell go as a concentrated beam of light as bright and hot as the sun itself struck her with immense force. Runa's wing was immediately incinerated and the beam of light struck her in the chest plate, turning it red hot. The castle-forged gold enamelled metal began to melt like molten lava. Runa, with an almost divine stroke of skill managed to get her iradinium sword up and block the beam of energy from doing anymore damage. Aunna's finger tips began to burn and bubble as she refused to back down. The fierce paladin got back to her clawed feet and began walking towards Aunna, gripping her red hot sword, however the iradinium would not yield to anything but Litore's primordial flames. Aunna called upon every last bit of divine power within her until her diadem shattered into a thousand pieces and the energy springing forth from her hand turned a viscous black with streams of blue and purple. The magic itself blackened her hand and sent Runa hurling backwards through a hut wall.

Aunna fought to the stop the magic for a split second before she lurched forward in pain, gripping at her wrist and quickly inspecting her corrupted hand. The pain was surreal but the visceral destruction around her quickly brought her back to the present situation. Aunna threw herself upon the corpse of Arta, she had died almost immediately. All around Aunna, Sesaran Soldiers repelled down into the cavern and began slaughtering the Sarnese. She saw burning homes, fleeing citizens, and battling warriors and knew this was her fault. She led them straight here and cursed herself for not foreseeing this. She saw Runa walk out of the burning hut she had been thrown through, head lowered and serpentine eyes glaring back. Aunna knew she could not defeat this divine warrior but she did not care. She could not let this manifestation of her corrupt religion have their way with this entirely peaceful community. She drew a dagger strapped to her thigh, a gift bestowed upon her by her surrogate fathers. Ivan and Ifan had crafted this spirit blade using their mastery in the Paladin and Cleric arts, designed to capture then obliterate any soul it touches across all time and space. The knife its self didn't look extraordinary in any capacity except for the face of an Oni embossed on the forte of the blade.

As the two pillars of the church walked closer to each other, Runa's unshakable rage cracked at the sight of this puny human facing her with a dagger.

"You gonna kill me with that?" Runa snorted.

Aunna said nothing, determined to land one solid strike, rummaging through her years of training as a Paladin for something that could help her here. When they were in range of each other it all happened in the blink of an eye. Runa swung down across Aunna's body, Aunna ducked and weaved the opposite direction and plunged her dagger into Runa's clavicle.

A light so bright it blinded everyone in the cave exploded from the wound. Aunna's ears rang like her head was inside a belfry. She was shoved back by an equally blind Runa and stumbled around for several heartbeats. Panicking, she took measured steps backwards to create some distance from her enemy, if there was even an enemy left. On her tenth step she tripped over a log and splashed into deep water. She felt something dragging her deeper and deeper, fighting and thrashing Aunna swam as hard as she could. In what direction she did not know as her eyes still burned white, the only she thing she understood was it must be Runa pulling her below. She fought, kicked and flailed until it occurred to her she no longer felt a grip. The next thought was that her feet had broken the surface of the water; like pulling a fish out of water. With a grunt she landed hard on a pebbled beach. Her eyes finally seemed cured and she felt the soothing midnight darkness against them. Knees sunk into the little rocks, she looked around and found herself to be alone and not in a tropical land, rather there was nothing around at all. An endless sea of ankle deep water.

"Still a thorn in my side are we."

Aunna froze, that voice, she had not heard it in over a decade. She had seen his death first hand and knew this to be some trick. She squeezed her eyes shut tighter than she ever had and told herself she was hearing things.

"Oh my little doe, it is okay, you may look." The voice was so calm and paternal. She felt a firm hand gently grip her chin and lift it but she refused to open her eyes. "Look at me, one last time." Everything in her mind and body told her to keep her eyes shut but she simply could not waste this chance to see him one last time.

Aunna opened her eyes to see a faintly translucent and shimmering Ifan Fjell kneeling before her, warm and loving smile as large as ever.

Aunna's purple eyes filled with tears.

"You've become more than I ever dreamed of, I'm so proud of you little doe."

"How are you here?" She asked reaching to hold his hand but it passed through his incorporeal form.

"You used the knife." he said sombrely. She nodded, a tear falling as she did. "It appeared to have back fired. Your soul was about to be obliterated when I pulled you back into this world.

"How? How did you even know what was happening?"

"The dead see more than the living. And there is no saviour without sacrifice." He smiled again and looked upon her with such pride.

"You didn't." Aunna said in more despair than disbelief knowing he had just given up his soul, his afterlife in eternity to prevent her ultimate demise.

"Any parent would. I'm so proud of you, Aunna Fjell Morningthorne, Daughter of Peace, Child of Sesara." He placed an ethereal kiss on her cheek. Aunna closed her eyes as he did, wishing to feel his kiss but knowing she would not.

"Don't leave," she cried softly.

CHAPTER SIXTEEN

Better Together

What are the limits of one's self? What amount of spiritual pressure does it take to crack one's being? For some, it could be the death of a loved one, an atrocious act suffered by another's hand, for others the loss of their home. Although there may be overlap in these scenarios, from what I have seen, every individual succumbs at a different point, but the metamorphosis to evil from tragedy is inevitable. Sooner or later, no matter the person, enough bad things will poison the good in them, leaving them vile and hateful. It has been so present all around me, my whole life.

Renic Devar died the most honourable elf I've ever met and far before his time was due. Queen Trilara, the closest thing I ever had to a mother, died with a good heart but still young. The tragedy that rocked Silva and loss of his mother turned Rexous into a veritable monster. My dear Vakar lost everything, and so too it would seem everything that made him good. It leaves me to ponder, if good can turn to bad, can the opposite be said? The optimist within hopes a soul can be redeemed, dark can turn to light and hate into love. I have to hold out for this truth. For I fear that person I was who first stepped outside the great rainforest is slipping away, consumed by hatred, barraged by failure.

At the behest of my closest companions, I abandoned the love of my life so that others may do what I always promised—keep her safe. I would rather have walked into Silva unarmed than live with the shame I carry now. I would rather kill and not stop killing until I had my beloved Scáth back.

- Ven Devar

* * *

Ven found himself seated on a rock beside the large pool of crystal, still water in the centre of Glowen'ashen. He watched with keen unwavering eyes as the reflecting moons and stars slowly moved across the water.

"You're not the most diplomatic elf I've met." Aolendìr approached and stood next to him, watching the reflection as well. "Far from the least diplomatic, in your defence."

"Kaiason," Ven echoed. "There is only one other who knows." Ven turned his heavy opalescent eyes upon the Solsta.

"Never assume anything, young Kyst. Do this, and you will be impossible to surprise." He gave Ven a disarming smile, trying to offer a piece of advice that could save him one day. The hunter noticed this and felt even more uncomfortable about his standing with this ambiguous elf.

"How did you know?"

"I've made it my business to track down the others of your kind. As fate would have it, I've found four Grimìr and counting in this forest alone."

Ven furrowed his brow at that. "Myself and Njor. Who else?"

Aolendìr smiled. "All will be revealed in good time. I suspect the Grimìr are drawn to each other. What truly matters is your next step."

"I'm going back to Shallowbay hideout. With or without new allies, it's time we started making real progress."

"I couldn't agree more." Aolendìr squared up to Ven, grabbed his shoulder cape and dipped into a bow. "I am at your service, Mighty Ven Devar. Say the word and consider it done."

Before Ven could accept or refuse this pledge of service, the rest of his troop returned with Wynn in the front. Ven stood to meet them.

"My people will help. I will go as ambassador to meet with Queen Saphier and discuss further cooperation between our people."

Ven did not speak but he offered a nod that hopefully extended his gratitude and relief. Wynn returned the gesture before looking to everyone and patting the sides of her thighs, indicating for the next move to be revealed.

"And our merry band grows ever larger and cheery," Rinya chimed in sarcastically.

"If it's all the same to our merry band, I'd like to get going now." Ven said and saw only agreement around the group. He ruffled around in his pockets and pulled out a smooth, sky-blue runestone, the one he received from Queen Saphier under the pretense that through their magical map, it should bring him back.

"Good to see old magic making a return," Aolendìr quipped, regarding the stone. Ven looked to him and received a smirk in return. "I suggest everyone grab hands."

Ven reached for Onstera and she grabbed his hand. Soon everyone followed suit until Aolendìr reached for Rinya's hand with a cockish grin. Rinya rolled their eyes and sighed heavily, clamping his hand like a vice. Against their better judgment they looked at him, hoping to see discomfort from the pain, but saw only a lustful gaze.

Using his free hand, Ven held the stone out in front of him and read the rune. It jumped out of his hand and bounced around on the ground inside the circle they had created. It jumped and hopped like a popping kernel until it exploded in blue smoke.

Scáth, accompanied by Kithlyn and Faenla, found their way back to the Shallowbay hideout by dawns first light. The two Scorn showed up exhausted, Scáth still suffering from nearly a month as prisoner and Kithlyn from shadow-jumping all night to keep up with Faenla. As they approached the beach that would take them along the seawall, Scáth caught sight of Agan waiting in the sand next to a dying fire. As he noticed their approach, he stood up and smiled larger than Scáth had ever seen. He walked up next to Faenla and helped his dear friend off the mighty wolfs back. She was stiff but nevertheless jumped into a long embrace.

"Good to have you back, Princess," he squeezed her tightly.

"Good to be back." Scáth pulled away but used Agan for support as she looked around. The half-orc gave Kithlyn a firm nod of thanks and the Shadow Mistress reciprocated, surprising herself to be so glad at seeing this reunion.

"Where is he?" Scáth asked the obvious.

Agan hesitated for a moment before deciding on the right words. "Let's go inside, they know more."

The hulking half-orc supported Scáth with ease as the four walked along the rocky shore into the cave system. Clearly an effort had been made to spruce the place up some; more sets of furniture were scattered throughout, a few braziers brought some warmth to the slick and damp interior. They walked through a series of twisting halls, each one growing colder until they came up to the War Room. A hunter and sage stood guard but immediately opened the door after seeing Agan and Faenla. Inside was Saphier and Ina, with that large glowing map consuming one entire wall. The two Kyst regarded the guests, and expressions of relief consumed them.

The tall and beautiful queen walked up to them with her arms raised in welcome. She stood in front of Scáth and bowed low.

"It is an honour to meet you Lady Scáth ShadowScorn, I've heard only extraordinary things."

Scáth smiled and thought she detected a hint of bitterness in those words. "Thank you, Your Grace. I am forever grateful for your help in recovering me from Vakar's wrath. Before we go on, where might I find Ven?"

Saphier squinted somewhat suspiciously at that but was quickly overtaken by Ina. "I left him a cycle from here, he was about to meet with the Gloom elves of Glowen'ashen. Ven has been trying his hardest to unite the clans of this forest against Vakar's kingdom." That brought a bittersweet smile to Scáth's lips. "I assure you it took a great deal of convincing to keep him from marching on Vakar's front door and rescuing you. As you can imagine, we couldn't let him throw himself to his doom like that." Ina seemed as though she was apologizing and Scáth recognized this.

"Do you know when he'll be back?" the Scorn asked, and Faenla backed her up with a stomp of his paw.

"When he has succeeded in his mission. The Mighty Ven Devar is crucial to this effort in restoring freedom to the Great Northern Rainforest," Queen Saphier butted in rather authoritatively. Agan and Kithlyn exchanged glances and Scáth held a hostile stare with the queen. Faenla sensed this and brought his body to a guarding position over Scáth.

After a tense moment, Ina cut it with kind words. "What can we do to aid your recovery, Lady Scáth?"

"A dark room and some rest would do me wonders," Scáth graciously requested.

"Follow me, if you will," Ina led her and Faenla to the room Ven had been using.

"Not overly tactful," Agan said gruffly to Saphier.

"I did what you said. I spent great resources to get this Shadow Mistress here and recover the Princess."

"I'm right here," Kithlyn said sardonically with a wave. "And you're welcome."

"She was a queen, your highness, and relinquished that title. Never in all my travels have I seen someone wise enough to shed that kind of power willingly." Agan laid it out plainly.

"It sounds like the easy route," Saphier replied indignantly. Agan stared back and considered what to say next. In his youth he might have roared and rambled at this level of scrutiny. He was wiser and calmer now, yet Kithlyn spoke up first.

"I'm new to this party and I just met Scáth mere hours ago, but I've studied humanoid behaviour my whole life. I've made it my art to scour one's heart and mind, know their weakness and exploit it. Scáth ShadowScorn might just be one of the most powerful people I've ever encountered, you'd do well to keep her happy and on your side because from everything I have heard, where she goes, Ven goes. That is why I am here, is it not? You found the world's greatest assassin to bring her here so Ven would fight in your little rebellion?" Kithlyn paused to let Saphier nod, and Saphier did so. "Then I suggest these three things; appreciate the skilled warriors under your thumb, don't piss on my hard work, and find me a room to sleep in because I've never fancied the daytime."

The group of adventurers appeared on the rocky walkway with a bang and a flash of light. They all quickly let go of each other to rub their eyes for they were momentarily blinded.

"What in the underworld is that crap magic?" Rinya complained as they stumbled around.

"Squeeze your eyes shut for ten seconds and open them," Aolendìr said calmly. Everyone did so and soon the evening sun could be seen reflecting off the lapping waves. They all took a collective moment to breathe deeply and consume the beautiful sight. It was a beautiful, warm sun-soaked eve on the coastline. Searavens flew overhead and the wind tickled their skin.

"Look who came back," Agan blustered as he came out of the cave to greet them, Ina close behind.

"With many allies in tow," Ina added, moving to greet them all. Ven walked up to Agan and made to apologize but the half-orc clapped a hand on his shoulder.

"All is fine, elf." He smiled and motioned his head inside. Ven nodded and pulled Agan in close to whisper.

"Keep an eye on the Solsta," he played it off and patted Agan on the shoulder before going to find Scáth. Ven walked into the hideout and saw the door to his room. He pushed open the reclaimed wood and saw Scáth asleep on the bed through the crack. He slowly stepped inside and noted Faenla's head pop up. The wolf lumbered up to his feet and over to Ven. The Kyst immediately sensed anger coming from Faenla. He couldn't be sure exactly what Faen was angry about but understood it was justified, so Ven got down to one knee and held his hand out. The wolf came over and sniffed Ven a number of times, even encircling him once before stopping eye-to-eye with the hunter.

"I'm sorry I left you," Ven whispered in kystin. "I wanted you with me but I was confused. I felt betrayed somehow when Āina replaced you. I know that's not your fault and you two are not the same. I hope you can forgive me." Ven lowered his gaze and felt the wolf judging him. A few shaky breaths later, he felt the fuzzy warmth of Faenla's forehead against his own, then a giant lick across his face. Ven stood up to wipe the slobber off his face and the wolf went and curled up next to the door, guarding his two favourite people.

Ven walked to the armour stand and removed his road-dirty leather chest and torso piece. Unstrapping his bracers, he hung his cloak up and quickly dressed into fresh underclothes. With every ounce of stealth he could muster, he slid onto the bed and laid on his side, head against the soft pillow. He could see Scáth's hair, now out of their braids, curly and misting away into the dark room. He wrapped one arm around her waist and fell asleep before his next thought. He awoke sometime later, judging by the candles in the room, many many hours later.

Scáth was rolled over now and facing him, those bright white eyes adoring him. Ven broke into a smile that consumed him.

"Hey," he whispered.

"Hey, lover boy," she said while placing her fingers on his cheek. Her smile turned serious as she pulled him in closer for a kiss, softly at first until she couldn't control herself. She was kissing him hard and passionately now. Squeezing his body to hers, wishing to feel every part of him as closely as possible.

"Wait," Ven, against his better judgment, pulled away. Scáth was embarrassed at first, but Ven's demeanour quickly extinguished that. "Come with me." He leapt out of bed, grabbed his trident from the armour rack and held his hand out to her. She smiled, throwing his cloak over her underclothes and took his hand. With Faenla taking up the rear to protect them, they walked outside into the night air. A clear sky, with the moons so close after the spring equinox of celestial harmony, where the three moons aligned perfectly. It meant the moonlight bathing the world was more purple than red now. Walking hand in hand, Ven safely navigated their way through the bio-luminescent forest, poisonous plants, and treacherous trails. It reminded Scáth of her first few days in the forest; it was a miracle she survived as she long she did before Ven found her. Only now she wasn't afraid, not because she walked beside her love, but because she was no longer the sheltered and defenceless princess she was back then.

Upon walking around one tree that seemed to never end, a great light danced against the low-hanging forest canopy. A pool of steaming water, the most beautiful colour of turquoise Scáth had ever seen, was being slowly filled and agitated by a tiny trickling waterfall. Overhead were blossoming flower trees, occasionally losing a petal to a gust of wind, creating waves of descending light as the flower petals fell lazily into the pool.

"What do you think, milady?" he asked with a coy smile. She looked to Ven with watery eyes as the perfection of it all was almost too much. "It's warm," he said kindly, not sure but hoping she loved it. She looked back to the water and skimmed her hand across it, warm as a bath she thought, warmer maybe. The tingling sensation was not lost on her, it invigorated her weary muscles. "Do you like it?" he questioned sheepishly.

She took a few steps forward and stopped just out of reach. She untucked her soft white undershirt from her black leather pants and slowly lifted it over her head. For the first time baring herself entirely to him, his reaction was predictable and dumbfounded. She turned away from him to continue undressing next to the pool before slipping into the water.

Treading water now she looked back to him, "Are you ever going to join me?"

Ven finally broke out of his stupefied state and began nervously removing his clothes, placing his weapons close to the pool edge for safety. She noted his natural white tattoo-like veins running down his lip to his back, chest, arms, and legs. So too did she notice great welts and black bruises across his entire body. He slipped into the water, and though he was almost more comfortable in the water than on land, his heart was about to beat out of his chest. She swam closer to him and wrapped her arms around his shoulders.

"I've seen you fight demons, stand tall against a dragon, march bravely into the unknown, but I've never seen you tremble like this. We don't have to." She placed a meaningful kiss on his cheek.

"No, I mean yes. Yes, I want this. I've just never…" he trailed off looking for the right words but she found them first.

"I love you, Ven Devar."

He pulled her closer. "I love you."

CHAPTER SEVENTEEN

The City of Ragos

The Horizon's Edge surfed the growing and crashing waves thanks to the amazing Captain Tsuni Tal and her crew. The Dragon-blood boy was bent over the taff rail, vomiting up his breakfast, his ivory scales now sickly white. The ShadowScorn teenager who had introduced herself to the crew as Hazi was rubbing his back and humming a comforting song. The sky was a swirling mass of grey and black, turning the sea into vengeful force. Snow was falling but the sea spray kept the ship wet enough from freezing. Captain Tsuni had been keeping them far from land to keep them off the Royal Navy's radar. She had announced the night before they would be turning for land now to make a straight shot for the City of Ragos. That had come as welcomed news to these two as the sturdiness of land was all they desired.

"Look," Hazi rubbed her hand against his and beckoned Spike to look up. The scaled lad did so and saw the famed city breaking through the stormy weather. The city itself sat high upon the Cliffs of Skölnir, a wide peninsula that was surrounded by the oddest walls the Scorn girl had ever seen. "What is that?" she asked.

Spike stood proud now as the sight of his capital filled his sick bones with fervour. The two were now surrounded by the Aquon lad and nearly the entire crew, for few could resist the urge to look upon the infamous city.

"The Leviathan," Spike answered in awe. "I've only seen it once before when I was barely a hatchling, but I remember the story well." Ivan was now gripping the rail as he himself had never laid eyes on this most unbelievable sight.

Spike looked around to see everyone staring at him. His blue serpentine eyes made contact with Hazi's black ones and her smile clearly requested he tell the story. Looking back at the city, he began.

"In the First Age, Skalgr the Diamond Dragon had fought with Nuada over the dominion of the dead. From the Underworld's deepest, most vile depths, Nuada sent the Leviathan to kill Skalgr. This would be the first of ten known Leviathans to rampage across the realms. When the God of Death met this foe, even he was at loss as how to defeat it. For the monster could wrap itself around whole countries, it brandished thousands of teeth, bore scales harder than Iradinium, carried claws so long and sharp it could carve entire canyons with a single swipe. Skalgr faced the beast and suffered greatly for it, nearly dying in the process, saved only by the Goddess Pirelia.

As the two gods fled, leaving the Leviathan to wreak havoc across Litore, they began to form union. From this union would come a child unlike anything before it. In a matter of cycles, the two had perfected their creation, granting it the power to consume death itself to grow in power as Skalgr did, and the gift of eternal rebirth and fire from Pirelia. From that day on, nothing would be the same as Ragos the Reaper was born unto the world. He was the first Dragon-blood, created in Skalgr's image, with eyes and wings of fire. His scales were an ever-changing weave of elements and colour, a spearhead created from Skalgr's own claw and haft forged from Pirelia's own fires. Their son was ready to conquer any foe.

Ragos flew from Celestia and struck the first blow against the Leviathan. The Reaper stood fierce against the monster and their war shaped the very land we walk upon. For cycles their battle raged, and Ragos suffered a hundred deaths, but every time his mother's gift of eternal life resurrected him to fight anew. Eventually their battle brought them to the peninsula that we now look upon. After the monster had gouged out one of his eyes, Ragos flew for its maw. Entering through a valley of teeth, the great Leviathan spewed an ocean of acid out, but too late, for the Reaper with his spear had entered through the Leviathans brain and out its eye.

Having defeated the One of Ten, Ragos grabbed its body and

wrapped it around the peninsula. The Reaper laid himself to rest amongst his enemy's bones. Seeing the feats of his son, Skalgr created the Dragon-bloods we know today."

Everyone stood in silence as the view became clearer and the giant bones covered in snow no longer looked like disjointed rocks. Some of the crew stood there, picturing the event in the most vivid parts of their imaginations, while others onboard scoffed. Spike looked at Hazi with glistening eyes and a prideful smile. She returned it before frowning as he bent over the rail to puke again. Ivan laughed before the sound of disturbed air reached his ears. He looked up and around then finally spotting three figures through the slate-grey clouds and whirling snow.

"Flyers!" he shouted for all the crew to hear.

Tsuni cursed under her breath and Tilly leapt atop a crate to view the Rhogarian's skimming the turbulent water, carried by their great leathery wings heading straight for the Horizon's Edge.

"If they find your cargo," Tsuni glared hatefully at the gnome, "we'll all rot."

The only response Tilly had was to adjust the spectacles on her little nose. The captain spun with a grunt of anger and rushed down to the poop deck. "At ease everyone, go about your duties. Alaana, Seerene, Ivan, you're with me."

Ivan turned to regard the three women but he turned back as the three elite Rhogarian warriors were seconds away now. They must know—perhaps the Pirate Prince tipped them off—why else send their best fighters? At the last second, one of the three flyers split off and soared straight up with incredible grace and speed. The other two hovered just metres away from the rail. Ivan looked up at them in awe. Their great wings, easily six metres across, were lined along the ridge with serrated blades so they could fly by their enemies with great affect, splitting them in two with ease.

"Are you the captain of this vessel?" the apparent leader asked with a coarse, rigid, militaristic voice. His scales were a grand gold in hue and he wore a helmet above his natural ridged brow with a single long spike. Ivan merely stood aside and swept his arm out to Tsuni.

"Well met, I am Captain Tsuni Tal of the Horizon's Edge. Have we offended your customs in some way?"

"Not at all my friend. I am the harbour master for our great city, this is merely a routine check for new vessels. I noted no distinguishable flag flown. May I come aboard, good captain?"

Tsuni bowed graciously and the two flyers landed easily. Ivan noted the second flyer was much younger, her breastplate lavishly decorated and lightweight. She was of a dark-red colour that highlighted her serpentine eyes with a ferocity unseen by many.

"I am Raz and this is my colleague, Kalix. What brings you to the great City of Ragos?" the harbour master, Raz asked. Kalix was eyeing up Spike with great interest.

"I believe your colleague has already guessed," Tsuni answered, motioning to the young ivory Dragon-blood in her care. "We found him in the cesspool of Port Noga when we stopped to resupply, along with Hazi over there and a young Aquon."

Raz seemed completely unconcerned by this and turned to face Spike. "Come here, lad." Spike looked nervously to Ivan who nodded confidently. He approached, merely half the height of Raz and Kalix but he stood tall.

"Is what they say true?"

"It is, sir. We three were locked in cages when Ivan here rescued us. He promised us we'd see home again." Spike spoke with great uncertainty in his voice, as any child does when confronted by a scary authority figure.

"Hmm," Raz bellowed as he contemplated his next words, never breaking eye contact with Spike. "And where is home for you, son?"

"I don't remember, exactly. I don't remember growing up anywhere per se. I was so young when I was taken. But I do remember my parents, and them always talking of the City of Ragos."

"I suspect his kin was on a caravan when he was taken," Ivan added.

Raz simply put a clawed hand on the young lad's shoulder. "You're home now." He walked to tower over Ivan, tall and intimidating. Yet, Ivan looked at him with tired and experienced eyes.

"It was simply out of the goodness of your heart you set these slaves free? Surely humans have the greatest affinity for slaving," Raz insinuated without fear. Ivan smiled dispassionately; he had chosen the right words, but not before Hazi interjected.

"It's true, he saved us." She came beside Ivan and intertwined her fingers with his in a show of solidarity. "I was taken by a band of elves, I'll have you know, before being sold to a human who had several of your species in his employ. Ivan is among the kindest souls I've ever met." She stood proud in this.

Raz laughed aloud and alone. "What they say about you ShadowScorn is true." Raz turned one last time. "Quite the crew you have here, Captain. His business is about freeing slaves, yet he is not in charge."

"He's currently paying the bills, so I take him where he wishes."

"Our capital has no use of mercenaries."

"None here, Harbour Master, just a ship looking to make berth." Tsuni bowed uncharacteristically again.

"Good, show me your cargo and manifest and I'll personally see to resupplying your ship on the crown's behalf for escorting Spike home," Raz cocked his head to Ivan, "and anything else we may offer to aid in your good deeds."

Ivan squinted for an instant, unsure if it was a threat or a genuine offer.

"Surely, we can come to another mutually beneficial arrangement? I might have just the artifact for you if gold is not up to your taste?" Tsuni questioned most confidently.

Kalix' nostrils flared with a puff of black smoke and Raz sidled up to Tsuni. Everyone on board froze. Alaana went for a flint-lock pistol but Sereene stayed her hand. Ivan slowly moved Hazi behind him for her own safety, but also so he could rest his hand on a dagger tucked against his tailbone.

Raz scoffed as he towered over Tsuni. "Show me the hold, Captain."

"Excuse me," Tilly's voice rang out and it took a second for Raz to spot her. "Yes, yes, over here," she said, clutching her tome a little tighter.

"Yes?" Raz said through gritted fangs.

"Tilly," she waved faintly. "As the ships purser, it would be my privilege to accommodate you with our manifest and show you every nook and cranny of our hold." She swept away a stray strand of blue hair from her face and fixed her spectacles once more. "If it pleases," she added with a smile only describable as uncouth.

"Aye," his voice strained. "Kalix, stay here while Captain Tsuni and

Tilly escort me below."

Kalix nodded and gave a hand signal to her flyer comrade above. Ivan watched most suspiciously as that flyer disappeared from sight. He met the gaze of Kalix and felt a familiar distrust.

As the three walked below, Raz asked for the manifest. Before Tsuni could respond with a well-planned lie—for she never fancied keeping a detailed list of her supplies or cargo, and in fact did not have a purser as Tilly so claimed—she was astounded by the gnomes next move.

"Here you are, Harbour Master," she flipped open her most curious and hefty tome for the briefest moment to pull out several pieces of parchment. Judging by Raz's expression, everything he found on the list was satisfactory. Of course, Tilly hadn't stopped filling his ear about where they had purchased what and at what rate. As they reached the third and lowest deck, everything appeared up to snuff. Tsuni was beginning to understand why Zerenies kept the river gnome around.

"Everything here is in order," he addressed Tilly before turning back around to face Tsuni who had been following without a peep. "So why would a captain with nothing to hide, attempt bribery?"

"Call me cautious, a few crooked harbour masters can taint a girls expectations." Tsuni said dryly and a thump from a closed room punctuated her lie. As Raz turned to the sound, Tsuni closed her eyes in frustration.

"Supply closet, mop likely just shifted, nothing of intrigue good Harbour Master," Tilly said nonchalantly. "Let me show you the captain's quarters to round out our tour and set your mind at complete ease." She began walking towards Raz to escort him out but he threw up his hand as another thump was heard.

"You'll show me that closet." His countenance was enough to make Tsuni's skin crawl. Tilly bowed and made for the closet door. Raz was close behind her, sure footed for whatever came next. Tsuni wasn't far behind, resolute to strike him down when he saw the dwarves. Tilly unlocked the metal latch, and without anyone seeing, opened and closed her tome while swinging the door open.

Tsuni had her rapier halfway unsheathed when she indeed found nothing but mops, brushes, and general maintenance supplies instead of the brig with four bound and gagged dwarves.

"Hmm," Raz grunted.

"Yeah," Tilly smiled with a nod and gently closed the door again. Tsuni quickly stood at ease, hands at her side.

"May we dock now?" she asked out of fraying patience. Raz approached and studied her for a moment, scouring for any excuse. He must not have been able to think of any as he handed her a sealed scroll.

"Bring this to our royal slip and they'll see you're accommodated for your efforts."

"Thank you."

Raz, without escort, made his way topside. Tsuni looked to Tilly with equal parts hesitation and admiration. "Nobody said you were a wizard."

The gnome waddled past and shrugged her shoulders.

Ivan was at first concerned to see Raz emerge alone and even more unsure as the harbour master strode right up to him. "Bring the lad to the Church of Ragos, they'll see him sorted out."

Ivan barely had the chance to nod before Raz gazed at Kalix and the flyers soared up from the deck and were lost in the clouds.

"Make for port, ladies!" Tsuni commanded now that her and Tilly were top side, and a weight of anxiety was swept off the ship.

Ivan sidled up to Tsuni and asked quietly. "How?"

She didn't say anything but wagged her chin at the gnome. Ivan looked at the peculiar creature standing awkwardly and clutching her tome tighter than a babe to its mother. A theory was beginning to form in his mind but not one he was yet ready to share.

"Glad to have her then," he said with an unconvincing smile to Tsuni. Ivan strode over to the taffrail and continued to admire the view. It wasn't long before Tilly was dragging a crate over and climbing on top so she could also enjoy the view.

"Who will you send to deliver spike?" she asked.

Ivan looked strangely at her. "Myself, of course."

"I strongly suggest you do not step foot in that city," she protested while giving a tight squeeze to her tome.

He looked from the tome to her with disregard. "Your pirate prince does not control my actions."

"This is between two servants of higher powers. Only evil awaits you in that city."

"And how would you know?"

She pushed up her glasses and looked out over the icy water again. "Knowledge is a powerful thing, wouldn't you agree?"

Ivan nodded slowly.

"If you insist, then I would like to accompany you."

"Into evil?" he clarified.

"To better understand something, one must subject themselves to it," she responded almost scientifically.

"How did you end up in the charge of a pirate prince?" he questioned out of genuine curiosity.

"So I'd be right here, right now."

It was now sundown but that did not deter Ivan, Tilly and Spike from entering into the City of Ragos proper. In truth, the once Arch Paladin of Sesara felt right at home, for this city was no less large nor magnificent than Serenstrom. He walked through the ancient, cobbled streets with his armour on and hood up attempting to blend in with the evening crowd, which turned out to be far easier than he surmised. There were floating lanterns in the air casting shadows of Timber, Cave, Desert and Lava-dragons across the streets. They figured this was some part of a greater celebration happening. Suddenly the earth began to shake, yet no one panicked, and when the quake had subsided everyone jumped and cheered. He grabbed Spike's shoulder and pulled him a little closer.

"Let's not get separated now," he warned softly. Spike agreed in awe and bewilderment. The young lad grabbed Tilly's shoulder to bring her a bit closer too.

The nearer to the city centre they got, the more packed with folk and buildings it became. The buildings were mostly a combination of stone and wood with layer upon layer of cracked and missing plaster, no doubt to insulate them from the arctic conditions. Every street swirled with snow dust and every structure had brown snow compacted neatly against its base. Ivan looked up to see the sky entirely obscured by crooked walls, balconies, and twisting roofs. Brightly lit windows spilled patches of glowing gold while folk clung to their balcony rails in all manner of leisure, some undeniably better suited for the privacy of enclosed walls. Ivan was nearly knocked asunder from his gazing as a group of drunken patrons erupted from one rowdy establishment. The party of Dragon-bloods seemed not to notice him as they stumbled through the crowded street.

They were on their way again and Ivan noted that the closer they got to the palace, which was the southernmost part of peninsula, there were less and less other species walking about. It seemed every nine of ten people they passed were Dragon-bloods of the finest calibre and social repute. Their scales, every colour under the rainbow, seemed to glow and glisten under the moonlight as the streets opened up, transforming into grand roads. Buildings that took his breath away lined the immaculately maintained causeways. And although the street was still busy, it accommodated the crowd with great forethought. Between the two roads that must have spanned fifteen-metres across each, was a divide of well-kept winterberry bushes, topiary's, and huge brazers, each one a different colour than the last.

He noted keenly the city guard were entirely replaced by Royal Flyers, their wings all lined with razors and the house emblem of King Dusanith emblazoned on their boiled-leather armour, that emblem being a dragon skull wreathed in a crown of flame. They patrolled in groups of five, occasionally the fifth one landing while another took flight. Ivan took care to make sure his sigil of Sesara was covered by his now rich appearing cloak.

"That must be it," Spike finally spoke up while pointing to a building on their left. Little doubt was left in their minds as they approached a massive temple with nearly 100 deep inset steps leading to an ominous grand entry, made all the more daunting in appearance by a twenty-metre tall statue of Ragos the Reaper himself, standing proud, wings spread wide with his spear planted dominantly and an eye patch covering the left side of his face. The statue stood without a plinth in front of two doors that appeared as though an army could march forthwith. Ivan had imagined just that scenario happening many times as they stood awe-struck at the base of the grand stairs. He looked down to Spike who was gaping at the sight. "Ready?" Ivan asked.

Spike looked at him and his expression said it all. Ivan returned the gesture before quickly glancing at Tilly, who was in silent contemplation. They made their way up and into the temple, but as they passed through the doorway, Ivan felt a pressure in his mind that he had not known before, an unrelenting feeling of congestion, and for a moment he thought he'd pass out until he was brought to by a voice.

"Welcome."

Ivan opened his eyes and found himself in a pitch-black room, if it even was a room, for he could not know. There was only blackness, save one Dragon-blood holding a single candle dripping wax onto the stone floor. They were grey, not a shade he knew was possible for their kind, and perhaps she was the oldest Dragon-blood he had ever bared witness to. Her wings were curled neatly against her back, her eyes completely glazed over by cataracts. The paladin quickly realized Spike was not with him.

"Where is he?" He demanded the truth, yet Tilly seemed completely unsurprised.

"Safe," she answered melodiously. "It is a bold thing for the former Arch Paladin of Sesara to step within these hallowed walls," she added just as warmly.

"I suspect you are right."

"Never, in fact, has someone of your faith walked these very stones that our saviour blessed with his own blood."

Ivan wasn't sure what her point was. "I mean no offence. The lad, Spike was in dire trouble when I found him. Honour alone would have dictated I return him safely to his people, yet the tenets of my faith demanded it." He bowed his head respectfully.

She smiled, then pursed her weary lips to blow out the candle. All was revealed as the three were now standing at the entry hall of the temple and saw Spike being cared for by a priestess. The young lad waved at Ivan happily, which warmed the old human's spirit.

"Most in your faith these days would have sold him for a profit."

Ivan shot her a glare but was at a loss for words, as he knew it to be true.

"You will help him find his kin?" he asked, almost insisting.

"We will."

"I'll say my good-bye then and leave you in peace." Ivan bowed once again and turned to Spike. Much to his surprise, the lad was being walked away by the priestess. "Spike," Ivan called out, but it yielded no response nor action from him. He looked back to the ancient Dragon-blood with disdain.

"You would deny me a final word to him?"

Another foreboding smile crossed her rigid and tight, leathery lips. "No." She walked closer to the paladin. Normally a Dragon-blood stands several heads taller than a human but her old, withered frame barely met his shoulder, as was evident when she reached to grab his chin. "We would deny you everything."

Ivan's expression became one of horror in the blink of an eye. He quickly turned to see the King of Rhogar, Dusanith Dreki, massive, imposing, and as yellow as the sun. He put a mailed fist in Ivan's face and the human fell in an unconscious heap.

CHAPTER EIGHTEEN

War in the North

The war room within the rebel hideout was full with adventurers. The room was dim; candles hovered aimlessly while larger sources of light illuminated grand trestle-table, yet the dark rock walls seemed to soak up light rather than reflect it. Queen Saphier sat regally at one head of the table, many in attendance still in awe of her legendary beauty, especially one Aolendìr Tardinian. To Saphier's left sat lead hunter Ina, then Ven, Scáth, Agan, Kithlyn, and Onstera. The Mistress of Shadow and the Sanguis Queasitor sitting next to each other appeared as polar opposite. Both physically strong and skilled with a blade, but Kithlyn's wisping black hair and shadow pooling around her eclipsing eyes was in stark contrast to Onstera's olive skin, platinum hair and piercing silver eyes. Aolendìr certainly didn't mind sitting so close to them as he somehow managed to secure the other head of the table.

To Saphier's right was a recent but important addition to their effort. There sat a Kyst male, small by their species standards with turquoise hair, skin that nearly matched, and a horrid scar consuming nearly the entire right half of his face. Surrounding the eye was a great blast of a scar that branched out across his cheek, up his forehead and down his chin, as if he caught a lightning bolt with his eye, which by Ven's account is exactly what happened. The Mighty Hunter had heard of this Kyst. Sŷna was the preeminent sage in River Luvium, the oldest settlement in the Great Northern Rainforest. It was no small thing managing to escape Vakar's rule and find the rebels.

Next to Sŷna was the prestigious dwarf Nordhum Ironboot, former commander to the entire army of the Dwarves of SilverRock, current master of the Willow Guild. He led the famous guild on innumerable quests and missions during the War of a Thousand Dragons. To his left sat the ever caring and indomitable Faye Walker, who stood bravely beside Nordhum on every journey. Cleric to the Care-Taker, Faye had guided lost spirits to the Evar Spring Glade for over a decade. Wynn Walker and sister to Faye Walker, sat together. Beside Wynn was Scarlet Albright, then Njor and Rinya.

"I thank you and offer the full extension of hospitality my good kin and kind can offer to each and every one of you. I know some of you have made a great journey to be with us and that will not be forgotten. Let me say that though many of us have just met, we all have something in common. Each of us has lost and sacrificed something dear to our hearts, else you would not join our cause as you have." Queen Saphier sounded like just that, a queen. It filled Ven with pride and a sense of hope that what they wanted to achieve was possible.

"What are you forces numbered at, your highness?" Nordhum politely inquired with his affable dwarvish brogue.

"1,000, mostly hunters, a few hundred sages. More trickle to our cause every cycle," Ina answered for her queen.

"What are we facing?" Rinya queried.

"6,000 fully trained hunters and sages from each of the five main kystin settlements," Ina replied heavily.

"No," a soft and diminutive voice spoke up, that of Sŷna. "Since this rebellion has been gaining traction, Vakar has outsourced some mercenaries."

"Who?" Njor SecondSpirit asked.

"The Soul Stealer's, or something moronic like that," Sŷna answered with an air of disinterest. In an uncanny second, Agan Dusk and Njor sighed in unison.

"Who are they, Agan?" Faye asked. The hulking half-orc raised his glowering eyes from his palms.

"I am sure a number of you here have at least heard of them, for those who haven't, well. Each mercenary carries a slightly curved, single-edged blade forged in the underworld and blessed by Nuada herself. To die by a Soul Stealer's blade is to spend eternity without hope in that domain of dread. Becoming a slave to the Power's every whim."

"That changes nothing," Ven interjected.

"The elf is right," Nordhum agreed, nodding to Ven as the two once shared a journey together in the Great Northern Rainforest at the beginning of the War of a Thousand Dragons.

"It changes much for us," Rinya announced. "It is a horrible thing for a follower of Lokor to fall in battle and not have their soul join him in Celestia."

"It is not too late to back out," Njor offered genuinely. Rinya looked surprised.

"You misunderstand, this just means wherever the Soul Stealer's are, so will I be, so I may kill as many as possible." Rinya roared with bravado.

"How many can we hope for from the elves of Glowen'ashen?" Onstera chimed in, looking at the two Gloom elf sisters.

Faye diverted her gaze to her sister. "620 warriors. Each and every one of them will fight twice as hard as any mercenary," Wynn answered proudly.

"Great, 8,000 against our 1,600," Kithlyn groaned.

"Wars have been won against worst odds," Scáth replied, clearly referring to their people's troubled past. Kithlyn gave an unconvinced grimace.

"Vakar's numbers mean little against a region of this size," Agan noted.

"Aye," Nordhum agreed. "He has many settlements, towns, and cities to protect now. He cannot leave any one of them vulnerable to attack, so his forces will be spread thin."

"The trick then is to pick a suitable target," Saphier added before declaring, "Green Wave."

That left the room in quiet for a short time. By all accounts it was the most isolated settlement and had the least to offer.

"Wouldn't River Luvium or Red Oak serve us better?" Njor asked doubtfully. He knew well the power that resided in those locations; the bloodlines ran deep and ancient, not to mention were more geographically advantageous.

"I'm afraid River Luvium is home to over 1,000 sages and 500 hunters, all fiercely loyal to Vakar." Sŷna paused a moment. "Red Oak, is better left alone for now."

Nobody asked why but many curious looks were exchanged.

"I was under the impression we were to launch a strike against Sanctuary Island, creating a fake offensive to draw out Vakar and strike a settlement. Why have you chosen Green Wave, so far away?" Ven rather harshly questioned Saphier and Ina.

"Vakar has chosen Green Wave as the permanent harbour for his navy. We lure him out with a siege as you described, then attack his harbour, removing any chance of him docking his formidable fleet."

"There are dozens of suitable natural harbours for him to dock at for that plan to be effective," Rinya rebutted.

"There are, but none suitable for repairing vessels. We burned our docks in Shallow Bay and there is no other settlement large enough to house the ships of his size. Which means when Vakar is forced to harbour in these protected bays and coves for a lack of any other option, we will burn every ship." Ina was unwavering in her confidence. Nordhum and Agan, two proven and battle-hardened leaders of entire armies gave each other looks of optimism.

"Good." Ven crossed him arms with finality. Scáth looked at him with worry in her eyes. This was not the disposition of her gentle and kind elf.

"So what of the attack on Sanctuary Island?" Faye asked, attempting to find a spot for which she knew she could assist well in. Saphier looked to Ina to explain their next course of action.

Ina stood up now and walked around the table, fingering a small wooden tablet. "We will split into two teams. The bulk of our forces will sneak onto Sanctuary Island, demobilize Vakar's forces there and wait for him to come take the island back."

"What makes you so sure he will risk anything for such a small island?" Onstera questioned.

"His attachment to the island is a strong one," Ven confirmed, extinguishing any doubt.

"How are we to sneak on an island that is by all accounts impregnable?" Kithlyn asked and was met by several intrigued stares.

Ina smirked at that before continuing. "With our secret weapon."

She placed the long wooden tablet that appeared more like a scroll tube against the base of a wall. She placed one finger on the centre of it and small kystin runes lit up. From it appeared the translucent map of the whole rain forest, bright and shimmering. Everyone was taken aback by the bright blue light and sheer scale of the map. Ven watched closely for Aolendìr's reaction, who until now was being unusually quiet.

The golden elf slid his chair back and approached the map. "I've never seen anything like it, and that is saying something," he reached out to put his hand through the map, but Ina snatched his wrist.

"Careful," she warned. Aolendìr smiled at her and pulled his hand back.

"It's miraculous, and it works?" Sŷna was now also up, inspecting the highly detailed map with a curious eye.

"I've tested it, along with Ina and Onstera. No complaints," Ven assured.

"That is how we will appear anywhere we want. It is how we will win this war," Ina declared.

"About these teams?" Scáth inferred they get back on topic. She caught a disdained glare from Saphier and returned the look. She did not sense Saphier desired Ven, but she was wise enough to understand the rebel queen did not wish him to be with a ShadowScorn.

Ina had a hard time lifting her gaze from the Solsta but returned to face the table. "It is my wish that our friends from Redwillow, along with our new Kintar allies and Solsta elf, will join me and my forces to take Sanctuary Island. The rest of you will head to Green Wave, scout the best way to dismantle their harbour, and burn as many ships as possible. Once that has been accomplished, Sŷna will send a message to me and our forces will retreat from Sanctuary Island."

"I assure you I'd be of much more assistance in Green Wave than Sanctuary Island." Aolendìr bowed most respectfully. "If the mighty hunter would have me?"

Ven eyed Aolendìr suspiciously and the two held that stare for many moments.

"I agree, the Solsta will give us a much-needed edge," Agan said, breaking the silence. He saw no real value in Aolendìr joining them; however, Ven had warned him to keep an eye on the Solsta and that's what he planned to do.

"It is settled then," Ina said, approaching and disabling the map, much to Sŷna's disappointment. "Prepare yourselves, we embark on our mission at first light."

It was then that Nordhum shared a concerned look with Agan and Scarlet. The half-orc nodded to the dwarf to speak, as it was as good a time as any other and they may not be joined around a table like this again. The famous guild master cleared his throat with a reverberation that startled most in the room.

"Ah, well, if I could just have everyone's attention for a wee moment." Nordhum stood, not really changing in height. "I am not sure what many or any of you have heard in recent years, but there has been a rumour buzzing in the west of late." Nordhum paused as he considered how best to say it, and by now everyone was at full attention. "We did not come from Redwillow to entirely help fight this war, although we will help how we can and are eager to aid. Aye, I'm not sure how best to say this so I might as well just spit it out—the gods are dyin', or likely dead." His demeanour was heavy with sorrow and everyone could feel it. The Kyst in the room, except for Ven, looked at him like he was mad. Yet when Ina and Sŷna looked around the room at everybody, it was as though they were the last in on some joke.

Ven looked to Scáth to gauge her reaction, as they had not discussed Ven's interaction with Kaia and Āina yet, nor had she told him of the dream under the black blossom tree. She gave him a knowing look and although it surprised him, he knew exactly what it meant.

"Well, what in Brailin's Beard, you all know this already?" Nordhum huffed. Agan and Kithlyn chuckled.

"What on Āina's green earth are you on about, dwarf?" Saphier demanded.

"Although he has been known to fumble his words, I do believe he was clear," Scarlet chirped. "I have not felt Pirelia's presence since my transformation, none in my religion have. Despite all my searching across the world, there has been no new Phoenix Folk."

"So the goddess of fire and birth has abandoned this world. Can we really be surprised?" Saphier shot back, unwavering in her faith to Kaia and Āina. Onstera, a non-religious person, still found a scowl for the queen.

"As a matter of fact, it is not just Pirelia, but Brailin too," Nordhum said with a defensive tone.

"Lokor as well," Njor declared sombrely.

"Aceia too, has disappeared from this realm," Scáth added with melancholy. Agan looked to Nordhum and Scarlet as Scáth had confirmed his suspicion.

"This cannot be," Ina begged as she looked around the table.

"It is not," Saphier roared. "I have felt the presence of our saviours, even now. The land is still ripe and the oceans are still the fruit of life."

"No." Ven cut the validity of the queen's statement before she had barely finished speaking. "No, their days are numbered. The first night I was here, they came to me... in the flesh. I did not want to hear their portents but it is undeniable. The gods are dying and with them, the Second Age of Litore. Each one of the twelve has placed a final child or chosen to unite the world in the dawn of the Third Age," Ven ended and looked at Aolendìr, who was predictably wearing a cock-sure smile. The famed hunter sat back down and stared at nothing, but Scáth grabbed his hand and held it firm.

"So now that we agree on that," Nordhum ignored the fact Saphier was shaking her head in denial while Ina and Sŷna sat there dumbfounded by the announcement and the overwhelming fact that all these people from different corners of the world were saying the same thing, "who here is Grimìr?" Nordhum asked still standing.

Njor stood proudly, "Chosen of Lokor, God of Battle."

Scarlet arose next and stated, "Child of Pirelia, Goddess of Fire, Birth, and Renewal."

Scáth stood up confidently. "Daughter of Aceia, God of Shadow and father of the ShadowScorn," she declared with unrivalled pride. She then looked at Aolendìr expecting him to stand, and when he did not she looked down on Ven with love and admiration.

Ven breathed in deep, angry as ever. It was all he could do to suppress an outburst of rage. He didn't want this. He didn't want to be at this table surrounded by these courageous folk, who knew what needed to be done and came to do it. He never had love for the gods growing up and now after Āina and Kaia made themselves known to him, and *told* him what to do, that he was their child, that they loved him...well, that fact burned in his life-blood. He hated Kaia and Āina. The feet of his chair scraped across the stone floor and he stood up slowly.

"I am no one's son." With no more ceremony he left the room, and nothing was heard within for many moments after his departure. As Scáth went to leave the table she noticed Onstera was already ahead of her to go after Ven. She looked to Agan, confused as to why that would be.

"She's training him, to utilize his anger instead of letting it consume him," he replied knowingly.

"What?" Scáth roared in a fashion entirely unlike her. "That's absurd. He needs to confront his anger so he may grow and heal, not live with it. Using it will consume him all together." She looked at Agan angrily, not something he was used to, and she promptly left the room.

"I need him," Saphier growled, looking accusingly towards Ina and Agan.

"Ven Devar has never let anyone down, he won't start now," Agan answered indignantly.

With that, the assembled heroes stood and began to trickle out. First, Rinya nodded to everyone and found their way to their room. Sŷna quickly went up to Aolendìr, sensing a fellow practitioner of the arcane. Faye, Nordhum, Wynn, Njor, Agan, Kithlyn, and Ina were standing in a circle now.

"You are the Scaleless Dragon, yes?" Njor asked of Agan, and Kithlyn looked at her old companion with near lust.

"I am," Agan said dispassionately. Njor extended an arm out and Agan clasped it at the elbow.

"It is a great honour to meet one of your renown. I hope to do battle beside you soon." Ina was quite surprised at the friendliness of this Kintar but it did her heart well.

"I've battle alongside many worshippers of Lokor, his power is a wonder. I count myself blessed to be fighting now, shoulder to shoulder with his Grimìr."

The two brooding warriors let go now as Nordhum interrupted with a snide joke.

"Yes, yes, a bunch of muscly hunks, we're all saved." Faye and Wynn both nailed him with a punch on either shoulder. "Most of you do not need an introduction, but for Ina and Njor, this is Kithlyn

Whisp, thee Shadow Mistress and the single most prolific assassin in Litore. Only she could have secured Scáth with such precision."

"I'm glad you have joined us," Ina said earnestly.

"What makes you so 'prolific'?" Njor asked skeptically.

Kithlyn raised a single brow in disinterest. "Stick around and find out, big boy."

Njor seemed stern for a moment, before cracking a wide grin. "This shall be fun."

"Oh aye, it always is with these two around," Nordhum chuffed lightheartedly.

"You all have a history?" Ina asked of the group. Wynn scoffed and Faye coughed at the understatement of that.

"Even I have met the famed willow guild," Njor declared. "What has become of your Templar companion, Corpsepaint?"

Nordhum and Faye looked to each other with heavy hearts at the mention of their dear friend, a Kintar berserker turned Templar of Lokor.

"Dead," Ironboot said flatly.

"An early causality in the war. He saved us from an ancient glacier dragon before the Quake of Harazune," Faye explained, not allowing her friend's sacrifice to go unspoken. Njor simply lowered his head and placed his fist over his heart.

"We all met at the beginning of the War of a Thousand Dragons. We've been crossing paths ever since," Kithlyn answered Ina.

"Do we call you something, Ina? A title associated with your rank perhaps?" Faye asked out of honour, understanding well the importance of such things in regimented organizations and militaries alike. Ina pondered that for a moment.

"Svar." Her face lit up. Njor was the only one who acted as though he understood, and thus the group looked to him to explain.

"It means 'great warrior', in Kintish."

"It means 'humble defender' in kystin." Everyone gave their Svar a reaffirming smile, and so too did Njor.

It was not lost on Nordhum that Scarlet was still speaking with Queen Saphier, and since Sŷna was chatting Aolendìr's ear off he took this opportunity to speak candidly. "How did the Solsta make his way into the group?"

"I found him wandering the forest at night, alone. I had considered it was him," Wynn answered.

"He's been attached to us like a sticky web ever since Wynn found him looking for Glowen'ashen," Njor said in clear annoyance. "He never shuts up," he added under his breath.

"He's slippery," Faye whispered.

"And has a knack for being present during catastrophic events," Nordhum said, making direct eye contact with the elf across the room.

Agan grumbled something unintelligible, which the dwarf thought was interesting, since these two had met in passing, yet it appeared Agan did not recognize him.

"Did he say what his goal is here?" Faye questioned the group.

"To bring peace and balance to this forest," Wynn replied, recollecting his speech from the conclave of elders.

"Then that's exactly what he'll do," Faye said.

"You just might not like how he does it." Nordhum had the last word on the subject and Scarlet and Aolendìr joined them as Sŷna was now discussing matters with Saphier.

"A genuine, understated pleasure to see you all again, my old friends." Aolendìr bowed with his shoulder cape in one hand. "Had I known we'd all be reconvening I would have worn my nice cape."

"Seen the gem lately, Tardinian?" Nordhum chortled and Agan's eyes narrowed.

The elf appeared flummoxed. "I haven't the slightest idea what you might mean, Master Ironboot."

"Hello Aolendìr, as charming as ever I see," Faye said in a slight mocking manner.

"My pale hearted beauty, is the north bringing any warmth into those cold bones of yours?" he replied with a knowing grin. Wynn scowled at him and Njor couldn't suppress a grin at the intrigue on display.

"And you," the elf turned and grabbed Kithlyn's hand to kiss it, "my black-heart love." He stood up straight. "Make no mistake, the half-orc was correct, this is the greatest assassin on Litore, if I remember correctly," he said with a wink. "And yes, I can be slippery when I need be." His smirk let everyone in on the fact he heard their entire conversation about him. The infamous assassin blushed and

Agan, Faye, and Nordhum's jaws nearly dropped.

"Kith," Faye nearly shrieked in disbelief. She shrugged again.

"Did I miss something?" Scarlet asked.

"Hardly. You remember Aolendìr," Nordhum replied.

"I do. Good to see you."

"Ah, see, thank you," the elf blustered. "Good to see you, Daughter of Pirelia." He bowed most genuinely.

"I do recognize a charlatan when I see one, Aolendìr." Scarlet crossed her arms, back straightening. Aolendìr cocked his head with a wry grin at that undeniable description.

"To address the four-ton bisonbear in the room, what exactly are you hoping to achieve in this civil war if you already find yourselves on a quest?" Aolendìr made his question directly to Nordhum.

"Would it be the first time we got roped into another's mess whilst tryin' to deal with our own?"

"The gods know it be true, ol' friend. Let us say you do unite the Grimìr, then what?" Tardinian asked, as if entertaining the hopes of a child.

"We keep the world from imploding as the gods die and a new age begins," Nordhum said sternly.

"Yet not all the gods are benevolent, literally the opposite for many of them, while others prefer to straddle the line between light and dark," the Solsta countered.

"Your point?" Ironboot questioned, losing patience.

"Not all the Grimìr will want you to succeed. I find it shocking enough the chosen of Lokor is acting so... peacefully." The golden elf eyed Njor.

"Yours is not to question his way," Njor growled, assured in his decision.

"You're all still missing the point," Aolendìr fired back, expecting that exact response. "There is no *them* anymore. Only *us*." He let those words hang in the air for a moment, as he saw many of them had not considered this most basic fact—soon, very soon, they would be the only divine creatures left on Litore. "Perhaps you should each take some more time to consider what comes next." He bowed once more before leaving the room.

That left the remaining to look around at one another for several silent moments.

"Gods, I hate him," Nordhum mumbled.

"I suggest you find rest, fulfill any pre-battle rituals," Ina said softly. "We meet upon the shoreline at first light."

Ven was sitting on the precipice of the rocky shoreline, nearly a fifteen-metre drop to the crashing waves. He had his legs hanging over the edge, attempting to calm the storm within.

"What are you doing?" Onstera asked judgmentally from behind him. Ven heaved a great sigh.

"Leave me be, I am in no mood."

"Precisely why I am here." Moving silently, she smacked him on the back of the head.

"Don't," he growled through gritted teeth as his hood fell down.

"I am here to make you strong, unbeatable." She slapped him again forcing his head to snap forward. He slowly turned to lay his piercing opalescent eyes upon her. "Do it again, and I'll fucking kill you."

Without changing a shade, she went to strike him again. He snapped his hand up and gripped her wrist, twisting it violently. Her arm bent and he stood to his impressive height and withdrew Hunter's Protector.

Her eyes swirled from silver to red, as if someone had dropped a single drop of blood into a glass of water. She leapt and spun in the air, landing on her feet so her wrist was no longer bent. She kept her momentum going and before he knew it, Ven was end-over-end and flat out on the ground. He seethed with anger and drove his shortsword into her foot. She let out an ear-piercing scream and with her free foot kicked him square in the jaw. He rolled over a few times, dazed by the kick.

Onstera dropped to one knee and grasped the sword by its intricately weaved hilt. She took several deep breaths and yanked; it did not budge. Judging by the amount of blade left above the earth, Ven had driven it deep into the rock. The Kyst slowly got back up to his feet as Onstera grunted.

He drew a knife from his chest piece. "What did I tell you?"

"I was wrong," she muttered through laboured breaths. "You have your mother's rage and no one can tame the sea."

He grabbed a handful of her platinum hair in one hand and held the ShadowScorn dagger tight to her throat. His eyes burned with pain. Onstera knew this look for she had given it to every man, woman, and beast she had slain.

"Do it. Please, end this. My life has been one tragedy to the next. No one on this gods forsaken earth knows happiness and the end of the Second Age will bring only misery. I beg of you, do it."

Ven was about to plunge the dagger through her throat when he heard, "Stop!"

Still in a fit of rage, he was more hunter than elf, so instinctively he turned and threw the dagger. It flew true to its mark, straight for Scáth's heart.

"No!" he screamed, realizing his mistake too late. In the peak of night, it was all too easy for Scáth to let this dagger pass through her body without harm. She looked down, half expecting to be skewered, and breathed a sigh of relief. She quickly noted the distressed state her love was in.

"Ven, listen to me." She slowly approached him, seeing clear as day the tears pouring freely down his stormy cheeks. "It was an accident, my love. I am okay, everything is okay." She was in arm's length of him now, reaching to place a soft hand on his face.

Scáth gave a hard and disproving glance at Onstera.

She grabbed the sword and pulled hard, for some reason it released with ease for Scáth. Dentoress fell back with a yelp of pain and relief.

"Go get yourself looked at," the Scorn declared harshly. Onstera limped away with great effort but not a sound of pain.

Scáth pulled Ven in close, nearly smothering him with her thick hair. "Let's find Faenla and go sleep."

"I am a danger," he softly cried into the crook of her shoulder.

"No, my love. You could never hurt me."

CHAPTER NINETEEN

The Battle of Hearth and Heart

During the calm and quiet of early dawn, several hundred warriors, sages, hunters, and wizards were gathered outside the rebel Kyst hideout. The morning dew clung to the forest and rocks about them; the cold fresh air filled Ven Devar's lungs as he stepped outside. Faenla stood proudly beside him, so tall and mighty. The wolf nudged his head sidelong and nuzzled Ven's face. Ven rested his arm around the colossal wolf and the two sauntered into the crowd.

He noted many of the warriors in attendance were from Glowen'ashen. Not a one of the twilight-coloured elves were without tattoos of stars and celestial bodies. Many of their tattoos stretched across their entire body and occasionally up into their fully or partially shaved heads. Most wore leather armour that was segmented for optimal flexibility; even the handful of their Diwyn's he saw carried the atypical yklwa and bore armour. The yklwa's were hafted with moonwood, an ashen hue that had dark purple carvings across them.

Ven stopped a moment at a particular Diwyn dressed in blue, grey, and white robes with a star pattern of silver stitched throughout. He had grown up hearing about the Diwyn's, a select group of Gloom elves who were so in tune with the universe they had achieved spiritual enlightenment. This meant that they could actually draw on the power of the universe to fuel their arcane abilities instead of the magic that oozed from Litore. It had always felt like a fairytale to him, and yet seeing the Diwyn's now he felt a sense that anything was possible. The war-wizard noted Ven's presence and offered him a firm but kind smile; the hunter reciprocated before continuing on with Faen.

As they approached, he was momentarily surprised to see Onstera standing with everyone bound for Greenwave. He tightened his grip on Faen's fur as a sense of shame hit him; it quickly shifted to anger, like a cloud passing across the sun.

"You appear no worse for ware," he chimed, saddling between Scáth and Agan. He received only curious stares, and one from Onstera that told him to shut it.

"Dentoress was just explaining she'll be joining 'Island Company'," Agan updated Ven. He perked a brow at her. Ven assumed she would be recovering from her wound, but by all means it appeared as it had never happened, and if she was suffering any discomfort, she was not showing it.

"The attack on Sanctuary Island is better suited to my talents," she said.

Nordhum, who was standing next to her added, "Aye, I extended the need for Onstera's unique skills and it so happens that the Redwillow Guild has a great deal of experience fighting beside the Sanguis Quaesitors."

"So it is," Ven replied. Aolendìr wasn't the only one who noted tension between Ven and Onstera but no one brought it up at present. With that, Nordhum and Onstera said their brief farewells and joined the mass of Kyst and Gloom's walking single file through the shimmering map.

"Who here has been to Greenwave?" Agan asked.

"Only once I'm afraid," Sŷna answered.

"A good number of times," said Ven.

"Really?" Scáth sounded surprised.

Ven nodded with a faint smile. "Renic took me once as a boy, then I spent many months there in my sixteenth year. Trilara sent me for their sailing academy which is best in all the north, the whole world some say."

"Good, then this mission belongs to you," Agan declared with a steadfast heart. The hunter's face screwed up and the two

ShadowScorn began to protest.

"I'm not sure now is the best time. You are a tested military leader, you should command us," Scáth reasoned.

"She's right, this is routine for you Agan. We've done missions like this a hundred times and you always led us to victory." Kithlyn tried to make the half-orc see reason. Ven was shaking his head with doubt now, but Agan remained firm.

"If it's any aid in this decision," Sŷna added, "I was hoping to follow the Mighty Ven Devar into this war." He planted a friendly hand on Ven's shoulder.

"No, I shouldn't, this is too important." He visibly withdrew into himself.

"Your closest allies will be there to guide you. I know a leader when I see one, Ven, you're ready for this." Agan reassured the group.

Ven was feeling another outburst boiling but was instantly humbled by the memory of last night's altercation and settled on a barely perceptible nod of agreement.

"Might I have a word in private?" Scáth insisted, rather than asked, Aolendìr. The golden elf bowed and held his arm out for her to lead the way. She took them to a quiet spot near the shoreline, away from prying ears.

"I'd like a moment as well, elf," the brooding fighter said to the hunter before walking off, expecting him to follow, which Ven did.

That left Kithlyn, Faenla, and Sŷna standing awkwardly together. After a far too long and uncomfortable silence, Sŷna caved.

"So you like... black?"

She looked at him through her hood and misting hair with those cold eclipsing eyes and Faenla's ears flickered at the question.

"Have you ever met an assassin that wears pink?"

"Hmm," he clearly pondered the question and even put his hand to his chin. As if struck with a stroke of genius he snapped his fingers and Kith's black and red leathers turned to hot pink. "Now I have," his face beamed with delight. The wolf hopped back in surprise before letting out a snort.

"Turn it back or Aceia help me I will throw your precious books into the sea." Her threat didn't carry the weight she wanted as the sage continued to laugh before snapping his fingers once more.

Scáth stopped near a low ridge that overlooked the crashing waves; the two elves skin glistened from the spray.

"What is it, Lady Scáth?" Aolendìr asked.

"Back when I was Vakar's prisoner, we first met. It appeared you were working for him."

He held her gaze silently for a moment before asking, "Why haven't you told them?"

"Because at best they'd make of you a prisoner, and at worst, slit your throat."

"Don't dodge a dodger, answer the question," he insisted.

"You showed me respect when I was a prisoner. So although you may still yet prove evil, I know there to be good," she answered.

He chortled, "You really are the wisest of us. I have fulfilled my bargain with Vakar. I found Ven and reported on him. As far as Vakar is aware, I've returned whence I came."

"You are lying." Her words were fast.

"If that is your verdict, then tell the others all that you know of me. Which I remind you is little," he smirked.

"But enough." She threatened and considered turning right around and telling her companions everything, but she had more questions. "You said Vakar is 'one of us'. Which god chose him?"

Aolendìr laughed lightly. "In truth, I'm still figuring that out. I will confess I may have led him astray when he asked me the same."

"Why would you do that?" she scolded. He gave her a look that told her that she clearly had the answer.

"You are the Grimìr of Mahem, aren't you?" She said the words slowly, as if putting it together while speaking them.

"It doesn't get you many dinner invites, yet the thing about chaos that no one understands, it is neither evil nor good—it's fair." He put the most serious tone he could behind the statement and Scáth nearly rocked back on her heels.

"Then you can't be trusted," she said with shaky resolve.

"Perhaps, perhaps not, as that is the point. However, you can count on me to topple tyrants and ensure Litore sees the dawn of the Third Age." He could tell she was not convinced. "I'll tell the group I am the chosen of Mahem, will that satiate your hunger for now?"

She nodded, and he bowed deeper than ever.

Ven and Agan were now standing next to a great tree and the elf leaned against its strips of soft bark. A look of disassociation was about him, and it was the very reason Agan had pulled him away.

"Look at me," Agan said, and Ven slowly raised his eyes. "I don't care what happened between you and Onstera. Rage has kept me alive my whole life, but a life of anger is one hardly worth living. I should have known it was not your way, and for that I am sorry."

Agan's sincerity startled Ven for it was a rare thing in the stoic half-orc. Ven thought about speaking, but Agan continued. "Do you know why I put you in charge?"

The Kyst considered it before shaking his head. "This is your home, your people, which means it's your fight to win or lose. I do not doubt your ability to lead, and by the gods you're the most clever combatant I've ever witnessed. Yet, if you go to war in this..." Agan looked the young elf up and down seeking the right words, "... mood, you will damn us all to a fate I dare not ponder. Listen and listen sharp. Nothing else in war matters except the soldier beside you and the enemy before you. Kill or be killed, Ven. Lock this woe within a dark recess of your heart and forget it there. You must do this for the sake of us all."

Ven's eyes were wide and watery when Agan laid a firm hand on the hunter's shoulder. Ven wanted so bad to hug his dear friend, but the feeling fleeted as Agan dropped his piercing, yellow eyes and walked back to the group.

The mighty hunter closed his eyes tight and breathed deeply, exhaling slowly. He did this many times and told himself when he opened his eyes, he would forget the unfortunate deeds of his recent past; not forever, he knew, but for a time during which he could perform as needed to accomplish the necessary.

He opened his bright, opalescent-green eyes; his pupils adjusted to the world around him, and for the first time in a long time, he felt himself.

Island Company came out of the teleportation magic with a bit of shock as only Ina had any experience with the process. Most, if not all, of the Kyst hunters and sages and Gloom warriors landed on their feet as the magic propelled them through space, descending from the sky to land firmly on the forest floor of Sanctuary Island. It was a different story for Nordhum Ironboot in his one-of-a-kind full cuirass of iradinium armour. He landed on his feet and ended up on his back with a loud thud, his horned head circlet rolling away. Njor offered him a large, red hand up and Nordhum took it reluctantly. Wynn came over holding his circlet and held it out to him.

"Gods, I can't believe I used to lay with you," she snickered.

"Aye, aye, you liked it," Nordhum said with a smirk as he took back his crown.

Nearly 1,000 rebels were in a large field of knee-height grass. They wasted little time regathering into proper formations. Ina was busy organizing their troops when Faye started to sniff the air. Rinya too was flicking their long elven ear as if catching distant sounds and Scarlet was whispering words of magic to herself. Nordhum stood close to Faye, as Njor did to Rinya.

"What is it?" SecondSpirit asked.

"I hear twigs snapping," Rinya answered

"I smell elven blood," Faye whispered to the dwarf. Nordhum gave a nod to Onstera to warn Ina. The Quaesitor slowly walked over to the Svar so as not to arouse suspicion.

"How many?" Nordhum asked Scarlet, who was using her divine blessing to sense hostile creatures.

"Too many," she replied bluntly. After receiving the update, Ina began looking around and blew a loud whistle signalling to move out. Before the rebels could begin moving to the tree line, a similar whistle was returned. It caught nearly everyone's attention as it was followed by another, then another, and another, until nothing else could be heard but a discordant wind of whistling. Then it suddenly stopped and the only thing that could be heard was the rustling of the grass. Just as Ina was about to command everyone to get out of the field, a single arrow buzzed for Rinya's head. With impossible speed, Njor threw his hand out and the arrow pierced the palm of his hand, just centimetres from Rinya's eye. A single tense moment of shock was shared before a rainstorm of arrows pelted the entire company.

"To the tree line!" Ina shouted as she began waving people to the right direction. It was catastrophic, for the arrows were assailing them from every direction. As the rebels began running into the tree line, they began dropping faster than ever. Nordhum summoned a magical companion in the form of a giant blue bisonbear. It materialized in a puff of blue smoke and the dwarf jumped on its back, leading the charge into the forest. Faye Walker was gone quicker than the wind and soon sensed the direction of the Kyst hunters loosing their bows. Scarlet took flight and soared low over the rebels, casting spells of healing and protection. Rinya yanked the arrow out of Njor's hand and they both roared their infamous Kintar Roar, filling the hearts of their enemies with dread. They took up the rear guard with Wynn, who was ensuring her people stayed close to the Kyst. It also helped she was one of few people here with a shield.

"How did they know?" Onstera shouted to Ina as they entered the forest.

"Someone clearly betrayed us." As she finished, the great Phoenix landed next to them.

"What are your orders?" Scarlet's feathers flamed brighter than ever in this moment of battle.

Their Svar looked around at their worsening situation. She knew dozens of her own were already dead or wounded. She saw Faye's form move with such speed from tree to tree it appeared as a blur, Kyst hunters falling like leaves behind her trail. Nordhum Ironboot moved briskly around their allies, drawing fire and offering cover.

"We need to draw them out. Gather any shield bearers and arcane users to create a perimeter around us," Ina shouted. Scarlet sent out a telepathic wave to a select number of their leaders to do as Ina instructed. With the level of efficiency and discipline Ina knew she could count on, the entire rebel force gathered in a circle. The Diwyn's, clerics, paladins, and sages, had a shimmering dome of energy protecting them in seconds. Every time an arrow struck the dome, a ripple of energy like rain on still water would spread across it. The number of arrows increased until a thick bed of them encircled the dome on the ground.

Faye was last to enter the barrier; as she slowly walked inside, she yanked an arrow out of her shoulder and the wound smoked before slowing stitching itself back together.

"Silver," she whispered to Nordhum and Wynn.

"They seem to have known a lot about us," Wynn said.

The barrage stopped and the only thing they could hear was the heavy breathing of their allies, as the dome blocked out all exterior sound. The rebels remained within for a long while, so long that shadows moved from east to west and darkness began reclaiming the land. Nordhum looked at Ina and he got the go-ahead. He took his shield of iradinium off his back and slowly walked out. His legs were sturdy and his heart steady. He scanned the woods around him and after feeling comfortable, let his guard down.

"Keep the dome up in case," Ina instructed, and she too walked out, followed by the rest of Island Company. When no more projectiles were fired, the magic users dropped their concentration and the wall of energy vanished like a mirage. The leaders gathered around to discuss their options.

"Well clearly there is spy in your organization," Nordhum pointed out indiscriminately.

"I thought there wasn't even supposed to be fifty hunters and sages on the whole island," Rinya said.

"There wasn't," Ina answered.

"This doesn't change anything. We have a mission to do, so Green Company can do theirs," Njor said resolutely.

"We have no idea what we're walking into. Vakar could have a thousand soldiers in wait for us in Hearth," Faye argued with Njor.

"Like Lokorson just said, that doesn't change anything," Rinya sneered.

"Aye, and he's not the only Grimìr here," Nordhum retorted. Their bickering was interrupted by the release of a rebel bow string and a Kyst hunter in Vakar's army fell from a tree with a sickening thud.

"Regardless, we can't stay put for long," Scarlet's voice crackled with flame.

"Njor and Faye, you two appear to be our fastest, take my hunter Keel and scout ahead. See what Hearth looks like. We will make our way there behind you." Ina's confidence was all it took, and the three scouts sprang off towards the town of Hearth.

After nearly an hour of breakneck speed running, Keel, a Kyst hunter, threw up his hand to stop Faye and Njor.

"It's just over this ridge." He referred to a steep rocky slope of bright green moss and slick stone.

"Split up, meet back here in ten minutes," Njor said and they all went different directions. Faye shot up the slippery slope with unnatural ease and when she crested the lip, she looked down on the quaint town.

It was nothing she like had imagined, for the town hugged the precipice of a huge cliff and the homes were small and built mostly of reclaimed wood. She had heard that the town was mostly inhabited by gnomes and that seemed evident, yet there was a great score of Kyst as well, all wearing the uniformed armour of Vakar's Kingdom. She figured that the guard towers were an addition since the new ruler had taken over, but from what she could tell, the town was not military. A handful of palisades were set up to hinder the easier entries which Faye counted few to begin with. The town of Hearth was well sequestered between a hillock and a cliff with thickets and trees offering decent protection. She noticed too a good amount of hunters were running to and fro, attempting to gather into formations and heed the commands of their leader, who Faye immediately recognized even though it had been nearly a decade since her brief meeting with him.

Njor had chosen silence over speed, although he made more noise than he wished as he was still adjusting to this new god-like physique. He came around a bend in a great bluff of boulders and heard much yelling and monstrous roars. He peaked his head around the rock and saw a huge metal cage, perhaps the size of a small cabin, rattling and nearly tipping on its side.

At least a dozen hunters and half as many sages were attempting to calm the beast within. It was something he had only witnessed once in his long life, for this beast was more legend than reality within the massive confines of his home—a Gründi, a feared and terrible beast once thought to be kin of dragon-kind. Later it was theorized to possibly be a troll breed for its hide which was thick and callous, great muscular arms and legs, yet its glowing green eyes were the omen of its true power. The Gründi is as likely to rip you in two as it is to breathe a cloud of noxious gas that can kill even the most powerful of creatures. The beast within this cage was bigger than the Gründi he remembered and sported wicked horns and spikes across its head and forearms. Two more things about this particular Gründi amazed him; one being that somehow the Kyst had muzzled them so it could not kill them all with its poisonous cloud; and the other being a thick-plated armour covered the back of the creature, running from its brow to its stubby tail like an armadillo.

Immediately discouraged by their odds, he slinked back behind the rock to reconvene. He met with Faye back at their rendezvous. They exchanged their findings and grew concerned that Keel had not returned. After several more moments and little debate, they returned to Island Company. The rebels were perhaps two kilometres outside of Hearth and Ina's spirit dropped when two, not three returned.

"Well?" She asked.

"It is not ideal," Faye admitted.

"The former prince of Silva is leading them." She let that hang for a second and everyone gave murmurs of despair.

"That's not the least of it. They have a Gründi," Njor added skeptically.

"No, they don't," Onstera interjected as if Njor was plain stupid. "Nobody *has* a Gründi."

"I know this is your particular type of business, but they have a Gründi, locked in a cage," Njor said simply. "And if I was to guess, they have changed it somehow, as my people crossbreed monsters."

"Then our best bet is to release it," Rinya suggested as if the answer was obvious.

"That's the single worst idea I believe I've heard from you yet," Onstera spat.

"Now just hold on a minute." Nordhum silenced the bickering. "What is a Gründi?"

"Death," Wynn said with eerie calm.

"Exactly." Onstera backed her up. Now the heroes of the group were arguing and speaking in such evil finite tones, the rebels began to whisper words of despair.

"It is Rexous we should be worried about." Ina brought the focus back to attention.

"I think we can handle a despoiled prince," Ironboot proclaimed.

"No, he's become... fell." She hesitated to speak the words as if saying them gave him power. "Take no offence good dwarf, but he is the equal of Ven Devar and no one here could go toe-to-toe with that elf on his best day."

"No offence to you, but while you Kyst were hiding in your forest I was fighting in the Great War. Don't dare to judge who might out-do me with a blade." Nordhum's friendly affectation dissolved quicker than a droplet to flame.

"Arguing is going to get us nowhere," Scarlet chimed in irritably. We have twenty dead and nearly double wounded but that still gives us a greater force by far. Ina is our Svar, what do you command of us?"

Ina looked around at the hundreds of expectant eyes holding their heavy and anxious gaze on her.

"They're built against a cliff, two roads in and a small hillock between. Archers and ranged sages line the top of the hillock and any advantageous trees. I want to confine them, box them in. The Gründi is unexpected but so will be its movements if released. We use it to our advantage if it comes to it. Spread the word so every last of one us knows, not a gnome will befall harm by our hands today. We will want them as allies and if nothing else, Vakar tore their life apart in the very beginning, let's give it back to them."

The Gloom elves thudded their fists against their shoulders and the Kyst bowed to her commands. The troops began to split up; archers and ranged spell casters took the height advantage while an even amount of Diwyn's and Gloom joined the two assaults on either side.

Nordhum, Onstera, Njor and Scarlet, along with the other half of the rebels, went in the direction of the Gründi, for they were considered to have the best chance in defeating it. Ina led her soldiers alongside Rinya, Wynn, and Faye. Ina walked the vanguard of her assault with caution and the traditional shortsword and trident combination. She favoured a unique stance that held her three-bladed trident out defensively at a forty-five degree angle, while her single-edged sword was held reverse grip, the flat of it tucked against the rear of her forearm. Much like Ven, her skin tone favoured the sea, hers being a soft coral hue, but her heavy pumasheep cloak aided in her camouflage. Her leather chest piece and spaulder were embossed with intricate depictions of the sea. Yet the next second brought a red arrow cutting a deep line across her spaulder. Before she could react, Rexous leapt down from a sprawling arbutus tree.

"Your aim needs work," Ina touted. Rex just shook his head with a grimace. Ina furrowed her brow and turned to see Faye Walker with an arrow feather protruding from her breast, the shaft made of pure silver and the head solid iradinium.

"Vakar knows what you're doing. Island and Green Company lost before they departed. It's over." Rexous spoke without compassion or malice.

Ina was in horror to see such a hero fallen, and the hatred towards Rex was now never stronger. She lunged at him and with her, the rest of her army. The two leaders clashed with fury and precision. Ina was impeccable, every muscle working flawlessly with the instinctual commands of her mind. Every thrust and every slice was made with the next four moves in mind. This was Ina Enallea, lead hunter of Shallowbay, on her best day. Wynn quickly dragged an unresponsive Faye out of the path of war and yanked the arrow from her chest. She removed the fur cloak from her own shoulders and placed it over Faye.

"Rest now sister, I will tend to you soon." Wynn stood up, unsheathed her hooked sword and shield, and leapt into the fray.

The rebels began pouring down the eastern road into Hearth as a good score of Rex's army lay in wait. As nearly half of Ina's forces were locked in melee, a small horn sounded, and a great explosion followed. From the road exploded a long spiked palisade coated in burning oil, effectively cutting off the rear guard of rebels. Ina caught this from the corner of her eye and saw Rexous smirking as he parried her impressive routine. More infuriating than the grin on his face was that even at her pinnacle of combat, she was barely making him work. She struck his left arm dirk out wide and moved in with a twist to deliver a gash across his face with her sword. He ducked and spun under the extended elbow with the blade still against her forearm. Throwing his weight down, he extended one leg and tripped her. She went end over end and before she could roll with her momentum, he kicked her in the head with his boot. The force utterly rolled her body over so she was sprawled on her back. Rexous made his way to stand over her and deliver the killing blow.

The second troop was making their way down the western road, with Nordhum riding his bisonbear. Nordhum, being the ex-commander for the entire army of the Dwarves of Silver Rock, was appointed to lead this force. Njor and Scarlet flanked him and his mount. They all stopped when they saw the cage that housed the Gründi was empty. Nordhum let out an audible sigh as the cage door squeaked in the wind.

A faded scream came closer and louder until Onstera soared through the air from behind a large boulder and collided into BB. That same boulder was lifted high above the ground as the Gründi held it above its head. Letting out a great roar, the monster threw it at the rebels. Nordhum jumped off his bisonbear as everyone dove in different directions to avoid the projectile. BB, however, planted his rear hooves and slammed his great, bear-like fore claws into the ground and met the boulder head on, literally. It shattered against his huge bison head into a hundred pieces.

BB let out his own roar and charged the Gründi. Running on all fours like some sort of ape, the Gründi met BB. The bisonbear was quicker as he used all his considerable weight to charge and ram his horns into the monsters' gut. With the horns deep within its innards, the beast lifted its two bulging spiked-arms and slammed down on BB's neck. The bisonbear fell to the ground with a pained moan and the Gründi slammed its huge moss-covered foot down on BB's head; in a puff of blue smoke, the statuette reappeared in Nordhum's hand.

The rebels helped each other back up in a panic as the monstrosity curled up and began rolling toward them with frightening speed. A number of hunters managed to strike it with arrows but the missiles ricocheted off its hard carapace. It continued to roll over half-a-dozen Gloom's and twice that many Kyst, leaving flattened, grotesque bodies in its wake.

"We gotta get this dealt with," Nordhum shouted to anyone with an idea.

"Your bisonbear had it right, its centre is the only soft spot," Onstera shouted to the group.

"I'll stop it, be ready to strike," Njor proclaimed before jumping several metres in a single leap to put himself in the path of the rolling monster. Njor braced his body with his hands stretched out. As if the Gründi knew him to be there, it picked up speed, kicking up a huge rooster tail of dirt and tree droppings. It struck Njor like a bolt of lightning, and sounded like it too, but the Grimìr of Lokor with his divine strength did, not, budge. A wave of dust sprang forth when they collided and Njor let out a groan. The Gründi shot open like a cannon, making Njor rock on his heels. It struck the Grimìr with its forearm and sent him into a tree, creating cracks and splinters throughout the trunk. The Kintar landed on the ground as he choked and sucked air back into his lungs.

A hailstorm of arrows, javelins, and arcane bolts peppered the monster's exposed belly. Scarlet Albright put her feathered hands into motion and her diadem glowed a fiery red. She was the last one to send forth a burst of energy in the form of a streaking jet of dripping lava. It struck the Gründi square in the chest and sent it barrelling backwards. It came to a stop and laid on its front, motionless. Onstera and many rebels cautiously approached. The Quaesitor held her matte-silver sword out and poked at it. She turned to give her nod of approval and turned back to drive her sword through its head for good measure. When she looked back, the eyes were open and it belched a huge cloud of poisonous gas. Instantly anyone within fifteen metres fell to their knees as their skin festered and boiled. Their eyes filled with blood as their internal organs corroded and burned.

Onstera was the only person of nearly thirty that did not drop dead. She went down on one knee and planted her sword into the ground to support herself as she fought the poison, her Sanguis Quaesitor modifications keeping her alive through the toxic fumes. Njor, Nordhum, and Scarlet were left dumbfounded by the sheer savagery and will to live that this monster possessed.

"Ah, this isn't working," Nordhum said, rather positively given the circumstances. Scarlet reached out her hand once more, as though an invisible tether was reaching out with sticky tendrils, latched onto Onstera, and yanked her out of the fumes. The Quaesitor's eyes that always turned a blood-red when in heightened situations were now streaked with veins of green as her body worked through the poison.

"Any ideas?" Njor asked of Onstera, who looked up from her pain to see three Grimìr looking at her helplessly. She peered back at the monster through hazy eyes and lingering fumes. It was in a state of panic as it tried to wipe away the molten lava on its chest, placed there by the Daughter of Fire.

"Njor needs to wrestle it down, Scarlet and Nordhum need to make sure its mouth stays closed, and I'll go in for the kill. Its belly is tough but BB and Scarlet have weakened it. Nordhum, send over our rebels to assist the east assault, they can only be causalities here." Onstera said confidently.

Nordhum ordered the Kyst and Glooms to join Ina and they did so happily. Njor offered Onstera his large red hand and she gripped firmly as he brought her to her feet. With that, the four heroes stood side by side and the Gründi recognized the challenge. Scarlet waved her hands apart and the residing fumes blew away; the Gründi roared in defiance. Njor sprang with impossible speed and strength, leaving a great divot in the earth. He landed next to the tree, his body cracked and splintered. He broke the tree clean right at the trunk and firmly gripped it. He used it like a hammer and brought it down right on the monster's head. Njor was already on the beast before it had even recovered. He wrapped his arms around its neck and clasped his hands together tight, forming a lock of godly strength. The Gründi rolled and flipped and did everything it could to knock Njor off, but Lokorson would not budge. Nordhum and Scarlet seized the opportune time when the monster's belly was exposed to leap into the fray. The dwarf had mastered the art of black-smithing long ago and held a gleaming chain of iradinium. Scarlet had flown up to the Gründi and cast a spell which produced two spectral hands that clamped the jaw and nose of the beast, slamming them shut. Nordhum, with speed and agility contradictory to his strong stout frame, deftly wrapped the chain around its mouth.

Three Grimìr was what it took to wrestle the beast just so Onstera could have a chance to deal the killing blow, and it was barely enough.

Rexous stood over the fallen Ina with murderous intent. Yet in the fear of Ina expecting her life to end with one foul swoop, she noted a hint of despair, or maybe even regret, in the eyes of Rexous. Time seemed to slow as he approached her, dirk at the ready, and he saw her sensing his true emotions which flared his red eyes with the fires of the underworld. The Svar of the rebellion could have acted, could have shifted from his blade, yet she did not move, and his sword went for the kill.

Centimetres from her throat, a hooked longsword caught the blade and spun it up and away from Ina.

"Males." Wynn stalked toward a stumbling Rexous. The once prince grimaced before readying his battle stance. The tumult of Kyst killing Kyst rang out around them, but it may as well have been waves crashing against rocks for it did not distract these two warriors. Wynn slammed the edge of her shield against her sword so it buckled, taking the form of two crescent moons stuck together, creating a far smaller, more agile shield, almost akin to a buckler.

Wynn sprang at him like a pumasheep, ferocity in her throat and eyes. The ring of their swords clashing was crystal clear above the battle. She quickly dipped and spun, striking his thigh, too slow though as he parried it. Still low, she spun the opposite direction and struck his other leg. She let out a war cry as it was met with another parry. She threw her hands down, hoisted her legs up, and slammed her ankles down his shoulder blades. With immense core strength she lifted herself up so her thighs were squeezing his delicate eleven neck. Rexous, like most elves of Litore (save the Kintar), was feather-light, dexterous instead of strong, and was struggling to stay on his feet with the sudden weight on him.

Wynn wasted no time. She drove her elbow into the crown of his head several times before shifting her weight forward to make him collapse on his back. Her weight shifted the same time a ball of shimmering, swirling light, like fog captured inside a glass orb, exploded next to them. It was as if being struck with a cannon ball and no sooner than they had flown apart, a dense fog filled the battle ground. Wynn rolled down a slight embankment and propped herself up on her elbows to look around. Everything seemed quiet somehow, the stillness only interrupted by the odd death scream. Occasionally a silhouette dashed through the fog, only to disappear again.

From the smoke cut a clear visage of a determined and furious Rexous, heading straight for her. She scrambled for her weapon, but he kicked her square in the temple. She rolled over with a spurt of blood, arms sprawled out at her side.

"You never forget killing a Gloom. The world simply seems, brighter." He plunged his sword down, and for the second time was thwarted when a fully armoured dwarf slammed him.

Nordhum Ironboot had the feathery Kyst down on the ground and was pummelling him with his gauntlets. Rex had his forearms up in an attempt to block the devastating punches, but it did little good. Nordhum punched, blood splattered his face, he punched again, more blood, again, and again until his fist ached under the gauntlet. The Kyst managed to deflect a strike away and headbutt Nordhum, but it broke the elf's nose and the dwarf laughed heartily. Then Nordhum wasn't laughing, as a dagger found its way deep into his arm pit. The sudden shock left Rex enough time to pull it out before sinking it even deeper the second time. Nordhum tumbled backwards off him, growled at the elf, then suddenly fell over unconscious.

Rex sat up on his knees and spat out a tooth. He grabbed his dirks, sheathed one and unhooked his trident as the magical fog was pulled away like a curtain, revealing the battlefield once again. It was clear his forces were sorely outnumbered and taking heavy losses. There was no retreat, no failure, only victory.

He stood up, beaten and battered, and recognized Scarlet as the one who dispelled the fog, unleashing devastating divine energy on his soldiers. He circled around her, cutting a clear path through the rebels and Gloom elves standing in his way. Soon they were avoiding him altogether for he made war seem like a game of his own creation. He could extinguish life quicker and easier than pulling a flower from its root.

As if she was feigning awareness of the fact he was approaching, she suddenly turned a beam of spluttering fire at him. He dodged, rolled, and weaved around it until he was close enough to strike her. She of course had the greatest advantage of them all—flight. She beat her huge avian wings and concentrated on keeping Rex in a state of defence. He rolled forward and with immense speed came out of the roll and hurled his trident straight for her. She dropped her spell and on instinct caught the weapon. Holding the haft, the three blades encircling the long spike-like centre, detached and struck her right in the chest. She fell from the sky like a songbird struck by a pebble. She hit the ground, a distinct snap echoed out, and she was wheezing hoarsely.

Vakar had a clear grin of superiority on his face when his right hand was gripped and his left wrist was snapped clean in two. His weapons fell from his hands at the searing shock of the broken bone. A large red hand wrapped around his neck. Njor Lokorson looked at him with a malice the prince had never known. He hoisted Rex up by the neck and fought the urge to snap it. It would have been as easy as breaking a twig, and Njor wanted nothing more. Rex kicked at the Kintar but he might as well have been kicking stone. His eyes started to flutter as the oxygen left his body. The last thing Rexous saw before falling unconscious was the hatred of millennia untold.

CHAPTER TWENTY

Celestial Renewal

Ven was laying on his back with his legs dangling over the cliff edge, where below the crashing waves broke against the stone and ricocheted back into the ocean. He hadn't done this since he left with Athvar and Scáth to return the lost Scorn home. Back then, he wished only for a life of adventure and belonging. Now that he had all those and much more, he understood he had never been so broken. He had gotten everything he wanted, everything he desired, so why did it all feel so wrong? Was what the heart desired nothing more than a farce designed to self-sabotage? Put there by the mind or the gods to corrupt the soul and lead you astray? He did not hear Scáth approach but felt her presence when she laid down beside him, intertwining her fingers with his. His heart calmed and knew, at least partially, he was wrong.

What is desire? Beyond seeing or envisioning something and claiming it for yourself. I had often found it interesting that there were the Gods of Litore, but also the Powers. At a glance, one and the same. Beings of such supernatural power that they changed reality. They controlled fate, could snuff out a millennium of culture and memories like blowing out a candle, or will an entirely new species into existence by merely dreaming of it. It was said the Powers represented aspects of existence, rather than the gods who merely bent it. For example, there was no god of love, but there was a Power of Love. There was no god of time, but a Power of Time. It unnerves me to know these powers are as real as the gods, but not as much as knowing the Power of Desire was also responsible for Greed. Nuada, ruler of the Underworld and Power of Fear, Greed, and Hatred. Does that mean then, that desire is evil? Surely one can want without it evolving into greed, but I've never 'needed' anything my whole life. Which has left me to do little but want. When I get what I want, do I feel less than I was? Angrier, even? The root of my rage has never been clear to me. I do search for the answer. I need the answer, I desire it. If I find it, will it do more damage than good? Or will it offer me the peace I need to live a fulfilled life. Peace, a domain of the gods; ironic, for the goddess Sesara seems little interested in her domain. Peace is thinner and more fragile than glass, and from my travels I saw life has little to no value.

If the gods are dying, perhaps it is what they deserve. Perhaps Litore itself is shedding their weight. From what I have seen, they do little good for anyone but themselves.

-Ven Devar

This was all he wanted and more. No matter what you got, be it what you wanted or not, the good always came with the bad. The Dark was never far away from the Light. The shadow of life hid all that was special and sad. Simply because you cannot see them does not mean they are not there. Trilara, Renic, Athvar, Arwr and Torvic all had died, but for a greater purpose than themselves. New relationships take root where old ones die, and bonds are forged in the crucible of ruin. What Ven knew to be most important then, was to protect his loved ones even at the cost of himself. He squeezed Scáth's hand tight and she rubbed her thumb across his finger.

It was nearly twilight now, and the two lovers were sitting, Scáth leaning her head against Ven's shoulder, their feet still dangling over the cliff edge. A piercing whistle tickled their ears and they turned to see the rest of Green Company standing around a fire and Sŷna preparing the map. As the two approached, still holding hands, they caught the tail end of Kithlyn arguing.

"If they might be dead, we need to regroup."

"No," Agan said confidently. "Faye was confident everyone would make it through the night."

"What happened?" Ven asked, sorry to have missed the beginning of the conversation.

Aolendìr chimed in happily. "Island Company has sustained heavy losses, hardly half of their forces remain. They were successful in their mission, however but your undead prince has defeated every Grimìr, except Lokorson."

Ven's eyes widened and glistened in the firelight. "What do you mean defeated?" He almost choked.

"Everyone will live, Faye has assured me. Don't forget she is Ward to the CareTaker." Agan reminded Ven she served the Power of Souls, the one Power Ven had actually met during his trek to Moon Mountain with Captain Sindrum Silver, now King of ShadowScorn.

"What happened to Rexous?" Ven asked next.

"Prisoner," answered Kithlyn, giving him a wink as she spoke. Ven wasn't quite sure what that was supposed to mean but he was relieved, surprisingly, to hear Rex was alive.

"I still don't understand why we can't relieve Island Company of their wounded before moving onto our mission," Sŷna questioned again.

"Because we have a mission that is time sensitive. To aid them would make their effort and sacrifice redundant and our mission incomplete," Agan explained.

"We sent a great number there and we can't win a war without soldiers," Sŷna continued. "Ven, many of those wounded are Kyst and other elves of this forest. I urge you to consider my proposal."

"Guilt or empathy do not offer coherent conclusions," Agan fired back.

Ven looked around at Green Company, the Grimìr and heroes staring back at him, looking for a decision. He looked up to Scáth who offered a heartwarming smile brimming with confidence. He felt his insides warm up and a sense of strength before looking at the party with an ease about him.

"We continue our mission as planned." He put a hand on Sŷna's shoulder. "Everyone in this rebellion will make sacrifices and those lost will never be forgotten." He nodded once at the renowned sage, who nodded back solemnly.

"Faye Walker is one of the most gifted healers in Litore, Island Company will be fine." That was just about the kindest thing Kithlyn could muster from the depths of her literal black heart. The sage's lip barely curled as he went to place the map down, brushing his fingers across the tube-like object, which activated with a glow from the glyphs. Aolendìr approached the map first, showing that he was clearly eager to use this one-of-a-kind item. Pointing his index finger to GreenWave, he was sucked into the map. Agan went next, followed by Sŷna, and Kithlyn. Scáth walked up to it but held her hand out low first. Faenla trotted over and sat on his haunches before putting his paw in Scáth's hand. She was always astounded to feel Faenla's great paw, for it was bigger than her own hand. She put her free index finger on the map and the two dissipated together.

Ven looked around the hideout, the Kyst and Gloom elves going about their delegated tasks. He looked back to where he and Scáth had been seated on the cliff edge and saw that Queen Saphier was standing there, motionless, staring at him. Her silken gown fluttered in the wind; her god-given beauty gave her an air and power no one else on Litore possessed. Her sharp jaw and angular eyes cut a menacing figure.

Ven furrowed his brow contemplatively as he looked back at her. A great gust of wind from the sea blew his heavy hood off and his hair, now tied up loosely in a half-knot, blew madly. He couldn't put his finger on it, but the look and feel he got was something between need and disdain. They exchanged neither nods nor expression. Ven turned his gaze to the ground somewhat woefully before touching the map.

The group landed safely atop the kilometre-tall waterfall of rich green water that doused GreenWave below. Scáth walked to the edge where the rush of falling water was nearly deafening. She looked out and it stole her breath. There were over a hundred longships moored to a network of docks, and more slips than not were empty, which meant the fleet had already left to take back Sanctuary Island. She saw what she could of the settlement before it dipped into the overhang of rock that the waterfall flowed over. The water was clean and vibrant with a dozen shades of green that shimmered in the dusklight. Ven walked up next to her, and as their eyes met, she was stunned again they appeared so much like the water below. Ven's ear flicked over the rush of water, then a thud was heard. They rushed over to the group that were standing over a Kyst hunter who had fallen from a tree, save for Kithlyn, who had just shadow-stepped out of said tree.

"That didn't take long," Agan chuckled at his old friend.

"Sharp as ever," she answered flirtatiously.

"I'll say," Aolendìr couldn't resist adding.

Ven walked over the fallen hunter and touched his neck. "He's still breathing, see if we can get some answers out of him?" He looked up at Agan. The hulking veteran nodded sternly.

"I brought the soft rope," Aolendìr quipped with a smile for no one but himself. He tied the Kyst up and placed a bronzed hand on the elf's temple. The hunter slowly opened his eyes and looked around as panic already began to set in on the imposing group before him. The Solsta elf stood and stepped back, allowing Ven to move forward and kneel in front of their hostage. His face was still partly obscured by his large hood, and Ven wanted to remain incognito for a time.

"What's your name?" he questioned.

"Ash," the hunter answer meekly.

"That's a strong and mighty tree, a good name for a hunter. You're lucky you didn't die in the fall, perhaps Āina has more planned for you," Ven said, trying to plant a friendly seed and watering it with the promise of divine intervention. As if Āina cared about him, Ven thought bitterly.

"The gods are mysterious, no one can truly know their plans," Ash answered.

"You might be surprised," Ven mumbled under his breath. "Are there more sentries up here?"

Ash offered up no answer. Ven pulled his hood off to look him in the eyes. He was surprised to see the hunter's eyes were an off grey, almost white. Not something he had seen more than handful of times in his life.

"I need you to be cooperative. A few of my companions won't have the patience I do and we're short on time."

Ash looked up at Agan, whose brow was heavy, and stared threateningly back. Kithlyn twirled the point of her dagger on the tip of her finger. As Ven looked up to see them, he fought a smile as these two clearly had a well-rehearsed intimidation plan.

"I'm sorry, but I can't betray the King of Kyst." Ash looked away in terror. Ven sighed heavily before standing up and motioning to Agan.

The fighter took a step forward but was halted by Sŷna. The sage approached the hunter and cast a spell over him, "There. Ask away," he said as if someone should have asked him to do that from the beginning.

"As I asked before, are there more sentries up here?"

"Yes, dozens. We have a special guest staying in our humble settlement," Ash answered happily.

"Who?" Ven pressed.

"Vakar the Cunning. It was sudden but we were honoured to host our King."

Ven shot straight up and didn't take his eyes from Ash, lost in thought.

"You can't be serious," Kithlyn nearly laughed.

"Tell me again, who is visiting GreenWave?" Agan said, needing to hear it again to believe it.

"The King of Kyst, Vakar the Cunning," Said the spell that made Ash happy to comply. Agan turned away from the group to think alone.

"I'm not usually the first to say it, but this does complicate things," Aolendìr said, putting his pointed goatee between his fingers.

Faenla padded over to Ven and nudged him out of his disassociation. Ven's eyes widened as he only now noticed the wolf's coastal blue eyes peering at him. It was Scáth's turn to kneel before Ash and question him.

"What is he doing here?"

"Going beneath the falls. There is an underwater tunnel that leads to a natural stone chamber. It's a great spiritual place for our people, but it's overrated if I'm being honest," Ash chuckled to himself.

"You've been inside?" she asked.

"Every Kyst born in GreenWave has. Vakar's entry will mark the first outsider to make the pilgrimage. The swim is dangerous, many die but that is level of our devotion to the Mother. There is nothing within but a single statue of Kaia." Ash sounded more serious at that declaration.

Scáth stood up and stepped back. "Thank you for your help." Then she turned to the rest of the company. "Well?"

"Do we think he knows?" Kithlyn asked to anyone.

"Most likely," Ven answered.

"He certainly does," Aolendìr said. Everyone looked to the golden elf. Agan slowly turned as well, as if something had dawned on him. "I promised the Grimìr of Shadow to be honest, so here it is. Some gods are benevolent, some evil, while one or two stride the realm between." He dipped into a low bow with his shoulder cape in one hand. "Chosen of Mahem, at your service."

Ven and Kithlyn managed to roll their eyes in unison. Scáth and Sŷna stayed quiet as Agan took several steps forward.

"You son-of-a-bitch, it was all you ,wasn't it?" Agan was centimetres from the elf's face. "I remember you now, at the Quake of Harazune."

Kithlyn visibly shifted. She was lost in the Underworld for over a year, fighting to survive and find her way back to the surface.

"I am impressed you remember, you were barely conscious when you saw me. I'm the one who got everyone to safety before you left my teleportation spell," Aolendìr chimed as if Agan should be thanking him. In a lightening swift motion, Agan headbutted the Solsta, and with a spurt of metallic blood, Aolendìr hit the ground.

"You played both sides of that War!" Agan nearly frothed at the mouth. "You ensured chaos ensued, keeping the Dwarves and Rhogarians in a constant bid for power. How many lives are on your hands?"

Aolendìr didn't budge; not out of fear, the opposite in fact. He simply wiped the blood away from his nose.

"Agan, you don't know that for sure," Kithlyn said after regaining a measure of her composure.

"Yes, I do." His demeanour was fire. "I had heard you were close with the then Queen Ranalia of Rhogar. You dined with Prince Corundrum and Princess Ametrine. You were the one who could get anything for anyone. You were even good friends with Valoris Rhoshal, that explains how the Willow Guild knew you and came into possession of the Dragon Horn and Gem of Domination."

Agan was seething, his hand slipping to the grip on his axe. Aolendìr noted this and let out a boisterous laugh.

"He's right..." That statement washed over everyone with disgust, "...to a certain degree." The Solsta elf gripped his nose and cracked it back into place. He went to stand but Agan held out his axe. "Please, do not start what you cannot finish. I was leading rebellions and stealing precious artifacts when you were a six-year-old street urchin getting the shit kicked out of you by the other orc kids with real families and homes." He stood up straight and Agan growled. Few to none knew about his younger years, yet somehow this one did.

"Explain," Ven said with his eerie calm he only brought out in tense situations as these. In truth, Ven needed Aolendìr if what Kaia and Āina said was true about reigning in the Third Age.

"I instigated events, yes. I offered my services when they were called upon, yes. I stole and I murdered. No more grievous acts than anyone here has committed. Even though I have started wars in the past, the Thousand Dragon War is not mine to claim. That title belongs to the now dead Queen Ranalia, eldest sister of now deceased Princess Vasenith and current King Dusanith of Rhogar."

"Blasphemy, you spit on the very lives who perished fighting for justice," Agan shot back.

"Ha! You forget the Dwarves of SilverRock worship Brailin StoneSower. Their very own ex-commander Nordhum Ironboot is the Chosen of Brailin Himself. No, it was Ranalia who planted the grey powder aboard the peace vessel you were on. She knew it would kill her sister and start the war, leaving the dwarves to hold the candle of blame. She captured the dwarves pretending to be Crookedhorn and worked her magic. You were just the fool too blind to see it," Aolendìr said without warmth or charm. He looked to Scáth. "Honest enough?"

Agan stood, his huge leather-wrapped arm shaking, verily hyperventilating, beads of sweat rushing down his forehead. Neither Ven nor Scáth had seen this kind of behaviour before and were unsure of what to do, but it was Kithlyn who walked up to the half-orc. She squared her body up to his and pulled her hood down, revealing a single long braid, misting away in a concentrated point. She looked at him with those black, eclipsing eyes and placed both hands around his angular face.

"It's over. You are not there anymore," she said with compassion and softness that none here thought possible from the stone cold assassin. Then she kissed him. Long and passionately. His vibrant yellow eyes squeezed shut as their lips met, finding each other like muscle memory. She pulled away from him and said, "Come on, let's do what we do best and complete this mission."

Agan let out a quivering sigh that might have been the closest thing Ven thought the half-orc got to a cry.

"You forgot one thing," Scáth said.

"Oh right." Aolendìr squinted at her, hoping she would not force this out. "Vakar hired me to report on you. I did so, telling him you gathered the Gloom elves of Glowen'ashen and then I refused anything else from him. Before you ask, no I didn't disclose the whereabouts of your hideout." Aolendìr sighed, thoroughly done with all this honesty. Ven simply shook his head, already nothing had gone right. Agan was a mess, which he didn't think possible, Island Company had suffered immensely, and more loss was on the way. He breathed in deep, collecting his thoughts, and exhaled his doubt.

"Kithlyn, take Faenla, Agan, and Sŷna. Complete the original mission, burn the docks and remaining ships. Perhaps Ash here can be of some assistance. Scáth, Aolendìr and I will head to the shrine and deal with Vakar," Ven ordered and Kithlyn nodded.

"Where should meet up?" the assassin questioned.

"Right here. If that fails, four kilometres up the river is a cave system. You can hide out there and we will find each other," the famed hunter answered, and everyone was in agreement. Ven, Scáth, and Aolendìr departed for the beach but before Ven could get far, Faenla stopped him.

"What is it?" Ven whispered in his kystin tongue. Faenla licked his face which brought a smile to his lips. "I'll see you soon, keep them safe, okay?" He wrapped his arms around the wolf and hugged his thick mane. With that, the trio got on their way.

Ven led the way down to the shoreline. The waterfall covered their sounds with ease but made the stone steps slick with algae. The entrance to the shrine was a good distance away from day-to-day activity, so the only Kyst they encountered was a small retinue of guards, no doubt Vakar's hand chosen hunters and sages to accompany him. There were four of them, only one being a sage and he was identified by a cowl obscuring much of face and a blue sash tied around his waist. The three were perched behind a fallen tree and were peering over to survey the situation.

"That's Pine, Vakar's lead Sage," Aolendìr whispered.

"You deal with him, the other three won't be a problem for me," Ven responded.

"I'll be by your side." Scáth's words rang confident, but Ven shook his head.

"Let me deal with them this time."

She studied him for a long moment before softly nodding. She would be ready at a second's notice if it seemed like he needed help.

"On your mark," the Solsta chimed. Ven did not choose stealth or a surprise strike; he very calmly stood up and strode the remaining distance. The other hunters were slightly confused by this tactic, the confidence he strode up to them with left them wondering if he was friendly. However, Pine quickly set them straight.

"That's Ven Devar. Stop him!"

Ven already had a dagger twirling towards the hunter furthest from him. The pommel struck the hunter in the temple, knocking him out cold. Pine was already moving his fingers and speaking the incantation for a spell. The two remaining hunters pulled out their tridents and ran for Ven. The famous hunter dropped low and swept the legs out from under an enemy. The Kyst fell and knocked himself out when his head cracked against the slick stone.

Pine shot a bolt of oozing energy at Ven, who had placed his shoulders and hands firmly to the ground and now lifted his torso and legs up. The bolt shot past where his waist had just been, then he pushed hard and sprang upright to land on the last hunter. Ven forced them both down and punched him square in the nose with his sword pommel clenched in his fist.

Ven, still kneeling over the last and now also unconscious hunter, turned his gaze to Pine. The serenity and confidence in Ven's eyes made the sage shiver, but that didn't stop him from casting another powerful spell of annihilation. What did, however, was Aolendìr appearing behind him and grasping his shoulder. Tendrils of electricity sprang from his fingers and Pine hit the ground stiff and convulsing.

Scáth watched Ven with a sense of wonder. She had seen him fight many times now but never with the intent and calm ferocity she just witnessed.

"Well done," Ven commended Aolendìr.

"A distracted wizard, is a useless wizard," he coyly remarked with a shrug.

The Scorn walked up to them and didn't say a word, replaying the event that was over in the blink of an eye.

"We took the position, where's the entrance?" Aolendìr asked looking around. Ven nodded into the water.

"Right," he replied with lack lustre.

"How long is the swim?" Scáth questioned.

Ven pursed his lips. "Just under an hour."

She scoffed. "Did you forget that's not possible for me?"

With a cold shoulder Ven pointed to the golden elf. "That's why I brought him."

She looked at Aolendìr quizzically. He walked up to her and fumbled around in one of the innumerable pockets he had. As he planted his feet in front of her, he held out his hand; resting in his palm was a small ball of brown goop. She looked back to him unimpressed.

"And?" She recoiled.

"Its bubbleweed," he answered all too cheerfully. "Keep it in your mouth, and it will release air. For the love of the gods, do not swallow it."

Scáth sighed heavily before grabbing the snot ball. Ven was already tying up the hunters and Pine together, then gagged each one.

"I suggest shedding any excess weight," he said, removing his cloak and hiding it in a bush. The other two did likewise, and soon the three of them were standing on the cliff edge, merely a metre above the water.

"Any idea what we might encounter down there?" Aolendìr cut the sound of the raging waterfall with his voice.

"Destiny." Ven began his deep breathing and the other two shared a look at his ominous comment. They both popped the bubbleweed into their mouths and the Kyst dived in. Aolendìr dove in seconds later and Scáth was on his heel. With a splash, the cold water nipped at her flesh and the sensation to take a breath overwhelmed her. A sense of panic overcame her as she began to have doubts about being able to keep up. She quickly realized you had to breathe through your mouth without opening to suck down the air of the bubbleweed, then exhale through your nose. Her mind felt all wrong, but she convinced herself this was how it had to happen and soon her body adjusted to it. The other two Grimìr were beside her now and she gave them a nod.

Ven kept leading them deeper. The water became darker and murkier as the fall's basin churned up sediment. However, the trio stayed close together as Ven led them through the murky green water.

The pressure began to build in Scáth's ears. Fortunately the seabed came into view and their descent stopped. With the clearer view they understood how the waters of Greenwave got its hue. A bed of vibrant seaweed covered the floor like fine grass upon a breezy hilltop. Great boulders pocked the ground that had fallen from the cliff, covered in brightly illuminated algae and weeds. Not far off in the distance was the border of a vast and fertile kelp forest. Scáth was torn away by the underwater vista when Ven grabbed her shoulder, pointing to a curious hole near the base of the seawall. He paused a moment to recognize that her skin had turned a grey almost like his now she was in the darkened depths. She looked back at him with a thumbs up that was distorted by an exhalation of bubbles and which had him appreciating the fact he was doing all of this on a single breath.

Aolendìr was standing on the cusp of the hole looking down its black maw, as the pressure on them was almost crippling. He sent a ball of light down the hole, then almost in slow motion jumped in feet first. An interesting choice, Scáth thought. Ven gave her a final nod and she dove in, letting the sheer weight of the water pull her down. He looked around the seafloor one final time before leaping in after them.

It wasn't long before Ven caught up to them as they were far slower swimmers. He took the lead as the tunnel began to narrow, coral and juts of sharp stone made it tricky to not get sliced as they swam through. He stopped the trio as the tunnel became so narrow; he knew they would have to squeeze themselves through one at a time. Fortunately, Aolendìr and Scáth were of similar slender builds to Ven so he went first, knowing if he could pull himself through, they could as well. He swam to the crack in the wall; putting one arm through, he managed to twist his head in just a way that he barely dragged his jaw on the stone. Slipping his other arm in now, he grabbed purchase and began to pull his torso through. Ven paused a moment to regain a measure of composure as the fear of getting stuck here rang in his mind like church bells. Hoisting himself through with all his might he got his waist, then legs on the other side.

Without a second to think he was swept further down the tunnel by a blasting current. His body was twirling and spinning out of control as the rushing water had full control over him. He attempted to balance himself out in a plank formation, but his back caught the tip of a stalagmite, tearing through his armour and the flesh on his back. He involuntarily let out a gasp of pain, which released most of the air he had left in his lungs. More out of luck than thought, his trident brushed his hand. Gripping it, he elongated the handle into a haft and buried each end into the stone. He clung onto it long enough to re-balance himself and delay long enough for the others catch up.

Scáth heard in her mind. "Go next, if you get stuck, I can help you through." Aolendìr's voice rang clear. She was not comfortable with putting herself in a vulnerable position with this one but she had already made the decision to trust him so she was not about to stop now. She nodded to him and began her way through just as Ven had. She found this process to be far easier, as she was slender like Ven but also far smaller. The one time she felt her hip snag on the stone she simply shadow-phased through it, a technique that was becoming easier with every use. Before her legs were even through, the sudden burst of current shot her onward. Aolendìr saw her legs get sucked through with great speed and furrowed his brow in confusion. He shrugged nonchalantly and simply blinked from one side to the other. As he reappeared, he was similarly throw off balance by the current and was tumbling through the narrow tunnel.

Scáth, like an arrow, was flying through the rushing water, weaving flawlessly around the odd stalagmite or bend in the tunnel. She saw Ven up ahead and whizzed past him as he had a firm hold on his trident. The hunter watched with pride as she went by and he knew Aolendìr would be shortly behind. He was right, however the Solsta elf was limply floating and a great pool of blood leaked from his forehead. The hunter reacted fast, shortening his trident and full body grabbing the unconscious elf. Ven knew the end of the journey would be soon, the water quickly shifted to a glass-clear freshwater reservoir and the current slowed to a standstill.

Scáth and Ven had met back up and she was surprised to see he had the Solsta draped on his back and was swimming for both of them. He motioned for her to keep going and the tunnel took a slight curve up. Neither of them realized they were about to breach the water for it was as clear as air. As soon as they did, Ven gasped for air harder than he ever had in his life. Scáth helped him swim Aolendìr to the shore and they hoisted him up together. Ven let out a groan of pain as a hunk of flesh was hanging off his back. After a moment to rest her weary muscles, Scáth went to inspect Ven's wound.

"Take off your chest piece," she instructed.

"I'm fine, we need to keep moving," he insisted.

"You know better than to make me repeat myself." She looked hard at him, and even with all the pressure he was under, the anxiety of knowing Vakar was in here somewhere, he could not deny her. Within a few moments he was bandaged up, albeit in great pain.

The two looked around and noticed a vast cathedral cavern. The air was stale and a few dozen paces in front of them stood a tall statue of Kaia. Ven walked up to it and found the sensation to be weird—the visage barely resembled the goddess he had met. It wasn't dignified enough, he thought. Yet, how do you capture the spirit of a higher being in a wood carving? He did, for some reason, despite himself, feel a strong connection to it. All he wanted his whole life was a family, a place he could belong as himself, not what those around him wanted him to be. He had found that in his new family, with Faenla, Scáth, Agan, and Athvar. He didn't want a parental figure past Renic and the fatherly lessons Athvar has imparted on him. So why did he feel as though he missed Kaia like only a son could in his mother's absence. Every night since their meeting, he cursed the two gods, disregarded their message and the love they offered. He did not need it, he did not want it, so why heed it. Yet, that wall he built up around the whole situation came crumbling down like a ton a of bricks, and with it, the hole he had buried his anger in just a few hours ago.

Scáth stood halfway between the unconscious Solsta and Kyst, watching her love with sorrow. He put both hands against the statue and sobbed silently. A moment later, Ven and his whole weight fell through the statue. He tumbled through ankle-height water before catching himself and looking around in hesitant awe. He saw nothing but blue sky and the ocean for as far as the eye could see. Looking back to where he had just stumbled through, he saw a mirror image of the statue, and Scáth fumbling through it to join him in wonderment. The water they stood in was eerily still, only agitated by their movement. When he looked at Scáth he saw three stone walls behind where they came, and a single Kyst standing between them. He nodded in their direction and Scáth put her hand to her hilt.

Ven slowly began walking towards the stone wall and saw that it depicted something; however, he kept his eyes trained on who he knew to be Vakar.

Without turning around, Vakar spoke. "Feels like a lifetime since we last breathed the same air."

Ven continued to close the distance, putting his hand to Hunter's Protection. "Simpler times."

"Happier times," Vakar added. Ven dare remove his gaze from Vakar to the stone wall. It reminded him much of the hieroglyph fortune he read in the Vampire hideout and old Kyst ruin outside Rushwater. Yet, this one seemed to depict thirteen beings arriving on Litore.

"You've been busy," Vakar interrupted, turning to face Ven. "Journeying around the world, saving princesses, squashing sieges, meeting Powers, climbing mountains, making family and friends wherever you go." Vakar all but sneered near the end.

Ven's face screwed up in shock. How could he possibly know all that?

"It all pales in comparison to you, torturer, betrayer, genocider, and all in the name of being the first ever King of Kyst. And why? Because the man you loved died, or your best friend left to help those in need outside of our forest?"

Vakar ignored him and set his sights upon Scáth. "Impressive escape. It managed to unify my people better than cutting your head off."

"Glad I could be of some help in the end after all," she said sardonically. "I must say, I've met many tyrannical rulers in my time as a princess, no one has quite done it like you."

"Why?" Ven immediately spoke after. "Why did you do it all?" He pleaded for an answer that made sense. He wanted nothing more than to believe Vakar did this not out of malice and even though he knew that answer was impossible, he wished for it all the same.

"How do you end violence?" he let his words hang for a moment.

"With violence," Scáth answered, but Ven gave her a disparaging look.

"A violence so hateful, so damaging, that it extinguishes all hope from your enemies. You have one out of how many surviving Kintar actually on your side in putting an end to me. I did what I had to, to make sure what happened to Silva never happens again in the Great Northern Rainforest."

"Conflict breeds only more conflict. You weren't king for single day before a rebellion was formed against you. That was one of your only flaws growing up together, you always thought you were right," Ven said in heavy condescension.

"And you always thought you were better than everyone," Vakar shot back before calming again. "Anyways, perhaps this will change your view on things." He stood aside and motioned for them to view the stone wall up close. Ven only took a few steps forward, keeping his awareness fixed on Vakar. Scáth, however, walked right up to the wall as if entranced by it.

It showed images of such perfect detail that they knew no mortal had crafted it. It depicted thirteen beings flying past a single moon and crash landing on what was clearly Litore. Out of the thirteen, seven were male and six female. They spread out across the land in continual contact with one other, often offering aid and support to each other in their exploration. Soon, a group of natives emerged from the land, and they labelled them as Powers, or at least that is what Scáth thought the translation was from Old Elvish, which she understood now was not elvish at all, but the original language known as Vox spoken by the foreign beings.

In time, two men and a woman met a celestial being who lived over the oceans and brought the weather at their whim. These three from space murdered this celestial being and the woman absorbed her divine power for herself, taking the name Kaia. Next it depicted a man living in a land where the sun never rose, bathed in darkness for many years, searching, hunting for someone. Finally, he found him and with great ease was gifted the divine realm of darkness, and took the name of Aceia.

Slowly but surely, the thirteen beings who arrived on Litore discovered the world itself radiated a power unlike anything else in the known universe, a power they called Tenticae. They became masters of it, pushing out the old gods and collecting their celestial seats one at a time. Eventually, one of these thirteen returned to the stars, never to be seen again. The gods started creating sentient life, the elves, dwarves, gnomes, dragon-bloods, aquon, vildfir, and watched them stumble through evolution and suffrage like entertainment. They occasionally offered glimpses of themselves to these lesser beings, giving them concepts like law, chaos, society, battle, justice, peace, and knowledge, demanding worship for a false sense of safety—a safety promised but never delivered upon. Only the opposite in fact, as these now evolving creations fended for themselves and were subject to the squabbles and tantrums of these gods.

And then the best fact of all, which made Ven clench his fists and Scáth gasp. The gods demanded fealty so they may grow in strength, and promised their most devout followers like paladins and clerics a piece of their divine power, when in fact, these people of Litore were never granted anything at all. For the power was in all of them, belief being the only ingredient to unlock it. Ven heard sniffling as Scáth's eyes were watering over at the barest realization of it all. Nearing the end of the hieroglyphs it showed thirteen more beings descending from the stars near the end of the First Age. From them, they brought incredible devices and minions to do their bidding. They called themselves Keeper's, and though they offered edicts to keep Litore safe, they immediately began siphoning the power of the gods.

Aunna Morningthorne had spent that last several hours, maybe even day, wandering the infinite waters of this plane that her deceased father had brought her to. She had at first assumed it was some area of the Void, but since her magic worked and there was a total lack of Mind Reapers, she ruled that possibility out. She screamed, more than once, in hopes of anything at all hearing her. Sound seemed to die out faster in this empty space. She collapsed to her knees, her silk dress floating around her waist in the shallow water.

It was all too much, seeing Ifan again, confronting Runa, seeing the kind folk of Nedea murdered in their homes by her religion. A religion she had devoted her entire life to. A religion built on peace and prosperity that offered only death and destruction. She punched the smooth, marble stone beneath the water and screamed, and kept screaming until her lungs were empty of air. A tear drop hit the water and rippled out, and a second later a ripple came back to her.

She curiously lifted her head to see a statue of Kaia, and behind her a three-stoned wall covered in hieroglyphs. She was immediately glued to the images, her eyes scanning each one hungrily until she got to a section that showed a tall woman walking through a field of billowing grass, stumbling across a celestial being with a chest wound. This tall woman sat in the grass next to the bleeding celestial and offered aid. However, the celestial cried out, "I am dying and so with me thy realm of peace; unless, thou child of thy stars takes thine place?" The tall woman was reluctant but with much convincing agreed.

"Put thou hand into mine chest, and eat mine heart of hearts, then thou will ascend higher than even thy stars as thou know them, child."

The tall woman did so, and with it became the new Goddess of Peace, taking the same name of Sesara. As she stood tall she was invigorated with a radiance of pure light. The deceased celestial was no longer laying in the grass, but tied by chain to the ground, her body marred horribly. A sick laughter filled the air as Zeries revealed himself.

"The others had all tried their best to get you to become one of us. But it was Mahem who convinced them to let me have a try, and now we know that not even the reverent Flo, or should I say Sesara, can resist my tricks," he bragged with a sickly grin.

Sesara weeped for cycles untold; in that time nothing knew happiness or contentment, until her tears filled the land that would form Litore Lake.

Aunna was torn from her mixed emotion of hatred and grief by a distorted sound from the statue. She quickly ran to the opposite side of the wall and hid.

"Now you know the Keepers as we know them are here to replace our gods and start fresh. We, the last Grimìr, were strategically placed to stop it," Vakar voiced, and Aunna, who was still undetected on the other side, knew she was listening to other Grimìr.

"I already knew that," Ven said, not really caring about Vakar's words as he was still processing this new intel, and would be for some time to come. Then, Ven did care about his words. "We?" he repeated and slowly turned to face his old friend.

"Chosen of Zeries," Vakar answered nonplussed. Aunna did everything she could to hold herself back from coming out and killing him on the spot for what his god did to her mother.

Ven scoffed, wanting to be in disbelief but hating how true it felt.

"Was this all a trick then? To get me here with Scáth so you could have your final revenge?"

"No, you did that yourself. You emptied your hideout of its best warriors, I stationed just enough of my soldiers there to keep yours busy and wounded. And no," Vakar said as if correcting Ven, "my navy isn't on its way to reclaim Sanctuary Island because that's where my road began. You erred in thinking me still sentimental. That defiant little sea-rat Saphier has already met her end, along with everyone else in the Shallowbay Hideout. The rebellion is over, Ven. There is nothing I do not know, nothing I cannot achieve." Vakar delivered his victory with such tepid emotion it left Ven and Scáth feeling sick.

"How did you know?" Scáth asked, "Queen Saphier told us the whole hideout was impenetrable to spying magic."

"I may be partially to blame for that," a fourth and familiar voice answered. Aolendìr had walked out of the statue, his head still leaking bronze blood. Ven's face screwed up, of course he was betrayed by this elf. "In my defence, I was tricked by the new God of Trickery and Lies." The Solsta bowed to Vakar in respect.

"Explain," Scáth demanded through gritted teeth.

"I have many magical items and artifacts spread across my body, more than a few are for spying. From what I could discern, Vakar the Cunning found a way to activate and use them from afar. I am sorry, I did not mean to betray your cause." Aolendìr lowered his eyes in apparent shame.

Ven's narrowed eyes turned back to Vakar. "I have had a persistent thought since my return to our forest. Is redemption possible for everyone? I have killed my own kind when they were helpless and fleeing my blade, and yet the only conclusion I consistently come to, is no." Ven unsheathed his artifact shortsword and trident. "The Kyst I once called brother will never return. The world has no use of your tricks so I will do what I must to end your terror, even if it further blackens my heart." He lowered his stance and squared up with Vakar.

The sounds of ringing metal were heard as Scáth pulled her scimitar out, but she held eye contact with Aolendìr to see how he would react to Ven attacking Vakar.

"You cannot kill each other. All the Grimìr are needed to defeat the

Keepers," Aolendìr reasoned but the others were past that. Vakar snapped his fingers and thunder rolled above, followed by a bolt lightening. The hunter saw the fingers move and instantly leapt forward. The water was electrified, but instead of shocking everyone, the stone wall exploded into a thousand pieces of shrapnel. Ven was blown back by the shock wave and landed in the water. Vakar was covered by a telekinetic shield and Aolendìr had projected something similar in front of Scáth and himself. Ven propped himself out of the water to see a small, dark-haired woman with lavender eyes and a ruined diadem around her forehead standing where the wall just was.

"Who in the Underworld are you?" Vakar seethed.

"Your worst nightmare," Aunna answered, and with her words came a ray of light from the sky so hot it sizzled Vakar's flesh. The beam of radiant energy was broken as Vakar lifted a gush of water above him. He looked back at her, his entire left eye burned and scarred.

"You have no idea the meaning of nightmare." Vakar conjured writhing black tentacles that lashed out at every single person here. One slashed Aunna's arm and the residual black goo left behind burned her flesh like acid. Aolendìr had drawn a wand and was fending off the tentacles with strikes and waves of his hand. Scáth, standing safely behind him, looked to Ven, who was fumbling around in the water for something.

The hunter had lost his trident and sword in the blast and was now looking around frantically for them. As he planted his free hand down to lift himself out of the water, it brushed a cold haft. He looked through the disturbed water and saw a handle made out of two helical pearls, the pommel a deep blue piece of coral that came to a serrated point. At the end of the handle was a trident head similar to his own, yet the blades were embossed with crashing waves and storm clouds. He picked it up out of the water reverently and felt a surge of energy wash over him, similar to what it felt like diving into the ocean. The opalescent green in his eyes were replaced by a stormy blue.

Everything and everyone around him slowed down so that their movements were almost barely perceptible, as if he was removed from time altogether.

"My beautiful, strong, determined boy." A voice he had heard only once before in his life echoed out behind him. He turned to see Kaia standing there, diminished and weak. "The ocean never stops—neither can you." Her voice still sounded sweet like lapping waves.

"I won't, Mother."

"Do not give up on the folk of this world. It is the point of everything; no matter how small or large, each one a soul as valuable as the last. We are all one, one and all." She slowly approached him. Even in her weakened state she was far taller and more grandiose. She grabbed his grey cheek in her palm. "Everything becomes clear as water in the end. I was wrong about much, yet the only thing I wish I could change was to have raised you, my baby boy."

Ven pushed his face into her hand, "Mom," his voice quivered, "I need you." Tears ran from his blue eyes.

"No, you have everyone you need." She gave him a look of loving serenity as the life faded from her eyes and she became one with eternal water. In a heartbeat, time resumed and the liquid field they were standing in gave way, as if a trap door had opened, and all five of them were plummeting into the waters of Greenwave.

CHAPTER TWENTY-ONE

Precipice

Sŷna was currently standing next to Faenla, who was looking out over the cliff edge, tracking the movement of Agan and Kithlyn below. The sage, however, was busy looking through a spell book, trying to decide which incantation would serve him best. Ash was still tied up to a tree but was now fast asleep from a well-placed punch. They had discerned from the hunter where the grey-powder was stored for the few cannons aboard Vakar's fleet. So, naturally, Agan and Kithlyn were off to steal the explosives and plant them throughout the harbour, and Sŷna was to ignite them from above. Faenla was, of course, standing guard to keep the sage protected, as even a Kyst was not to be trusted to watch out for their own surroundings when otherwise occupied with books.

Agan and Kith had made their way to the town proper, using all means of shadow and objects to make their way undetected. He was reminded of the old days as he struggled to stay out of sight, and if Kithlyn wanted to disappear, she simply would. Fortunately, the harbour was built off to one side of the town and there were not many civilians to dodge. As they neared the underground bunker built into the cliff wall, Kithlyn made a gesture to Agan to stay put but be at the ready. He nodded and took up position behind a large stack of crates and fishing traps.

The assassin vanished into the shadows and reappeared behind the two guards in front of the bunker. She rolled her eyes visibly as neither of them noted her materializing behind them. She swept the legs out from under one while driving a knife pommel into the head of the other. She stomped her boot on the temple of the fallen one and looked unimpressed while doing it. She lifted a set of keys off of them and opened the bunker.

"Never gets old watching you," Agan said, walking past her inside.

"Wish I could say the same," she teased. The pair entered the bunker as Agan dragged the unconscious elves inside. Upon entering, the room was illuminated by magical cases of light, displaying a long narrow corridor a cathedral in length, filled floor to ceiling on both sides with kegs. Agan's heart skipped a beat as he knew this much grey-powder could level one of the great cities like Serenstrom or Three Gates. He became short of breath and the nerves he spent a humans lifetime hardening to glacier forged steel came crumbling down. He lost his balance and reflexively grabbed on to the wall. An entire section of barrels shook under his sudden weight. Kithlyn quickly grabbed one arm and put her hand to his chest to keep him steady.

"What's gotten into you?" she almost scolded him. He put his huge hand around his neck as if to claw at it.

"I can... can't... I can't do this." His voice was coarse and his lungs empty. Kithlyn quickly bolted the door and Agan slid to the ground. She came back to kneel before him and was nearly brought to tears, for he was whimpering between fits of ragged breathing.

"My sunset, please, tell me what is happening." She grabbed one hand and breathed evenly, hoping his body would mimic hers.

"I've done too much wrong, I've seen too much pain. I haven't been the same since my memory came back. I can't handle the trauma I've inflicted and suffered, there is no reconciling it anymore." He looked up at her, his eyes red and brimming with tears like a child begging for help. She sighed sadly, unable to offer advice. "How do you do it, Kith?"

"I'm dead to the world, Agan. I haven't cared about a cause since the Adazji Guild was together. I kill slavers and pretend it's the right thing to do. I maim and murder because I told myself that is my purpose in life." She hung her head in defeat.

"We've done so much bad in the name of good and much worse because we had no other choice," he clutched his chest again, "I need it to end, all of it."

"You know I've always taken comfort in knowing everything good and bad comes to an end. This pain will pass, you have overcome every struggle in your life, you will conquer this too."

The half-orc closed his eyes and took many deep breaths before slowly opening them again and expressing a thank you.

"Let's finish the mission," she stood up and offered him her hand. He took it and together they filled enough leather wine skins to the cap with grey-powder to blow up a castle. They left the bunker and went to separate ends of the harbour. Agan first donned one of the hunter's cloaks so he could walk along the docks with greater ease. Keeping his head down, he stopped at every other piling and left a sack of grey-powder either hidden under a crate or hooked around a docking cleat hanging over the side.

Kith finished distributing her entire stash of powder in a matter of minutes as she shadow-jumped from section to section, avoiding any guards with ease or circling back to a spot after they had moved on. Agan was making good time and had even passed a handful of guards; with nods of recognition exchanged they were none the wiser.

The fighter was nearly 200 metres offshore and nearing the end of the harbour arm when he was yelled at for hanging the bag off a cleat. He recognized the language as kystin, and that was all he could discern. Agan slyly let the wineskin hang as he stood up to regard the elf. He quickly noted three more hunters coming to check out the situation.

"No need to cause a fuss, I'm just here doing a routine check on the pilings," Agan said in the common tongue. The hunter that first approached him had seafoam-coloured eyes and a look that spoke of a couple hundred of years on this coast.

"Only those in the king's army are allowed on this harbour," the hunter threatened as if it wasn't a threat at all.

Agan lifted his arms knowingly. "It's why I'm here."

By now the other three had arrived and created a wall around Agan, with the half-orc's back facing the water. They were all speaking kystin. This went on for a number of moments and it became clear they were arguing amongst themselves now.

"If that's all, I got a job just like you and need to get my work done before the night sky is in full." Agan went to move between them, but the old hunter shoved him back with a firm hand.

"Everyone in the king's army speaks kystin."

Agan looked the hunter dead in the eyes for a long time before caving. "Screw it."

A small coin slipped between his fingers and as it struck the ground, an echoing bang sounded, followed by Faenla's howl reverberating over the town. From above the waterfall, dozens of individual flames flew out; each one heading for a different sack of explosive powder. Agan had already turned to jump in the water but he felt a sting and something grip his ankle. One of the hunters pulled a whip out and tried to stop him. Agan was nearly 160 kilograms, and the Kyst, well he didn't come close to that.

The half-orc kicked the tethered leg out, causing the hunter to stumble forward into Agan's waiting elbow. A crack was heard, followed by the first explosion which made them all rock back on their heels. The whole section of dock they were on began to sink as the pilings continued to explode, sending wooden shrapnel in every direction.

"Don't let him escape!" the lead hunter barked and all three Kyst jumped at Agan. He grappled the first hunter but the other two were on top of him, dragging him to the slick deck. Agan was roaring, flexing every bulging muscle to shake them off but all three of them were pinning him to the ground. Even the fourth, whose nose Agan had apparently broken, was now brandishing a scimitar and climbing up the half-sunken dock to end him.

The veteran began to panic again as a lifetime of war and struggle came rushing back to him. He roared so menacingly it would have made any Kintar proud, but no matter how hard he struggled to break free, the hunters would not lessen their grip. The hunter holding the sword high was about to plummet it through Agan's neck when a light blinded them, and an explosion left them deafened. The last sack of grey-powder Agan just placed exploded, the dock they were left on was annihilated, and all five of them were thrown through the air.

Kithlyn had just finished off two Kyst hunters that gave her more trouble than she would have cared to admit when she spotted Agan's silhouette rag doll through the air before splashing into the darkened waters. She was about to dive in the water to retrieve him when she spotted five other figures appear at least forty metres above the fiery mess and a large pond's worth of water. Ven went headfirst, arms and trident extended to a point as he slipped into the water, barely making a splash. Aunna magically decreased her momentum just before hitting the water. Vakar managed a quick spell of teleportation, landing on a massive structure of floating dock. Aolendìr cast a spell on Scáth and himself, surrounding their feet in liquid mercury, allowing them to land harmlessly atop the sea water. Ven sunk deep into the black depths and found the trident was pulling him through the water without any effort on his part. The speed was immense and with blind luck, he saw Agan sinking to the sea floor. Letting the trident pull him through the water, he tucked one arm under the unconscious Agan and began their ascent.

"We have to put an end to Vakar's reign," Scáth told Aolendìr, but the elf didn't seem convinced now was that time.

"We can't kill him," he insisted.

"We don't have too." Scáth began running atop the waves towards the floating dock, with difficulty at first before she got the hang of it. She saw a bright beam of light heading for her, and she pulled the natural shadow around her snuffing out the spell with sheer darkness. She continued her stride with Aolendìr close behind. Looking to her right, she noticed Aunna swimming for the same platform.

"Help her!" she shouted with a point of her finger.

"Yes, your highness," he mumbled under his breath, and with a point of his wand Aunna was lifted and granted the same water-walking spell. He then shot her a wink and Aunna looked hesitant. Vakar continued to send missiles and bolts at Scáth and she continued to dodge or let them pass through her. With a grunt of anger, Vakar lifted both hands and a huge wave grew between them and headed straight at the trio.

Ven and Agan shot out of the water, Kaia's trident leading, and they landed on the floating dock like fish jumping into a boat. The harsh landing forced the water out of Agan's lungs and Ven was quick to realize he landed on the same dock as Vakar. He slowly stood and Vakar focused hard on his coastal-blue eyes.

"Please, Vakar, end this madness, I do not wish to harm you," Ven nearly begged. Vakar noted Ven's grip on this clearly powerful weapon, and with it the ocean began to churn and agitate around them. Storm clouds rolled in and a streak of lightning lit the sky.

"You already did. I needed you, you were my brother and you left me. Abandoned me in my weakest hour." Vakar's tone was one of the saddest Ven had ever heard from the once jovial elf. "There is nothing more you can do to me." His final words were harsh and bit at Ven's heart profoundly.

"If I had known or realized," Ven said, knowing it wouldn't make a difference.

"There comes a point in everyone's life, where your very being stands upon a precipice. For some, we stand there in contemplation, for others we're shoved off the edge and never look back. This was our fate."

"I will not fight you, Vakar."

"So be it." The King of Kyst lifted his hand and from his fingertips shot forth a bolt of viscous tendrils. The Mighty Ven Devar closed his eyes with a smile and reflected on a lifetime of inner turmoil for handing out death so freely to the innocent and guilty alike. He knew in his heart that this act of pacifism was the right one. He would not kill someone he once loved so dearly. Ven heard the bolt strike and was ready for death to take him, yet several heart beats passed and still he heard the waves and rain. He opened his eyes and Agan Dusk was facing him, a calm look on his face.

"The world, it needs you, elf. I've done all I can for it." Agan fell forward and hit the deck, with all the flesh, muscle, and sinew on his back burned away to the bone. Ven's eyes immediately brimmed with tears as the realization hit him. From the shore, a great scream was heard as Kithlyn was stuck in a whirlwind of hunters and sages all trying to capture her. Ven looked up from Agan's still body to Vakar, malice and hatred clear on his face.

His hand squeezed the grip of Kaia's Trident and several bolts of lightning struck the ocean around them. For the first time since Vakar began his takeover of the forest, he knew fear. His fingertips sent a fan of flame at Ven but he slashed it away with his trident as it sent a crashing wave to extinguish the fire. He was only a few steps from Vakar when the sage sent another bolt of necrotic energy at him. Ven rolled under it and sent a dagger into Vakar's thigh mid-roll. The sage dropped to one knee and reached out for Ven. He gripped the hunter and static electricity leapt out for him. Ven was unbothered as the trident absorbed the power. He grabbed the hand that just cast the spell by the wrist, and with a twist he snapped it clean. Vakar screamed in agony, pulled the dagger from his thigh and drove it into Ven's shoulder. The hunter barely grunted at the stab, instead taking the opportunity to rip the pendant off Vakar's neck. It clattered to the ground and Ven held his artifact trident, crafted by Kaia herself, to Vakar's thin, frail neck. He twisted the grip and another bolt of lightning forked across the sky and the waters roiled.

"There's no redemption for any of us. You've always been a killer, the best there is, and we cannot change who we are," Vakar wheezed through the gritted teeth. Ven pushed the trident deep into his neck, ready to slice his throat open.

"Stop," Aolendìr said calmly. Ven looked back and now everyone made their way onto the dock. Even Kithlyn appeared from the shadows, covered in blood and bleeding from many wounds. She was kneeling next to Agan's unmoving body, while Scáth, Aunna, and Aolendìr stood near the two Kyst. "We need all the Grimìr to defeat the Keepers," the Solsta continued.

"I don't care what you say. He's done too much harm, it's who he is." Ven went to slice his throat but Scáth spoke up.

"This isn't you, my love. The Kyst I first met would never have dreamt of killing someone at his mercy."

"The ocean kills those at its mercy every day." Ven's throat became thick as he tried to convince himself this was who he was—a killer.

"And it brings life to the whole world," Aunna said, surprising everyone. She wanted to see Vakar dead more than anyone, but in her heart she knew it was not right.

"Who are you to speak of life and death?" Vakar groaned in anger.

"I am the Daughter of Sesara. Zeries doomed my mother from the start, we cannot usher in the Third Age by killing each other."

"If you don't kill him, I will." Kithlyn looked back at the group surrounding Vakar. Black tendrils of shadow always poured from her eyes but now they wept black tears.

"Agan gave his life so you wouldn't have to take another. Please Ven, take him as a prisoner instead." Scáth pleaded for Ven to not make this mistake, to not throw away Agan's final act. The hunter looked to Kith who was hunched over Agan, begging with her eyes for Ven to take revenge.

With a grunt of rage, Ven kicked Vakar onto the ground and stood up. "Chain him." The hunter glared at Aolendìr, who obliged. Cuffing his hands in anti-magic iradinium. Ven looked to Kithlyn as she stared at him hatefully. Aunna went over to Kithlyn and Agan. She placed both hands over the smouldering flesh of Agan's back and dim light radiated from her palms. "Do not be hopeful, but I will do what I can," Aunna said.

CHAPTER TWENTY-TWO

Son of Death and Fire

Ivan awoke chained up to a stone chair in a palace throne room, the likes of which he had never witnessed. His chair shook and the blazing chandelier above him threatened to fall. When the quake ended he spotted Tilly, not tied up and still clutching that damned tome. He looked at her confused before committing his senses to take in his surroundings. Ceilings well over a 100-metres in height and width held dozens of dragon eyes staring down at him, occasionally one of them lighting the ceiling up with a burst of flame, ice, or lightning.

In front of him was a huge dais and throne, at the base of the stairs was King Dusanith, wielding a greatsword of gleaming iradinium. He was standing above the dwarf prisoners they transported here, each one shackled and kneeling.

"What is this?" Ivan asked still dazed. King Dusanith said nothing, instead replying by cutting off one of the dwarves' head. "Stop!" Fjell yelled.

Dusanith moved behind the next dwarf in line. At the same time, a tall figure appeared from behind the throne to fill its seat. Ivan was immediately filled with a dread he had never known, yet somehow it reminded him of that fateful day he breached the walls of ShadowScorn and became an avatar of Sesara. The Dragon-blood figure was huge and glistening, his scales almost translucent with hard lines like diamonds. His eyes flickered with a cyan flame as he licked his serrated teeth. Ivan knew without doubt this was Skalgr, the Diamond Dragon, God of Death and the Final King. Yet for all his terror and divine power, he could tell the god was diminished.

Dusanith struck one more dwarven head from its shoulders, and Skalgr appeared momentarily rejuvenated.

"What a final gift for thy Final King." Skalgr's voice carried a hiss to it. Ivan did not know if he possessed the courage to speak. "Sesara's Revered has paid him a visit in thy final hour. And with thee, thy Daughter of Zemez. He doth love when things cometh together."

Another quake occurred and Ivan was nearly knocked over as the chains prevented him from balancing. Skalgr saw this and waved his hand; the iron melted off Ivan and hit the floor in a fresh slag. Still, the paladin dared not move.

"Speak!" Skalgr roared and he was echoed by the dozens of dragons above, all screeching in drekin.

"I never thought to see you in the flesh. This must be a momentous day and my final hour indeed," Ivan said, regaining a measure of calm.

"Thou hath fed mine more than any else upon Litore. Thou would taste delicious upon mine own tongue as a final meal, yet a new era will need death upon its cradle," Skalgr spoke and his whole body shrunk in pain before sitting upright again. Dusanith struck another dwarf dead. Ivan felt as though the death in this room would claim his life quicker than a poorly placed strike from Skalgr himself.

"I have only served for peace in Her name." Ivan rejected Skalgr's claim.

"Thou wars have made mine stronger than mine children ever had," The God of Death sneered with uncouth delight. Hearing this made Ivan feel so low he wished he could take his own life then and there.

"Please, feast upon my soul as your final death. I beg of you. End me. End this," Ivan begged, turning his eyes to the floor. Dusanith took another head and it rolled into Ivan's line of sight.

Yet another quake shook the room. "Little one, bound in leather tells the story of future and past. Thyself must proclaim to him thy destiny."

Tilly sighed and looked for the first time back at Ivan. She flipped open her tome to no particular page.

"Ivan A. Fjell, destined to be a great human from the sewer district of Serenstrom. From the filth will rise a man all around him can cherish and follow in sound mind and heart. He will win countless victories around the world and further expand the name and tyranny of Sesara. He will lose only one war, and it will change the course of the world. He will raise the Daughter of Sesara like she was his own. He will flee his home in pursuit of the enemy that he treats as an ally. He will fight alongside the Grimìr and command great battles in the War for Litore with only one other strategist of his equal. He will die in that war atop an unnamed hill, his bones will return to soil in an unmarked grave," Tilly read from its pages and closed the tome with finality, hardly missing a beat as she spoke aloud.

Ivan's eyes ran with tears as his whole life was recited to him, yet the tears he bore were for another. "Aunna? Is the daughter?" he said aloud, more than asked. "Tell me, what is to become of her, I beg."

"The fate of the Grimìr are not recorded in her text," Tilly answered.

"You hold the Tome of Zemez, all is recorded in it," Ivan cried out.

Tilly simply shook her head. "Not for us."

Another great shake and thud were felt throughout the palace and Dusanith cut the second to last dwarf down.

Skalgr hissed in delight. "Thee prodigal son returns. All dragons are mine children, yet I only bore one unto this world. From Fire and Death he was made, and that will be thy legacy." Skalgr stood from the throne of Rhogar and began to twist and contort, his limbs, neck and wings elongating and expanding to impossible lengths. He writhed and curled around the room until he nearly filled all of its empty space. He was magnificent, gleaming, his scales truly made of diamond. His enormous draconian head settled between Dusanith, Ivan and Tilly.

"As one reign ends, another begins," Skalgr's voice boomed and all the dragons roared and screeched as the Diamond Dragon lifted his head to release one final breath of pure, bubbling energy. It disintegrated the entire roof off the palace and in a great swirling mass, every dragon within flew into the stormy sky.

The floor exploded next and through it flew a Dragon-blood wreathed in flame, spear point leading. He was easily thrice the size of the largest Dragon-blood ever born and landed in front of Skalgr. He looked up to the God of Death with his one eye and spread his terrible wings as a burst of flame exploded around them.

"Son," Skalgr hissed with knowing delight.

"Death is the final king," Ragos the Reaper spoke and thrust his spear through his father's jaw and out the crown of his head. The Diamond Dragon fell into a heap before turning to ash and floating up throughout the open ceiling. Ragos the Reaper in his true form was over ten-metres tall and slammed the bottom of his spear to the ground, sending out a ring that was heard across the entire city. The Grimìr of Death looked down to Ivan and Tilly. He shrunk to just under half his natural size and squared up with Dusanith.

"What is the age?" The air around his maw rippled with heat as he spoke.

"My Lord, it has been 112 years since you last awoke. The end of the Second Age is upon us," Dusanith declared with a measure of confidence the others were surprised by. Ragos turned to face the King of Rhogar.

"King?"

"King Dusanith, my Lord. Of the line of Dreki preserved for over 3,000 years." Dusanith dipped into a half bow.

"Good, ready the country for war," Ragos ordered and Dusanith nodded before exiting the chamber. The Grimìr faced Tilly now, looming over her.

"Daughter or Chosen?"

"Chosen," Tilly answered. Ragos snarled slightly.

"Unfortunate. Why is there a human amongst us?" he asked Tilly, disregarding Ivan entirely. Ivan remained still and silent.

"He is a true follower of Sesara. Very important in the war to come," Tilly said earnestly, trying to sell the fact they needed Ivan. She really could not be sure if Ragos would even entertain mere mortals.

"Your book say that?" he asked, sending his one good eye gazing at the tome.

"Mhmm," Tilly squeaked, unhappy about his eye resting upon it. Ragos grunted in irritation.

"He better not hinder us."

"In what, exactly?" Ivan pointed out. "You just woke up from nap while the world has been struggling. Your own country fought in a war that most the world took part in only twelve years ago. Do you have any idea what is going on?"

Tilly squeaked again and Ragos finally paid Ivan heed. Ragos stared him down and smoke poured from his leathery nostrils. Then the corner of his lip curled up.

"I suppose that is why you are here," Ragos chimed, not unhappily. "What is the plan then?" He crossed his impossibly large arms.

Ivan and Tilly both looked at each other in semi-astonishment. Neither would have guessed him to act this amenable.

"Well, finding the other Grimìr seems to be the best course of action, as Zemez did task me to do so," Tilly explained sheepishly.

Ragos grunted, somewhat introspectively this time, "Ale." Tilly flicked her head in surprised confusion and Ivan ever so slightly leaned in with raised brows.

"Come again?" the paladin asked.

"Has there been any advancements in ale? I'm thirsty," Ragos declared and began exiting the palace. The two remaining looked at each other, lost somewhere between amazement and sheer confusion.

"Wait!" Tilly cried, running after the Grimìr with her tiny legs against his massive strides.

They finally caught up and were exiting through the great bailey at the front of the palace. Ivan slowed his stride a touch as he noted all the Dragon-bloods were falling to their knees in reverence at seeing Ragos the Reaper with their own eyes. He even noted a handful of folk crying in apparent relief at his return. Ragos was as mythical as one could be while still being real. He had been around since the birth of Rhogar and before. Many Rhogarians to this day chose to worship Ragos as their chosen deity over Skalgr because he was seen as the true shield of Rhogar. He only ever surfaced when the royal family awoke him from his tomb under the palace, in the original castle Ragos had first built; which only happened under the most dire of circumstance. Every time he was risen, the threat facing their country was quashed like a fly between two fingers.

Ragos continued into the upper city and walked as if he was any other citizen. Tilly was in a full jog as her height only reached the knee of Ivan, and even he was having to walk quickly to match Skalgrson.

"Where are we going?" Ivan dared ask in irritation.

"Do humans still forget to use their ears? Ale." Ragos emphasized the word 'ale'.

"I'm sure your palace would have had ale," Tilly pointed out between heavy breaths.

"The best ale comes from the local taverns. It has been over 100 years since I filled my tankard. Sleeping works up a thirst," he explained, not really giving them his attention, but rather looking for a particular establishment.

"Well could you at least slow down?" Tilly asked, now breaking a sweat.

"Doesn't your book tell you the answer?" Ragos almost made himself chuckle.

"Of course no-" She was cut off from answering as his massive red-scaled hand scooped her up and threw her on his shoulder, which was more than big enough for her to sit comfortably. Ivan was now astounded by the apparent playfulness of death incarnate.

"Pee-yoo, we need to get you clothes that aren't 100 years old," Tilly stated matter-of-factually. Ragos didn't reply nor smirk from what she could tell.

The giant Dragon-blood took a hard turn and squeezed himself through the door of a tavern known as the Golden Talon. The interior of the tavern did appear golden as it was built from light-coloured wood and danced with golden light from two blazing hearths and dozens of torches. Only a few patrons were inside at the time and every one of them stopped as if caught in a petrifying gaze; all save for a band of what must have been adventurers, as Rhogar was a free-trade city with one of the largest ports in Litore. It attracted every sort from around the realms, and this particular group did not seem to notice the reverence the others were paying Ragos, for they continued to celebrate drunkenly. Ragos, with Tilly still riding shotgun, approached the barkeep who appeared as though he was seeing a lifelong celebrity crush.

"One of your finest ales," Ragos demanded as politely as one of his nature could. The barkeep stood there looking up for some time before shaking himself out of whatever was preventing him from moving and went to pour a tall, frothy tankard of ale.

"Look at this cock-eyed brute," a Solsta elf nudged his adventuring companion who happened to be a larger than large orc. Tilly turned her head to look at the adventurers, who had a sack of gold sprawled out between them. She shook her head discretely at the party, which included two degenerate-looking humans, as they were all staring at Ragos. The Grimìr of Death paid them no heed, instead taking the ale just given to him and downing it in hurried pleasure. He placed the empty mug down and cracked his neck.

"Nourishing. Another please, and one for each of my," Ragos paused to look from Tilly to Ivan, clearly deciding what to call them, "work associates."

The barkeep nodded and Ivan smiled despite himself. The celebrating crew continued to cackle and talk about Ragos, however.

"I bet you could take 'em, Grog," one of the humans egged on the orc.

"Fifty golden scales say the Dragon-blood pisses himself," the other human wagered.

"Deal," the higher than mighty Solsta said. Grog downed another ale before standing up, sending his chair tipping over. The other patrons in the tavern were torn between running for their lives or witnessing what few ever had—Ragos in action.

The orc was no slouch. Typically his species stood around 2.7 metres in height and not much less in width. Natural born warriors with fearsome tusks capable of ripping jugulars open like fruit. In the time it took him to lumber over to the bar, the keep had dropped off the two ales to Ragos and Tilly, who promptly leapt down from his shoulder. The barkeep walked over to Ivan who was seated at a small round table. Ivan knew fear better than most, and he could tell the barkeep was terrified.

"Must you?" Ivan said to Ragos. He received no reply. Tilly jumped down from the bar and made her way to sit with Ivan; better to gain some distance, she thought.

"My friends over der said I could beat ya up," Grog chortled with a drunken snort. Ragos did not turn his head, favouring a sip from his fresh drink.

"Well, here it comes," Grog said stupidly, winding up to punch the demi-god. Grog hit him square in the jaw and Skalgrson did not budge. Grog looked confused; clearly that had never happened to him before, so it wouldn't a second time, surely. Ragos caught the hand, his huge, clawed grip covering Grog's entire fist. He put his tankard down and gripped the orc's head in the palm of his hand and hoisted him up high. Skalgr kept one hand free for no other reason than he could. Grog kicked and punched to save his life, but each blow was like striking solid stone.

Ragos cocked and slightly turned his head, putting his one good eye on Ivan. Ivan met his gaze and felt a wave of worry wash over him, amplified ten-fold by the smile Ragos gave him. Ivan's eyes widened as Grog began to scream and the huge hand of Ragos squeezed tighter and tighter. Ragos never looked away from the Revered Paladin of Peace as Grog's skull cracked and covered Ragos' smiling, sinister face in blood and brain. He extended his unnaturally long serpentine tongue and licked the blood off his face before dropping Grog's headless corpse to the ground. The Grimìr looked to the other adventurers with something that could only be described as lust. All three of them scrambled to collect their coin and ran out of there.

Ragos grabbed his tankard and went to sit with his 'work associates.' No one said or moved for several long moments. Eventually Tilly handed him a handkerchief to wipe Grog's brains off. Ragos took it reluctantly, clearly preferring to have stayed covered in blood.

"I must admit, at first you seemed, almost, affable," Tilly trailed off, unsure if that was the right word to use. Ivan gave her a furrowed look. Granted, he wasn't what he might have assumed, but affable didn't seem to hit the nail on the head, perhaps equitable.

"I serve one purpose, and this is to kill," Ragos explained with a hint of melancholy.

"But the legend says you are born of both Skalgr and Pirelia," Ivan added.

Ragos conceited. "Hers is to burn."

"And give life," Tilly added. "All that is burned is given bed to grow again."

"I do at times feel duelling desires in my heart," Ragos admitted.

"And what is that desire?" Ivan prodded.

"To see what comes next," the son of death and fire answered. Ivan pursed his lips in contemplation. Never did he expect this to be the entity that is Ragos the Reaper.

"Explore that side of you. You are older than most if not every other living thing on Litore, yet you do not truly know who you are," Ivan suggested amiably and Ragos only looked back at the paladin blankly.

"We need to start actioning, else the Third Age will have begun without us," Tilly interrupted.

"I just found out about all of this, you are one of the few Grimìr throughout the realms and have had apparent time to devise, what do you suggest?" Ivan said a little harsher than he intended. Ragos too stared at Tilly expectantly.

With a brief sigh she gathered her thoughts. "There are thirteen Keepers. The amount of Negators is unknown but believed they come and go form our world into the stars above as needed," Tilly explained but was predictably interrupted.

"Who gives a damn about the Keepers?" Ragos asked and Ivan agreed; as far as he was aware they were here to help. He just recently met one atop the Spire Lakes to dispatch The Macer.

"They are why the gods are dying or dead. As the gods we have known replaced the gods before them, the Keepers aim to do the same. When they have ascended, they will wipe away all life on Litore and start the world anew, as they see fit. No past wars, no feuds between species and nations, just a blank slate."

"That cannot be. The gods created the world and all we know. There was no world before them and the Keepers have only helped since revealing themselves. They would not possess the power to kill our gods," Ivan retorted, not wanting to hear this story.

"This is the tale Zemez revealed to me," she said plainly.

"You believed it?" Ragos questioned.

"The gods gain nothing by deceiving us." Tilly pushed her spectacles up with her index finger. "To hide anything from us would only give their ultimate enemy, The Keepers, an advantage over us. Our gods put the final Grimìr across Litore to ensure that everything they created does not die with them."

Ivan slumped in his chair; he could not understand how he was supposed to react to this. He did not have the training to prepare him for a divine war against all-powerful extraterrestrial beings. He did not even want to begin to think about the consequences if they lost this war, let alone the inevitable loss that will come by fighting in it.

"Hmm," Ragos snorted as he slammed down his tankard. "My mother once said, 'the world cannot know peace, for it was born in blood, only the end will save it.' Perhaps this is the 'end' she referred to. A unifying cause for everyone to believe in," Ragos suggested with surprising wisdom.

"Belief is the most dangerous thing in the world," Ivan recited under his breath.

"Who said that?" Ragos chortled with obvious brevity as he knew he was the most dangerous thing in the world. Tilly, however, looked at Ivan in awe of his simple truth.

"Me," Ivan answered.

"So we kill the Keepers. Simple," Ragos declared with an air only the son of death could. Ivan was still lost in thought.

"It will take all the Grimìr to kill the Keepers, if indeed that is the route chosen to end them," Tilly explained.

"I beg to differ. Where are they?" Ragos asked indignantly.

"All over the world," she answered.

"The closest one," Ragos barked.

Tilly rolled her eyes. "The Blue Waste."

"Good," Ragos said, and for the first time, with a smile.

CHAPTER TWENTY-THREE

Grimìr

Green Company found themselves abruptly appearing in the town of Hearth to a devastating scene. The local gnomes Ven remembered so well were out in full, attending to the wounded soldiers of both sides. Yet the gnomes themselves looked dirty and starved, and the once beautiful town of Hearth was but a shadow of its former self. Gloom elves and Kyst littered the town and surrounding forest, many screaming in agony while others were eerily still, staring off at nothing. Even more stared at nothing but the afterlife.

"Look at your good work," Vakar whispered snidely to Ven. The hunter clenched his fist and moved into town while Aolendìr kicked Vakar's knee out from under him, forcing the sage to sit.

"If you wish to live, I suggest you shut it. Even I have limits in your defence," Aolendìr said standing over the former King of Kyst. Ven made his way up to a gnome he thought he recognized.

"Tolmie?" Ven asked sensitively, still unsure if this was indeed the kind leader of Hearth that helped him through his struggles after the fall of Silva. The gnome was clearing rubble away from the entrance of a collapsed home when he turned to face Ven.

"Ven? Is that really you?" His voice quivered. Ven simply nodded.

"I'm so sorry Tolmie," Ven offered him his condolences and felt like an idiot for doing so. This was all his fault, no matter what anyone told him.

"Me too," he replied before noticing Vakar chained from a neck collar that bound his wrists and legs. "You brought him back here?" He sounded almost horrified.

"He's our prisoner. It's over, Tolmie, I promise." Ven's voice was soothing, but the gnome was on edge nevertheless.

"Best keep him out of view. We may be small folk but he turned us into hardened creatures." Tolmie quickly turned to hatred. The hunter nodded, fully understanding the good folk of Hearth would want their revenge. Ven ordered him into the closest dilapidated structure. The Solsta took him inside along with Kithlyn and Aunna carrying Agan's limp body inside. Aunna went to work, casting every spell of healing in her repertoire to help Agan Dusk through his life-threatening injury. The flesh was melted deep, and she could sense his life-force was fragile at best, but it was a testament to his strength that he still drew breath.

She looked to Kithlyn and spoke. "I am weakened, I must rest to have the energy and will to cast again." Her lavender eyes were bloodshot and brimmed with tears, and even Kithlyn could tell they were not tears over Agan. Kithlyn looked back down to Agan, resting on his front, clearly appearing helpless. Aunna recognized this and pulled out a jar of salve. "Apply this to the rawest parts of his flesh before bandaging him." She rested a comforting hand on Kithlyn, and for some reason the cold assassin was indeed comforted. It faded the second Aunna's hand left.

Kith's icy, eclipsed pupils peered at Vakar after the Grimìr of Peace left the hut. It said everything. Vakar didn't shift uncomfortably but Aolendìr did.

"Don't, Kithlyn," the Solsta warned with soft tones. He did not want to escalate the situation, for not even in all his confidence and power was he sure about defeating this one.

"One day," the assassin promised before treating her dear friend.

Ven and Scáth walked through Hearth as they once did the previous year. They paused at the breathtaking vista of the northern archipelago that stretched as far as the eye could see before eventually merging into the Magma Isles. It didn't fill them with the awe or inspiration it once did, for the smell of smoke and death was too pungent.

"Look who still draws breath," Onstera echoed.

Ven and Scáth turned to face her, her platinum hair and dark eye shadow were stained more red than silver.

"Sounds as though you had a hell of time," Ven responded coldly.

"Everybody here but one fell to your old prince."

"Take me to him," he demanded.

Onstera nodded and turned to lead them with a wave. She took them to another familiar place, that of the old town hall. Ven noted the same seashell handle on the grand door; upon opening it he saw a scene he never thought he would. Nordhum Ironboot was in his leather pants and nothing else, black and blue all over with a great bandage, blood soaked and covering most of his torso. Scarlet Albright was in a similar state and both heroes rested on cots. Faye Walker was upright and attending to wounded Gloom and Kyst alongside her sister Wynn.

"Nobody had seen a warrior so fierce and determined as Rexous was that battle." She pointed to a spectral cage that held Rexous within. The cage was currently being watched over by Njor, and Ven sighed at having to now confront Rex.

"I'll go attend Faye and send her to Agan, she will surely want to aid him." Scáth squeezed Ven's hand before leaving him. The hall was quite large, but even so Rexous managed to lock onto Ven as he approached. Njor turned to follow his gaze and even found a smile at seeing the Kyst.

"Good to you see, Kaiason," Njor said respectfully.

"Likewise. You managed to stop him?" Ven asked.

"He tore through every Grimìr here like wind through smoke," Njor answered quietly.

Ven swatted his impossibly huge bicep. "Save for you."

Njor smirked and Ven closed the distance to the cage. The once-prince was seated cross-legged so Ven remained upright.

"I believe absolution is in order," Ven started.

Rex chortled. "You wish me to beg for forgiveness?"

"No," Ven fired back quickly and hotter than anticipated, so he paused to breathe deep. "No, I want to apologize. In our youth, I often alienated your tendency towards anger. I stole time and love from your mother to fill the void of not having one of my own. We often fought like brothers but never loved as such. I am sorry that I was there for your mother's final moments and you were not. For what happened on Glass Mountain and everything in between."

Rexous stared up at Ven, his cherry eyes boring into Ven's green ones. "What should I say to that?" he snapped and stood up. "Guardian of the North,' 'The prince that should have been,' 'The Mighty Ven Devar' comes groveling for forgiveness. You expect a few apologies will make a lifetime of rivalry and envy disappear?" Spittle flew from Rex' lips. "Do you beg for mercy because none of you stand a chance at stopping Vakar and need me to do your dirty work once again?"

"I have him in irons," Ven stated flatly. Rexous immediately cocked his head back.

"Liar."

Ven shook his green mane of hair. "We captured him outside of Greenwave. I was about to kill him, but..." he trailed off.

"Weak," Rex spat.

"No, courage I think. It was the easiest thing to slit his throat and yet not doing so was difficult."

"You sound like your snivelling Scorn," Rexous insulted with a hint of glee.

"She has proven to be the wisest of us."

"Not the smartest," Rexous said under his breath.

"No, I believe that would belong to the Grimìr of Knowledge," Ven quipped. Rex' face screwed up at that and Ven laughed for how trivial this all seemed. "What do you want now?" the famed hunter asked.

Rex furrowed his brows even more. "I don't get to want. That is your luxury."

"Perhaps, I am offering it to you now."

"Who gives you the authority?" Rex argued.

"Stop," Ven shouted. "Just stop it. What would you do with your freedom, or by the bloody gods that live I will throw you off a sea-cliff and watch the waves consume you." His threat carried throughout the hall and the hunter did not heed the stares, but the prince saw them all and the fear they carried.

Rex turned his eyes back to Ven. "I first committed murder when I donned your cloak. I haven't stopped till your friends captured me. Perhaps I know nothing else now." He didn't take his gaze from Ven, letting his honesty pour into his counterpart's heart.

"Then you do not believe all are capable of redemption?" Ven asked like a kid again.

Rex thought long. "No," he said with finality before sitting back down.

"On this we may agree," Ven admitted in defeat.

"If I may," Njor said from a few metres away. He walked up to them tall and proud. "Excuse my intrusion but you are both wrong. I was once like you and worse," Njor confirmed, looking at Rex. "Lokor teaches that strength can only be measured by one's perseverance. Commit yourself to an idea, to redemption if that is your need, and do not falter. If you fail once, commit yourself again and again until you have become who you wish."

Rex looked at the Kintar and simply laughed in his face. "That is pious puma-dung if I've ever heard it."

Njor stared him down before turning away again. Ven watched the Grimìr leave in retrospection.

"Think on what I've said," he added before leaving Rex in his cage alone. He went outside and saw everyone, including Nordhum and Scarlet, heading to the cabin that held Vakar and Agan. He was about to join them when Ina stopped him.

"Devar." The Svar walked up to him and embraced him uncharacteristically. He hugged her back, resting his chin on her much taller shoulder.

"I am glad to see you unharmed. You led a great victory here," he commended her.

"It does not feel that way," she admitted. "Barely a quarter of us remain in fighting condition."

"Have you had contact with the hideout?" Ven thought to ask, and he did so with panic.

"After the battle yes, but not since. Why?"

"Come with me," Ven instructed and the two hunters headed towards the others. They entered the hut that had one wall missing facing over the ocean. A fire was lit in the remainder of the hearth. Faye and Scarlet were attending to Agan while Nordhum sat slumped against a wall, staring at his old friend's limp body.

"You captured him," Ina said in awe as Vakar sat there in even more chains than before. Ven looked around and did not see Aunna.

"Did anyone see where the Sesaran went?" he asked.

"The beach," Kithlyn answered, still hovering over Agan. He nodded and left to find her. Making sure he had Faenla, the two walked down the familiar winding path down to the water, one of only two known paths on the entire island. He quickly spotted Aunna sitting on a bed of pebbles. Much to Ven's surprise, an all too familiar searaven was flying around her in a large circle. She was in quiet contemplation looking out over the calm sea and keenly heard Ven approach.

"May I sit?"

She looked up at him and smiled before looking to Faen. She did not fear the wolf, which is more to be said than most. She patted the pebbles beside her for him to sit. He did so and Faen curled up into a huge fluffy ball beside the hunter, resting his massive head on Ven's breeches.

"Beautiful animal," she commented, as Faen looked up at her with his eyes.

"There is something to be said about the companionship of animals. I don't know if I've ever loved something as I do Faenla," Ven said passionately and the wolf licked his forearm as if to say, 'I love you too.'

"There is a unique bond between the species and animals of Litore. It's not one forged from language. It's all feeling. No room for misinterpretation." She looked away from the wolf to Ven.

"I am Aunna Moringthorne, by the way." She feigned a brief smile.

"Ven Devar, Kaiason. Good to finally make your acquaintance," he replied earnestly. They both enjoyed a moment of peace and quiet.

"How did you come to be in that realm?" he asked, speaking of the place with the stone wall left by Kaia.

She chose her words for a moment. "A spirit took me there."

"Do you know what it was?"

She shook her head. "At first I thought it to be the Void, but I've never known there to be anything truly material in that plane."

"I felt Kaia pass there, she gave me the trident." Ven pulled the trident off his belt and handed it to Aunna.

She took the weapon and inspected it; it reminded her of her days as a paladin before converting to the school of healing as a cleric. "It is magnificent. Do you know what it does, truly?"

Ven shook his head and she handed it back. "How does Agan fair, in your words?"

She looked grim. "He appears strong, but the wounds, may rest even beyond my skill." Ven looked crestfallen at that, so she quickly turned the conversation around.

"How many Grimìr are here?"

"Well, you and I, Scáth, Njor, Aolendìr, Nordhum, Scarlet, and Vakar."

"That leaves four more to find," she whispered.

"Well three," he answered, and she looked unsure as to what he meant. "I am the son of Kaia and Āina."

"That does not mean Āina did not sire or choose another," Aunna pointed out. "If the hieroglyphs showed anything, it is that each god put a Grimìr on Litore."

It made sense, Ven thought. He did lose Āina's weapon Hunters Protection when Kaia gave him the trident. He did not like the idea of having to find yet another one the gods descendants though.

"Listen, I don't care who is the child or chosen of what. All I know is, somehow, we are to put our differences aside. You are the daughter of peace, I was hoping you'd know best how to do that," he explained hopefully. Her whole upper body expanded as she breathed deeply. She went to speak several times but stopped, eventually hanging her head.

"Nothing is as it seems. It's all gone. Broken from the start. An endless cycle of hate and death." Her voice wavered.

"Yes, it is," Ven said empathetically. "That is why we are inheriting the realms; we can break the cycle. Together." He put a smile on her that reminded him of his old self. He knew he wasn't his old self and never would be again, but he could find pieces of that Ven and bring them to bare.

She smiled back at him before it faded once more. "Some may not be so willing to cooperate. Vakar and whomever the Grimìr of Death come to mind."

"Consider it all part of the fun," he smirked before ruffling Faen's thick mane and the two predators stood up. Ven held out his hand for

Aunna to take. She brushed her silk dress of sand and seaweed before taking it.

"I'll be needing to borrow something warmer," she said as a harsh breeze nipped at her body.

"In our forest, there will always be a pumasheep cloak for those in need," he said, removing his own cloak and putting it around her. The cloak tails hung on the ground and the billowing sleeves were an entire arm's length too long. "Until we get you your own," he said with a laugh while running his hand through his hair. Faenla trotted ahead and Ven looked up for the searaven but it was no longer circling.

A short time later, they all arrived in the cabin and were finally seated together. Ven found comfort next to Scáth as he intertwined his fingers with hers.

Everyone looked around the room, yet no one said anything. Scáth could tell tensions were thinner than parchment and was concerned for what was to come.

Finally, it was Nordhum who broke the silence like a rock through glass. "Well, you've never shut up before, why start now, Goldie?" His tired dwarven eyes stared through Aolendìr.

The Solsta smirked. "I do not pull speech from my arse such as yourself. When I need to speak, I will."

"That's a first," Faye said, face and hands covered in blood from those she healed.

"At least I don't drag my sister everywhere to fight my battles, blood-drinker." He squinted at the Gloom elves.

"Faye has proven more trustworthy than you have yet," Onstera pointed out, being the resident monster hunter.

"And why has she need to prove that at all, I wonder," Aolendìr sneered with delight.

Most around the room gave Faye queer looks, but Scarlet interrupted.

"Please, we are not here to discuss the qualities of each in attendance."

"Personally, I'd love to know why he refers to the Ward of Souls as 'blood-drinker,'" Rinya piped up with a curious expression.

"I will not tolerate this. My sister has done nothing but heal your injuries." Wynn sprang up in fury.

"She did suffer a mortal injury and was as healthy as fruit freshly plucked," Njor pointed out.

"Are your ears full? She is Ward to the CareTaker, her wounds are healed by another. There is no justice in this persecution," Nordhum roared. All the while, Faye looked at her lap in sorrow.

This infighting continued, and the whole time Ven watched the merriment grow in Vakar. "We're not here to fight amongst ourselves. The opposite in fact. In Greenwave, we were made aware of the history of the gods." He brought the conversation around to a productive side.

"Oh good, the history of the gods. This will make things easier, I wager," Nordhum offered up cynically. Onstera actually smiled at that but Scarlet scowled, for her reverence of the gods rivalled even the most devout.

"Ours gods as we know them came here much like the Keepers did. They removed through various means the old gods and claimed their power for their own. The Keepers are doing the exact same," Scáth explained, without humour, while laying a heavy look upon Nordhum and Onstera.

"So what?" Kithlyn spoke up, looking away from a bandaged and still unconscious Agan. "The gods never showed love to us. You don't need to read some divine note to understand that. They only took, never gave, end of story." Everyone in the room felt a cold chill as the assassin spat her hatred. Scáth looked at her fellow ShadowScorn with empathy; it was true no one here could or ever would come close to understanding the hardships dealt by the gods unto the Scorn.

"Want to know something even richer?" Aolendìr couldn't resist.

"I've heard just about all I can stomach of you today," Faye shot back.

"Too bad," the Solsta answered. "The gods didn't grant their worshippers divine power. They demanded undying fealty and said the most pious and deserving of us would receive a portion of their power. As it turns out, those willing to believe in something so devoutly was what granted them the power to harness magic. In other words, it was in us all along." The ever-smug Solsta felt especially self-satisfied.

"Lies," Scarlet snapped with her beak.

"Why do you think paladins and clerics and other followers around the world continue to cast even though most of our gods are dead already?" Aolendìr retorted as if speaking to a child. Scarlet stood up and the flames clinging to her body rose in heat.

"Stop," Aunna begged. "It does not matter. None of it matters now."

"And who are you, exactly?" Njor asked not unkindly.

"True born Daughter of Sesara." Aunna placed her big purple eyes on the Kintar then around the room. Kithlyn made a point of scoffing heartily.

"Forgive my fellow Scorn but your faith is directly responsible for the most brutal sieges against our entirely peaceful kingdom," Scáth answered for Kith's disrespect.

"Among many other atrocities," Nordhum added.

"Far more than you could imagine, good dwarf," Aunna surprised them all by admitting. "Before my deployment to the Magma Isles, I sat on the High Council of Sesara. Although many in my religion, such as my adoptive fathers, believe in the old tenets of our faith, most fell victim to its finer offerings."

"That's a polite way to put it," Onstera mumbled.

"I'm still missing the part as to why we need to stop the Keepers? If that's even possible, that is." Wynn said. As a Gloom elf she paid only heed to the stars above, and never put any value in the gods.

"If they are to succeed in becoming the almighty as we knew our gods to be, then they will surely cleanse Litore and start anew." Ven let his words hang in the air as all digested them.

"How do we know if the Keepers have ascended or not?" Faye questioned. No one had an answer for quite some time.

"Ask the last one standing," Vakar said while staring only at Ven. The hunter stared back and the room fell silent again.

"We have more pressing matters," Ina spoke up for the first time. Her mind was focused on one thing alone. Everyone looked at her expectantly, and she stared back, dumbfounded as they all seemed to have completely forgotten the destruction outside. "The restoration of the Great Northern Rainforest." Her ire fell upon Vakar. "Why is he still alive?"

"He is Grimìr," Aolendìr answered.

"So he gets to go free? He committed genocide against my people,"

Rinya nearly shouted. Vakar grinned at that and Rinya leapt at him. Njor and Ven both jumped up to stop them.

"If your people were so strong, they would not have died like bugs under my heel," Vakar added and Rinya threw Ven off; however, it was Aolendìr who punched Vakar in the jaw to shut him up.

"I warned you," he said flexing his fist. "I'm protecting you out of necessity, not because I like you."

"She's right," Nordhum answered. "It is my responsibility to uphold the world's justice. Brailin is no more. He's committed irredeemable atrocities in your country. Vakar must pay for his actions against the Kintar and Kyst."

"Your kin and kind have done such a wonderful job at spreading justice," Aunna couldn't help but point out. The dwarves for many centuries had waged unrelenting wars, claiming what wealth they could regardless of its ownership.

"You're right, we have. Now that I am Grimìr of Justice, my people will be hence forth known as Keldör, Stone Kin in our native tongue. Once these Keepers are dealt with and we usher in the Third Age, as I know we will, I will see to it my people return to our values of kinship and living harmoniously with the earth," Nordhum declared proudly and he saw many approving faces.

The moment shifted as a great crack of thunder and a streak of red lightening blinked across the sky and they all viewed it from from cabin. Nordhum stood up and walked to the missing wall that overlooked the ocean.

"I know that lightening," he mumbled. Aolendìr completely disregarded Nordhum's sudden interest in the weather.

"His penitence will be bringing an end to the Keepers," he continued on, regarding Vakar.

"Not good enough," Ina said with derision.

"For once I agree with the Kyst," said Rinya.

"Until we know more, he remains a prisoner. I promise." Ven swore to this. "I need a team to come with me to the hideout."

"We should all be heading there, Sŷna simply needs to recover the map," Ina replied and Vakar laughed. The Solsta elf exhaled in restraint as he was about to backhand him.

"What?" Onstera hissed at Vakar

"They're all dead,"

"What?" Ina growled and Ven gave Njor a knowing look. The brutish berserker walked up to the Sage and knocked him out with one swoop of his back hand.

"We don't know anything yet, more than likely he is just trying to sow division." Ven tried calming Ina down.

"I'm getting Sŷna to ready a teleportation spell." Ina barked while leaving the cabin.

"I'm coming too," Nordhum pressed and Ven nodded.

"Me too," Scáth declared and Ven wasn't going to argue it, and he wanted her by his side anyway.

"Njor, I need your aid. I am bringing Rexous," Ven announced confidently, which caused a stir from everyone save Lokorson.

"No offence, but I've never seen you fight like him. It took all of us to capture the hunter, many of us almost dying in the process, and now you want to release him?" Onstera seemed to be eliciting doubt from the others but Ven remained steadfast.

"Thanks," Ven said flatly. "I can take Rex, and if it comes to that, I'll have all the backup I need," Ven answered eyeing Njor.

"Let me join," Faye and Wynn said together.

Ven chuckled. "I need healers here to care of Agan and the other wounded. This task won't require much time. I trust you will all watch over Vakar diligently."

"Best gag him before he wakes," Rinya said jokingly, but proceeded to wrap a rag around his mouth.

"I have a contact who may know where to find a few Keepers, I will start there," Aunna offered and Aolendìr added,

"I know there is one hidden in your great forest somewhere, just a bit of the proverbial, 'needle in the haystack'."

"Start digging," Ven said before leaving with Njor, Nordhum, and Scáth. Faenla was waiting outside for them and led the group to Ina and Sŷna.

"You're able to send us magically? We can sail if need be," Ven suggested but Sŷna had a spell of recall ready to take him back to the Shallowbay hideout at a moment's notice.

"Ready when you are." Ina's hasty tone betrayed her calm exterior.

"We need one more guest," Njor said, already walking towards the old town hall. Ina gave a worried look to Ven but the hunter shrugged it off.

Ven and Njor walked up to the cage and Rex stood up this time.

"Do you have your answer for me?" Ven said harshly.

"I do. I want what was stolen from me—to be reunited with those I've lost," Rexous answered so candidly it brought a sense of respect from Njor.

"I'll give you a war in which none of us stand a chance at surviving," Ven said before looking to Njor who nodded in brief agreement at that approximation of survival.

Rex rolled his eyes and Ven went to open the shimmering cage when he said, "And if you try anything, everyone here will make sure you spend the next one thousand years locked in a cage half this size."

Rex wanted to smile at the threat but scowled instead. Ven opened the cage and the former prince of Silva stepped out and cracked his neck. The two fiercest hunters in the north shared a tense and loathsome stare until Njor shoved the dirks and trident into Rex's chest.

They walked to the group and could see from a distance the skeptical stares from Ina and Sŷna. Scáth appeared pensive, leaving Ven with shaky confidence.

Faenla surprised Ven as the wolf went up to Rexous; standing on all fours he was almost taller than the once prince. Faenla's hackles looked like a crown atop his jet-black head from Rex's perspective. The wolf snarled and brought his huge fangs to bare as drool dripped and his throat crackled with threats. Rex had to mentally force himself from taking a step back, if not from fear than simple instinct. After all that, Faenla licked his cheek and padded back over to stand next to Scáth. Clearly that settled the Scorn's doubts as she smiled reassuringly at Ven.

"We find the map, we make sure the site is safe and help any survivors," Ven instructed and the gathered nodded in satisfaction.

"There won't be any," Rex said quietly.

"Any what?" Sŷna asked the obvious.

"Survivors." Rexous turned his cherry-red eyes on everyone and they all knew he spoke only the truth. Ven gave Sŷna a look and he finished the spell; a light surrounded them, a pressure in their eyes built then released as the light faded, leaving them on the stone shoreline of the hideout.

It was carnage. Black smoke poured out the entrance to the cave and the small holes that acted like windows. The wide shoreline of solid grey stone was strewn with the bodies of rebels and Vakar's soldiers. Blood soaked the rock more than seaspray. The sheer number of crates and furniture about indicated the attackers were looking for something outside of pure destruction. Ina and Scáth went to fallen rebels, checking their vitals. Faenla let out a singular, melancholic howl. Ven gave Rexous a hateful stare and felt his blood boil again when Rex showed no kind of remorse. Njor walked nearer to the cave entry. He saw out the corner of his vision a rope tied to the ground leading up and into the smoke over the entry.

"Sage, do away with this smoke," he bellowed and Sŷna all too happily obliged. It took several moments as the sage funnelled the smoke from every corner within the hideout out into the open air.

They all stood in horror as Queen Saphier, hanging by the neck above the entry, swayed in the wind. Ina fell to her knees and stared up at her defiled leader. The three moons of Litore bathed her once divine beauty in deathly gloom. Ven looked to Njor and they both knew to get her down. As the Kintar went and stood under her, the Kyst cut the rope. Njor caught her as effortlessly as catching a babe. He rested her gently on the ground and grabbed a loose blanket to cover her. Ina knelt beside her fallen queen and began to sing a song in Vox that was equal parts beautiful and haunting. Everyone dared not move, but rather took in the devastation around them.

Scáth looked at Rex and wondered what he was thinking. She thought there was a part of him that truly cared about all of this, yet it was known that when your soul was taken from the afterlife, you never returned wholly you. Rexous stared blankly at the covered corpse, forcing himself to listen to every word Ina sang, willing himself to feel again. Hating himself. Wishing, wishing he was different.

Ven was pulled from the lyrics when he spotted Faenla's ears prick and his head dart up to the cliff top above them.

"Go," he whispered to the wolf in kystin. Faenla bounded off with purpose. Ven looked once again to Njor and then Scáth, and motioned for them to investigate what they could in the hideout. They went to do so and he grabbed Rex by the shoulder, shoving him towards the cliff face.

"Eh, wait for me," Nordhum shouted, chasing after the wolf.

The pair of hunters scaled the rocks with ease and grace and surfaced in thick grass. They each put their hands to hilts when they spotted a figure run behind a thicket of bushes. Then they caught sight of Faenla's impressive form dart through the trees without a hint of sound. The two hunters kept low with vigilant eyes though the grass. Ven couldn't help but feel a sense of nostalgia wash over him, as so often did the two of them go on hunts in their youth.

"This way," Rex whispered and darted in front of Ven to lead them around an upturned root system two stories tall. Ven caught the tail end of a heavy cloak flutter behind the roots as Rex led. The two hunters weren't five heartbeats from rounding the tree, when the sixth heartbeat had them dive in separate directions as a loud bang and a bolt of red plasma nearly carved a hole through them both. Ven came out of his roll into his low defensive crouch, Kaia's trident in hand, and Rex stood similarly with one dirk out right and the other held defensively across his body.

Both their faces wore confused expressions as they glimpsed their attacker—a humanoid cloaked in heavy black canvas and body armour that was rigid and of a material neither had seen before. Most shocking was the full helmet and two glowing red slits for eyes where a visor might have been.

"Where is Vakar?" his voice sounded robotic and had an almost static tone.

"Who are you?" Rex questioned with a hostility Ven thought unwise. A throat-grumbling snarl was heard and two piercing blue eyes peered behind the humanoid as Faenla slowly stalked closer to his prey. This outsider dressed in futuristic armour drew a second pistol that Ven at first thought was a flintflock before realizing it was far too sleek and small for that. He aimed it right at Faenla and the wolf lowered his head, teeth flashing.

"You're out numbered, put the weapons down and this can be resolved peacefully," Ven urged, and all he saw in response was an angular helmet incapable of showing emotion staring back at him. Ven looked at Rex who did the same and they both considered who would strike first. Faenla let out another threat from deep within but the humanoid holding the weapons was unflinching.

"Avon!" Nordhum shouted out happily, having finally caught up.

"Ironboot?" The unnatural sounding voice almost squeaked in surprise.

"Aye, aye, put your pistols down ya fool." Nordhum walked up to him like an old friend but stopped when Avon trained his blaster on the dwarf.

"What are you doing here?" Avon asked. Nordhum drooped his brow at the sudden hostility.

"I'm helping the Kyst. I'd ask then the same of you?" Brailin's chosen questioned right back.

"I'm here to collect the King of Kyst. The Keepers won't be denied, Nordhum," Avon said with a warning. "I like you better than most, dwarf, but get in my way..." he dared not speak the words.

The two Kyst were clearly aware there was a shared history between these two that left Rex feeling uneasy. He did not like Nordhum and had no reason to trust him.

"I know the damage you could do here, Avon, but he's not ripe for the picking I'm afraid," Nordhum said keeping his hands raised, wanting no trouble.

"There is a war coming, you and the other Grimìr won't be enough. Don't die alongside them fighting for a cause not worth saving," Avon nearly pleaded for Nordhum to see sense.

"Where's the Keeper in the north hiding?" Nordhum asked. Avon stared back at him with those unblinking red slits. A small light flickered where his ear should have been, and after a moment Avon's mood changed suddenly. He holstered his two weapons and stood at ease.

"I would hurry back." Avon's words left their skin crawling as he touched his bracer and vanished. The three of them looked at each other in fear as the realization set in. They all sprinted back to the cave entrance, their minds running faster than they were at the possibilities of treachery awaiting them. Ven figured they had only been gone from Sanctuary Island nigh an hour, but that was plenty of time for a great many things to go wrong.

Nordhum forced his short thick legs to push harder and carry him faster than he ever had. The mother to his son was there, Faye who he loved as a sister, Agan and Kithlyn, dear friends the both of them. He thought back to those times during the Thousand Dragon War, the adventures they all shared, the scrapes Avon had saved him from and wondered if this is what it was all leading towards.

Rex was sprinting through the foliage, outpacing his two allies. He didn't much care for the safety or well-being of anyone on that Island, but he knew if Vakar was set free again it wouldn't be long before he tried to dig his claws back into his life. Forcing him to do whatever he commanded, keeping him alive, away from those he wished to be reunited with in the afterlife. Rex was torn from his thoughts as his ankle caught something metal and he hit the ground hard. A fury washed over him, with Ven and Nordhum not slowing their pace, he looked to see what tripped him. From the upturned and half-decayed forest floor, a sword hilt with a searaven-head pommel emerged. Or at least he thought it was, for within the blink of an eye it resembled a pumasheep head. He looked back to see the other two disappearing behind a curtain of ferns. Mesmerized, he crawled over to the hilt, wrapped his hand around it, and pulled. Two leaves formed the cross-guard and the perfectly straight blade was engraved with an impossibly fine filigree of vines and leaves.

"A weapon of strength, grace, and above all, protection." The voice sounded like rustling leaves and moaning timber, it did not startle Rexous, rather soothed his pain. The once prince, then assassin, turned to see a magnificent Kyst, at least he thought the elf before him was Kyst. Rex stood and only came to shoulder height with the stranger, who was looking at him with a familial smile.

"Who are you?"

"You know. You've always known that the destiny of Vakar the Cunning, Ven Devar Kaiason, and Prince Rexous RealmShield were intertwined from dawn till dusk."

"I am no shield." Rexous let the sword clatter to the ground. "I've killed the very innocent I swore to defend, defiled the forest that raised me."

Āina moved face to face with Rex and bent down to grab the sword before rising. "The land betrays those who call it home, not out of malice but nature. The land burns and it crumbles, but it never loses strength." The God of Land and Forest cut his hand open on the blade and let the dark brown blood flow down the filigree. "I found my way slower than any other, in the end though we all find it."

Rexous dropped his eyes from Āina to the blade, understanding what it meant to take the grip in his own.

"What if I fail?" he asked in a stern voice.

"My poor boy, you never accepted that the road to success is paved by the steps of failure." Āina spoke with a fatherly love. Rexous made eye contact with Āina and his dark brown eyes spoke of infinite wisdom and years hard lived. He took the sword Hunter's Protection and Āina offered one more smile before his spirit was carried off by a gust of wind into the bioluminescent forest.

No sooner did Rexous feel a surge of power coarse through his veins, did the wind die, did the waves fall still, did the air feel thin and toxic, did the moons lose all shine of colour and glow, did the stars flicker as if breathing their last, and all the Grimìr knew —the last god of Litore was gone.

CHAPTER TWENTY-FOUR

Requiem of Celestia

Faye had just finished casting her most powerful spell of healing over Agan's grievous wound before slumping over in exhaustion. Onstera was across from her, pouring a black liquid of her own creation over his charred flesh, and Kithlyn sat cross-legged in front of them.

Onstera gave Faye an uncharacteristic smile of vulnerability. Faye returned it, thinking fondly on their time together over a decade ago.

"What could you two possible be smiling about?" Kithlyn scolded.

"Listen, the three of us may be some of the most powerful gals in Litore, but we cannot fight amongst ourselves." Faye tried to disarm Kithlyn's anger.

"My only love lay here, likely to die, and you want me to be sunshine and rainbows?" she spat hatefully.

"You know I love him too," Faye answered honestly.

"Everyone is doing what they can to keep him alive," Onstera said evenly, delicately pouring her potion over the half-orc. Faye noticed Kithlyn staring down Vakar, who was currently being guarded by Scarlet and Rinya. The sage was returning the stare with a passionless one.

"If Agan dies, so does he," the world's most dangerous assassin declared.

"That we can agree on," Onstera said capping her potion bottle.

Aolendìr was outside with Aunna, both flipping through tomes provided by the Solsta elf.

"I know it's in one of these," he said half-minded.

"Why won't a simple message spell work?" Aunna asked, tossing one leather bound book aside for another.

"The Great Northern Rainforest muddies the arcane, like light through water. It's just one of many reasons why the sages here are so powerful," Aolendìr explained, wetting one finger before vigorously flipping through more pages.

"So get a sage to do it, or a Diwyn," Aunna said before rubbing her eyes with index finger and thumb.

"No, they'd call me mad, or chaotic for trying it," he said with one corner of his lip rising. "They'd be right of course."

"For casting a spell?" she asked in confusion.

"No, for reaching out to an ancient Water Dragon." He turned his golden eyes on her lavender ones to gauge her reaction, which was unrewarding for she gave him no satisfaction.

"Hmm," she mused.

"What do you suppose we do with Vakar?" he asked nonchalantly. She put her book down to look at the Solsta.

"You like to play games?" she asked rhetorically.

"It's in my nature," he admitted.

"Well peace is not in mine. I was raised and trained by the fiercest, most honourable men in my religion. The leaders turned that once wholesome religion into a synthetic version of itself until it became little more than a game for power. So do not think your theatrics and ploys will go unnoticed here. I was weened on them," she warned him without threat, but her tone was tense.

"It was just a question," he said sheepishly.

"We can't do anything with him, so the question was heedless." She put her eyes back into her book. He smiled and too went back to his tome. No sooner than the two of them regarded their reading, then a war horn sounded.

Everyone in the cabin turned their head towards the horn blaring.

"Watch him," Faye instructed Scarlet and Rinya as both jumped to attention. The three tending Agan rushed out into the town.

Wynn ran past them with a dozen Gloom elves towards the horn bearer. They followed suit until they came around a bend in the road and saw a force of nearly fifty warriors cutting a clean path through the remaining Kyst and Gloom.

Many of the unknown warriors carried long flintlock rifles that were firing bolts of red and green plasma at rapid speeds while the others brandished vicious swords and spears that crackled and sparked with a similar energy. A stray bolt was about to strike Faye when Wynn lifted her shield up; it caught the energy and left a smouldering pockmark in the fine metal.

"Get word to Ina we're under attack," Wynn told Faye and no sooner did the Ward of the CareTaker try to send a magical message to Ina, did she find she simply could not.

"I'm afraid it may be time," Faye said direly to her sister. Wynn didn't have to respond as these peculiar soldiers were devastating the remaining warriors. Faye breathed deeply and the astral star-like dots in her eyes turned red, her fingernails grew to an impossible sharpness, and finally two wickedly serrated fangs elongated in her mouth. In a true blur Faye was gone, and in the next second a soldier's throat was torn out and they fell to their knees dead. She was gone in a blistering blur again until three more attackers had their heads or hearts removed from their bodies. She skidded through the dirt to a halt, mouth and hands dripping with blood, inviting these foreign invaders to try their best.

Aunna sprang up and went to run towards the chaos, but Aolendìr gripped her forearm.

"What?" Aunna spun, ripping her arm away and snapping at him. The Solsta just kept his eyes to the ground in thought. He turned his pointed beard to the hut with Vakar inside. Aunna nodded and they both made their way in that direction. When they reached the cabin, a gout of scarlet flame burst through the door, followed by Scarlet herself gripping a soldier clad in light synthetic armour and a great-sword with electrical currents skipping up and down the blade face. Scarlet beat her great fiery wings and smashed the soldier into the ground, dragging him through the dirt. The pair kept pace and entered into the cabin.

Agan was still unconscious, Vakar was doing everything in his power to remove his bindings, and Rinya Witblade was swinging their dragonbone sword for their life against a being unlike any of them had ever encountered; a creature long and thin, standing several heads taller than any of them, four spindly fingers attached to a pale and wide hand. Its head was taller than wide, it all but lacked a nose, instead having two slits like a snake and impossibly large dark eyes that appeared too bulbous for its otherwise sleek head. Rinya's stocky muscular frame was rendered sickly as the Keeper caught the sword in its palm, the weapon turning to dust on contact. Its next motion was smooth and precise, materializing a blade thinner than a scalpel from the dust and opening the Kintar's throat. Rinya's eyes sprung wide and they put their hands across their throat, fumbling to keep the spurting blood within.

The Keeper turned towards Vakar as if Aolendìr and Aunna didn't exist. The Solsta elf took apparent insult at that, pulling a wand from the many folds of his many cloaks and releasing a streak of lightening. The Keeper kept moving deliberately towards Vakar, simply raising a hand at the golden lightening. The forked energy skipped off his hand and struck Aolendìr square in the chest, sending the elf through the cracked walls of the hut.

"What do you want with him?" Aunna decided to ask, seeing two far superior fighters taken out. Vakar looked at her like she was insane, but the Keeper turned their huge eyes towards the human.

"What we want with you all—" it turned its glare back upon Vakar, "—death." The word fell out of its mouth like a yawn.

"You won't do it," Aunna answered defiantly. The Keeper turned their attention on Aunna and took a great hunched step towards her.

"Peace," it whispered and smelled the air around the blithe human. "A lie told by the strong to ease the weak."

"No, an ideology meant to encourage kindness, love, and aid. I hate that Kyst in the corner, but it is my tenet to help those in need. So what will you do now?" she stated plainly and asked kindly. The shards of gem left on her once glorious tiara glowed with light, which the Keeper saw and showed its stubby teeth in a wet smile.

"Nice try." The Keeper stood to its full height and walked back over to Vakar. Rinya let out a Kintar roar and leapt, plummeting a dagger into the Keeper's back. The Keeper hissed in pain, spinning, and back-handed Rinya in the temple so hard Aunna heard the Kintar's skull shatter. The Daughter of Sesara quick stepped, determined to unleash her spell. She gripped the Keeper's free hand and searing light disintegrated its fingers, hand, and entire arm. As the alien recoiled in horror, she ran for Vakar to get him out of here, but the Keeper gripped her long dark hair and yanked her so hard her back hit the ground and the air left her lungs. It lifted its long leg and stomped it onto Aunna's shoulder, sending a resounding crack throughout the room, and the human gasped coarsely in pain before passing out.

With its one remaining arm, the Keeper grabbed a still chained up Vakar and the two vanished from sight. When Aunna awoke, all was quiet and she could not have said what had happened. She moved and pain she never could have imagined washed over her. She tried moving her right arm but found it unresponsive. After several deep breaths she craned her head back and saw an unmoving Rinya and Agan but no Vakar. She steeled herself and sat upright with a tortured scream. She rolled off her cloak and could see the bones in her shoulder sticking horribly through her skin. Casting a brief spell of healing on herself did little but ease the pain. She stood up and when her senses came to she could hear the sounds of fighting outside. Peaking her head outside revealed Aolendìr laying in the dirt, a steaming hole in his chest. She also saw dozens of soldiers running down Kyst and Gloom elves as if they were rodents. She stumbled through smoke and debris over to Aolendìr and put her left hand on his chest. With a few murmurs his eyes opened and the wound on his chest closed.

"Ow," he whined.

"Vakar is gone. Rinya's dead. The town is being slaughtered."

"Get word to Ven, they need to..." Aolendìr stopped mid-sentence as everything natural in the world fell silent and their voice and movements began to echo unimpeded. The moons above turned monochromatic and the stars seemed starved of light. Every living creature, no matter how small or large, stopped to regard this unfathomable phenomenon.

Aunna put her hand to her temple; as if trying to pull something away from her, she clawed for relief before succumbing to the excruciating pain and wailing a great scream. Aolendìr felt as though a mountain giant was stepping on his chest. He rolled onto his hands and knees and sucked for air, yet no matter how much he breathed, a crushing weight left him feeling empty and purple faced.

Off in the woods a great echoing screech was heard as Scarlet underwent a similar sense of torment. After a short time that felt too long, a sense of right in the world filled the Grimìr again and sounds of nature returned along with the colour and light in the sky. Wynn was already rushing towards them as the few remaining of her Gloom elves fought relentlessly against the soldiers.

"We need the others or need to leave, fifty have cut through 200 like nothing and Faye is hard pressed," she shouted at the two recovering Grimìr. She lifted her shield to catch a stray shot of energy and by now there wasn't much left of it.

"I can't." Aunna could barely get the words out, for the agony that left her clawing at her own scalp had worsened her shattered shoulder.

Aolendìr was already trying to get a spell off when a great flash of light and smoke exploded a dozen paces away, revealing those who went to the Shallowbay hideout.

"Who are these jesters?" Rexous asked cynically.

"Negators, pets to the Keepers," Nordhum said amongst his companions. Njor snarled and Faenla lowered his massive head, baring those great fangs and blue predatory eyes. Ven withdrew his trident and his eyes turned sea blue again, followed by a rumbling thunder.

The Negators all stopped to regroup which allowed Faye, Scarlet, and Onstera a moment of reprieve to join their friends. Faenla let out a howl that acted as bell to begin, and the fourteen heroes charged against the thirty Negators. Ven, Faenla, and Rexous quickly fell into a comfortable routine together. Faenla leapt and tore a throat out, breaking apart a line of Negators that was quickly filled by the two hunters. It was a duel unlike either hunter was familiar with, for the Negators parried and dodged their precise blows with grace. Nevertheless, despite all that happened, Ven and Rex knew each other's every move and switched opponents so regularly that every time a Negator felt confident, they were fighting the other Kyst again and on the defensive once more.

Scáth and Kithlyn naturally felt a connection to one another and Scáth's time training with the Ghosts of Aceia proved invaluable. The two ShadowScorn pressed the same target at a time, blinking in and out of the darkness in such acrobatic coordination few foes in all the realms could have stood a chance. Their Negator had a large pistol in one hand and an electric dagger in the other, which made reaching him nearly impossible despite their ability to move from one place to another through shadow. Kithlyn, a life-long assassin, dodged his bolts as if she knew where each one was aimed before the Negator did. Scáth's experience was severely lacking in comparison yet she had such control over her phasing that every time a bolt was to strike her, she let it pass harmlessly through her. Kithlyn found herself envious of Scáth's unique and unheard-of abilities as a Scorn, and made up for it by driving a dagger through the Negators eye.

Woe to any enemy who crossed paths with Njor Lokorson. His large frame was unmatched, as was his strength, dexterity, and sheer will. He shot himself into the fray of Negators like an arrow through hay, burying himself deep into the combatants where he could offer the most pain. His enchanted mallets shattered their synthetic armour and left their bones in broken ruin. He was on his fifth kill before he suffered a stinging sensation and saw a small smoking hole in his leg from an plasma bolt. He glared at the Negator who shot him and threw his mallet; it hit him square in the chest and didn't slow down as it reemerged from his spine. Soon, no less than six Negators were beating and stabbing him. Njor let out the infamous Kintar roar and grabbed an arm poised to strike him. He snapped it like a twig and hurled the soldier like a whip into the others around him. Njor then sent his improvised weapon flying into the air like a ragdoll in a random direction. He lifted one forearm as an electric sword shattered against it. Njor smiled, picked up the now weaponless Negator and broke his back over his knee. This was all but child's play for the Chosen of Lokor, God of Battle; no, he realized then, he *was* the God of Battle.

Nordhum could barely swing his axe, his body still recovering from the wound dealt by Rex but that did not stop the headstrong Keldör. He was right there next to Faye, Wynn, and Scarlet, all of whom had fought together countless times over the years in Redwillow and abroad. He watched the Walker sisters in awe as he always had, their distinct combat styles complimenting each other well. They were a living reminder to him that Justice was well and real, both having endured the unthinkable and coming out the other end stronger for it. So when Wynn's head flicked back violently, he didn't register anything truly terrible had happened until she staggered to the side, and faced him. He his heart stopped, for a great smoking hole had replaced her eye and a chunk of her face.

Nordhum dropped his axe and ran to her, cradling her in his thick arms. Faye slashed her nails so hard across the attackers face his neck twisted and snapped, and she too was quickly beside her dying sister.

"Don't go Wynn, I need you, our boy needs you." Nordhum choked on the words. He cast a spell of healing on her but it did nothing. She looked up at him with her one starry eye and smiled faintly, willing her face to cooperate. She held out a hand for Faye to take, and her sister hadn't gripped her so tight since they were little girls in the Kermon range, scared of monsters under the bed. The battle still raged on around them, all the heroes and Grimìr locked in mortal melee—except for Rexous. Having just slain a persistent Negator, he stood slightly to the side of them, eyes affixed on the dying Wynn.

"We can bring you back, sister," Faye reassured, "We can find a way."

Wynn simply shook her head no. "Not again." Her voice was coarse and raspy. She looked away from them to die staring at Rexous. Nordhum curled over her body, sobbing silently. Rexous stared back at Wynn as the life left her, and for the first time since his resurrection, he felt again.

He didn't move until the battle was over, instead staring motionless at the mourning Keldör and Gloom elf. He was joined by everyone; Ven Devar, Scáth ShadowScorn, Faenla, Kithlyn Whisp, Njor Lokorson, Scarlet Albright, Onstera Dentoress, Aunna Morningthorne, Aolendìr Tardinian, Ina Enallea, and Sŷna. Each and every one of them watching silently at the stark reminder of what they stood to lose.

The next night, the survivors of Sanctuary Island held a funeral for the slain Kyst and Gloom elves, and at the head of the funeral pyre was Wynn Walker. It was customary for Kyst to either be buried at sea or beneath the forest so that their soul could go on and find rest. The coastal elves of Litore felt that in death they could still be visited by the living in this way. The Gloom elves chose solely to be burned, envisioning it to be the fastest way for their soul to reach the stars above.

Njor had insisted on cutting the logs himself and building the pyre that would send Rinya Witblade to the afterlife. He built the funeral pyre down the beach and away from everyone. He placed Rinya atop the oil-soaked wood and looked at them for well over an hour, unable to find the right words. He sniffled once and lit the torch, placing it within the wood. As the flames took the body, he said, "We have fought beside each other since we could walk. There was never a stronger elf in body or mind. You were loyal to the last and I would not be here if weren't for your constant protection. Never will our people see the likes of you again. I know in my heart there is a place for you in the Hall of Valour, I'll meet you there when this is all done so we may fight together once more."

Ven, Scáth, Faenla, and the remaining gnomes of Hearth took the opportunity to finally lay their sweet Athvar to rest. For the gnomes of Hearth it was a joyous thing to have his remains laid rest in the place he chose to call home. They opened the lid of his BlackGlass casket and looked upon his little frame, the spell of repose kept him looking the same as the day he died. For Ven and Scáth, it felt as a chapter in their lives had closed, with the sacrifice Athvar had made in the Siege of Shadow now complete. They had both said their goodbyes to him in the crypts under shadow palace, and so neither of them spoke now, but simply reflected on all the good Athvar had done for them and the wider world.

Aunna had her shoulder set and was now cradling her arm in a sling. She walked over to the casket and removed the spell of repose. They buried Athvar the Undusted in a grassy glade, surrounded by trees and critters with a BlackGlass marker that read 'Generous, Wise, and Compassionate to the end.' It was late into the evening when they had filled the grave and all in attendance had left back for Hearth. Except Ven, Faenla, and Scáth.

She placed an arm around his waist and kissed his stormy cheek before silently slipping away. Ven sat in the grass staring at the upturned dirt with Faenla laying beside him doing the same. Hours had passed since either of them moved, the light of the moons above shifting across the glade. The two noticed a small chipmunk scurry out of the grass and up the glass marker. Ven knew it couldn't be 'Chips' but smiled all the same. It gave a couple squeaks before leaping down and bounding off again.

"Thank you," the words escaped Ven's mouth, and Faenla stood up and nuzzled Ven's hair. The Kyst stood and the two strode back to

Hearth.

Ven gathered the other Grimìr and only the Grimìr. They stood around a massive bonfire blustering in the night winds.

"I'm sorry for the passing of Wynn and Rinya," Ven offered his condolences.

"Don't be, Rinya died fighting. It's the best they could have wished for," Njor said honestly.

Nordhum Ironboot however remained silent and gruff as only a Keldör could. Ven looked around and Aolendìr, Aunna, Nordhum, and Scarlet were still reeling from their wounds. The Keldör and phoenix were giving dark glares to the Kyst.

"Shouldn't he be in chains when not in service?" Nordhum spat.

"Come and put me in them," Rexous snarled.

"Gladly, killer." Nordhum leapt up from the crate he was resting on and Rexous withdrew his new artifact short-sword. Njor was quick to intercept but not before Ven spoke up.

"That sword, where did you come by it?" he asked in shock.

Rex turned his dark eyes upon Ven, surprised by his comment. "In the forest," was all he said, not wanting to further explain his encounter with Āina and the subsequent upheaval of the world. As it turned out however, most in the room remembered Ven sporting the one-of-a-kind weapon.

"I thought it belonged to you," Njor said to Ven.

"It did, but Kaia took it away from me when she gave me the Storm Trident. Āina crafted Hunter's Protection." Ven spoke slower as if a realization was overcoming him. Rexous looked away almost bashful.

"This must be some jest, he's murdered, betrayed, and worse." Njor nearly burst.

"Wonderful," Nordhum said under his breath.

"It does seem unlikely," Aunna almost protested while Aolendìr smirked, all too pleased at this turn of events.

"Why would the gods pick such a vile excuse for an elf to safeguard the land?" Scarlet tried to make them see reason.

As the Grimìr argued amongst themselves, Rex peered over at Scáth and met her shadowy eyes. "Do you have nothing to add?" he wondered honestly. She continued to look at him in contemplation. "I treated you as vermin when you entered Silva, I tried to kill your love, I stole you from his arms and imprisoned you, to the Underworlds I even aided in your torture."

He was trying to elicit something from her, anything, but Scáth ShadowScorn and Daughter of Aceia looked at him with a sagely wisdom.

"I know. Although I haven't forgiven you, I don't blame you. I can say I know who you are and I believe Āina was right in his choice." She didn't show much emotion in her reasoning and it surprised Rex as much as it made Ven proud of his partner.

"We're not here to argue the decisions of our dead gods. If Rexous is the Realmshield then so be it." Ven left no brook for debate.

"Do we think that monster is still on this island?" Scarlet asked to no one and everyone.

"Avon said he was here, but I doubt anymore. When the Keepers are found they habitually change locations," Nordhum explained.

"You know this how?" Aunna asked earnestly.

"Experience," he answered sullenly.

"So we're back to the beginning, no leads, no information other than the fact one Keeper went through three Grimìr as if we were children." Scarlet's fiery voice raged.

"It is clear they drained the gods of their power over time so I would suggest action sooner than later," Njor added.

"There are still three more Grimìr we do not know yet, we must find them if we hope to overpower the Keepers and their Negators," Scáth reminded everyone in serious tones, adding to the weight of their reality.

"Perfect," Rex said bitterly.

"We're already down several of the world's finest fighters before the war has even taken full root," Nordhum reminded. That left the room quiet for several minutes before the ever-resolute Aunna Morningthorne spoke.

"This would be a good as time as any to add unfortunate news." All eyes fell to her, but she did not waiver. "Macer O'Donnel is still reeling from his defeat at the Siege of Shadow," she looked pointedly at Scáth, "so he set his lust for conquest upon the one place in the world that has avoided him and the church throughout history."

"The Magma Isles?" Scáth asked cautiously.

Aunna shook her head. "The Isles offer little that cannot already be bought from pirates. The Great Northern Rainforest for a start, I am afraid."

Njor laughed as if drunk. "Our forest will swallow him whole, leaving not but his flesh and bones to rot and nourish the land." The Kintar didn't get the response he was hoping from the two Kyst present.

"Don't be so sure," Scáth said disheartened.

"I met him once," Rexous shocked the room by announcing. "At the time I thought myself wicked and cunning, but that vile human was surrounded by the world's richest army and pious zealots so disillusioned they'd eat shit from a latrine if he told them it would grant them his favour." Rex locked eyes with Aunna, not a hint of humour in his smooth voice.

"It's true," Aunna agreed with a curtain of shame above her brow. "The Kingdom of ShadowScorn is strong but it lies on the opposite end of the world. Serenstrom and the bulk of its followers hold strong in the west, they are building forts and staging grounds as we speak for an invasion on your door step."

"And you were to stand by and aid in this invasion?" Nordhum accused, rather harshly for his nature.

"I left my mark clear on the military stationed in the Magma Isles. I went from Arch Cleric to Arch Traitor." She laid a harsh smile on him.

"The gods of old did not prepare us for this. The harbingers of peace wage unrelenting war. Rhogar has never been so closed off. The Keldör are all but starved for their war crimes. The east continues to devour itself while an alien species kills our gods and spent an entire age watching, plotting, and discerning the perfect way to bring our existence to a decisive end." The words chilled everyone but even more so coming from the ever suave and confident Aolendìr Tardinian.

Ven had never felt a room so sombre and disheartened. It served as a ragged reminder that even the most powerful folk in Litore were subject to despair. The words of his parents rang in his mind, a warning that he would have to unite the Grimìr against the Keepers and all that threatened Litore. He wondered if that meant now. How was he supposed to? He was barely an adult by elf standards and one of the most inexperienced among them.

He felt his heart pumping as he moved to stand. "I don't entirely know what to say. I know that most of us in some form or another have a long-intertwined history. Unforgivable acts and feuds that go back beyond our memory. I've seen first-hand the destruction that can be wrought, but I've seen too what happens when past wrongs are set aside to forge a brighter future." He paused a moment to look at Scáth who gave him that smile she always did. The one that made him feel like anything was possible. "A responsibility has been thrust upon us, the likes of which no other living being has ever bore the weight of. I'm not sure if we will succeed, but it was the will of the gods that we should do this thing that not even they could do themselves. Let us agree now there is nothing more precious than Litore itself and that we will all gladly give our lives to see it brought safely into the Third Age."

Ven looked around to see faces of confidence, courage, and conviction. He held out his hand for Scáth to take. Her ghostly white skin touched his stormy grey hand. The others stood and followed Ven Devar as he led them to their greater destiny.

CHAPTER TWENTY-FIVE

Epilogue

Deep in the Blue Waste of Rhogar, the winds wailed and the snow fell upon the icy terrain with wrath. The territory was all but uninhabitable for there was nothing but a thousand square kilometres of barren tundra. Ice shelves a hundred metres tall, frozen boulders the size of cathedrals and temperatures that could freeze the heart of a Lava Dragon. Glacier Dragons, PolarElk, and Sabretooth Rams however, were in abundance, with each one likely to kill you before you knew they were there.

In the very heart of this frozen hell was the great hall of the Keepers, known to them as the Silent Sepulchre. Its jagged and spiked exterior spoke nothing of Litore and its architecture. The Silent Sepulchre appeared as though it sprouted from the top of a great mountain, however it was so ancient that the ice and snow had formed a natural sloping exterior to the hall. Not a single light shone from the structure that loomed over the Blue Waste, nor did any window appear from an outside perspective. There were smaller circular huts that surrounded the Silent Sepulchre in a ring shape, each one equidistant from the others. The huts were made of the same metal material and were capped in similar peaks and spikes.

Inside one of the small buildings was a harsh and cold interior. The walls were black metal, albeit smooth and refined with intricate patterns. A long oval window offered very little in the way of a view, as the terrain was perpetually blue and white. There was a cot against the round wall and opposite that, a small table with a few trinkets strewn about it. The circle on the floor began to illuminate in waves of cyan and a constant beep was heard. As if being pieced back together with imperceptible speed, the cloaked and helmeted humanoid appeared on the circle. The same one Nordhum spoke too and known as Avon. No sooner than he reappeared, the room lit up a soft green and a voice softly projected out.

"Master Avon Crim, I am pleased to see you are home." The voice was melodic but synthetic in nature.

"Hey, J.U.N.O." Avon stepped off the teleportation pad and placed a leaf from a sword fern on the table.

"How are you feeling today, Sir?" J.U.N.O asked with exaggerated kindness.

"I can tell my sensors are working, Joons," Avon replied, fingering a trinket on the table. This one was a jade dragon figurine with one wing broken off.

"I know, Sir. I just thought it polite to ask. You are displaying clear signs of depression and fatigue. May I offer a remedy?" As soon as J.U.N.O finished speaking a slot on the wall opened up and a drink was revealed, bathed in golden light. Avon turned his crimson slits for eyes towards the drink before turning to his cot.

"Change the view would you?" he asked softly through his helmet.

"Certainly," J.U.N.O changed the natural window into a screen that appeared as though you could reach out into it. It turned into the nothingness of space with a far-off celestial body, and after a moment it turned into a vast ocean with tall islands in the distance.

"How many years?" the Negator asked.

"Till what, Sir?"

"Since the beginning," Avon answered.

"4,908 years," J.U.N.O answered as if having to think about it, but of course it knew the instant he asked the question. A great sigh was heard through his helmet as he watched the screen change. It turned to a vista above the clouds, then it faded into a desert, then a dense and loud jungle.

"There," Avon said, crawling into his cot and rolling to face the screen. "There," he said in barely a whisper. The constant sound of insects, birds, and rustling foliage filled the room.

"Sleep well, Sir," J.U.N.O said before dimming the green lights.

Sometime later, Avon's helmet chimed inside and he was jolted awake, nearly made sick as he had just fallen asleep. He pressed a button where his ear would be to silence the noise, yet it persisted. He pressed it again and again in frustration, but the chiming continued. He yanked his helmet off and threw it at the jungle screen. It shattered and a gust of arctic air filled the hut. Avon's jet-black hair was tousled by the wind and he stood there silhouetted in darkness as he peered at the moonlit snows. The lights finally turned on followed by J.U.N.O's voice.

"My apologies Sir, an interference momentarily shut my faculties down."

Avon raised his gloved hand, a magnetic thrum whirred and his helmet was sucked into his hand. He hid his face again and with a sigh of relief the chiming inside had ended.

"What's the summons?" Avon asked his artificial intelligence.

"A full counsel has been convened and all Eyes are summoned to appear before their Keeper." J.U.N.O was serious and slightly impressed at the gravity of the request.

"A full counsel," Avon expressed to himself, lost in thought but J.U.N.O took the time to reiterate the point.

"Yes, sir. All thirteen Keepers are inside the Silent Sepulchre, now awaiting their Eyes."

"You're with me this time, Joons," Avon instructed and soon he heard the voice of his companion projected within his helm.

"Glad as always to join you, Master Avon." J.U.N.O sounded genuinely excited. Avon made his way from the hut into the blistering winds of the Blue Waste. He immediately felt his suit begin to pump hot air within to keep his body temperature at the perfect level. Avon made the long journey through crusty snow towards the hall which was much more like a great castle or tower. There were nearly 100 levels within the Silent Sepulchre, each one serving different purposes, from living quarters for Negators to tech rooms where new instruments were created. His eyes were set on the top level, the counsel chamber for the Keepers. There he would find the thirteen, including the Keeper Sinian whom he had served for over 3,000 years.

He had been bestowed the title of Eye eons ago, and at the time it had meant everything to him. Yet, as Avon was exposed to everything

Litore had to offer, it began to feel more and more like home. More of a home than he ever had in the stars; a planet he could barely recall and the images of a family that were mere strangers to his mind now. The gift of science and limitless technology he grabbed at hungrily had become his only passion, one the Keepers were keen to encourage. Avon had become the most tech savvy of any Negator in a score of millennia. He used that knowledge of technology to create a suit of armour unlike any other possessed. He mastered the art of fractal-projected imaging to become invisible in any environment, thrusters were installed in his boots for flying, and of course, his trademark helmet—autonomous sentry, night vision, language translator, and direct feed to the ever-versatile J.U.N.O who carried every piece of recorded documentation since the Keepers arrived on Litore.

Avon hadn't even realized he was at the entry when a hand grabbed his shoulder and the constant voice of J.U.N.O was calling for him. He spun and saw the Eye of Keeper Orthéthea.

"Avon? Are you okay?" Negator Clarissa looked at him with concern.

"Clarry, good to see you again." She was a mousy figure, with grey hair and oval eyes completely void of pupils. Just a solid grey colour peered back at Avon. She kept a rifle nearly as long as her strapped across her back and a glacier forged dirk at her hip. She moved past him and put a hand to the only discernible object against the wall of ice. The square tablet scanned her hand and a door-sized hunk of ice slid into the ground, revealing a dark interior.

"Come on, Sinian might not punish you for being late but Orthéthea takes pleasure in it I swear." Clarissa walked into the darkness and Avon followed. Her milky-grey eyes and Avon's red slits were all that could be seen in the blackness. Although they could both see through darkness, neither needed to after the amount of times they had walked through the halls of the Sepulchre. Good thing too, for there was no light nor sound emitted in any of the halls, corridors, or elevators of the Sepulchre. That part always bothered Avon; he had adjusted to the lack of light and when he created his helmet the first thing he did was equip it with night vision. Yet, no matter how hard he tried, he could never beat the deafening lack of sound. It was torturous, your own breath was without sound, which gave your mind a horrid sense that you weren't breathing at all. Then there was the sound of your heart, it was enough to make your eardrums think they would burst. You became hyper aware of the fact your blood was rushing through arteries and bleeding through veins. It crippled most Negators their first time in the Sepulchre, and it certainly did him in. It was one of the few memories that lasted these 4,000 years, though he wished it would die with the rest of them.

They found themselves in the elevator rising to the top floor in a matter of seconds. When the door opened, their senses were assaulted by an antechamber dimly lit by lights in the floor and the static sound of shifting air. As they approached the door adjacent the elevator, it slid open for them with a quiet whir. The door took them to a railed platform overlooking a tridecagon shaped room with high-backed chairs in each wedge. Seated on the throne chairs were the Keepers of Litore, their chosen 'Eyes' standing at their right hand.

The platform Avon and Clarissa stood upon levitated them down to the centre of the room and they both found their spots. At the back of each wedge on the wall was a long window overlooking the Blue Waste and a banner that was the sigil for the Keeper in front. Keeper Sinian gave Avon a nod as he approached, and the Eye took a knee before his Master and stood again to stand beside him. Avon peered over his shoulder, as he always did, to regard the banner—a four-pointed star with a grotesquely detailed heart at its centre.

The thirteen sat around in fine clothes of tight fighting fabric, by no means colourful but not entirely monochromatic. Their lanky frames were capped by their tall thin heads and bulbous eyes. He keenly noted that Keeper Joraxa was missing an entire arm, the stub that used to be his bicep capped with a metal bandage of sorts.

Sinian opened his slim and small mouth to start the proceedings. "Congratulations are in order. The twelve gods of Litore cease to exist and we have another in our midst."

Avon could feel the tension in the room grow as his Master revealed they were in possession of not one but two Grimìr. He waved his hand over the armrest of his throne and a wide tube was projected up from the floor. Contained within was a human of light brown skin, black hair with a shock of blue and dark eyes. She was held within the glass confine and looked as though she had been in there for some time. Her gold and black robes were weathered and torn. A sigil of Ordo still gleamed through the disrepair of her raiment, and she lifted her dark eyes up towards Avon. Avon felt his stomach churn, but no sooner did he make eye contact with Dame Autumn Sapphire of the Vingardo did her cage slide over and another emerged from the floor. Within was Vakar the Cunning, looking bewildered and furious all at once. The Kyst did not rant or rave about his imprisonment but observed most diligently.

"Two in our midst, is it enough?" Keeper Orthéthea asked in a more feminine tone but there was no discernible gender apparent to any of the Keepers.

"You know it is not," an old and raspy voice echoed back. Vakar looked to the one who just spoke and was surprised to see it was the only Keeper here who looked of a different age than the others. Of course, the language they were speaking was something wormy and slithering which he had no hope in understanding.

"Who are you?" the short human asked. Vakar turned to regard her as if just realizing she was there now. The tall, proud Kyst looked down on the hard lines and strong flesh of this being.

"Vakar," he answered disinterested.

"Dame Autumn Sapphire, Chosen of Ordo," she declared proudly despite her terrible condition.

"Do you so pompously declare that to everyone?" sneered Vakar.

"If there was a god of jerks, I'd suppose you were the chosen."

"What makes you think I'm Grimìr?"

"Right about now, the last gods standing are us." Autumn watched as the Keepers squabbled amongst themselves. "Once they have all twelve of us, they'll be the only gods of Litore."

"Hey," Vakar shouted at the Keepers. "Any of you speak the Known Tongue?"

"All of us," the thirteen Keepers answered in unison. That unsettled Vakar more than he showed.

"You need all of us Grimìr so you can be the gods of Litore and create the world anew?" he asked rhetorically, and when he got no reply, he continued, "Yes, is the answer your stunted lips were looking for. I have no love for this world. So allow me to help."

The room remained silent but Vakar could tell that was a good thing. They spoke in their alien language again for some time and the Kyst refused to regard the Knight beside him.

"What do you propose?" Keeper Sinian asked, leaning slightly forward in their throne.

"Those you fight have everything to lose and now they know your intent. You've lost your only advantage, which was working from the shadows, but the gods of old told them all about you. To put it plainly, you'll lose this war."

"Remind me again, who are you the Chosen of?" Keeper Orthéthea spoke.

"Zeries," Vakar answered plainly, assuming they obviously knew the answer.

"We cannot trust anything you offer," they replied with a sort of twisted smirk.

"You can trust my desire to live," he said with a vigour not shown to many in his life.

"Traitor," Autumn spat in her cage.

"My Lords," Avon interrupted, "We have a perimeter breach."

"Go," the Keepers said in unison once more and all the Eyes left the room.

"Case and point. You need me," Vakar pressed the point.

A Keeper known only as the Fist approached Vakar and Autumn. They walked with long strides and looked down on them as if they were children. "You err in wanting us as allies. Our objective is annihilation."

Vakar had the perfect retort when an earth shattering crash made him duck and the entire roof collapsed in on them. The whipping snow was let in and by the time the rubble had settled, a fine white dust covered everything and everyone. The two Grimìr were perfectly safe in their cages and it didn't take long for Vakar to notice his was splattered with the gore of the Fist.

In the centre of the room stood a 20 metre tall Dragon-blood with a spear taller than most trees and a golden eye patch. He held a Keeper in his hand and dragged his impossibly long tongue around its whole head before he bit it clean off. He dropped the dead Keeper and spat the head at the breathing ones.

"Foreign blood, foreign flesh, death comes all the same," Ragos the Reaper boomed. He unleashed a blast of fire that not even the Underworld could produce.

Vakar's elven ear flicked as he heard Autumn's cage unlock and saw a middle-aged human dressed in lionwhale boots and bisonbear furs helping her get out. He watched as the two of them walked over to a blown-out wall and Ivan told the knight to hide. He then made his way back to Vakar and began unlocking the cage.

"Who are you?" Vakar asked.

"Ivan,"

"What are you doing here, Ivan?"

"The big guy wanted to meet the Keepers, I'm just along for the ride." Ivan got the lock open and swung the door free for Vakar.

Ragos closed his huge jaw to view his good work as the smoke dissipated. He was somewhat angered when he saw that not even the stupid robes they were all wearing showed any sign of scorching. He threw his spear at Keeper Sinian but the projectile stopped mid-flight as if an invisible hand caught it. It floated there and Ragos held out his hand; the spear disappeared and reappeared back in his hand. The Son of Death stood towering above the Keepers as they moved to surround him.

"We need to go," Ivan urged Vakar. The elf stepped out of the cage but had a hard time looking away from Ragos, as even he had heard the legends of this greatest of demi-gods. Birthed by Pirelia herself, fathered by the Final King. Everything he knew about the Reaper told him this war was to end right now. It could be over before it ever truly began.

Ragos flew towards Sinian, spear point leading, but before he cleared even a metre he felt a great weight on his wing. It didn't halt him completely at first, but after a few heartbeats of struggling, both his wings and legs were rendered utterly useless. Vakar watched on as all the Keepers focused their entire energy on levitating or paralyzing Ragos. He slowly began to float into the air, and he let out a deafening cry of defiance. Even Ivan could not look away from the sheer power on display.

Keeper Sinian approached and lifted a hand before throwing it down; in perfect timing the left wing of Ragos was torn clean off his back. A similar motion tore the other wing and with it a horrifying cry of pain.

"We need to go," Ivan gripped Vakar's arm, but the Kyst would not budge.

The next thing to go was the last eye of Ragos. Ivan let go of Vakar's arm and ran to the missing wall where Autumn was waiting most perturbed. In a horrifying display of collective power, Ragos was eviscerated limb by limb, till there was nothing but a pile of flesh and bone. Vakar looked on in terror. The pile of ichor was smoking and one Keeper walked over to it and grabbed a handful of the remains. The smoke had increased until the whole body burst into flame. The Keeper screamed but not for long as he was rendered ash. A great vortex of fire swirled madly until Ragos was reborn from the ashes. He looked at the remaining aliens and roared before turning and flying back for his companions.

Autumn, Ivan, and Tilly leapt onto his back and he flew them away into the whiteout of the coldest place on Litore.

As they flew further and further away, the room grew quiet save for the howling winds outside. Vakar stepped over the pile of ichor that was the Fist and the headless corpse of the other Keeper. He walked into the centre of the room, staring at each of the Keepers in tense hesitation. He expected them to have eyes of wrath and clenched fists, yet they remained eerily neutral. Vakar dropped to one knee as the remaining aliens surrounded him.

"I pledge my life to you. My will is yours to command. I will serve you until the last life on Litore's green lands has been snuffed out and the final dawn cloaks the world in darkness."